W9-CCZ-935

ANYONE
WHO HAS
A HEART

ALSO BY JACQUELINE POWELL
Someone to Catch My Drift

ANYONE WHO HAS A HEART

JACQUELINE POWELL

WARNER BOOKS

An AOL Time Warner Company

This book is a work of fiction. Names, characters, places, and incidents are the product of the author's imagination or are used fictitiously. Any resemblance to actual events, locales, or persons, living or dead, is coincidental.

Copyright © 2003 by Jacqueline Powell
All rights reserved.

Warner Books, Inc., 1271 Avenue of the Americas, New York, NY 10020
Visit our Web site at www.twbookmark.com.

An AOL Time Warner Company

Printed in the United States of America
First Printing: August 2003
10 9 8 7 6 5 4 3 2 1

Library of Congress Cataloging-in-Publication Data

Powell, Jacqueline.
    Anyone who has a heart / Jacqueline Powell.
        p. cm.
    ISBN 0-446-53174-X
        1. Triangles (Interpersonal relations)—Fiction. 2. African American women—Fiction. 3. Sexual orientation—Fiction. 4. Female friendship—Fiction. 5. Saint Louis (Mo.)—Fiction. 6. Divorced women—Fiction. 7. Bisexual men—Fiction. I. Title.

PS3566.O8318 A8 2003
813'.6—dc21   2002193351

Book design by Giorgetta Bell McRee

To my husband,
Robert Jeff Johnson

You are the gallant king
that I prayed for and the friend
I'd only dreamed about

ACKNOWLEDGMENTS

The sweetest gift that I've been given is the ability to weave a tale around people who do not exist, giving them habits, hurtful moments and hearts of gold. It has made me a more compassionate human being and dedicated scribe. For this, I want to thank the Creator for giving my life a purpose during this time that I am here on earth and when I am gone. Thank you for loaning me to my wonderful and supportive parents, Williemenue "Penny" Powell and Larry Powell. Sharing me with my sisters, LaNita, Valerie, Carla, Kim, Joy and Dawn. Shining through me for my nephew, Curtis L. Powell. Helping me to inspire my nephew Grady Gatewood II. As well as my other nieces and nephews (too many to name . . . some people have to go to work in the morning).

I have to say a special thank-you to my cousins Dave and Doris Jennings. Thanks for the great time in Houston! I love you two. Thank you Mr. Jerae "Fix it til dawn" Smith and Celeste Smith for your support. Thanks to you all and Opal, I know I've got family in Dallas. Thank you McKinley Payne for the radio plug in Dallas—told you I wouldn't forget.

My buddy from way back Reginald Mitchell and his wife, Brandeis, cannot be forgotten either. You all pushed my book in

Acknowledgments

D.C. and Maryland like I'm sure no one else could have done. Many blessings to you both . . . Bunchie and Charlie too.

I'm grateful for the love that I got from John and Claudia Gatewood (the best aunt and uncle a human being could ask for), Paula Hughes, Demeatrius Brooks and Lisa too. Ellen and Charles Cobbins, Dorothy Henderson (my #1 fan), Norene Thomas, Dorothy and Larry Hubbard, Antoine and Theresa Coffer and "Brenda-Bren" Watson.

T.A., and M.K. at Legacy Books, Bro. Simba and everyone at Karibu Books, Bro. Adekunle at Nu World Books, CushCity, Clotilde Pettis at Jokae's and everybody at Black Images Book Bazaar. Jennifer and Vera at Community Book Center in New Orleans. Marcus and Stacey at Ujamaa Maktaba Books took care of me and so did Floyd Boykins Jr. Thanks for the spectacular article in *Spoken Vizions,* the magazine for the creative soul—everybody needs to grab a copy *today*! Another thank-you goes to Sankofa Books and Mekhat at Napps (Natural African Peoples Professional Styles) for lettin' me promote from your spot. A special thank-you goes out to all of the book clubs who supported *Someone* . . . sisterfriends.com, The Sistah Circle book club, The Cover Story book club, sista_friendz bookclub, The G.R.I.T.S. online book club, Sisters Sippin' Tea book club, A.P.O.O.O. book club, Black Expressions book club, Soulful Expressions book club and many others.

I've met authors during this journey who have been extremely helpful along the way. Jacqueline Jones Lamon, we started taking these baby steps around the same time—thanks for being my sounding board when stressful publishing left me unable to do anything but crack jokes. Eric Jerome Dickey, you know where it all began. Thanks for seeing my potential. Timmothy McCann, Jacqueline Jermayne, Earl Sewell, Brenda L. Thomas and the Eugene B. Redmond's Writer's Club.

Thank you to my agent, Sara Camilli, for having my back.

Acknowledgments

Colin Fox, my editor and advocate at Warner, what can I say but you made all the difference in the world. Thanks for giving my ideas a shot. My publicist, Linda Duggins, I want to thank you for showing me what I needed to do in order to make it in this business—whether you realized you were or not.

Last but not least, I want to thank my husband, Robert Johnson. Thanks for being you. You are more than enough.

If I forgot to thank you, email me at Rache49957@aol.com and tell me all about it.

Many Blessings to all.

JACQUELINE POWELL

ANYONE
WHO HAS
A HEART

Prologue

If I've learned one thing in life it's that peace of mind and a clear conscience are priceless. Lacking them is like watching a flower slowly die: Each day you expect to find it in worse condition than before. The weeds of circumstance wrap around and choke the life out of it by way of unresolved issues, other people's expectations and self-contempt. But in rare instances, when the heart is truly pure, the universe will conspire to keep that flower alive and remind it of its purpose. Even when we can't think of a damn thing to keep living for.

PART ONE

"I'm Crying Everyone's Tears . . ."
—SADE

Theresa

"Theresa, you okay in there?"

I gave a mumble resembling that of a sane individual. Due to the circumstances, that was about as close as I was gonna come. Pretending the queasiness in my stomach that had caused my knees to buckle, leaving me doubled over on the commode, hadn't gotten the best of me.

The light in the bathroom was off. Nothing but the illumination from the Glade plug-in deviated from my plan. I was not to look in the mirror under any circumstances. Not even to rescue loose lashes from drowning in the tears that were decorating my beet-red face. My eyes were irritated, burning. My bare feet had paced the carpet until my path was visible—to the door and back to the tub. Someplace in between I was supposed to make sense of it all. Make what was happening to me somehow appear to be real.

"All right, I'm going back to bed."

Vince's voice was too close for comfort. He had pressed his face against the door, expecting the frame to hold his exhausted mass of weight. He'd just come in from getting my son Dameron some pull-ups when he caught me in the middle of another full-fledged, arm-flailing nightmare. This was the seventh in just two weeks. They were becoming more frequent, more real. And so had my habit of drinking. Rum, vodka, a cooler, whatever was around. Even found myself passing out once while Dameron was at a sleepover. That night Vince happened to stop by unexpectedly and threatened to leave me if he ever caught a whiff of alcohol on my breath again. My mother viewed it as a noble deed. But to me, it only meant I had to sneak.

My son's father, Don, was the primary reason for my pain. He died before he even knew that I was pregnant. He was a fire-fighter. One who lost his life in the line of duty. We were engaged to be married and planning a future together. Then suddenly he was dead. Dropped all of those dreams in my lap and left his baby to fill my womb. I took his death extremely hard. I'm even sad to say that I tried to take my own life. And though I know in my heart that Dameron was God's way of helping me cope, and even with counseling and some of my girl-friend Nikai's meditation tips, I haven't been able to get back in control of my own destiny, let Don rest in peace and bury the past.

The darkness engulfed me as I stared at the door to the linen closet. There was a fifth of white rum shoved behind some cleaning supplies and a cardboard box. I had hidden it there the day before just in case my nerves got bad. Just in case the sooth-ing sounds of the ocean on a tape that my momma sent me from Atlanta to help me sleep didn't work. And it hadn't, which meant that a watered-down swig was in order.

A pair of Vince's *Sean John* jeans were hanging on a hook. I stood and checked his pockets for a lighter. Reached behind me and lit the two yellow and black candles with Asian writing that translated to "wisdom and sincerity." Grabbed a Dixie cup and drank to them both. If I was lucky, one of those virtues would become part of my being before the sun came up.

As the reflections of the flames danced on the wall, I remembered the night I realized that Don wasn't coming back. The feeling of emptiness was simply surreal as I sat in the same pink sweat suit for days, surrounded by his clothing, pictures and heroic plaques. The very ones that I occasionally pull out of my secret compartment in the wall of the hall closet just to hold and smell. I can remember thinking that I'd never love again. But now that almost three years have passed with hardly a decent night's sleep, I'm coming frightening close to *knowing* it.

Vince was the first man I'd shared myself with since Don was laid to rest. There was one after that, but Vince was the most memorable. I guess because he said everything I thought I needed to hear: *Theresa, you didn't die with him; life goes on.* And the one that really anchored my panties to the floor: *Widows are worthy of love too.* That one made me feel sorry for myself. Sorry that I had to go through such heartache. I felt so damn sorry for myself that I began to view sex as a treat or reward for not trying to commit suicide again. Felt I owed it to myself for holding up so well. But in actuality, I didn't deserve a reward for the simple stuff people do every day.

I shook my head in disgust and snatched the colorful satin scarf off of my wrapped auburn hair. Ran my fingers through my oiled scalp. Rested my elbows on my knees and listened to the quietness in my apartment. There was a small portion of peace surrounding me, demanding I take notice. Instead, I took another swig.

Rrrriiiiinnnnnngggg!

I hadn't even had time to place the cup back down before someone with bad timing was ringing my phone. I hopped up and tried to grab the doorknob. I missed it and ended up sending Vince's jeans falling to the floor. The flames that calmed me only seconds earlier were now beginning to confuse me. Even blurred my vision, made it hot in there. Harder to breathe.

Rrrrriiiiinnnnnngggg!

7

I turned the cold water on and splashed some in my face. Bugged my eyes and caught my damn reflection. Saw what I didn't want to see—the eyes of a self-destructive woman.

Rrrrriiiiinnnnngggg!

This time when I tried to grab the knob it was like ice-skating uphill. I turned to dry my hands and began knocking things over—the bottle of antibacterial soap, a hand towel and three Dixie cups. The flames moved when I moved. Scrambled atop the candles like they didn't have a clue which way to go. Seemed as though they were aware of the urgency, how badly I needed to get to that phone before it woke Vince. I picked up the hand towel, got a good grip on the knob and opened the door.

Vince was sitting on the bench in front of my brass vanity. One hand was propped midway up his thigh. The other was slowly waving the phone in my direction. His navy-blue pajama bottoms were almost as wrinkled as his brow. I could tell from all the way across the room that his right cheek was twitching as he grit his teeth.

"What's goin' on?" he asked.

I looked blankly at the phone. Had to play crazy and keep some distance between us so that he wouldn't smell the rum on my breath.

"I was trying to come out here and grab it before it woke you."

"Yeah, I heard. What were you doing in there?"

I opened my mouth to speak. I really can't say if what was about to come out was a lie or the truth, but a loud shriek cut me off and changed the subject completely. Wisdom, sincerity and the smoke detector all conspired while my back was turned and was givin' up the goods in surround sound. Telling what little business I had left. Vince ran past me into the bathroom and picked up the candle that must've fallen and ignited the cover on the commode. He grabbed a towel and smothered the flames.

Stepped back into the doorway, and looked at me with fury in his eyes.

"What in the hell is wrong with you?"

He was holding the bottle of rum, and just to add insult to injury he turned the light on so that I could see the crushed Dixie cups lying on the floor. The stench raced out and met me like an impressionable military inductee. Held my attention, damn near sobered me up.

"I was thinking."

"Thinking about what? What could be so wrong that you have to drink?"

Vince was so livid that he didn't take the time to stop the smoke detector from alerting the neighbors that I had issues.

"Stop that thing before it wakes Dameron," I insisted.

"You're not concerned about Dameron, or otherwise you wouldn't be sneaking and drinking. What is it, Theresa?"

It seemed the frustration had seeped through his pores and been replaced with the desire to understand. His tone was more distraught than angry. As though he were at a loss for words, the end of his rope.

"Theresa, you told me about the nightmares with Don. I wanna help you, but this is not the way."

Self-pity, coupled with the alcohol, took hold of me and wouldn't let go. I stood before him crying and trying to prove my worth.

"I'm scared, Vince. Don keeps showing up in my sleep. Tellin' me about how he loves me and misses me. Saying he's ready to be with me. I'm trying to help myself but I know how you look at me like I'm crazy when I explain it. Those looks make me feel so alone, so I drink. I drink so that I don't think about the dreams."

I buried my face in his chest as he reluctantly wrapped his

long virile molasses-toned arms around me. Finally the smoke detector gave way to the moment.

"So what do you want me to do? I can't get inside your head and make sure Don doesn't show up in your dreams. You're not giving me very many options."

I whispered, "Help me."

There was silence and then a lengthy sigh. Another forced hug and then more empty words that sounded strangely close to surrender.

"I wish I could."

Vince pulled away and handed me the bottle of rum. Never looked me in the eye. Not even when he began to pack his things.

"It's one in the morning," I said.

"I know. That's why it's so important for me to go. One of us has got to be able to keep our word."

I didn't rebut, and that's not like me. A schoolteacher always has a response, should always be prepared to answer anyone at any given time. Even at one in the morning.

"But it's not about Don" was all I could mutter.

Vince pulled his white T-shirt over his head and asked, "Then who is it about?"

Silence took over the moment.

"It's about us," I finally told him.

His mouth fell open as he stared at me like an unsolvable equation. Removed the gold band from his left ring finger that we'd exchanged six months ago as a sign of commitment to one another and placed it on my dresser. Then Vince resumed with packing while shaking his head in disbelief.

"You're wrong again, Theresa. There is no more us."

I lay across my bed on my back and stared at the ceiling while listening to the door catch as Vince left. It took him all of ten minutes to gather up everything he owned. I spent nine and a half of those begging him to stay. It wasn't an all-out beg for mercy on my alcohol-inflicted soul but one that let him know there was supposed to be more between us. Substance that was thick enough to bond us through tougher times than these. I glanced over at the digital clock across the room. It read 1:14 A.M. Wondered who that was calling me so late. I reached over on the nightstand and grabbed the gray and white phone. Pressed the review button. The Caller ID screen read: Nikai Parker. I dialed her back and she picked up on the third ring.

"Hey girl," she answered.

I rolled onto my back and said, "Nikai, you called?"

She whispered, "Yeah, but I can't talk right now."

"Kalif in the room?"

"He's in the kitchen. What are you doing this weekend?"

"You know I'm taking Dameron to Atlanta with me to visit my mother."

"Wait a minute. Hold on."

She put the phone down as the faint sounds of Lauryn Hill's "MTV Unplugged" acoustic performance reverberated throughout the loft they lived in on Tucker near downtown. Nikai and Kalif were night owls; they stayed awake all night and never got up before noon. He was a music producer. She was a singer who had sung the *"I cain't get a record deal to save my life"* blues for three years. She swears it's not important to her anymore but I see that as a defense mechanism. True friends always see one another clearly.

"Yeah, I'm back," she told me.

"So what's goin' on?"

"I thought Kalif still had company but he doesn't. So now isn't a good time to talk. Mind if I come by the school tomorrow during your lunch?"

"I don't care. But you're okay, right?"

11

She became quiet. It was the sort of quiet that made me wish we were face-to-face. Nikai and I had both lost and survived a lot together. She was there for me when Don died and I was there when her ex Robert's memory had done the same. She didn't sound well. Not at all like the gutsy woman who had confided in me last week that she was ready to tackle another battle with infertility again.

"I'm losing it, Theresa."

I sat up and tucked my feet under the powder-and-navy-blue plaid comforter on my bed.

"Welcome to the club. I can't maintain a relationship strong enough to withstand a bottle of Puerto Rican rum."

I chuckled. She didn't. That scared me. Nikai was sillier and more sarcastic than I've ever been. She rarely passed on an opportunity to laugh.

I asked, "Do you need anything?"

She didn't respond. I could tell that she was preoccupied with something else.

"I'm sorry, Theresa. Now what did you say?"

"Nothin'. We'll talk about it tomorrow. I asked if you needed anything."

"Yeah, I need you to not be judgmental."

The stench of burned carpet and melted wax wafted out of the bathroom and shook its shimmy under my nose. I turned away, only to rest my eyes upon Vince's ring. Rejection in the highest form. It was taunting me. Reminding me that I'd failed. Reminding me that I was losing again.

"I've got no right to judge anyone," I told her.

"Don't speak so quickly. You've got no idea what's been running through a sista's mind."

"Will it get you five to ten?"

"No, Theresa. Now I've gotta go. I'll see you tomorrow."

Vince

I woke up at my own place this morning and I have to admit that it is truly underrated. There was no warm, soft body next to me longing to be cuddled, but it felt damn good not being awakened with an elbow jab to the trachea. That's what I had to look forward to when I spent the night at my lady, Theresa's, place. It's not that I'm ever worried about her *seriously* hurting me, even though that term is relative. But psychologically, the thought of her allowing a man who is no longer amongst the living to occupy her thoughts, whether consciously or unconsciously, has begun to take its toll on me. Not to mention the drinking habit that she's forming. Most of the time I feel sorry for her. And to tell you the truth, I walked out last night hoping to jar something in her. Sorta how when people in comas are taken off of life support in hopes that they'll fight for a life that you want nothing more than to share with them. But I can't do it for her. I can't make her desire to live.

I stood up from my king-sized dark walnut sleigh bed covered in grape Calvin Klein sheets and glanced outside my downtown-facing bedroom window. Stared across the skyline at the Arch towering over the city, with the old courthouse, where many decades ago Dred Scott fought for freedom as a slave, resting in view. Today was gonna be a good one, regardless of what comes my way, I thought. Since I'd taken the day off, aside from my ritualistic trip to the YMCA to lift weights the only thing I had scheduled was to help my older sister Rayna's melanin-challenged husband, Luke, move some furniture into a new house they had built out in St. Charles. And if he keeps his mouth shut, maybe this time an EMS unit won't be necessary. Rayna has no one else to blame but herself for the last incident that left his arm in a sling. I told her not to let him call her "Sissie" in front of me 'cause it made her sound like a slave fresh out of the cotton field. She told me that it was a pet name that she liked. Said it made her feel safe, helped her relax. I told her to smoke a joint. She told me that was for urban thugs and rappers. I shook my head and walked away. She was not only brainwashed but dumb enough to think that I was serious. Sometimes I swear to God, the only reason I keep in contact with her is because she looks so much like my momma.

Mable Lowery died of a heart attack when I was eleven and Rayna was eighteen. Shortly afterwards, Luke snatched my big sister away and my pops fell in love. By the time I turned twelve, he was spending every night he could next door with Ms. Irene. Her son Ramone and I became best friends since we were the same age, were in the same classes at school and both hated our lives at home. He wanted to go and live with his father in Minnesota. I can't really say if at that time I wanted to live at all.

My friendship with Ray became all that I would look forward to. We talked about what car we would drive when we got older, and what girl we would "get" in the backseat when we finally did. But another two years flew by and things changed *again*. Ms. Irene got "saved" and stopped seeing my pop. They moved out west to California with a man she met in church. Pop fell in love again—just not with the idea of being part of a family anymore. I became a loner until I was eighteen and old enough to leave home. Played basketball for a couple of years at Missouri University, fell head over heels for a sista named Jennifer and followed her back to St. Louis. Back then it was hard for me to adjust to the whole idea of family. She wanted one and I wasn't ready. Hell, I didn't even want to be bothered with the makeshift family I already had. I guess maybe that was Pops's influence. I had spent so much time studying his ways in order to avoid them that I ended up coming dangerously close to being just like him. But it's funny how fate has an irony about it. Now that age has stripped my pops of his machismo persona and half of his head of hair, he wants to bond with his children. More so Rayna. So I give him time when I have it, which is usually every third lunar eclipse. And I always remind him that a man's got to eventually pay for all of his sins. The last time I visited him he said that my momma used to say the same thing. I winced and told him to keep her name out of his mouth. He asked me why. That's when I told him how I felt watching him casually replacing the woman who meant so much to me, and how I had longed for stability most of my childhood. He gave me a look of disdain and asked if I wanted him to raise me all over again. I answered with a dry and lifeless, 'Again?' "

I try not to allow Pops to invade my thoughts that often. I've got enough to worry about meeting deadlines for Ringlord Books. I've been editing great works of fiction for four years now. But my goal is to represent authors. Squeeze myself right in between the publishers and the writers and get *paid*. I've got an appreciation for the art but I also want in on some royalties. See, what I plan to do is move out of this condo by next winter and buy a home out in West County with a two-car garage and an in-ground pool out back. Thought for a long time that Theresa would be the one plantin' a bed of flowers in a garden out front, where I would pick her one before walking in to greet her each day. But now I'm not so sure that's what she wants.

My homey, Leland, has been tellin' me to leave her since I

first started complaining about the way she leads with her left during the night. But he doesn't see what I see. I would imagine few men do.

I met Theresa almost two years ago while I was picking up my nephew Percy from the school where she teaches. In fact, he was in her class. I asked her out to lunch the next day and I could tell right off the bat that she still wasn't over this Don cat. She'd bring him up at the most inappropriate times, which often resulted in one-way conversations. Before I knew it she would be crying in a crab salad and asking for a minute to gather herself. I know what you're thinking: What could be attractive about that? Well, there's more.

Theresa has got to be the most sensitive, nurturing woman on the planet. When Percy was killed by a drunk driver later that year, she kept me from killing Luke with my bare hands. I believe he hated Percy because he reminded him of the fact that Rayna had had sex before he came along. I'd seen Labradors receive a more respectable burial than the one Luke was attempting to give Percy. And the thing that bothered me most was that Rayna refused to say anything about it. So Theresa and I took care of the funeral and burial arrangements ourselves. That drove a wedge between my sister and me for a long time. I hated to see her coming. My father never said a word. He's cowardly like that. Everything I never wanted to be. To this day he tells me that a disrespectful child shortens his days. I remind him that I'm not his *child*, I'm his son and a grown man. But I guess it's hard to know that when he wasn't around to witness the transition.

Leland swears that he could get somebody to make Luke and my pops disappear but I'm not cut like that. Honestly, there's a dark crevice in my heart that allows me to love my father. And as for Luke, I just want him out of my sister's life. I take that interracial stuff personally. But I would never let her know how it hurts that she wants to share something as precious as her life with a man who looks nothing like me or any other man with the same blood that she has flowing through her veins. Sometimes it makes a brotha feel like maybe he's not good enough. The black man's got enough struggles as it is with racial profiling, police brutality and unjust imprisonment without feeling like his partner, the most precious species on earth, has given up on him.

I stretched my pecs as I stared at my six-foot-two, two-hundred-and-ten-pound frame. I was in pretty decent shape but I could tell that my spirit was aging. What I wanted out of life was beginning to change. Turning thirty-one will do that to a man with no children and waning prospects for a wife. I know that the average brotha would disagree, but I ain't the average brotha. I don't do anything average or in a mediocre fashion. I'm either not touching it or goin' for broke. And I'm smart enough to think my shit through first, which is why I packed up last night. I needed some space and so did Theresa. I needed time to decide just what I'm willing to put up with in order to have this woman, or at least the portion that firefighter cat left behind. Theresa was dying inside and she didn't even know it.

I strolled over to my stereo, pressed play and allowed some hip-hop to get me into workout mode. Dropped to the floor wearing nothing but a pair of hunter-green boxer briefs and had started on three hundred push-ups when the phone rang.

"Hello," I answered, stumbling to my feet and turning the volume down on Kardinal Offishall's "Quest for Fire."

"What are you doing?" Theresa asked.

There was little warmth in her voice.

"I just got up. How you feelin'?"

A long sigh.

"I'm fine. I was calling to let you know that if you left anything, you'll need to get it by Friday night. I'm going to Atlanta to visit my mother this weekend."

I opened the middle drawer to my dark walnut dresser, slid into a pair of black mesh basketball shorts and walked into the kitchen.

"When did you decide to do this?"

"Last month. Remember?"

If I know Theresa, she was hoping that I'd tell her not to go. But I couldn't. Part of me didn't know for sure if maybe she didn't need to.

Then she asked, "Did you leave anything?"

"No, I'm pretty sure I got all of my stuff."

More empty silence.

"So what are you thinking?"

"I think you should stop drinking."

"Look, Vince, no lectures, please. I didn't call to argue."

I grabbed a glass from the cupboard and poured myself some orange juice from the fridge. Leaned against the counter and crossed my feet at the ankles.

"I'm not interested in arguing either. But I want to know that you'll be all right."

She gave a dry "Point well taken."

"I don't know that it is. You almost burned your apartment down last night."

"And you walked out on me last night."

"I walked out on the nightmares and the drinking. Not you."

Another sigh.

"How long are you gonna be gone?"

"Two weeks."

I placed the glass on the counter, massaged my eyes with the tips of my fingers and said, "Just make sure you come back."

"What's the hurry? There is no more us, right?"

"We were friends first. Remember that, ah'ight? I don't have to make love to you to care about you."

I could hear sniffling as her sorrow stretched across the line.

18

This was killin' me inside but it was for her own good. She had some growing to do that I simply couldn't help her with. I don't read minds and I'm not Freddy Krueger, so I can't join her in the dreams. Maybe this was for the best.

I asked, "You packed?"

"Tomorrow."

More sniffling. Then came a faint "Will you spend the night with me tonight?"

"I don't know if that's the direction we're tryin' to move in."

"Vince, I need you."

"Theresa, you need help."

"Fine! Bring me back my key!"

She hung up in my ear. Two seconds later the phone rang again. I picked up before the identity could register on the small screen above the keypad.

"Yeah?"

"What's up, Money?" Leland asked.

I laughed. Nobody could lighten the mood like my homey from way back. I met Leland about ten years ago when I was interning at a newspaper in Columbia, Missouri. He was slaving in the mail room and harassing the sistas on every floor. When we graduated from MU, we both decided to come back home. I got a job as the low man on the totem pole over at Ringlord, which translates to my duties were just above holding a light plug in the wall. If they needed someone to run and make copies, brew a pot of coffee or take messages from pissed-off literary agents who were trying to track down royalties, I was that brotha. Since then, I've graduated to an actual editor. Leland got a gig at the post office doing what he calls "slinging letters" all day. He was the type of brotha who grew up running the streets and mistook leaving the criminal-minded cats alone as a sign of weakness. He wouldn't be "keepin' it real" if he moved out of the hood. He reminded me of Rayna. Both had bought into reverse psychology: She didn't know that living in a pre-dominantly white neighborhood didn't make her any less black and he didn't know that staying in the hood didn't make him any more.

"Whassup, Leland? You still following that chick from the DMV?"

"Kill the jokes, bruh. You near a TV?"

"I can be. Whassup?"

"Turn it on Channel eleven. They're talking about my wife."

"Your wife?!"

"Yeah, the broad who runs that club down on the Landing."

"Discretion?"

"Yeah. Her name is Zenobia but they call her Z."

"And what do you call her?" I asked sarcastically.

"I ain't callin' her shit *yet*! Gimme some time. That chocolate ass is gonna be *mine*."

"You know what you doing, Leland? I know I've seen this chick hanging around that cat that plays pro ball."

"Who, Payce Whittington? The nigga who ain't blocking for shit? You think that cat's money is betta than all the fuckin' personality I got?"

"Yeah, I guess you're right. Especially if she's interested in being cursed out in five-point-two seconds flat."

"Fuck you, man. What's goin' on tonight?"

"I don't know yet. I may be trying to catch up with Theresa. She's leaving town soon."

"Well, listen, I need you to run through the spot with me after the finals."

When he said "the spot" he usually meant a string of clubs. And considering his newfound interest in the dark-skinned sista named Zenobia, I was sure Discretion was on the list of places to hit.

"I got a new one I'm tryin' to check out called Whose Is It.

20

Heard the freaks ain't scared to set it out for a cat. Drinks on me."

My other line rang so I told Leland to hold on a minute.

Rayna greeted me with, "Hey baby brother."

"What's up, sis?"

"Since Luke's brother Josh is in town we stayed up late last night moving a lot of stuff. You know, so people wouldn't see exactly what we were doing. This neighborhood is mixed so I'm not trying to make anybody think we have something worth breaking in for."

I could've gone somewhere with that comment but decided to let it go.

"So you're saying you're all done?"

"Almost, but I won't be needing your help. Hey, by the way, you know Josh is into real estate, and I told him that you were about to look for a house. Although he hasn't finished moving himself, he says that he could put you in contact with the right person. You interested?"

"Is the person white or black?"

"What difference does that make, Vince? If the house wasn't *built* by a black person will you not want to buy it either?"

I rubbed the top of my head and said, "Give him my e-mail address, Rayna."

"Hold on a sec. Let me get a pen. Okay, here we go. What is it?"

"MrVLruns@emg.com."

"All right, got it. You talk to Daddy lately?"

"No. Have you?"

"Yesterday. He didn't sound too good. I may need you to go by there and see about him."

"I don't think that's possible. I've been working on some editorial letters for six months. My time is valuable."

"And so is your relationship with your father. You have one

21

parent left on this earth and you can't kiss a little booty to get back in his good graces before he passes on too?"

"Kissin' ass is your bag, not mine."

Her tone quickly shifted. "And what's that supposed to mean?"

"Look, don't ask questions that you already know the answer to. I'm happy to hear that you got all of your stuff moved in but I gotta go."

"You remember what Mama said, Vince? A man's gotta pay for all of his sins before he leaves this earth."

"Try reciting that line to your husband."

Click. She hung up on me for the third time in two weeks. Just like Pops, Rayna didn't deal with reality too well. Quick to flee the scene. When I pressed the flash button again, Leland was gone. That brotha could never sit still for longer than a minute, either. Sometimes it seemed everyone around me was changing pace. Or maybe it was that longing for stability that made me seem stagnant to others, and more so to myself.

"Whassup Vince?"

This clown behind the front desk was yelling all the way across the entrance of the YMCA. I nodded my head and lifted my index finger, indicating that I'd be up there in a minute. I was holding the glass door open for a sista coming down the sidewalk with a bag the color of sunshine secured diagonally across her chest. The black strap matched her leggings and the tail of her white T-shirt cradled her backyard as she lowered a pair of shades, smiled and scooted past me. I hurried on in behind her while keeping just enough distance to respect her personal space.

"Hi, Jesse," she said, handing her ID over the counter.

"Whassup Bridget? What you know good?"

With unblemished skin the color of sand, she glanced back at me and tossed a white towel over her shoulder. It hung about the length of her light brown ponytail, which was down to the middle of her back. I stepped up, placed my ID on the counter and flexed in the black T-shirt that I'd cut the sleeves off of this morning.

"I know that chivalry isn't dead."

Jesse looked surprised. Snatched our cards and walked out into the middle of the floor.

"Who you talkin' about—Vince? Babygirl, Vince is the rudest cat you gon' come across. A brotha like me has been on my job for eight years, don't have no kids and ain't scared to let my lady use my credit cards."

We both laughed at Jesse's tactless attempt to pick up women. I stepped around Bridget, grabbed a towel and pressed the button for the turnstile to open. Headed down a hallway decorated with a bank of colorful posters giving instructions for CPR, maintaining a healthy diet and promoting a positive and friendly environment. As I approached the stairs to the men's locker room, I heard Bridget call my name. When I turned around she was doing a light jog in my direction, her ponytail bouncing.

"Hey Vince, I was wondering what you were going upstairs to do. Thought maybe you could help me lift some weights."

She laughed, lowered her head and continued, "I have no idea what I'm doing."

Then she looked up at my arms. "But it looks like you do. Mind if I meet you there?"

I shrugged my shoulders. "Sure. No problem."

"Okay, see you in a sec."

We separated and I put my bag in a locker on my way up the stairs. When I opened the door to the weight room she was standing in front of the ceiling-to-floor mirror with her feet shoulder-width apart, lifting five-pound free weights to her shoulder and above her head. She smiled at my reflection in the mirror and then sat down on the bench behind her.

"Don't let this fool you. I'm killin' myself here."

She wiped her palm on her leggings and extended her hand. "How rude of me. I'm Bridget, your new student."

"I guess that makes me Professor Lowery, huh?"

She stood and wiggled her hips like she was auditioning for Mystical's next video.

"I'm a dancer and I need to get in shape. I mean, not that I'm out of shape or anything but there are just some spots that need to be touched up."

She wound her hips in a circle and did a 360-degree spin. Broke out into a full-fledged routine that caused the other four or five guys in the room to stop working out. She was what Leland called a silent freak. Never had any intentions of giving up the goods, never even promised them to you. Just showcasin' what you'd never get a chance to enjoy. I took a step back so the others would know that she was public domain. When she finished she was on the floor in what looked like an uncomfortable swastika position, with sweat beading on her forehead. Ponytail ruffled around the edges. A smile on her face like she was used to paparazzi being present when she performed.

"That was nice, Bridget. Do you teach dance or something?"

"Let the other girls tell it; I don't. But I've taught them everything they know. When I came to the group they were doing jazz numbers. *I'm* the one who incorporated hip-hop and African dance into our routines."

She spoke with bitter passion. That million-dollar smile was bundled up in her towel.

"Maybe you can come see us perform one night."

"Uh, I don't know about . . ."

"C'mon, it'll be fun. We can hang out afterwards. Grab something to eat or go for a walk. Maybe even catch a movie, or just go somewhere to sit and chat. We'll be performing at the Caman Cultural Center this weekend. We'll be doing African dance."

She could talk a dog off of a meat truck with her persistence. What part of my reluctance didn't she get?

"Bridget, no offense but I'm really not interested."

"In what, supporting a black woman in her . . . You know what? Forget it."

She stood to her feet, snatched her towel off of the floor in front of the mirror and stormed across the room. Strutted with the intention of showing me what she was working with. That sort of strut that got women in trouble in a roomful of men. Bridget sat down on the bench press underneath twenty-pound weights and gripped the bar, illustrating about as much experience as a blind man with no arms.

I ran over and stopped her before she killed herself.

"Hold on, sis," I said, lifting the bar and removing it.

She stared up at me. "Thought you weren't interested in being my instructor. I don't want to cause you to compromise your integrity by doing something you're not 'interested' in."

"I won't be, if this is all you need me to do."

She sat up and turned halfway around to face me.

"When I want more, Professor Lowery, I'll ask for it. Class dismissed."

She got up and disappeared through the double doors. I stood there for a second holding on to the weights. Women like that made me glad to have found Theresa. I may have had to knuckle up and guard my grill at night but at least I could honestly say that she wasn't simpleminded. A man won't take a woman like that too seriously unless he's got shit to prove to himself. Unless he wants to know that he can tame her, in order to feed his own ego. Something my pops would do in a heartbeat.

But not me. Sometimes strength comes in recognizing that a challenge is too grand.

About an hour later, when I'd finished lifting and had retrieved my duffel bag from the locker room, I stopped by the front desk to get my ID. There was a white guy in his early twenties entering data into the system as I dropped my towel into the slot near the entrance.

"Vince Lowery. I need my ID."

"Sure, no problem."

He rolled the chair backward across the floor and sifted through about fifteen IDs. I brushed the sweat from the top of my head with my hand and wiped it on my T-shirt. The cool air was giving me a chill that caused my muscles to tense up. All I wanted was a shower and to catch the rest of the NBA playoffs. I had money on the Kings against the Lakers and tip-off was in thirty minutes.

"I'm sorry. There's no Vince . . ."

"Vincent R. Lowery. It should be in there. I gave it to Jesse when I walked in."

"Nope, don't see any Lowery or Vincent . . ."

I leaned over the counter. "I know it's back there. Just look under that—"

He lifted his hands in the air. "Hey, dude, I'm new here. Take it easy. If you left it, it should be here."

"Where's Jesse?"

"Jesse's gone for the day. I'll get Rebecca. She's been the one giving and receiving IDs."

"I'd appreciate it."

"No problem, big guy. Hey Becca! You wanna come here for a minute?"

A tall, slender redhead appeared from a back room wearing a navy-blue staff shirt and khaki shorts. Asked if there was anything that she could help me with.

"Yes, you can tell me where my ID is. My name is Vincent Lowery. I gave it to Jesse about an hour and a half ago. Now, you-all are telling me it's not here."

"Hang on. What's your name again?"

She tossed a few things around on the desk and then stopped and looked at me as if a siren had gone off in her head.

"Heeeyyyy, I remember that name. Bridget took that ID. She said you had already left and were waiting for her outside."

"What? I don't even know *Bridget!*"

"Well, I saw you two come in together," Becca countered. "That's the only reason I gave it to her, Mr. Lowery. I'm like so sure that I saw you holding the door for her. She's not your girl-friend?"

"Are you?"

She took a step back and did that dramatic damsel-in-distress motion where she placed her hand over her heart and left her mouth hanging open in shock. I didn't care. I was sick of white people assuming that because black people were cordial to one another we had to be intimately involved. Luke was known for pulling the same crap. When I could spend more than fifteen minutes around him without my blood pressure going up, he'd ask me the same stupid questions. I was supposed to screw every black woman I wasn't fighting.

I took a couple of deep breaths and asked Rebecca, "Could you please write down her phone number so I can get my ID back?"

"Mr. Lowery, we aren't allowed to give personal information. That's against policy."

Go figure . . .

"So what do you suggest I do?" I asked.

"We can issue you another ID if you would just wait about twenty minutes to get your photo taken."

I glanced up at the clock on the wall.

"I don't have twenty minutes."

"Then how about when you come back? We'll be happy to do it then."

"Fine."

I could hear her apologizing as I descended the steps and pushed through the glass door. The sun felt good on my skin. Warmed me over. Reminded me of what I told myself this morning. That today was gonna be a good one. But that was before Theresa and her denial, before Bridget and her games. That was all before I rounded the corner and read the note she'd left on my windshield.

Hey, if you want your card back, you'll have to come and get it. Call me if you'd like to see it . . . or the card sometime. Bridget/555-0112

I balled the note up and tossed it in the backseat with my bag. Like I said, simpleminded.

Zenobia

Whoever said the best things in life are free ain't even walked a city block in my shoes. In this world, you gotta work for everything. Even for the stuff that doesn't seem worth it. Hell, I've been dancing and grinning for almost five years and I can't get respect, recognition or a minor percentage of the business that I've practically worked my butt off for and turned into a huge success. Even earned Discretion a mention on the news early this morning for being one of the hottest-growing night clubs in St. Louis next to Whose Is It, which is still holding the number one spot.

But those are only minute points on my lengthy list of issues. I told myself two years ago that I'd never give my heart to another man until I saw proof in the form of at least one and a half carats. Everything in between will be dress rehearsal for the real thing.

See, men lie and cheat for sport. And the sooner women realize that they can't be taken seriously, the better off they'll be. My ex, Mike, is the one who sealed the deal for me. I thought I loved him but hell, I also thought that he was separated from his wife. And when the six-month mark of sleeping with a man who's still reluctant to take you home to meet his family hits, any self-respecting woman with a half an ounce of dignity will snap.

And that's just what I did. Tossed his pants, shoes and stupid baseball cap over the balcony of my apartment. Surprisingly, he had the nerve to stand in my living room wearing boxers and socks arguing over a television that he *may* have put three hundred dollars into. I told him my chocolate pudding was worth *way* more than that. He countered by insinuating that I was sellin' my coochie and if that was the case I owed him at least two more shots. That was when I shoved him into my six-foot ficus tree and called my ghetto brother. Told him I had some strange, half-naked man in my living room trying to take my big screen and callin' me a hooker. Needless to say, that relationship ended without either of us regressing.

My next issue is that I'm convinced that Payce, my daughter's father, is out to get me. My girlfriend Lainey is convinced that he's not over me yet. But Payce plays professional football, is a small-time millionaire (if there is such a thing), qualifies for the cover of *Black Women* magazine and is into chicks from the islands. I realized three years ago that aside from getting one last screw for old times' sake, I was lodged in his mind way back there next to what Reggie Jackson is doing these days.

Payce is the one who came up with the idea of opening a club in St. Louis. This was six years ago, when we were a semihappy couple and occupied the same hole in the wall in Chicago.

Lainey and I drove her red Festiva out there the summer of '95. We were both twenty-one, playing hooky from University of Missouri–St. Louis and trying to find ourselves. Lainey found Cedric, whom she married almost immediately. I found Payce and a red line on a pregnancy test. He and my parents played tug-of-war with me during my first two trimesters. They wanted the child of their bachelor degree–less, unwed daughter to be raised in a structured family environment. Once I reached seven months, they gave up on the idea of me coming home and of being able to frame anything with my name on it beyond a high

30

school diploma. Shortly afterwards, my father had a massive heart attack and died. Momma and my younger brother, Maurice, blamed that on me. Apparently I'd driven Daddy to an early grave. Absurd accusations like that are what caused me to pack my things after only three weeks in St. Louis and head back out to the Windy City. I hadn't been back there for six months before my momma passed away in her sleep. The coroner said it was an aneurysm. Maurice said that *too* was my fault. So with two deaths, a newborn, the task of handling a promiscuous, recently drafted football player and the antics of a wanna-be-a-thug-for-life little brother under my belt, I was well equipped for the loony bin.

The only thing that did work out in my favor was Payce being drafted to play in St. Louis. We moved immediately, and he began to cheat almost as quickly. Making me manager of his club was an effort to convince me that he was serious about his family. That is, until he got sloppy and women started showing up here acting a fool. After his recovery from a stab wound, compliments of some Cuban chick's brother, Payce started keeping his personal affairs behind closed doors. That's when I threw the towel in on hopes of an intimate relationship and began maintaining one strictly based on business. He didn't argue when I told him that I was leaving, either. Begged me not to drag the system into our personal affairs via child support. Bought me a two-hundred-and-fifty-thousand-dollar home out in North County, deposited forty-five thousand in my checking account and practically snapped my Achilles tendon when he closed the door on my heels. What I didn't know at the time was that that was all I was gonna squeeze out of his tight ass. Nowadays, he wouldn't put two cents on a pack of ramen noodles for me. But the feelings are mutual.

We only talk about our five-year-old daughter, Zaire, and the club. And lately he's been avoiding me on both. During the school year, we've been ping-ponging Zaire back and forth, alternating weekly visits. And then we take every other summer. This summer belongs to Payce. So I've signed up for a tae bo class to fill my time when I'm not keeping the finances straight and watching employees like a hawk from my office overlooking the dance floor. Sometimes I hate this job, but every time I mention getting someone to come in and work in the office so that I can have a break, Payce starts hollerin' about how he's in a financial bind at the moment. The brotha has got more excuses than a pregnant virgin for why he can't do this, that and the other.

But on one particular night during the summer before last, I'd had enough of him not returning my calls about some help around here. I drove to his place after I closed the club and beat on the door until it all appeared before me crystal clear. Payce had been leaving my baby with another woman while he was flyin' all around the world during off-season but telling me that they were bonding. Even had Zaire call me a couple of times just to make the story stick. Brea was his victim's name, I think. Tall, skinny chick with a thick accent, no brains and an attachment to my little girl. I asked her where Payce was and she didn't know. Couldn't even tell me when he was coming back. So I packed up Zaire's things and took her home with me. About six months later, Payce promised me we could work something out so that we were all satisfied but as soon as the police put my house under surveillance thanks to Maurice and his broke derelict friends trying to run marijuana in and out of my back door, I didn't have a leg to stand on. And Payce took every opportunity to throw it in my face anytime I fixed my lips to call him a bad father. This became extremely convenient for his new woman, Cammie, who's been spending time with Zaire, planning their summer as a family. But now, after six years of putting in long hours, coaxing a slightly more focused Maurice through

his last year of high school and struggling to move past the untimely deaths of both my parents, I've decided that I want half
of Discretion and a bus to run over Payce.

I was sitting at my desk in the upstairs office staring at a picture of Zaire sporting her toothless smile with two ponytails secured at the top of her head. Payce was supposed to be calling
me back about if and how we'd split this place. I looked up at the
gold and black clock on the wall next to my favorite black-and-
white framed print of Marvin Gaye. It was five minutes after
twelve. He was late and so was the bartender that I was scheduled to interview. I'd just opened the folder in front of me and
glanced over his application when there was a knock at the door.

"Come in!"

In walked a brotha who looked to be in his late twenties.
Faded haircut, peanut-butter-brown skin, perfect teeth, slight
five o'clock shadow, hunter-green Ralph Lauren button-down
shirt, dark brown Polo pants, a little over six feet, with a slender
build. Appeared confident as he stood next to the burgundy and
black chair in front of my desk.

"I'm Beacon M. Gaines. But you can call me B."

I stood and extended my hand. "I'll just call you late. Would
you care to have a seat, Mr. Gaines?"

"Thank you. I want to apologize for being tardy. There was a
problem in traffic."

"Sorry to hear that," I said, folding my hands in front of me,
"but let's get to the reason we're both here."

"I'm seeking employment at Discretion. I've completed my
training. I'm a team player, goal-oriented, and a self-starter. I
have—"

"You have obviously done this before."

"I haven't actually interviewed in a while but I do know how
to sell myself."

I opened his file and read his application again.

"Let's see, it says here that you've worked in retail, construction and as of lately bartending. What makes you want to be a bartender?"

"Well, when I was in college, I'd throw parties and mix drinks myself. I got pretty good at it and fell in love with the whole scene."

"So you're in it for the atmosphere?"

"I guess you can say that. I mean, I've always thought if you had to work a job it might as well be one you enjoy, right?"

"True. So it says here you graduated from SIUE. Southern Illinois University of Edwardsville."

"That's correct."

"So tell me about one of your parties and how you would be an asset to Discretion."

"I know that when you make a trip to a club an experience, people come back. By that, I mean themes, live performances and feeling comfortable with the staff. I'm not just a bartender—I'm a confidant to customers. You have to let people know that this is the place to relax and unwind. Let all of the stress subside. This is where your friends are. And we—the DJ, owner, bartender and other staff—*are* your friends."

I leaned back in my black leather executive chair and said, "Well, I'm impressed."

He nodded humbly. Had a boyish innocence about him.

"When would you be available to start?"

"As soon as possible."

"Can you be here tomorrow?"

"If I have a job here."

I smiled and asked, "And if you don't?"

"I'd still come by. Just to see how much 'discretion' is being used."

"That's cute. Be here at ten in the morning. I'll have someone take you through everything you need to know."

"Believe me, they won't have much work to do."

"I hope not, Mr. Gaines."

"Call me Beacon."

"Okay, Beacon."

He stood and shook my hand. His grasp was firm. But his hands were supple and unscarred for someone who had worked in construction. As he left, my phone rang. I thought about Payce and started feeling a headache coming on. By the third ring, I took the call.

"Zenobia Hall."

Maurice said, "I'm just letting you know, I'm about to shoot down to Dallas real quick."

I pushed my lengthy jet-black extensions behind my shoulders and reached into the drawer for lotion to put on my mahogany hands.

"What do you mean 'real quick'?"

"Just for a couple of days and then me and Self are comin' right back."

"I know you are legally grown but I've told you about hangin' with that guy. His name ought to tell you what he's all about."

"That don't mean nothin'. You think just 'cause my name is Lethal—"

"That's not your name! Momma named you *Maurice*. And you don't know how *stupid* you sound callin' yourself that."

"You about to start again? 'Cause Self is in the ride waitin' for me."

"Be careful, Maurice, and make sure he has insurance and it's actually his car he's driving and—"

"I gotcha, Z. I'm out."

He hung up like Ed McMahon was at the door wielding a sofa-sized check. I glanced up at the clock again and it was half past. I wasn't surprised at Payce, but frustrated.

There was another knock at the door but this time the person didn't wait for permission to open it. Lainey stopped with the door cracked and finished her conversation with whomever she was talking to in the hall. I knew it was Lainey, because she was complaining. Sometimes I think her motto is: Have breath, will argue. She finally walked in wearing a knee-length ultrasuede dress with custom-made sandals to match, her shiny dark brown hair pulled back away from her vanilla face and into a bun. She slammed the door and stood in front of me with her handbag tossed over one shoulder and the other hand on her hip.

"Let me slip and fall 'cause these people can't remember to put a wet-floor sign out and I'll show Payce what it feels like to pay a sista off! I've been *lookin'* for somebody to sue so I can quit my job."

Lainey was always talking trash. In fact, it's her big mouth that's always gotten her into unusual situations—for example, her marriage. She was so busy running her mouth that she couldn't hear or see anything. Didn't try to get to know Cedric first. Didn't make sure that they were sexually compatible first. If you ask me, I think it may all be in Lainey's head. I mean, Cedric has never been what one would consider a tough guy, but being a neat dresser with a sense of style and a low sex drive is no reason for folk to start tossin' around labels. And I tried to get Lainey to see that but after a year of what she has been getting, or shall I say "not getting," there was little I could say to deter her assumptions. So now that she's at the end of her rope, I'm expected to run around and play private detective with her while she spies on Cedric to find out if he swings both ways.

"So what did you find out?" I asked.

"That I can't sit in a car at midnight for three hours without falling asleep."

I laughed and said, "I meant anything other than that."

"Nothing. I parked behind the company truck, waited for him to go on lunch and he did just that. With about six other guys."

"So maybe you're wrong. You're running around like a lunatic based on the man having a low sex drive. It could be stress. Have you discussed that possibility?"

Lainey walked over, sat down on the windowsill, folded her arms and sighed with a look of seriousness. "Ask me the last time he's tried to kiss me."

"When, Lainey?"

"New Year's Eve, and I truly believe that's only because we were in a roomful of other couples who were locked in an embrace. Since then, I've initiated *everything.*"

"Well, I'm shocked that you haven't come out and said something by now. It's the end of May already."

Lainey's eyes became misty as she lowered her head in what I perceived to be shame.

"But what if . . ."

"What, Lainey?"

"What if it's not him? What if he's just not attracted to me?"

She lifted her head, resisting the urge to cry. It was as though those words reminded her of the dignity she needed to maintain, no matter what.

"That's impossible. Look at you. You are beautiful and—"

"I know," she said, pretending to hold back a laugh. "That's why it doesn't make sense."

"So ask him. Just imagine how you'll feel if your suspicions are true and you've continued to waste your good years."

She pulled a compact from her purse, opened it and began admiring herself.

"You're right. I'm too beautiful for this shit."

"That's right."

She lowered the small brown circular case and asked, "You been to lunch yet?"

"No. I'm waiting to hear from Payce."

"Yeah, *right.* Girl, c'mon so we can go get some margaritas."

I stood from behind the desk, retied the string on the side of my lavender one-piece dress, adjusted the sling on the back of my black sandal—and then the phone rang. The Caller ID revealed that it was the call I'd been waiting for. Lainey and I looked at one another. She squinted her eyes and said, "Don't play his game."

I sat back down and said, "What took you so long to call me back?"

Payce sounded unmoved. "I was taking care of business. What's up?"

"Well, you know we were trying to schedule a time to get together and talk."

"About what?"

"About Zaire and my percentage—"

He cut me off with, "Oh, not that again. Zenobia, I told you I've got family singin' the same song about wanting part of the club, and starting next week this will be my summer with Zookie."

I pursed my lips, slammed the bottom drawer of my desk and shook my head in frustration.

"And what about hiring somebody to come in and help manage the place. I'm the only one here making sure things go smoothly."

"And I never come through?"

"Not when it counts, Payce!"

Lainey whispered, "Tell 'im, girl!"

"So I see you're still showin' out for your little girlfriend, huh? I don't have time for this."

"Wait! I'm taking off tomorrow. And I want Zaire."

"I gotta see what Cammie has planned."

"Payce, I'm her *mother*! Cammie may be gone by the end of the year. I'll be here forever."

"I'll hit you back in an hour and let you know."

When I hung up Lainey asked, "What did he say?"

"He said he would call me back in an hour."

"Why do you let him string you along like that?"

"If you've never had the lines between business and personal matters blurred then you wouldn't understand."

"I don't need that to know that Payce has always had you just where he wants you. If he asked you about getting back together for the sake of having a family, you'd probably do it."

I busied myself stacking papers on my desk and rolled my eyes to the ceiling. She had a lot of nerve trying to size me up— I mean, *she* was still doing guesswork on her husband's sexual orientation!

"He steps on your toes like he gets a high from it, and you don't even have the balls to quit this job for one you'd be happy with." She laughed to herself and continued, "He's got Zaire calling every woman in the St. Louis metropolitan area Mommy and you're still *beggin'* for a weekend."

That was it! I scooted my chair away from the desk and slammed that stack of papers on top of the file cabinet resting next to the window.

"Shut up, Lainey, 'cause you don't know what you're talking about!"

"I may not have my own shit figured out but I can smell yours comin' a mile away."

"That figures. Misery loves company, doesn't it?"

"In most cases, but not this one. I'm your friend and I think you should stop chasing a dollar, get your child and cut Payce loose."

"Without Payce, I don't have a job."

"Without Payce you don't have *this* job. And I don't exactly know just how bad that would be."

"Yeah, well, if you had told me that three years ago I

might've agreed, but I've put in too much time and work to walk away now. I want what's coming to me."

"All right, Z. But be careful what you wish for, 'cause you just might get it."

I got home from having drinks around three that afternoon without receiving so much as a page from Payce. As soon as I closed the door behind me, I stepped out of those black three-inch-high sandals and tossed my black handbag in the vicinity of the coat rack. It went well with the mess Maurice left as he'd made a dash for the Texas border like he'd forgotten that was Bush's old stompin' ground. There were Platinum Fubu and Phat Farm denim outfits and sneakers of every shade strewn across the living room floor. I stepped over an empty bottle of ketchup and remnants of a veggie flame griller on a paper plate. His obsession with filth was getting ridiculous. I shook my head and tidied up the way my mother would've done. Besides, it was either clean it up or let it sit there until he returned sometime in the next week and a half.

By the time I was done vacuuming, my margarita buzz had disappeared like a prop in a magic trick. I walked upstairs to my bedroom, stepped out of my dress and played my messages. The first five were from Maurice's unofficial fan club. There was one from Lela, the sista who lives across the street from me, asking who braided my hair and how much they charged. Another was from Payce issuing an insincere apology for not calling me back when he said he would and informing me that he'd be dropping my baby off tomorrow around twelve-thirty. I soared with relief, then listened to the last message. It was Jeff, an optometrist I'd met in line at the bank a little over a month ago. He was tall, muscular and pecan-brown with a good sense of humor, his own practice and a fiancée. Which was fine by me 'cause until he was married, he was still single and available to consider other options. We had made plans the day before yesterday to get together tonight and he was calling to confirm. I grabbed the cordless off its base and dialed him back on his cell phone. He picked up on the third ring.

"I thought you were considering standing me up," he joked.

"I wouldn't do that to a man who makes a slammin' eggplant pasta."

"Can I get that in writing?"

I giggled and said, "Seriously, you can be here by eight. Dinner will be served at nine."

"Will there be anything afterwards?"

"All the conversation you can stand. You remember the directions?"

"I've got 'em right here. I-170 north to I-270, make a right off the Elizabeth exit and go down to Tenner's Way. Eight o'clock it is. Should I bring anything?"

"No, I've got it all."

"You sure do."

I could hear him drooling over the phone. The only thing that bothered me about Jeff was the fact that sometimes he made me feel like prey. Like at any moment I might need to take off sprinting across the room to get out of his reach. Hugs and a kiss or two were okay but anything further would require us sitting down and having a serious heart-to-heart about where we stood. I've never been interested in playing second fiddle. And a hefty 401K makes Jeff no different from the rest of the male species.

"All right. See you then."

I hung up and hopped into the shower. Got dressed in a pair of cotton shorts and a T-shirt. Caught the other half of *Oprah* and then started on the quilt I was making for Zaire. When I was finished there would be a square for every country in Africa. Each one would be trimmed in a red, black and green pattern to represent the blood that has been shed, the beautiful color of our skin and the land from which we come. It was my mother's idea to trace our roots back to our original home, pinpoint exactly what area of soil my ancestors dwelled upon. I can remember the day she realized it was the country of Zaire. Momma read several books about the land and bought a map of the African continent so she could begin sewing. But she never got past the seventh square. So I picked up where she left off. I cut out the first piece and I keep it with me at all times. Tuck it in the side of whatever handbag I'm carrying at the time. I don't know what it is but rubbing the material is relaxing to me. Reminds me so much of my momma's hands, so soft and comforting. I plan to eventually give the completed quilt to Zaire and explain its significance, since she'll probably never know exactly how much her grandmother loved her. She'll never know the feel of those hands.

Once *Oprah* went off, I got up and made some vegetarian lasagna, Italian rolls and Caesar salad and sliced up some fresh fruit. I decided I'd give Jeff his choice of water, apple juice or Merlot.

At about six-thirty I went to the closet to try and find something to wear. After an unsuccessful thirty minutes had whizzed by, I opted for a simple black ankle-length skirt and a cute little plum sleeveless number I snatched up in Macy's during my last trip to Chicago. My feet were bare except for a silver toe ring. I sprayed a tiny bit of my mother's favorite perfume, Alfred Sung, behind each ear and then tied my braids into a gorgeous upsweep. Lastly, I adorned myself with a pair of silver hoops and silver bangles. Stood in front of the mirror and said aloud, "Damn, you fine!" I'd turned to observe how much smaller my butt had gotten since I put my little lady on strike two years ago when the doorbell rang. I looked at the clock on the nightstand and it wasn't quite seven yet. As I descended the stairs I could see through the glass on the front door that it was a female. My first thought was that Jeff's fiancée had followed him over here and beat him to the door. But when I opened it, I could see that this girl was no thirty-five-year-old by the puffy light blue vest, baggy jeans and zigzag cornrows she wore.

I asked, "May I help you?"

"This ain't McDonald's! Where Lethal at?"

"Excuse me?"

"You excused. Now where Lethal at 'cause I know he got my messages."

She was standing there popping gum like it was a learned trade. I looked over her shoulder and saw an old-model silver Buick Skylark running—the driver another ignorant child. She started blowing the horn and yelling, "Yeah, tell 'im I'm out here too and I wanna know what's up!"

I said, "Look, Maurice is not—"

"Who is Maurice? I'm lookin' for Lethal. And who are you?"

"Somebody who prosecutes trespassers. Now I would suggest you and your little girlfriend take this elsewhere. Maurice is not here."

She rolled her eyes and rebutted, "Well, give him a message for me."

"What is it?"

"I'm late. And Renee right there, she late too."

"Well you *do* know that Maurice is not employed right now, don't you?"

"Wait a minute. You his sister that came to visit last year and never went back home?"

Maurice was at it again. Running around trying to convince people that he had more than two wooden nickels to rub together. I glanced at my watch as a white Cadillac Escalade pulled up behind the girl parked in front of my driveway. The little Miss Hip-Hop on my porch followed my gaze from my wrist to the street. When Jeff got out, she turned to me and said, "Keep it in the guest room."

"Honey, Maurice doesn't own a car. Why would you think he owns this house?"

She sucked her teeth and shook her head at me like *I* was the one dreaming.

"He said you'd say that too."

She turned, got three more pops in on that gum, hopped down the steps and gave Jeff, who was carrying a bottle of Pinot Grigio and half a dozen red roses, the once-over as she passed him.

"You look great, Zenobia," he said, presenting me with the flowers.

"Thank you."

I closed the door and took a small leather bag he'd brought.

"You doing some mentoring?" he asked.

"Yeah, the worse kind."

"What kind is that?"

"When you don't sign up for it."

"Well, let's not allow it to spoil our evening."

When Jeff opened his arms to give me a hug, I sized up his outfit. He was into the whole Gap look. Khakis, a black V-neck cotton shirt and some black casual Kenneth Cole shoes. His haircut was fresh, his thin beard neatly shaped up. I inhaled the scent of his cologne as I buried my face in his massive chest. He felt good. Or maybe it was the fact that I hadn't allowed a man to hold me like that in a long, long time. Whatever it was, I felt a tingle in my bones and a sense of security in his tight grasp.

"Would you like something to drink while I put these in a vase?"

"Water will be fine for right now."

I showed him my CD collection in the living room and headed for the kitchen.

"What's in the bag?"

"I brought some music of my own. I didn't know you had such a huge collection."

After I finished my floral arrangement, I grabbed two wineglasses out of the cupboard and filled them with cold bottled spring water. I could hear that he had chosen well as Stevie Wonder's "Joy Inside My Tears" permeated the air.

I sashayed down the steps and into the living room. Jeff was standing in front of the fireplace looking at pictures of my momma and daddy, Zaire, Maurice and Lainey with Cedric on the mantel.

"Who is this couple?"

"That's my best friend Elaine and her husband Cedric."

"You ever plan to get married, Zenobia?"

"When I find the right person."

There was an awkward moment between us.

Then I said, "I guess there's no reason for me to ask you that question."

"I'm not so sure about that. I just don't believe in getting married under the wrong circumstances. There's nothing wrong with taking the necessary time so you don't make mistakes."

"There's no need to sound like you're defending yourself, Jeff."

He shook his head and took a sip of the water.

"I guess I sound like that because that's just what I've been doing to her parents and family."

I scrounged up a fake "Really?"

"Yeah, she's getting close to thirty-five so she's sprintin' to the altar, with me in tow. But enough about Leslie. What's gonna happen between us?"

"Well, I don't have much time in my life for meaningless relationships. Especially with uncertain men who are being 'dragged to the altar.' I've got to work and maintain order in my life."

"By that you mean . . . ?"

"Gotta pay the bills. Makeshift love won't keep a sista's stomach full, or her heart either."

"True. What kind of monetary help do you need?"

"I'm not interested in any more debt. Thanks, but no thanks."

I stood, took his glass and started toward the kitchen again.

"Is the groom ready to eat?"

"That's not funny, Zenobia. I'm tryin' to see what will blossom between us."

"I can see now that you may not be my type, Jeff."

"And what exactly is your type?"

"Men who are in control of their lives."

He stopped mid-stride and gave me a look of insult.

I smiled and continued, "I mean that with the utmost respect. You have truly got too much on your plate right now. You couldn't keep a woman like myself happy for very long."

Jeff walked up from behind and placed his family jewels against me. Wrapped his arms across my 36Bs and rocked to Stevie's crooning from the other room.

Then he asked, "What would you say if I told you I think I *can* make you happy?"

"I'd say, 'You need to think with your other head.'"

"You're not feelin' me?"

"Oh, I'm feelin' you all right."

"Then what are you looking for?"

"I'm looking for a love I can call my own, Jeff. What are you looking for?"

Jeff spun me around and held me by the shoulders. Gazed deep into my eyes like he was considering giving me something more than a good stiff one. He leaned in and planted a soft, moist kiss on my neck, and then another. Leaving a trail to my earlobe. He pulled away and smiled as he hoisted me up onto the counter. I thought about resisting. Really, I did. And if it weren't for the way he fondled his lips like Denzel did in Spike Lee's *Mo' Better Blues,* I wouldn't have opened my mouth and invited his tongue inside. I could feel his hands traveling south. Nestling in between my legs. A sense of urgency drove me to indulge in the feeling. And then the moment I closed my eyes, I pictured him at the altar raising the blusher on a veil and gawking at whoever the lucky contestant on *Land That Groom* was.

I pushed him back as he cupped my right breast.

He asked, "What's wrong?"

"Jeff, you gotta ask yourself what's *right* with this."

"Everything. I'm into you."

I hopped down off the counter and whispered, "Not if I can help it."

He looked at me like a lineman waiting to rush the quarterback.

"Mind if I use your bathroom?" he asked, adjusting the bulge in the front of his pants.

"You know where it is."

I grabbed a tray of fruit and set it on the table. Lighted two candles and then went down into the living room to trade Stevie for Rachelle Ferrell's *Individuality.* I heard Jeff open the bathroom door as I did a slow groove in front of the fireplace. Closed my eyes and swayed to the often high pitch of Rachelle's voice as if it were my own. Jeff walked up behind me, held me around my waist and kissed the back of my right ear.

"You smell and look wonderful. It's almost unfair."

I smiled and turned to him. "Unfair to whom?"

"To me. I wish I could have you to myself."

"And why can't you?"

"Because you're one of those independent no-nonsense

women with no patience. I told you the day we met how I've been feeling pressured by her family and how I was waiting for the appropriate moment. I don't know. It's just that I'm tired of pretending to be happy when I know damn well that I want to be anyplace but there. Particularly here with you."

I took him by the hand and pulled him over to my eggshell-white sofa.

"Then let's stop playing games here, Jeff. If you don't plan to get married, I wanna know now."

"Truthfully, Zenobia, I have no plans of going through with it."

"Well look, we've been seeing each other for four and a half weeks. I enjoy your company and you seem to enjoy mine. I may appear evasive, but I do see potential for us. We both love jazz and Italian food, and our long walks near the fountains in Kiener Plaza have always been fun. It would be a shame for us to waste an opportunity like this. There's nothing *wrong* with being happy."

"Then happy is what we'll be."

He slowly leaned in and kissed me again. This time I let go. Allowed his hands to travel uninhibitedly—down the back of my skirt and right around to the inside of my thighs. I was tingling in places I'd forgotten existed. Jeff lay me down and removed his shirt. That was about the time that little voice in my head started screamin', *Z, this is not a good idea, give it some time.* But the way this man was lickin' around my ankles and up my leg with the agility of somebody with a point to push, I felt I had no choice but to take in the moment.

"Ooh, you taste so good," he said, tossing my skirt over his head.

Z, think about how you'll feel once he goes home.

Jeff hurled one of my legs over the back of the couch and

started unbuckling his belt. He fumbled for a minute and cursed in frustration. All the while leaving a trail of kisses up my thigh.

"Need some help?" I asked him, sitting up on my elbows.

"Not unless you really want to."

We switched positions, with me now on top. I did a slow grind as I freed his little man—emphasis on "little"—and I'd just removed his cell phone to place it on the wooden coffee table when it unexpectedly rang in my hand. We both jumped. Stared at it for a minute like answering was still an option.

"Didn't clear your schedule?" I asked, holding it just out of his reach.

"I—I don't . . ."

"Here!"

I handed it to him and hopped up in one swift movement. I could hear him pushing the button to answer as I went into the bathroom to remove my moist panties and finish the job of bringing my horny tail back to the Land of Reality. Standing over the sink, I could hear him walking around and pushing a lot of buttons. Sounded like he was getting a party line started as I took a washcloth and cleared his trail of kisses to my little lady. I stepped out of my purple thong and threw it in the white hamper under a gold-framed picture of a mother and daughter sitting on a bench sharing a quiet moment. Thought about Zaire and what kind of example I was being for her, even if she couldn't see me messin' up. That's when the front door slammed. I stood there in a trance for almost ten minutes, ready to beat myself up emotionally for losing control. I leaned forward against the counter and saw tears forming in my eyes. I had done it again. Ignored the warning signs and tried to rush things. Attempted to convince a man that I was the best thing walking before it was determined whether or not he was worthy of all I had to offer. Had confused my longing to be loved with a longing to be desired.

It was at that moment I decided that I had been mishandled for the last time, had gone against my original agenda and trusted a man for the last time. The next one would have to work overtime and then some. I looked in the mirror and chanted, *Protect your heart, Zenobia. You are obligated to live and learn.* I wiped my face and took a deep breath. Inhaled the odor of over-cooked lasagna.

"Oh, shit!" I yelled, bolting from the bathroom and down the hall.

I pulled the door to the oven open and smoke filled the kitchen. As I raced to the window, I noticed my cordless sitting on the table, partly because it was ringing but mostly because I knew where I'd left it, on the base in the family room. I picked it up, read the Caller ID and got ready to rip Jeff a new one.

"You don't have the fuckin' decency to—"

A woman was panting heavily on the other line. She stopped, tried to get a word out and finally broke into an ear-piercing scream.

"Hello?!" I yelled.

More panting. Then she brought herself to ask, "Yes, is Jeff still there?"

I put one hand on my hip and demanded, "Who is this?"

"Ouch! My name is Leslie. Oh God, help me! Please, I can't have this baby alone."

"What?!"

"I'm anemic. Please! Oh God, please!"

This can't be happening.

She cut my thought short with, "Please, stay on the line with me. I just spoke with him a minute ago from this number. How far do you live from University City?"

"He called you from *my* phone?!"

"Ouch, ouch! Shoot! It hurts! His cell went out. Pray with me, please."

I threw my hands weightlessly in the air and shook my head. My ego and sense of morals were playing tug-of-war.

"Are you there?" she asked.

"Listen, honey, I'm not religious."

"You don't have to be . . . Zenobia."

My jaw dropped in astonishment. "How do you know my name?"

"Ooh, ouch! Jeff—isn't the wisest man I've ever met. Now please lead us in prayer."

There I was standing in my smoky kitchen with no panties on, fresh out of a spread-eagle position, talking to the *other* woman and asking the Lord to listen to *me*.

"This is ridiculous, Leslie. I almost *worked Jeff over* tonight so maybe you need to find somebody else to do this with 'cause it just doesn't feel right."

"Lord, please forgive Zenobia for any of her wrongdoings as I have. And I ask that you show mercy on me in my time of need."

I sat down at the table and rested my forehead on the tips of my fingers as she continued.

"We realize that you are steadfast in your . . ."

"Excuse me."

". . . love and mercy."

"Uh, excuse me."

"Wait a minute. Zenobia, he's home! Thank you so . . ."

I could hear Jeff in the background asking how she was feeling, and whom she was talking to. And then came the muffled sounds of a phone being dropped.

He finally scooped it up and asked, "*What* are you doing?"

"Seeing you for who you truly are."

"I told you the other day that I needed time, Zenobia," he whispered.

"Jeff, you already have exactly what you need—a damn fool."

Theresa

"Deon, park it in your seat or you'll be sitting here making small talk with me after school."

My class clown gave me a look of disdain for cutting his rendition of *The Original Kings of Comedy* short and slowly took his seat amongst the group of thirty children who were dressed in about six hundred thousand dollars' worth of clothing.

There are days when my girls in the front row have better handbags than I do. Pedicures are regular and one child once even had the nerve to offer me a referral to her beautician. The boys usually strut around like they're stuck in a rap video with no desire to escape. I stop the pant-sagging and bling-bling medallions at the door. "You came here to learn. This is a classroom, not a runway."

Some immediately begin to dislike me for that reason alone. Others feel a sense of safety; they know someone is willing to draw the line between fantasy and reality. Mix the "shop for less" kids with the "finer department store" kids so they know they have more to carry them through life than the best-dressed award.

The Summertime Fair was our next major event, and I've always been big on celebrations. The kids and I decorate the classroom for every holiday and season I can think of. Easter,

Halloween, Thanksgiving, spring, winter, Groundhog Day. The level of importance doesn't matter. If it's written on a calendar someplace on this earth, I'm racking up on construction paper, ribbons and Nativity scenes.

And like just about every teacher, I have my not-so-favorites. This year there were a boy and a girl on this team. I refer to them as a team because they seemed to work in that manner, tagging one another out when their partner got tired. My counteracting opponents were the infamous Tiwana and Deon. Both were bona fide class clowns in search of a *Comic View* audition. Some days it appeared that they even had prewrittten material.

Tiwana informed me, "Ms. Downing, this glue not workin'."

"I beg your pardon."

"Ms. Downing," Tiwana repeated, "this glue isn't working."

"Let me see it, Tiwana."

They were cutting out flowers, grass, clouds and the sun and pasting them to a large white poster that was being used to welcome the sixth-grade class for the following year. Those who felt they were too mature for that got to write everyone in the class's name in calligraphy or to set out fresh flowers I'd gotten from Soulard Market that morning. The rest were on the cleanup committee.

And then there was Deon. In the last row holding his own private discussion with his usual group of followers who sought popularity.

"Who is that snapping their fingers?" I demanded to know.

"Deon," they all answered in unison.

"Front and center, Mr. Coleman."

He approached my desk with his hands stuffed into the pockets of his baggy jeans. Dragged his heavy, untied sneakers across the floor like they were filled with lead. He stroked the top of his head and then along the faded sides. Tilted it to the right like he had someplace to be and I was keeping him.

"Empty your pockets."

He sighed and shifted his weight from one blue Air Nike to the other. Emptied the contents onto my desk and turned to walk away.

"Hold on one second. Didn't I ask you not to bring dice to school?"

All I received was a nod in response.

"Take the dice and follow me."

I took him into the hall, then made him stand just outside the door and shake the dice until his arm came close to falling off.

"Stand here, and every time I see someone pass you in this hall you better apologize for shooting dice in this school."

At that moment a third grader came walking by. I looked at Deon. He looked at me. I looked down at his aching arm.

"I'm sorry for shooting dice in this school," he told the little girl in the green dress.

"No. Say, 'I'm sorry for shooting dice in this school and being silly enough to mistake it for a back alley.' "

He repeated what I said and grunted. I shook my head and walked back inside in time for the lunch bell. Students scrambled to clear their desks and then waited for permission to line up at the door. I could hear his frustration as his classmates teased him on their way out, so I asked him to step inside and have a seat, but he wasn't allowed to stop shaking the dice.

I sat down at one of the computers in the far corner to check my e-mail. Logged on and leaned back in the metal folding chair. I looked up and spotted him crying silent, angry tears. His face was twisted as though he smelled something foul in the air, but his arm never stopped moving. Three pieces of mail popped up and as I attempted to open the first, Deon dropped one of the dice. It hit the floor like a bolt of lightning ripping through a peaceful midnight sky.

"Come here," I told him.

54

As he took his time doing the lead-foot drag, I heard someone tap on the door. I turned around and found Nikai standing on the threshold wearing a white Moroccan-style shirt with a three-quarter-length denim skirt and flip-flops. Her locks hanging freely. A frown upon her face.

She asked, "Theresa, you busy?"

I waved her in. "No, sit down. I'll be done in just a second."

I told Deon, "Today is your lucky day. Go on to lunch, but when you come back you'll need to assume the position."

He turned and had broken into a slew-footed stroll when I yelled, "Pull your pants up, boy!"

Nikai laughed. Took a seat in the desk adjacent to the computer and set her black leather purse in the chair next to her. She tossed her locks over her shoulder and gripped the edge of the desk. Stared at me with eyes that danced with mischief. She was up to something, something so sinister that she couldn't keep it to herself.

I removed my hand from the mouse and asked, "What did you do?"

The smile she wore faded as she fell into the back of the chair and sighed loudly.

"I thought I could do it."

"You thought you could do what?" I quizzed.

"I thought I could just speak and keep going."

She glanced out of the window and needlessly tossed her locks over her shoulder again.

"He says he's not seeing anybody. I find that hard to believe."

"Who are you talking about?"

She turned her head swiftly in my direction, tilted it and raised her brow as if to suggest that I should already know.

"Think about it for a second."

"Look, I 'think' for a living. Tell me who you're talking about."

She lowered her eyes and toyed with her short, manicured nails. Then she whispered, "Firefighter Hayes."

"No! Nikai, no!"

Robert Hayes was an ex who'd snatched three years from her life. He was Don's best friend. He was Dameron's godfather. He was a tall, dark, bald, attractive and muscular firefighter whom women neglected common sense for, but he was also a part of her tattered past. She had credited him with helping her grow into the person she was today. But I could see him turning her into the insecure woman she was back then if she wasn't careful. Robert was a good person at heart. The last I'd heard from him, he was moving back this way from Arizona, where he had followed "some woman." I love him more than a brother, but that's been his thing for some time now—following women.

Nikai shook her head. "I don't know. This feeling just came over me. It's been so long. It was like I couldn't breathe or somethin'. When I saw him coming down that escalator in the Galleria, it was like everything I have in my life melted away."

I rested my arm over the back of my chair and asked, "Do you remember the love of your life—Kalif? Are you keeping in mind that these two men have had a physical altercation over you? Has the whole *Karen situation* escaped you, too? Remember, the woman he thought he'd impregnated while you two were living together?"

She fanned her hand at me. "Did I say that I was leaving Kalif for Rob? No! I just said I saw the man, damn."

"No, you said, 'It was like I couldn't breathe or somethin'.'" I mocked her lovesick behavior with a Scarlett O'Hara impression.

She laughed, but not for long. Looked up at me. Her eyes sought approval.

"He asked me to call him."

"And are you? You know I'm gonna talk about you bad if you do."

"I haven't decided yet."

"Yes you have."

"Shut up, Theresa! I'm just tryin' to see what the man's been up to—over dinner."

"What?! Okay, I don't know who you two think you're foolin' but you're treading on thin ice, Nikai!"

"I'm driving my own car and meeting him there. That's it! He says now that he's back in St. Louis he wants to spend more time with Dameron."

"What does that have to do with you going out on a date with a man who is single when you are not?"

"Look, I thought you would be happy to see that we can be cordial toward one another. Especially considering the way things ended between us."

"I am, but I don't think it's a good idea for you to get involved with him, Nikai. I'm telling you, when the chickens come home to roost you're gonna regret it."

"Well, since it's not that type of party, that's not a concern of mine, country girl. Now what's up?"

"All right, if you say so. I'm going down to Atlanta to stay with my momma for a week or so. These dreams have been getting the best of me."

"Maybe you should see somebody about them."

"That takes money. I think I just need to relax and spend some time someplace where nothing is expected of me."

"You need me to keep Dameron while you get packed?"

"Would you, please? That would be a big help. The landlord is having our apartments exterminated and I hate for Dameron to be there possibly inhaling fumes."

"No problem. How's your friend?"

"Who, Vince? That's *all* we are is friends. He left the other night. Says he has a problem with my drinking every now and then."

"Maybe that's an issue that affected his family."

"It isn't. And even if it was, he was in no position to yell at me."

"'*Was* in'? Sounds like it's over."

"He packed up his belongings and left, right after he willingly handed me my bottle of rum back."

"Ooh yeah, that's a done deal. Did you tell him you're leaving?"

"Yeah, he knows. But I guess what bothers me is that deep down I wanted him to ask me to stay."

"Sheila used to talk about me bad for that. Not saying exactly what I wanted and expecting other people to read my mind."

Nikai's friend Sheila was the owner of a new and progressive Afrocentric bookstore named African Impressions. She's supposed to be some kind of guru on life or something. Let Nik tell it, she's studied under Gandhi, Moses *and* Iyanla Vanzant. She's got herbal remedies for everything from toe jam to cancer. And if you sit quietly enough, she can tell you your next thought.

Nik reached out and held my hand. But it didn't make me feel any better. Pity was something that I'd had more than my share of.

"When was the last time you were home?" she asked.

"Almost two years ago."

Nikai nodded her head. "I think you're long overdue. I just hate that you won't be here for me to give you play-by-play on my dinner with Rob. It will be nice to catch up."

I shook my head. "I don't believe you, Nikai. The chances you take are so unnecessary."

She lifted her finger in the air. "Um, excuse me, Ned the Wino, you've got very little room to talk."

We both laughed.

"I don't have a drinking problem. My problem is that I'm a magnet for retarded women who chase firefighters who've already broken their hearts."

Nikai's laugh dwindled down to a chuckle. "I know that I love Kalif. Call it closure but I've got to know that I've gotten over Robert."

"And if you haven't gotten over him?"

She tossed her locks over her shoulder again and grabbed my hands. "Then we'll both have to do our part to get these firefighters out of our systems."

I shook my head.

She grinned and leaned back on the desk. "By any means necessary."

Zenobia

I was jolted from my sleep by the sound of the doorbell. I glanced at the silver watch on my wrist. It was already noon. As I stood to my feet, I kicked the empty bottle of wine I'd drowned myself in while toasting to a safe delivery for Leslie. She called me around midnight once Jeff went down to the nursery, to give me the *good* news—depending on who you are in this sick trio. I say that 'cause she asked me to start going to her prayer group on Monday nights. At first I thought I stood nothing to lose but with her being so dim-witted and her man being so delectable, I was sure the temptation would leave everybody layin' hands on me and tryin' to rebuke the lust from my soul on a weekly basis. So I decided to pass.

I rubbed the sleep from my eyes and asked, "Who is it?"

"Lainey. Open up."

I turned the locks over, opened the door and sauntered toward the bathroom.

Lainey asked, "What happened to *you* last night? You look like hell!"

"Shut up, Lainey. Jeff came by."

"And?"

"And he had a baby."

"What?!"

She dropped her backpack by the door and detoured my route into the living room. Picked up the empty wine bottle off the floor and set it on the coffee table.

"Now back this up and start from the beginning."

I took a deep breath and put my feet up on the sofa while Lainey unlaced her Nikes and did the same.

"Okay, I cooked dinner, which happened to burn when I was taking my panties off. But anyway, he was over here tellin' me all about how unhappy he was with his fiancée and how his days there were numbered, so to speak. Well, you know I ain't had a good piece in years and you *know* what that man's lips look like."

Lainey leaned forward and high-fived me. "Girl, somebody needs to teach him how to use 'em!"

"Well, he started kissing on me and things got serious and the next thing I know Leslie, his fiancée, calls on his cell. Well, you know by then I was pissed. I got up and went to the bathroom to regroup. That's when his black ass disappeared. So I'm standing in the bathroom cryin' like an idiot, when I smell the food burning. I run out in time to catch her phone call, which ended in a prayer session. Needless to say, they had a boy."

Lainey's mouth was still open by the time I finished recounting how my feelings had been stepped on for another man's personal gain.

"Did he even bother to tell you that he was expecting a child?"

I looked at Lainey like she was retarded. "Would *you* if you were him?"

"Well, be glad you found out sooner than later."

"I guess. What's the latest with you?"

"Absolutely nothing! I know paraplegics who get more action than I do. I spent almost two hundred dollars in Victoria's Secret last week. Put one of those come-get-it outfits on last night and woke up wearing the same damn thing this morning. Now who can miss a *lime-green thong?* Ever since Cedric got into the whole part-time real estate thing, our relationship has changed. He's about as bad as you are when it comes to chasin' a dollar. He goes from his mail delivery job to those stupid seminars and then home and straight to bed. It's like I don't know him anymore. My goodness, he's my *husband!*"

I didn't know what to say. I mean, Lainey was beautiful. A five-foot-nine, light-skinned sista from Louisiana with long dark brown curly hair that made her Creole background very apparent.

"Sit the man down and talk to him, Lainey. For somebody who can figure everybody else's problems out, you're taking the long route to get to the bottom of your own."

"And just what do you think he's gonna say, Z?" she asked.

I shrugged my shoulders. "Guess I see your point."

"The only way I'm gonna *get* to the bottom of this is if I keep quiet."

"Yeah, if you don't lose your mind first, and it sounds like you're halfway there."

I got up and went to the bathroom to brush my teeth. Lainey stuck her foot out to trip me on the way. I hopped and caught my balance on the ottoman.

"See, it don't pay to be ornery," I said as I flipped her the bird and sashayed out of the room.

"So what do you have planned for today?" she yelled from the living room.

"Payce is bringing Zaire over. We're gonna spend the day together. Maybe go to the Science Center, the Zoo and out to eat. What's up with you?"

"Nothin'. Mind if I tag along? Maybe if there's enough time we can go to the bookstore and buy one of those guides on how to sexually arouse a corpse."

I laughed. "Yeah, maybe I can get some books for Zaire.

There's this new Afrocentric bookstore down on Washington. It's pretty big, even has a small deli inside."

"Oh, you're talking about African Impressions. A woman I work with was just tellin' me about a jazz night they have there."

I ducked my head around the corner with toothpaste running out of the sides of my mouth and inquired, "They've got jazz there?"

"Yeah, she said a couple of local artists were there last Thursday and the crowd was huge."

"So what's up for next Thursday night? We goin' or what?"

"Hey, I'm free all week."

I could tell that hearing herself say that out loud was about to have Lainey sulking back down into her funk. Luckily, the doorbell rang. I looked up at the clock over the fireplace and realized it was about time for my baby to arrive.

I asked Lainey, "Would you get that for me?"

I ran back to the bathroom, shut the door behind me, rinsed my mouth out, washed my face and let my braids fall across my shoulders. Studied the mother-and-daughter picture in my bathroom for a minute and then opened the door. Lainey was standing there with an ambiguous look on her face and an envelope in her hand. She passed it to me and pulled me toward the front door.

"Hurry up, and get a look at this."

I started down the front steps as Zaire stood on the driver's side of a white Chrysler Sebring with Cammie inside. She looked at me and started the engine while telling Zaire to back away from the car. Zaire wouldn't. She seemed attached, almost as though she felt abandoned.

"Cammie!" I yelled, holding on to the inside of the passenger window. "Wait! Wait a minute!"

She abruptly shifted the gear into park and sighed. Banged on the steering wheel and reluctantly turned to me without uttering so much as a word. Her mocha-colored skin was bruised around the bridge of her pointy nose and her exotic, slightly slanted eyes were now swollen. There was a half an inch of stitches along her jawline and her middle finger was in a splint.

I instructed Zaire, "Go in the house with Aunt Lainey. She's got some ice cream she wants you to try with her."

Zaire pulled at one of the two twisted ponytails that hung on each side of her head, reluctantly moved around the front of the car, then walked across the driveway to Lainey and took her hand. I opened the passenger side and sat down. Placed the envelope with my name on it in my lap and searched for the appropriate words.

"Cammie, I don't intend to tell you how to run your household but Zaire shouldn't be seeing this."

She shook her head and buried her chin in her chest. I reached over and rubbed her shoulder.

"I know what you're dealing with. Well, Payce has never hit me but I do know his temper and how irrational he can be at times. But the only way he'll learn is if you show him that you won't tolerate it."

She nodded her head and remained silent. I felt like I was talking to Zaire more so than to a grown woman.

"Do you want to talk about it?"

There was a moment of silence. Then she said, "It was his wrongdoing, Zenobia. He was the one who got caught cheating, not me."

"And what happened?"

"I busted him!"

Cammie became angrier and somewhat louder as she recalled the incident in her mind.

"In *our* bed! He even had the nerve to yell out that he *loved her*! She'd been eating my food the entire weekend! Rollin' her funky ass around on *my* sheets like my picture on the nightstand

64

came with the damn frame or somethin'! She *knew* he wasn't single!"

Those last words hit home like a tornado rippin' through Kansas in spring. I had pulled the same stunt the night before. Disrespected a union like I didn't know it existed, like I didn't know it would cause another woman severe pain.

"So what happened when you walked in, Cammie?"

"I was frozen. I couldn't believe it, the way they were screwin' until they'd slid onto the floor. And even then they didn't stop. After about five seconds, I just snapped and started throwin' stuff across the room at them both. I was so mad, Zenobia, I even grabbed his momma's urn and threw that. He caught it in mid-flight."

Cammie gave a seemingly psychotic laugh and stared down at the splint on her finger.

"You should've seen him. It was the first time I'd seen fear in his eyes."

Then she looked over at me with a slight grin.

"It felt good."

I tried to chime in with a minimal amount of amusement but I could tell that something about Cammie just wasn't right—she had reached a breaking point.

"Well, that's when he charged at me and beat the hell outta me right in front of her. You think she stopped crawlin' across the carpet long enough to call the police?"

I didn't say anything, although she was staring at me like she didn't realize that was a rhetorical question and didn't require an answer. The little I could see of her eyes was pitiful. I could imagine how they gazed up at Payce begging for mercy. So I reached over and gave her a hug.

"I'm so sorry, Cammie. You know I have nothing against you—it's Payce that I can't stand."

"Don't worry, Zaire will be fine. I love her. I really do. And I know you love her too. That's why I wrote you this letter."

"What does it say?"

"Just read it. I gotta go. I've got a plane to catch. I'm moving back to L.A. in the morning."

"And Payce?"

"*Fuck* Payce!"

"Well, what about—"

"Read the letter, Zenobia, and you'll know all you need to know."

After Cammie backed out of the driveway, I quietly walked into the house and closed the front door behind me. Leaned against it and tapped my leg with the envelope. Lainey and Zaire were in the kitchen laughing about something. I closed my eyes and thought about how much I'd miss hearing Zaire's giggle every morning for the next three months. It was high-pitched, unyielding and innocent.

"Z, is that you?" Lainey called out.

"Yeah. You two saving me some ice cream?"

Zaire yelled, "Come on, Mommy. Aunt Lainey gave me a lot."

I stepped into the kitchen and pretended to put on a sad face.

"Can Mommy have some of yours, Zaire?"

She wrapped her skinny cocoa-brown arm around my neck as I stood next to her stool and let her feed me a couple of spoonfuls.

"Oh thank you. Lainey, isn't my big girl thoughtful and sweet?"

"Sure is. She says she's gonna be our tour guide at the Zoo today since she knows the whole park by heart."

"Well, let me hurry up and get dressed so we can go on the Miss Zaire Whittington tour."

I kissed her on the cheek and rubbed her back through the pink and white jumper she was wearing. She kicked her legs back and forth, laughed a little harder. On my way up the stairs, I stopped, turned around and admired Zaire's smile. It was my mother's. The sight almost moved me to tears.

As soon as I made it up to my bedroom, I grabbed a piece of my comforting quilt from the side of my handbag, sat down on the foot of the bed and ripped into the envelope. There was a single sheet of paper inside. I unfolded it and began to read Cammie's handwritten letter.

Dear Zenobia,

I know we've never been the best of friends but there is something I must tell you. I no longer want to be with Payce. I used to think of leaving him as throwing away a part of my life, but Payce tossed that out of the window the first time he cheated on me and unfortunately, the first time he beat me. I remember that night like it was yesterday. All of the promises and even the tears he shed. I was convinced that if he was willing to cry over me, maybe he needed me. Maybe I meant more to him than I'd imagined. But I was wrong. Wrong for more than just staying but for allowing it to be witnessed through the eyes of an innocent child.

One night I was watching a show about interpretation. That night I realized that Zaire might've been interpreting this dysfunctional behavior as normal or warranted. That's when I knew something had to change.

Payce didn't tell you but I left with Zaire once. We stayed in a hotel for three days until he tracked us down and begged me to come back home. Again, he cried. He only did so in situations where he was certain I had had enough and was about to leave for good. I enjoyed watching him grovel. I took pride in the abil-

ity to make a man so strong belittle himself for me. So again, we went back.

I'd tell Zaire stories of how someday a prince would come galloping over the hills for her and he wouldn't treat her the way Payce had treated me. I thought that would help. I thought that would somehow repair the damage Payce and I had inflicted in her delicate psyche. It didn't. So I'm letting you know that she cries in her sleep sometimes. She cries because she doesn't want to be asleep. She thinks that Payce will beat me if she isn't around to keep watch. I'm sorry for what has happened to her. And I ask that you forgive me. I'd rather see her with you than with Payce, any day. That's why I have to tell you that he may be getting traded to another team and taking Zaire with him. Please, if you can, save that baby from any further damage. Payce will never change, only the women he hurts.

Call me if you need me. I'll be at my mother's home. 210-555-7194.

Cammie

Vince

I left the office early with the intention of stopping by Theresa's place to drop off her key. As much as it hurt, I had to honor her request. But only that one. I'd promised Dameron a colorful red, blue and yellow desk for his room and I intended to make good on it. Truth be told, I'd grown attached to him. Maybe wanted to be the father to him that I never had, or maybe I just wanted to prove to myself that I could be anything other than the father I had.

When I pulled up to the redbrick apartment building, I got out, pulled the desk from my trunk and headed upstairs. I wanted to get in and get out before she had a chance to get home and suggest that my gift would only make things harder on Dameron. I unlocked the door as the scent of vanilla air freshener invited me in. I loved Theresa's place. Used to be my home away from home. Her apartment was decorated in soft hues, plenty of orange colors and reds ranging from copper to burgundy. Fine art by black painters hung from her walls and a taupe chenille throw was carelessly draped over the back of the sofa in front of sheer curtains. Books were stacked on the end of a mahogany coffee table that was adjacent to a black chaise lounger.

I maneuvered my way through the living room with haste and

opened the hall closet. Readjusted Theresa's damn near three-and-a-half-foot hanging shoe rack and accidentally caused a piece of wood to fall from the wall. When I bent down to re-place it, I noticed that there were things inside of this space. And as soon as I reached into the hole, there was a knock at the door.

"Exterminator!"

"Hang on a second."

I put the shoe rack back and took the desk down the hall to Dameron's room. Temptation ate away at me as I walked back past the closet and closed the door. But snooping around would do me no good. I know a firefighter's helmet when I see one.

I'd left the key on top of the desk, along with any hope that we'd ever make things work.

Zenobia

"Ah c'mon, Z. I just got in."

"Look, I told you that this time it's an emergency, Maurice."

We were standing in the foyer arguing about whether my request for him to baby-sit was unreasonable. When I got out of the shower, he and Self were coming in the door dropping bags and opening the refrigerator like either one of them had job stability or a dime to contribute.

"If I wanted to sit around with kids all day I'd have some."

That reminded me of the dumb duo who was looking for him a couple of nights ago.

"Well, I wouldn't speak so quickly. Some little girls came by here looking for you claiming that they've missed their periods."

"Ah, that's just Trish and Baby."

"And you're just unemployed and borderline homeless! Speaking of which, you need to get a job, not just for them but for yourself. Now, you can either watch Zaire today or have half on the utilities by sundown."

I turned, rolled my eyes at Self, who was sitting in the living room with his hands in his lap tryin' to look like he didn't have a police record as long as the damn coffee table, and stomped away. I went back upstairs and got Zaire dressed in a hurry. Her denim skirt and aqua-blue T-shirt were still wrinkled as I pushed and pulled her little sleepy limbs in and out of them. I fought to hold her head up as I brushed her hair into an Afro puff at the top and then let her lie back down in her bed. Maurice could make her breakfast. I was in too much of a rush. The guy who was supposed to train Beacon didn't show up the other day and had the nerve to call this morning sayin' somebody he grew up with died in his apartment late that night. That was the worst part about my job, trying to tell a lie from the truth without offending anybody.

I threw on some hip-hugger jeans and a white cotton sleeveless shirt that tied on the side. Jumped into my pearl-rose Altima and stabbed out. By the time I made it down to Discretion I was exhausted and had a headache. You know how you wake up too fast startled by something like the phone and it seems all of the blood has rushed to your head, making you jumpy and irritable? Well that's the mood I was in.

The first face I saw when I stepped through the door was Beacon's. He was sitting at one of the wooden tables in our black and gold T-shirt that read *Use Your Own Discretion* on the front and a pair of jeans. He had pulled the table and chair near the bar and was glancing through a *BE* magazine. When he heard the front door open, he folded one corner down and smiled at me.

"Sorry about you having to come in today," he told me, standing up from the table.

"That's okay. I was coming in anyway. I'll be back down in just a few minutes. I need to get situated."

"Oh, the owner came by looking for you this morning around ten."

It was well after eleven at the moment. I asked, "What did he say?"

"He just wanted me to tell you that he was looking for you."

"Thanks, Beacon."

I climbed the stairs to my office. With every step, my head beat a little harder. I wished for my quilt piece, which I'd accidentally—and quite uncharacteristically—left at home, as I realized nobody had even bothered to come upstairs. It was completely dark. I started down the long narrow hall and saw a light coming from under the door to my office. When I reached it, I found Payce sitting at my desk in some workout gear, with his feet propped up and staring out the window.

I held on to the doorknob and asked, "Is there something I can help you with?"

"What's up, Zenobia?"

I stared down my nose at him and waited for him to explain what he was doing chillin' amongst my personal stuff.

"What's up with *you*, Payce?"

"Seen Cammie?"

"Is that who gave you permission to unlock my office and come in here like this?"

He tilted his head and nodded it for a minute like his patience was wearing thin. His dark brown hands were folded in his lap as he rocked his feet back and forth. He bit his bottom lip and then repeated his question.

"I've been movin' so fast this morning I haven't seen *anybody*," I said, setting my purse down in a chair. I stood behind it for a minute and tapped my unpolished nails on the back while we played the intimidation game.

"Where is Zaire?"

"She's being taken care of."

"I didn't ask you that, Zenobia. I asked where she was."

"And I asked you who in the hell told you it was okay to come in my office!"

Payce snatched his feet off the desk and stood up abruptly. "This is my fuckin' club! You don't tell me where to go and where not to!"

I stood up straight and walked around to where the floor was clear of furniture just in case I had to break one of those unpolished nails.

"I told you before about coming up here. These are my *personal* belongings!"

Payce seemed to calm down a bit, moved around to the other side of my desk and leaned against a file cabinet. His keys, which he had tied on the drawstring of his sweat shorts, were jingling as he walked and getting on my nerves. Reminded me of when we were together, when we did everything including work out together.

"So who's the new guy downstairs?" he asked.

"His name is Beacon. He's the extra bartender you said we needed."

"He any good?"

"I don't know. I'm here to train him. Kevin called me at home this morning and said he couldn't make it."

"Did you give 'im the axe?"

I shoved my chair against the desk and yelled, "No, Payce! You said I could only hire, not fire, remember?!"

"Would it make you feel a little better if I gave you the power to do that?" he asked with sarcasm in his voice.

"No. What you could do is give me a percentage of this place."

"I'm letting you keep Zaire. That's not enough?"

"'Letting' me?! She's my child too! And the only reason you're not trying to get her back is because Cammie is gone! Otherwise—"

"So you *have* seen her?"

"Yes, I have. And that's a shame, Payce. I can't believe you did that to her, and in front of Zaire!"

"What are you talkin' about? Zookie wasn't even there that night."

He opened the door, laughed and said, "You're wearin' those jeans, girl."

"You'll never get close enough to know how well."

Beacon appeared in the hall behind him and started to go back downstairs.

"It's okay. He was just leaving, Beacon."

"I'll call you about that bike, Zenobia."

"That's fine."

Payce walked out and pulled the door shut behind him.

"What's up?" I asked Beacon.

"I thought maybe you'd forgotten about me."

"No, it's just taking me a little while longer to get situated."

He was walking around my office and looking at the pictures of me hugging Maurice at his graduation and another of my momma on the wall. Then Beacon stood in front of the two-way mirror that gave a bird's-eye view of the entire club. His hands were behind his back and he was disturbingly silent.

"Is there something you wanted to talk about, Beacon? Because if not, I don't allow employees to hang out in my office with me."

He jumped like I startled him and answered, "No, I'm fine. I was just gonna wait on you."

"Well, you can do that downstairs. I've got some phone calls to make."

"Okay."

I watched him as he slowly walked out the door without giving any eye contact and without uttering a word. Weird, I thought. Then I picked up the phone to call Lainey at work.

"Accounting Department. This is Elaine. May I help you?"

"Hey, what's goin' on?"

"I hate my job and I want to walk in that office and resign as of yesterday."

"That's a given, Lainey. Beside that."

"Cedric got e-mail from a MrVLRuns and a Joshsells4u this morning."

"What did it say?"

"It was pretty vague, and then Ced walked in on me so I had to shut the computer down. But the guy gave him an address."

"To his house?"

"I guess so."

Lainey left a moment of silence and I knew the dreaded was coming.

"You gonna go with me?"

"And do what, sit outside the man's house? If it *is* the address to a house."

"This is my *husband* we're talking about here, Zenobia. Please, you gotta."

I rested my forehead on the tips of my fingers and said, "I hate I called you."

"You know it would've been only a matter of time before I called you. Who else can I go to?"

"Try a fellow stalker!"

"Not funny. So when can you go?"

"According to my schedule, never."

"Okay. So I'll let you know when the plans are made. I'd like to go tonight just to scope things out but I know you're busy. About a thousand people have called me saying they saw you on the news or read the article in the paper about Discretion. And they all plan to be at the party."

"Well, I hope so."

"So what are you wearing?"

"I don't know yet. I've got to figure out how I'm gonna get Maurice to baby-sit after being stuck in the house all day."

"Well call me later."

"All right. Bye."

I hung up and called home to see what they were doing. Nobody answered. I paged Maurice and put my cell phone number in so I wouldn't miss the call while I stepped out of the office. Then I pulled some guidelines and Beacon's folder out of the file cabinet and headed downstairs. He was behind the bar mixing a drink. Poured it into a plastic cup and handed it to me.

I smiled and asked, "What's this?"

"I call it Numbing Nobia."

"Nobia, huh? What's in it?"

"It's a secret. Taste it."

I took a small sip. It was fruity like a Bahama Mama but with the punch of a shot of tequila. I slid the cup back to him.

"It's good. I hope you know what you're doin' mixing stuff like that."

"I'm an expert, Zenobia. Trust me."

I opened his file, perused it for a minute and then said, "Uh, Beacon, I see here that you've gotten a hepatitis shot but I've noticed that you don't have any references. You think you can come up with three for me?"

"Yeah, I guess so."

"Great. Oh, and Beacon."

"Yeah?"

"I know this isn't your job but I was wondering if you could do me a favor and pick up some decorations I ordered for this weekend."

"No problem. Anything else you need?"

"If you've got a drink called Peace of Mind back there I'll take a shot of that. Heavy on the peace."

Beacon winked at me and leaned on the bar. "Ah, it can't be that bad. How about some lunch after my training?"

I shook my head. "Sorry but I've got a ton of things to do, Beacon. But why don't you ask Melinda back there. I think she may be single again."

Beacon's eyes dropped immediately. He began wiping the top of the bar with a wet rag in a rapid circular motion.

"I didn't say I wanted a date, Zenobia, just a little company while I ate lunch."

Now I felt a slight twinge of guilt come over me.

"Well maybe we could—"

Beacon held up his hand and said, "No, forget about it. You've got work to do and I've got a job to learn."

"No, really, I could—"

"I'm all right, Zenobia. Really, it's no big deal."

"You sure?"

"Positive. Now where do we start?"

I leaned on the bar and told him, "We can start by you telling me why an attractive guy like yourself is still single."

He gave me a look that let me know that if I weren't his employer he probably would've reached across the bar and clocked me upside the head for getting in his business. I stood up straight so that we both remembered our roles.

"Only fools chase love, Zenobia. I'm convinced that love will come around and find me. In the meantime, I keep my eye on what I want so that I know just what to do when the time comes."

Theresa

"*Mistreating him?!*" I yelled.

The following morning was off to a rocky start. I was running late because of some last-minute packing for the Atlanta trip and when I finally made it to work, I received an urgent message from the principal about a meeting with Deon's father. And as usual, *I* was the culprit.

"Yes, that's what he says: You are singling him out. Now I can't write this off because it isn't the first, second or fifth time that he's complained."

I leaned back in the beige chair and rolled my eyes to the ceiling of the principal's office.

"Well, did he tell you *why* I had him standing in the hall?"

"Deon stated that you made it clear that everyone does not have to participate during Creativity Hour. Some students cut pictures out of construction paper, some talk amongst themselves. On that particular day, he wanted to play Monopoly with some of his classmates. As soon as you hear dice fall, and a little excitement that had nothing to do with your project, you send him into the hall. Is this true?"

"I heard dice and fingers snapping! That's why I called him up to my desk."

Mr. Edwards, the principal, looked at me like he was speaking to a special ed group and asked, "When did finger-snapping become a crime?"

I jumped up from my seat and yelled, "He was shooting dice in my classroom!"

"Keep your voice down! His father is right outside that door and accusations like that can cause big problems for this school. And frankly, with Tiwana coming forward as a witness, this doesn't look too good for you. Now, are you ready to sit down like mature adults and talk this over?"

"Send him in," I replied.

"*Are you ready,* Ms. Downing?"

"Yes, please send him in."

A short, heavyset black man followed Principal Edwards into the office and took a seat in the empty chair next to me. I extended my hand and he shook it firmly enough to let me know he wasn't in the mood for any bull.

"I don't have long," he started, "so let me get right to the point. I have a job to work during the day so I can provide for my family. I don't have time to take off and run up here every time my sick child is accused of something."

"*Sick?*" I asked, sitting forward in my seat.

Mr. Coleman shot a quick "Yes, sick! Deon is epileptic and he has fits when he's upset. Now, I send my child to school to learn, and in the evening *you all* send him *home* to be disciplined. He can't learn from the hall so I don't see any reason for him to be out there. This isn't the first time we've had this problem with Ms. Downing and I will not—I repeat, *will not*—subject my child to mistreatment."

"But I'm supposed to be subjected to his inappropriate behavior because he knows that you will come along and clear his name?"

"Ms. Downing!" Principal Edwards yelled.

Vince

"Booty's on duty!"

Leland was yelling and doing a little two-step to a reggae tune as we entered Discretion at about eleven-thirty Friday night. I patted him on the shoulder of his tan mock-neck short-sleeved shirt and told him to chill out. He'd had a couple of drinks before we left his place and was becoming a prime candidate for getting tossed out before the clock struck twelve. All he talked about on the way over was that Zenobia chick. It was becoming annoying and brought about a bit of concern on my part. He doesn't deal with rejection well. And from what I could see, she was a brick house who wasn't in the mood to be harassed. All of that coupled with Leland's two shots of Grey Goose vodka could be a recipe for trouble.

I had to admit that this place was nice and when they said Caribbean jam they meant just that. Some tables were decorated with grass skirts, leis or straw hats while others had miniature palm trees and plastic fruits that grow in the tropics. The lights over the dance floor were low and rotating from red to blue to orange to green every few minutes or so. The music was bangin' with the kind of vintage reggae party tunes that could raise Bob Marley from the dead. And there were enough sexy, sarong-clad sistas in there to generate a baby boom in this city alone.

When I turned around, Leland had disappeared. Probably chasing the tail of some poor woman's skirt. I stepped over to the bar and a brown-skinned brotha with a low haircut, wearing a black T-shirt that read *Use Your Own Discretion,* took my order for a Hennessey and orange juice. I tipped him, and made my way through a crowd that was growing in size. Fellas wearing two-ways *and* cell phones were putting their primary assets up front as they approached women who were satisfied with a fling that would probably last no longer than mid-winter, depending on whether or not they made the final cut.

The DJ switched the tune to one of Bob Marley's slow jams that sang of freedom. I finished my drink and placed it on a nearby table. Felt a soft hand grab hold of mine. When I looked down there was a woman with skin the color of pecans, wearing a short floral-printed skirt and a black leotard-like top, smiling at me. She tilted her head to one side and asked me if I wanted to dance. I obliged. Followed her to the dance floor watching those flowers growing on her backyard. She had the legs of an athlete. Firm, made for high heels. I held her close and rocked with her as she wrapped her arms around my neck and lay against my chest like she knew me.

Then she pulled away and said, "I'm Elise."

"Vince," I told her.

I closed my eyes for a split second and allowed the music to do our talking. She didn't say much else. Probably because she didn't get a chance to. When I opened my eyes, another woman was standing behind her like a bully summoning lunch money. Elise stepped to the side and revealed that it was none other than Sticky Fingers, a.k.a. Bridget. She was standing there in a black full-length dress that looked like it had been airbrushed on, with a made-for-TV smile sprawled across her face.

"Professor Lowery! Imagine meeting you here. And is this your friend?"

Elise introduced herself and gave me a look that asked whether or not she should be moving on. Let go of my hand and took two steps back.

"Elise, would you mind me cutting in on your dance with Vince? We've got a lot of catching up to do."

"No, don't mind at all. Maybe I'll see you later, Vince."

"No doubt," I told her as Bridget stepped closer and wrapped her arm around my waist.

We walked to another end of the dance floor. The colors had switched from blue to red. She gave me that same devilish grin she did the day we met, placed her rack as close as she could get it to my chest and winked at me.

"So, did you decide to come and watch me perform Sunday?"

"I thought I told you—"

"Yeah, yeah, you're not interested. But that's only because you probably haven't seen African dance before."

I shrugged my shoulders as Bob went on about a misty morning straightening out his tomorrow.

"Why don't you trust me, Vince?"

"I don't know you well enough to trust you, which is what I had to tell the people at the Y when you *stole* my ID."

She pulled back a bit and looked up at me.

"Now, wait a minute. I didn't 'steal' anything. I had every intention of giving it back. It was only a matter of you coming to get it."

I asked, "What's the deal with you?"

"What do you mean?"

"You ask me to help you out with the weights and when I don't agree to come and see your little performance—"

"'Little performance?'"

"I didn't mean it that way. What I meant to say was, 'What is it that you want from me?'"

"I want to be friends. Is that okay?"

"Just friends?"

She laughed and shook her head. "Yes, Vince. Just friends. I'm not in the market for a relationship. Can't you understand that?"

"Of course."

She was quiet for a minute. Like she was celebrating her victory of holding my attention this long.

"So are you seeing somebody?"

"What difference does that make, *buddy*?"

"Just trying to get to know my friend a little better."

"Well, just so you know: Yeah, I'm seeing someone right now."

"Is she nice?"

"If she wasn't, I wouldn't be seeing her."

"Do you think she'll want to come to the performance this weekend?"

"She's going out of town."

"That's okay. We're performing next weekend too. Maybe she can come then."

"Maybe. I still don't know if *I'll* be coming."

She smiled as the song ended, stepped back and held me by my hands. "Oh, you'll be there. What were you drinking, Vince?"

I gave her a look of skepticism.

"How long have you been watching me?"

"Since you and the guy over there at the tableful of women walked in the door. I wanted to see how you act when you don't think anyone's noticing."

"Oh, really?"

88

"Well listen, Bridget, I don't want to tie you up for the rest of the night."

She gave me an indignant stare.

"Oh, is this your way of tellin' me to push on?"

"Naw, but my partner over there has had a few tonight and I just need to make sure he's still being nice to the ladies. You can understand, can't you?"

"I understand that you're tryin' to get rid of me. But that's okay. You'll come around, *buddy*."

She rolled her eyes and walked away without looking back. I headed over to the table, where Leland was letting some unsuspecting victim have a seat on his lap. As I maneuvered through the crowd, I heard a light-skinned brotha dressed in a tan tailor-made suit call my name.

"Babyboy! I don't believe this shit."

As he came closer, I realized that it was a face from my past: Ramone Lippons. He looked like he was doing well. He was alone. But bringing a woman to Caribbean night at Discretion was like taking sand to the beach.

"Ray, man, what's goin' on? I ain't seen you since we were like this," I told him, lowering my hand to my stomach.

"Yeah, my mom moved back out here about four years after we left. That wasn't a good idea at all. Hey, how's your pops?"

"The same. The man you knew when you left is the man he is today."

"Well, the one thing you can ask of people is that they remain consistent. What about everybody else?"

"Rayna got married and had a son who was killed."

He shook his head and moved to the left a bit so a line of people could get through.

"Damn, Babyboy, I'm sorry to hear that. How's she doing?"

"She's happy, I guess. She married some peckerwood from the South so she's making the best of that situation."

"Sounds like that didn't sit too well with ya'."

"Should it?"

"Well, if he makes her happy, that's all you can ask. Hey, let me buy you a drink. What are you having?"

"Henny and OJ."

Ray stopped a waitress in a canary-yellow sarong and a matching bikini top that covered what looked like mosquito bites and placed our orders. She playfully batted her eyelashes and promised to return momentarily.

Ray turned back to me and said, "Yeah, Babyboy, so you heard about Whose Is It, haven't you?"

"Yeah, they mentioned it on the news the other morning when they were talking about this place."

"That's me. Built that shit from nothing. But I don't have to tell you. You know my humble-ass beginnings as well as I do."

"What are you doin' in here then?"

He leaned in toward me as though he were telling a secret. "Checkin' out the competition. Gotta see exactly what it is this Zenobia Hall is offering that keeps the crowds coming back."

"Well, look around. It ain't hard to tell. If you can promise the place will stay stocked full of women like this, that'll keep a line wrapped around the building every night. Look at that chick over there near the steps in that see-through outfit."

Ray gave me a look that was hard to read and then switched subjects.

"So what's up? I'm sure my mom would love to see yo' ass, Vince. She hasn't been feelin' her best lately. I think an old face would really make her day."

"Oh yeah, Ms. Irene could make a pound cake, couldn't she?"

"Still does. Got one at my place now. Matter of fact, why don't you swing by my house one day? It's a little ways out in Lake St. Louis but it's worth the thirty-minute drive."

"Life must really be good, huh?"

"Hey, Babyboy, I've earned it. Let me give you my card. Come by tomorrow night and we'll watch the Lakers spank that ass again."

"What? You think New Jersey got this far to mess it all up?"

"What I'm sayin' is that the Lakers are gonna dominate until they get somebody in the league who can fuck with Shaq. Otherwise it's over!"

I laughed, took his card, dapped him up with the black man's universal handshake that consisted of several movements of the wrist and pulled him in for a hug. I glanced over his shoulder and spotted Leland taking off after the owner, Zenobia, like he was being hypnotized by her walk.

"Ah'ight, Babyboy. Holla at me."

I stepped around Ray and caught L just as he was reaching out to touch her from behind. Placed my open hand on his chest and pushed him back.

"Leland, man, you trippin'! What are you doin'?"

He looked up at me with eyes that were bloodshot-red. He had bypassed his max probably about two drinks ago.

"Nothin'! Whassup witchu?"

"Ey, you don't know nothin' about that sista and by the looks of things, you ain't ready to meet her."

He pushed my hand away. I grabbed him by the arm. I was much bigger than Leland and he knew this but Jose Cuervo was convincing him otherwise.

"Chill, L!"

"Vince, I came all the way down here to meet this bitch and that's what I plan to do! Now, *you chill* and get the fuck out of my way!"

I had no choice but to snatch him up in the chest and push him toward a back wall. He stumbled, lost his balance, fell on a sista with a chip on her shoulder and got schooled in a crash course of Profanity 101. I apologized for him and wondered why so many black women felt all of that was necessary to get a point across. What they thought made them appear savvy really made them look like they had a limited vocabulary. Plus it gave an asshole like Leland every excuse he needed to be disrespectful. And me, another reason to apologize on his behalf.

"If I don't get her today, I'm comin' back, Vince."

I shoved him toward the exit so we *both* could get some fresh air.

"Then that's just what you'll have to do, Leland. Try it again at a later date."

Theresa

I awoke to the sound of a vehicle door closing. I shot up from the bed and peeped out my bedroom window for a clear view but the streetlights were out. I saw nothing except lightning darting across the sky. I closed the mauve blinds and pulled the sheer curtains back. My television was still on, showing an infomercial on how to get rich in ninety days. I grabbed the remote and pushed the display button. The time read 3:49 A.M. Too early to be awake but too late to try to go back to sleep and still arrive at the airport feeling energetic. I pulled the blankets back, got up and went into the kitchen to make a cup of coffee. As soon as I flipped the switch, the bulb blew. And then came the car door closing again. I jumped. Tried to slow my breathing as I felt around to a drawer crammed with candlesticks and flashlights. I lit a candle on the stove and placed it in a holder. Gathered the bottom of my long peach satin gown and walked back to Dameron's room. I'd witnessed him sleeping quietly and then turned to open the utility closet when someone pressed the buzzer outside.

I picked up the apartment phone and asked, "Who is it?"

"It's me—Vince. Can I come up?"

I hesitated for a moment as the sting of rejection resurfaced, and then buzzed him in. Unlocked and cracked my front door before making a beeline to the bathroom to freshen up. Brushed my teeth, snatched my scarf off and sprayed some fragrance across my chest. I put my diamond studs in my ears and teased my auburn bobbed hairdo until my look appeared effortless.

I stood on the threshold of my living room as Vince walked in and slowly closed the door behind him. He was wearing a pair of light blue denim shorts, a yellow T-shirt with light blue embroidery and a pair of brown sandals. His eyes were heavy and tired.

I asked, "Where have you been?"

"Watchin' the game with Leland and then we hung out for a while. Had to make sure he got home in one piece. Then I drove back to my place but couldn't sleep."

He rubbed the top of his head toward the front. His skin was flawless, and his jet-black eyebrows, full goatee and scattered freckles brought character to his face.

"What made you decide to come?"

"I missed you and I know that I'll miss you even more next week."

My shoulders slumped as I leaned heavily on one leg.

"Vince, how is this going to work? You can't keep doing this to me."

"Doing what, Theresa?"

"Loving me from a distance until you wanna get up close again. And if things aren't picture-perfect, you're ready to leave. I can't live like this."

He flopped down on the black leather chaise lounger in the corner of the room and held his head in his hands. The light from the moon shone through the sheer curtains and upon his face as he extended his massive arm to me. I stepped closer. Allowed him to hold me around my waist until he began trying to kiss me through my gown.

I pulled back. "Vince, c'mon."

"Theresa, I love you. That won't change."

"But our relationship has."

He ignored my cries for clarity and planted his face in my haven. I moaned as my legs became weak. Slowly, he lifted the satin until nothing stood between him and joy. His soft, moist lips danced with mine while Vince slid from the chaise to the floor, never allowing more than a millimeter between his face and my hips. Gripped my bare ass as though he'd hold on forever. I placed my hand on top of his wavy, neatly cropped hair and navigated the guilty feeling until our liquids had blurred the line between quivering thighs and a relationship that now lacked commitment. When he stood to his feet, he took my hand and led me to my bedroom. I stopped just inside the door.

"I thought you said that you didn't need to make love to me in order to care about me."

He continued to disrobe, completely ignoring every reservation I had. Vince stood up straight, with the body of a warrior. His frame was so powerful and exquisite that he was able to summon arousal without even trying. His piece was growing and beckoning me.

He stroked it in his hand and said, "C'mere."

I joined him on his side of my dark bedroom. When he lowered his eyes, instantly I knew what he wanted. It was the same thing he'd been asking for since last December. But my feelings about it had not changed. That was the one thing that I would never do to a man. I allowed my gown to gather at my feet and wrapped my arms around his neck. Pressed my warm body into his with hopes of diverting his attention. Inhaled the scent of alcohol and the faint scent of another woman's perfume.

I asked, "Did you have a good time tonight?"

"I was mostly baby-sitting Leland."

"Then who was watching you?"

Vince pulled away and gave me a confused look.

"What are you talking about?"

"Us, Vince."

"Why now, Theresa? I don't want to argue. Here, let's put some music on."

He walked over to the CD player in the corner. Grabbed my Bilal disc, inserted it and pressed number eleven. Vince's body was one of my weaknesses. His method of lovemaking was one of the others. And by candlelight it was on anotha' level. Vince knew how to take control of a woman. Made me feel as though my lovin' gave him the energy to navigate through this world by the way he'd grab my thighs and put me in positions I didn't know I could manage with all of my vital organs still in place. Bilal serenaded our act of giving with a tune entitled "Queen of Sanity" while Vince gripped the wooden headboard and rocked back and forth inside of me. Sexed me like he was trying to find the route to my dreams, like he was trying to leave an imprint of this moment in my mind that would last me the two weeks that we would be apart. Then, as the piercing drum continued its beat, he lay beside me at a ninety-degree angle, placed one of my thighs between his legs and held the other in the air. Lifted my hip with his free hand, got a hold on my ass and pulled me toward him fervently, repeatedly and knowingly.

I fell limp onto the saturated sheets when he turned me loose. My body knew Vince, recognized his touch. My nipples stood at attention as he drew a line with his finger from my breast to my navel and then wrapped his arm around me. Kissed my slightly perspiring forehead and told me that he loved me. I believed him. What I didn't believe was that his love for me was enough to make him stay.

I said, "So since I'll be gone, this should be our time to get clear on some things."

He looked over at me and removed his arm. "I agree."

"I mean, I would really like for things to be different when I get back. And I don't just mean with you. I mean with myself as well. It'll be like we're starting over. What do you think?"

"I think it's a good idea. But what about until then?"

I sat up straight and pulled the cover over my breasts. "What do you mean?"

Vince rubbed his forehead and pulled at the bottom of the sheet so that his feet were exposed. "I mean, how should we be thinking—thinking like single people or people who are involved?"

I snatched the sheet off and kicked him in what felt like his shin as I stumbled to my feet. "What do you mean, 'thinking like single people'?!"

He tilted his head like I was being unreasonable. "Theresa, let's not pretend that Don is not still here in your heart, in your mind. Hell, the cat's still in your fuckin' dreams!"

I felt tears welling up as I yelled, "But you're in my bed, Vince! Not Don, you! And now it seems that what's in my heart isn't even important anymore because you're *insecure*!"

"'Insecure'?! I have to be insecure to want to know that another man isn't bringing the woman I love to tears? I have to be insecure to wanna take care of you and know that you can love me completely? That's what you call 'insecure'?"

Vince sprung from my bed, brushed past me and ran into the hall. Opened the closet that housed my memories of Don, the closet no one was supposed to know about. Yanked my shoe rack down, and removed the piece of wood blocking the compartment as I covered my eyes. He was ranting and raving like a madman and when I looked up all I saw was Don's clothes, pictures, favorite western books, navy-blue uniform, helmet and badge being thrown across the hall, leaving dents in the wall. Items that I pulled out and stared at, dusted and sometimes even kissed. And that's when something in me snapped. I ran at top speed, shoved Vince to the floor. He turned over and hurried to his feet. Grabbed me by the shoulders.

"What are you gonna do, huh? Kill me? Don't *tell* me you don't still love him!"

He began perspiring as he shoved me on my chest over my heart with his index finger. "Don't tell me he's not still in there, Theresa! That's where I need to be but you won't fuckin'—"

I covered my ears and yelled, *"I hate you!"*

My words had deflated him, and tears ran down his cheeks. His shoulders slumped; his face was no longer angry but wounded.

I wanted to take those words back but I couldn't because at that moment I did hate him. Not only for not being Don, but because I hated my life and he was a part of this madness. He was giving me what he thought I *wanted*, but it wasn't about desire anymore. And if it had been, what I *wanted* was for Don to be alive again, what I *wanted* was to wake up every morning ready to live. But my situation had little to do with that; it was about what I *needed*. And that was to be still, and to heal.

Vince wiped the tears from his eyes with the back of his hand and whispered, "I know you hate me, Theresa. It's impossible to love two men at once. And you've never stopped loving Don. But that's cool, because now I don't feel so bad about beginning to hate you too."

Zenobia

Lainey stayed the night over at my place and kept me up until three in the morning flipping through a photo album that reflected a happier time in her marriage. But she had depressed the hell out of me with her trip down memory lane. What Lainey didn't realize was that she was showing me more than mere smiles that were evidence of a time with fewer worries and a carefree attitude—she was taking me back to the point where *my* life had changed. She'd only gotten married. Managed to finish up at UMSL a year later and prided herself on the fact that her husband had done the same. I was the one who was pregnant and chasing a fairy tale with a happily-ever-after ending. Payce had made several promises and one of them was that I'd never want for anything. But now that I thought about it all, what I wished I had back was the one thing he couldn't give me—those life-altering moments.

I lay there all morning, thinking about where I was in life and why I always came up short when it was an issue of personal accomplishments. At one point, being important to Payce was the only thing that mattered, the only thing I considered a victory. I was so busy losing—my parents, valuable semesters, my mind— that I guess he and Zaire were the two things that I didn't want to believe would ever escape my grasp.

I shook the memories loose and made the decision to go out and get another job. But everything in my salary range required a degree, I thought. Something I considered a waste of time back then, since Payce was gonna take care of us. I had seen the quarter-of-a-million-dollar checks, even went out to have the first two framed in a shadow box and hung them in the family room of the very house that he was currently sharing with another woman. I balled up my fist and pounded the pillow resting next to this morning's paper. Something had to give. I gathered up the courage to glance through the Employment Opportunities section, hoping there was something that fit my criteria and vice versa. There were openings for staff accountants, application and training productivity specialists with engineering firms and a director of systems in technology services with the public schools. I was two seconds from flinging the entire section across the room into the wicker chair when my eyes fell upon a position for a corporate human resources manager. Of course, the position required a bachelor's degree, but I knew I was able to fill the other requirements. I had established training and management development programs, advancements and terminations. I knew the ins and outs of benefits/compensation and people development/intervention as well. I opened the top drawer of my nightstand and retrieved a marker. Circled the ad, propped the pillows up behind me and placed my hand on the phone. Stared at the words: *competitive salary* and *outstanding benefits package*. This job had my name all over it. I picked up the phone, tossed my braids over my shoulder and dialed the number. There was a recording that already knew what my problem was. Asked me to leave my name and number or to fax my resume over. I decided to do the former. I hadn't touched my resume since Zaire was teething, so I knew there was some work to be done on it.

"Hi, this call is for Jim Shoner. My name is Zenobia Hall and

I noticed your ad in the *Post* for the human resources position. I'm very interested in applying for it. If you would please give me a call back at 555-6773 at your earliest convenience, I'd really appreciate it. Have a great day!"

That last part was corny, I thought. Made me sound desperate. I guess the same way I had made others feel when they were simply trying to make a living. Speaking of which, I still had some calls to make in reference to the next Caribbean party the following week. I picked up the phone and heard a conversation being whispered. Recognized Lainey's voice and struggled with the idea of eavesdropping.

An unidentified man asked her, "So Alexis, what can I expect you to be wearing, since you imagine the place will be packed?"

Lainey put on a voice so deep it would've made Eartha Kitt sound like a soprano. I covered my mouth to muffle a laugh and continued listening.

"Alexis will be in red, Daddy."

"Heels like I like it?"

"Ooh, anything for you. Now what are you gonna do for me?"

"Give you a night you won't—"

I cleared my throat.

"Listen, Daddy, someone needs to use the phone but I'll see you at Discretion around ten."

"Whose is it?"

"No, baby, I said Discretion."

"I'm not talking about the club, Lexi, I'm talking about that—"

"Uh, look, I'll see you later. Ah'ight?!"

Her boy toy hung up as my ability to hold back the laughter faded.

"'Lexi'?" I asked from my end of the phone.

"Lexi, Lainey. What the fuck's the difference? And why don't you know how to let somebody know when you wanna use the phone?!"

"Same reason you don't know how to let people know that you're married."

"Shut up! Well, I'm happy to see you're finally up. Zaire's down here in the living room watching TV. Think we'll get around to that bookstore today?"

"Yeah. Think you'll get around to tellin' me about your little friend?"

"That's my spare. Any other questions?"

"Yeah, Lexi. Who did you think you were turnin' on with that James Earl Jones impersonation?"

"Yo' mama! That was a sexy voice."

"Yeah, for a sea lion in heat."

"Just hurry up and get ready!"

CLICK!

"So what are you gonna do?"

We were sitting at a small square table inside the bookstore down on Washington. Lainey had just finished reading the letter that Cammie had written and I was staring blankly across the room at Zaire, who was sitting with a bunch of other kids her age and watching one of the store owners act out children's tales. The guy was hopping and wobbling to and fro. His dreadlocks were swinging back and forth, poppin' him in the face. The kids were chuckling and loudly recalling times when they'd seen a real bunny and saying that it looked nothing like Byron. At least I think that's what he said his name was. I'd been in a daze part of the day. Hoping and praying I'd get a call about the position I was interested in as well as thinking about the Mexican drama queen from Cali that Zaire had developed an interest in. Spent hours wondering what was going on inside Zaire's little head after seeing Cammie like that and to what lengths I'd have to go to keep Zaire if Payce got traded.

Byron's wife, Sheila, who wore an Afro and a large blue loose-fitting dress, brought us the cups of tea Lainey ordered and sat down at the table with us.

Then she asked, "So you need to get your husband's attention, right?"

Lainey took a sip of tea, forgot all about my problems *and* the letter. I had to snatch it from her before she used it as a coaster.

"I'll take that. Thank you."

She gave me a look that said: Get your panties out of a bunch. I rolled my eyes and redirected my attention to the décor. There were a lot of pieces of pottery, tribal masks decorating the walls, plants lining a high shelf along the entrance and plenty of large colorful sitting pillows for reading. That's where the kids were, which happened to be down about five steps in an open area. Up where we sat was the deli and plenty of chairs, a vending machine and piles of chess games.

I heard Sheila ask, "And what advice did *you* give her?"

"Who, me?" I asked, snapping back to the moment. "I've been celibate for almost two years."

Lainey said, "Not voluntarily."

I nudged her with my elbow.

Sheila laughed and said, "Well, I'll tell you what keeps Byron and me going."

Lainey got quiet and leaned over in the woman's lap like she was givin' directions to D'Angelo's house.

"Sis, I just *take* what I want. It makes him feel sexy. The fact that I can't keep my hands off of him is a turn-on within itself."

Lainey shook her head and rebutted, "I'm dealing with something totally different than that. If it were that easy I would've done that six months ago."

"How long has it been?"

I answered for her. "Forever."

"Well, you ever considered the *Kamasutra*?"

"The feathers, the oils and the whole nine."

"And what did you get?"

"Definitely not 'the whole nine.'"

Sheila peeped back at her performing husband and asked, "Nine?"

Lainey nodded her head and confirmed, "Nine."

"Well, in this case we've *got* to find a solution. That's just being wasteful."

We heard a little *ding-dong* over our continued laughter as the front door opened and two guys walked in helping one another carry a large box. Byron stopped doing his rendition of a wounded rabbit long enough to show them where to set it. They both wore light blue denim shorts and T-shirts. The taller one with the deep raspy voice and the caramel skin was starting dreadlocks. I watched his movements from upstairs. The way he stood with his feet shoulder-width apart and busied his hands at all times is what really caught my attention. He had full facial features and a slight mustache, curvaceous lips and high cheekbones. He turned around, smiled and waved to Sheila.

She waved back and asked in a whisper, "Zenobia, you married?"

"Not—"

"Cliff, Dave, come up here for a minute. I want you to meet some of my friends."

"Hold on a second. Just gotta get a few more things out of the truck."

Sheila turned back to us and said, "Cute, aren't they? Zenobia, what do you think? Would you like to meet a couple of Byron's oldest friends? They moved here from the Virgin Islands two and a half years ago, don't have any children and haven't been able to find any mentally stimulating sistas to keep company with."

"Are you serious? Even the one with the baby dreadlocks?"

The door ding-donged again as they continued piling boxes in the back of the store.

When they finished and started our way Sheila asked, "Quick, Zenobia, which one?"

"Baby dreadlocks."

"Good choice."

"Greetings, sistas."

The one with the faded haircut extended his hand toward us.

"Cliff, David, this is Elaine and Zenobia."

David was his name and he had a barely noticeable accent when he spoke. When I repeated his name aloud as I shook his hand, he gave me a sheepish grin. It made him look about twenty-eight although I could tell he was a little older. Our eye contact lasted about five seconds and then he went back to his shoulder-width stance. David was tall. Maybe about six foot four, and built to last. The sleeves of his T-shirt were rolled up twice, which gave me an opportunity to check for tattoos—none so far. I glanced down at his sneakers. They were clean—another plus. David was headed for the homestretch of surface approval when Zaire ran up the stairs and hopped into my lap.

He smiled and confirmed, "She must be your daughter. She's beautiful."

"Thank you."

"You always come for story time?"

"No, we just happened to stop in for books."

"Ever come in for the book signings? Sheila and Byron know just about every writer this side of the equator. I write myself."

"Oh really?"

"Yeah, mostly fiction but a little poetry too. I guess you've never been to any of the poetry slams either?"

"Nope, not one."

"Well, that explains why we haven't met. Mind if I pull up a chair?"

Sheila interjected with, "You can have mine. I'm about to help Elaine find the books she came in looking for."

David pulled up a chair as Cliff joined Byron downstairs.

"'Zenobia,' that's different. I like it. And what's your daughter's name?"

"Zaire."

David reached out to shake her hand and she held on to me for dear life.

"She's picky," I joked.

"I can see. Well, as pretty as you are, you *should* be able to choose whose hand you shake. How was the story?"

Zaire wasn't feelin' David. Ignored him like he wasn't even sitting there.

He laughed, turned back to me and asked, "So you read a lot?"

"Not a whole lot. I really need to start."

"I didn't when I first moved to the States but once my money was invested in this spot I started spending more time here. Found myself reading more than anything."

"Sounds like your date book is a little thin."

"Well, I'm waiting to run into the right sista. I don't want to start anything that I can't finish."

"What do you mean?"

David folded his hands on top of the table and answered, "Well, a man usually knows whether he'd be interested in seeing a woman based on the first conversation. I like to get it all out during the initial meeting. That way nobody's time has been wasted."

"I guess that makes sense. You're a lot better than most of the men out here."

"Think so?"

He gave me that grin again. That's when Zaire asked for a juice.

"I've got it. What's your favorite flavor, Zaire?"

"Really," I told him, "you don't have to do that."

"Maybe next time I see her she'll be willing to shake my hand. I mean, if I get a chance to see you again."

I batted my eyes. "Are you asking me out, David?"

"Yes I am, Zenobia. That is, if Zaire doesn't mind."

I playfully asked her, "Can Mommy go out with the nice man?"

She quickly shook her head no.

"Well, I guess I'll have to settle for just running into you over the next couple of weeks or so. You've heard about the open mike tomorrow and the jazz on Thursdays?"

"Yeah."

"So, will one of those be my lucky day?"

"We'll just have to see."

"That beats a no any day."

Elaine walked up the steps carrying about four books and slammed them down on the table next to ours.

"Looks like you sistas have got your work cut out for you."

David stood, gave Lainey his chair and Zaire a dollar. She slowly took it and then offered him a look of dismissal.

"I think she'd rather you get the juice for her."

I nodded. "I think so too."

"Well, it was nice meeting you-all. And I hope to see you around, Zenobia."

As he walked down the stairs, Lainey looked at me and said, "I know this is not the same black woman who said she'd never take another man seriously unless he's handin' her one and a half carats, is it? 'Cause that sure looked like a *dollar* to me!"

"Shut up, 'Lexi.' *Your* love comes that cheap, not mine. I'm just gonna meet him here to listen to some jazz."

"Excuse me. Mommy, can I have a juice now?"

Sheila overheard Zaire and brought her a bottle of apple juice. When I tried to hand her the dollar, she refused. Told me it was on the house. I told her to bring her husband with her to Discretion. She agreed to come but asked if she could bring a couple of girlfriends instead.

"How many?"

"Just two."

"Sure. I'll give you some passes when I come next week."

"Oh, so you're into jazz and poetry, huh? I see we're gonna get along. So what did you think about our friend David?"

When she said his name, she dragged the ending out like she suspected an interest already.

"He seems nice. Real—"

I covered Zaire's ears and finished, "—sexy and easy to talk to."

"Now that's a good brotha right there. Responsible, ready to settle down and focused. Did he tell you he published a book of poetry?"

"No, he didn't."

Sheila nodded and continued, "Real modest, too. He's working on a book now."

"What is he doing in the meantime?"

"He's out at Chrysler, and you know their employees get paid well. He just bought a house. It's just a starter home but hey, it's just him."

"So what's wrong with 'im? There's got to be a catch."

"Nope, no catch at all. You can't waste love like that. I've seen him bend over backward for sistas who don't appreciate a damn thing. Pardon my French, but the thought makes me mad. How many brothas do you know who will work all night, pay all of the bills and then rub his *woman's* feet when he gets in?"

Lainey butted in with, "Okay, here it says erogenous zones are the key to arousal. How in the hell am I supposed to figure out his erogenous zones when he won't come near me?"

"Go to him," Sheila suggested.

"And if he runs?"

I cut in, "Call Big Daddy, Lexi."

Sheila and I laughed. Then I turned back to Sheila. "Rubs his woman's feet, you say?"

"Dave and Cliff learned from watching Byron, so they were schooled well. He's got a couple of years on them."

"How old is David?"

"Thirty-two. How old are you?"

"Twenty-nine in a matter of months. I hate to think about it."

"Girl, you betta' age gracefully and enjoy life while you can. If September eleventh wasn't enough to make folk change their thinking, I don't know what will. Sis, *live your life.*"

I nodded in agreement.

Sheila looked back at the three men standing in a huddle by the door. "And get a foot massage while you do it, okkaaaayyyyy."

We'd apparently broken Lainey's concentration when we high-fived across the table. She gave me a look of annoyance, like she'd expected a little more concern from my end. I shrugged my shoulders and turned back to the front door, but David was gone. Byron continued to talk to Cliff while the kids talked amongst themselves.

"Zaire, you wanna go back downstairs and play?"

My observant child began to scan the room just as I loved to do from my office at the club. She was like me in so many ways that sometimes I found myself looking for traces of Payce's characteristics in her. When the laughter rose, she hopped down and joined the others.

I was watching Zaire play when suddenly I heard Sheila say, "Looks like somebody can't get enough of you, Ms. Thang."

I turned around, and David was standing in front of me with a stack of papers in his hand.

"Whenever you get the chance, I'd like for you to take a look at this. It's an excerpt from the novel I'm working on."

I blushed and asked, "What's it about?"

"It's about a man and his desire to be loved by the women in his life. His mother, his sister, an ex-wife and the daughter that he isn't allowed to see are his strengths and his weaknesses at the same time."

"Sounds interesting."

He smiled like a child seeking approval. "Well, just read it and let me know if you still feel the same afterwards. It's deep. Takes you into the heart and mind of a good brotha who can't have what some take for granted."

I winked and asked, "A good brotha, huh?"

"That's right."

"Let me ask you something. A lot of authors write about themselves or weave their own stories into the books they write. Will this book help me get to know a little more about you?"

David laughed and clasped his hands together.

"All it will do is show you how my mind works. It's fiction. You want to get to know me, show up here for jazz night. I'll definitely be waiting."

Vince

Rayna called the next day and asked me to come out to the house to help her set up some furniture while Josh and Luke went fishing that morning. My intuition told me that it was her way of getting me by myself so she could corner me on her turf and make me promise to go see Pops. What she didn't know was that she had a better chance of living to see a hurricane roll through the Midwest than she had of making that happen.

But I was relieved to learn that the guy Josh intended to hook me up with was black. Or at least his name sounded black. Cedric Cummings is what it was. Rayna told me that Joshua e-mailed him with my address so that we could arrange a meeting to discuss exactly what I was looking for. I told her to tell 'im that I wouldn't be free for another few weeks. I was so behind with editorial letters that putting anything else on my plate would have required sideboards.

Leland called me that following morning after the poison in his system wore off. Wanted to know why his bed was empty when he'd bought drinks for at least three women at Discretion. Leland was my partner in crime, no doubt, but his lack of control was starting to get on my fuckin' nerves. Felt like I was baby-sitting everybody around me. Tellin' 'em when enough is enough. Part of me felt like it was time to say that to myself in reference to the give-give relationships I was maintaining. And Theresa put the last nail in the coffin last night. If I was unsure before, I'm real clear now: She is not ready for love, a relationship or anything else.

I pulled up to Rayna's house and found a white guy outside who looked like a younger, cleaner version of Luke. He wore his dirty blond hair like Brad Pitt did, with that untamed flair. He was lean, with a tan and a walk that made him hard to size up.

He greeted me as I stepped out of my black Honda Accord.

"Hey whassup? I'm Josh. You must be Vince, Rayna's brother."

"Yeah. How's it goin'?"

"Pretty good. So you're looking for a home, huh?"

"Yeah, three-bedroom, two-bath."

"Well, I'm in the process of relocating to Missouri from California. Rayna and Luke have been kind enough to let me stay here until I can get things in order. But I'm sure she spoke to you about my buddy, Cedric. He's new with real estate but he knows his stuff."

"Hope so."

Luke walked out of the garage looking like he'd just rebuilt an engine with a speaker wire and a candle. Dirt all over his clothes and shoes. He stepped over to his red pickup truck and placed a toggle box on the bed. Didn't speak to me. I reciprocated the gesture.

Then Josh asked, "So what bracket are you looking at?"

I kept an eye on his brother and said, "Two hundred thousand. No more than two fifty."

"That's doable."

Josh attempted to distract my attention by asking me who would take the NBA finals. I told him that I had hoped on New Jersey but common sense would tell anyone that the Lakers had it. He agreed and then asked if I was married.

I looked at him and said, "No."

He watched as his brother walked back into the garage and up through the kitchen. Then he turned to me and said, "You'll have to excuse him. Luke likes to throw his weight around. I doubt he needed anything out here. Just wanted you to know whose property you were standing on."

"Yeah, I figured that was the case."

I looked him over again and tried to read him. Couldn't tell if he was one of those young white liberals who smoked marijuana and thought the world was truly one race or if he was just setting me up for what his brother had in store for me.

"He tells me that you two don't get along that well."

"He married my sister. What do you expect?"

Joshua took a dirty rag and wiped the handle of a fishing rod.

"You have something against white people?" he asked.

I flexed my chest and gritted my teeth. "Yeah, they have a tendency to marry into my family."

He laughed the sort of laugh that you come to expect from a smart-ass. "Then maybe you've really got something against your sister."

"Don't get yo' ass whooped," I warned.

"And don't test waters just 'cause you think they're shallow."

I stared at him for a minute. He was holdin' his own, stood his ground. Whether he was doin' it for his race or just to show me that he was a man who demanded respect was no longer the issue. I extended my hand. He dapped me up like he'd been places, seen some things. Something, I didn't know what, was different about Joshua.

I excused myself and went into the house to see Rayna. She was in the kitchen talking on the phone while making sandwiches. I walked up and hugged her from behind. She turned around as much as she could without dropping the cordless and waved a butter knife with mayonnaise on it, at me. The mid-length, blue dress she wore did nothing for her complexion. When she'd been in the sun, Rayna had a hint of red that spilled forth in her skin tone, just like my mother. I noticed that her dark brown shoulder-length hair was thinning like Mama's too. She grabbed a dry erase pen off a Velcro pad on the fridge and wrote *This is Daddy* on it. I shrugged my shoulders. Then she wrote: *Pick up other line.* I shook my head. Then she wrote: *He loves you & so do I.* The guilt trip worked. I walked around the corner of the family room and grabbed the other phone.

"So what do you want me to bring you, Daddy, food or cigarettes?"

"Both. I don't know when I'll see you again so just bring both."

"How about I bring something else?" Rayna asked.

"What? A peach cobbler?"

"How'd you guess?"

"'Cause I knows my baby girl loves me. That's right. Bring yo' daddy a nice big, juicy peach cobbler just like Mable used to make. Boy, that woman knew what to do in the kitchen."

Then Rayna said, "You know, Daddy, I talked to Vince the other day. He asked about you."

Pops didn't say much for a moment. And then he sighed like a man with unresolved issues in his life.

"I don't know about that boy. He act like a sissy sometimes the way he's always livin' in the past. Don't never wanna get over stuff. Hmmm, how's he doing?"

Rayna peeped around the corner at me. "He looks great. I'm proud of him. He's about to buy a house and everything."

"Well, it's about time. He have any kids yet? He ain't a real man 'til he's had some kids with a pretty woman. Somebody like ya' momma."

"I don't believe he's had any children but I'm sure there are some in his future. Why don't you ask him sometime."

"Ain't got nothin' to say to that boy. He clam up like a sissy, I told ya. Real man ain't got no time for that! When he grows up, he'll come to me like a man. Until then, Rayna . . . I, I really don't care if I see him."

I slammed the phone down in its cradle as Rayna shrugged her shoulders at me and yelled, "Yeah, I'm still here, Daddy. Must have been a bad connection."

I agreed. Only we weren't speaking in the same context.

When Rayna got off the phone, she called me back into the kitchen. I was in no mood to hear her justifying Pops's behavior, because her love was the blinding type. She saw what she wanted to see.

"Sit down, Vince. I'm sorry you had to hear that. Daddy's older and you know how older people can be. They don't see the err in their ways. All they know is what they see."

"And with you, it's what you *choose* to see."

She sighed. "What do you want me to do? If I turn my back on him, he'll have no one, because you sure won't be there."

"Too bad that thought didn't govern his actions when we were coming up. We might have turned out halfway normal."

"I am normal!"

The garage door slammed as Luke walked in and stomped through the kitchen and over to the mudroom like maybe he thought he'd escaped our minds in those few minutes. Then he doubled back and yelled, "Sissie! Sissie, get in here!"

Rayna jumped like she'd been struck by lightning, glanced at me and scooted her chair back. I grabbed her hand, wouldn't let go.

"You aren't going anywhere. Sit still."

Quiet crept through their home as Rayna's palm began to sweat inside mine.

"Sissie! Get in here. What the hell are you doing?"

"I'm—"

115

I almost reached out and covered her mouth. Pulled her hand tighter so she couldn't move even if she tried. Luke stormed around the corner, looked down at my hand on top of my sister's. Holding her, protecting her.

Then he looked at Rayna. "Sissie, didn't you hear me?"

Rayna stared at me and then turned around toward him. Tried to retrieve her hand. Pulled away from me, broke the bond. My eyes fell upon hers, waited for her to realize that she was safe. Able to decide what she really wanted, not what she had been programmed to do.

She scooted the chair away from the table and mumbled, "I was just walking Vince out. He was just leaving. Weren't you?"

Rayna stood, walked over to the garage door and held it open for me. Let me know in so many ways that I was no longer welcome and, depending on what day, no longer mattered.

"I guess there's really no reason for me to stay, Rayna Michelle. But I shouldn't have to be here for you to remember who you are."

After I was basically put out of Rayna's house, I headed out to Ray's. His directions were pretty simple, and once I'd made it out that far to Lake St. Louis, it wasn't hard to tell why Ray had relocated. St. Louis is in a valley and the farther you moved from the city, the more you could appreciate the view. His house had a lake in back, a four-car garage, a winding extended driveway with some impressive landscaping. When I pulled up, the front door opened and a fair-skinned guy dressed in black slacks and a short-sleeved black muscle shirt walked down the steps and pointed toward the back of the house.

"I think Ray is expecting you. You can take the path around back to the patio."

I did as he instructed and walked underneath a white awning with vines growing up the side of the house. When I came out the view before me was unreal. Small boats were docked on the lake just feet from nearly impeccable green lawns that seemed to go on for days. To my left was the patio, where Ray was sippin' a Bud Light from the bottle and looking about as out of place as Leland did at a Sunday service.

"Babyboy! Whassup? Get yo' ass up here."

He was stretched out on a lawn chair wearing navy-blue slippers, khaki cargo shorts and a white T-shirt with the words *Fuck What You Heard* written in brown. His haircut was the same as mine, faded on the sides and low on the top. Now that we weren't in the darkness of the club, I could see that he'd gotten much taller since we were twelve. Ray now stood about six feet even and weighed in at roughly one eighty-five or so. I could tell that he'd been to the gym but he wasn't lifting what I was capable of. Not even close.

"Whassup, Ray?"

I walked up three steps and extended my hand to dap him up.

"Pull up a chair. Game don't start for another thirty minutes. I'm sittin' here trippin' off this shit."

He lifted a stack of paper from a glass end table where he'd placed two empty beer bottles.

"What's that?" I asked.

"Insurance. That's got to be the biggest scam in America. Pay anotha' man *just in case* some shit happens. Then they wanna know everything just short of what you did last night. Asking me if I've smoked tobacco in the last six months. Hell nah! You think I don't know what that stuff does to the black man?"

He lifted his half-empty bottle and continued, "I sticks to a brew and an occasional joint. Oh, my fault, Babyboy, you want a Bud Light? It's plenty in there. If you want something stiffer, make a left and fix ya'self somethin' at the bar."

I got up and headed for the glass patio door, which I expected to lead into the kitchen, but instead I ended up in a sitting area.

Didn't spot one photograph of anyone in his house. Not Ms. Irene, not even one of a special woman. As much as I hate to admit it, I had pictures of Theresa around every corner in my condo. But I don't think Ray was letting people that close to his heart.

There weren't any curtains up. Ray or his decorator had placed a long charcoal-gray marble-top table with large stained-glass artifacts in front of the windows to catch the sunlight. In front of the table was a cream leather and fabric sectional with navy-blue pillows trimmed in cream. An odd lamp hovered over one end for what I assumed was reading purposes. And a white rug that looked like it had been torn off a Pomeranian's back rested in the center of the room, along with a glass coffee table holding the Rundu Collection and a black-and-white photography book about dreads. Across the room, in the opposite corner, was the bar I'd been looking for. It wasn't as though I'd miss it considering the way he had it lit up from the bottom shelf, giving the colorful bottles enough appeal to send a recovering alcoholic into relapse.

I poured myself a glass of vodka, added some cranberry juice and then headed back out to the patio. When I reached the glass door, Ray looked like he was cleaning up the mess he'd made out there in order to come inside.

When he looked up and spotted me he asked, "You good?"

I lifted my glass. He smiled. Then he said, "We can take this party to the basement. Damn sun is killin' me out here."

I followed him through the sitting area and down some steps while trying not to act like I'd never been anywhere this nice. But his house was impressive as hell. And when we made it to the basement, it got better.

Ray turned to me and said, "I would take you on a tour but I'm too fucked up. Maybe you can check it out yourself during halftime."

"I can say right now that you've done well. All of this is from the club?"

"Hell nah!" He laughed to himself and continued, "Insurance. I had a couple of criminal-minded cousins who were livin' foul and I knew their last days were coming. I let them stay with me so when my suggestions fell on deaf ears, I did what any man would do: Take out a policy."

"I guess that insurance ain't so bad after all."

He took a swig from his beer. "Depends on how you play the game. Get 'em before they can get you."

"I hear ya'."

We sat down on the black leather sectional which was adjacent to a picture of the St. Louis skyline at night that he'd hung on a wall decorated with brown Canyon Stone.

Ray turned to me and said, "Moms wants to see you when you get a chance."

"Ah, you told Ms. Irene you saw me at Discretion, huh?"

"Yeah, told her you were up there turning down the desperate women like you been hitched for ten years."

"Nah, I had to let 'em know that I'm not for games. You know how twisted things can get."

Ray didn't respond. I chalked it up to him being drunk. His eyes were heavy when he leaned over and pulled a plastic container from under the sofa sectional. He removed the lid and let out an odor that smelled like a skunk had been skippin' through an open field with a stink bomb strapped to its back.

"You smoke, Vince?"

"Not often."

"Babyboy, ain't nobody here but me and you."

He pulled out some papers and proceeded to roll a joint. Scooted down to the end of the sectional, which was like a chaise lounger, put his feet up and bent his right knee in order to rest his arm.

I asked, "So how long you been staying out this far, Ray?"

"Three years."

"And where is Ms. Irene staying?"

"Sometimes out here. Other times she stays at home in the house I bought for her. She says this place is too flashy. She's a southern girl. I think that's why she hated California so much."

"How long did y'all stay out west?"

"*Maybe* six months, and then we moved down south to Tennessee to help my aunt take care of my grandmother. The guy Moms up and follows out to California decided that working a job just wasn't for him. We were on our way to a homeless shelter when Moms decided that enough was enough."

"Damn, never imagined that was goin' on. I always pictured you out there meetin' movie stars and practically livin' at Disneyland."

"Yeah right!"

We placed a bet on the game but I went ahead and paid up by the beginning of the fourth quarter. There wasn't a team on the planet that could beat the Lakers unless Shaq was blindfolded and Kobe had gangrene in at least one leg. When we cut the game off the sun had gone down, and Ray plugged up the next best thing to sex: "Madden 2002" football on his XBOX. We played a couple of games of twenty-one, which meant that if either of us scored that amount before the second quarter the game was over, and I beat him every go at it.

"Ah, get outta here! The computer's been helpin' you the whole time!"

I laughed as Ray dramatically jumped up and swung at nothing in particular.

"I had five cats right there and this dude comes all the way across the field?! That's some bull!"

"I don't wanna hear that! You weren't in the inzone, Ray! You gotta get the ball in the inzone."

He flopped down on the couch next to me. Started rollin' another joint.

He asked, "You want somethin' else to drink or you're cool?"

"Yeah, I'll take another one."

I started to get up and get it when Ray put his hand on my leg. Way up and too fuckin' close to my sack. I froze for a minute and then realized that he must've stumbled. I grabbed his arm and stood to my feet to get his weight off of me.

"You a'ight, man?"

"Yeah, just sometimes shit gets hazy."

"Maybe you need to lay off smokin' the trees for a while."

"What, you gon' write me a prescription next?" he laughed, then said, "C'mon so I can show you the rest of the house, man."

I followed him up the stairs to the third floor where the bedrooms were. He showed me where Ms. Irene slept when she visited, his lavish sleeping quarters, another guest room and what he said was a friend's room. He wouldn't let me see inside that one.

We were on our way back downstairs when Ray turned to me laughing and asked, "Do you remember that time when we stole money from your pops's dresser drawer when he was spending the night over at our house for the first time? How is your old man?"

"He's still alive."

"Not getting along?"

"We don't create opportunities to get along. Gotta be in contact for that to happen."

"Believe me, I know how it is. I tried to contact my father when I was about sixteen and all the dude had to say to me was that he was laid off. Translation: You ain't got nothin' comin' so don't even ask."

The one thing I could say good about my father is that he

made sure his children ate and had a roof over their heads. Now attention, support and an ounce of affection were far-fetched requests in his eyes, but the basics he had down to a science.

"What about that time when we walked from downtown over my cousin's house? And the time we were in the locker room at school?"

I remembered the daylong trek from downtown all the way over to Bircher near Riverview to his aunt's house for the fresh sweet potato pie she always kept, but the locker room didn't ring a bell.

"Nah, what happened in the locker room?"

"Nineteen eighty? Mr. Sullivan's gym class?"

I sipped my drink and insistently shook my head.

"Think about it. I guarantee that the shit'll come to you."

I lifted my glass for a toast and said, "Well, until it does, to the past not meaning a thing anymore."

Ray clinked his beer bottle against my glass and smiled.

"It don't have a *damn* thing to do with who we are today."

PART TWO

"... Can't Run Away from Yourself"
—Bob Marley

Theresa

Mama left me a message letting me know that she wouldn't be able to pick me up from the airport because the Women of Triumph support group that she'd started volunteering with had two members who needed a ride. She suggested my stepfather, Richard, give me a ride back to their Smyrna suburb just outside of Atlanta but I declined. We've never gotten along. I'm sure it had a lot to do with the timing. All of my life, it was just my mother and I. We were girlfriends, best friends who were inseparable. The transition wasn't smooth for any of us. I was a sixteen-year-old who now had to listen to someone who was occupying the valuable time I cherished alone with my mother. Not only that but the rules were changing. When some single women invite a man into a ready-made family where there are already children, they have a tendency to prove to the man that he is the head of the house, and present their children as sacrificial lambs in a desperate attempt to prove their loyalty. And my momma was no different. My curfew had gone from ten to eight forty-five. My allowance had vanished before my eyes and the car I'd saved up two years for was given to Richard when his broke down. And all of the tension left little room for a level of respect. He and I were both protecting our ground. The only thing was that we both wanted my mother by our side on it.

When the cab pulled up to their two-story brick home, my mother's car was still in the driveway. I paid the driver and gathered up my belongings. Put Dameron on my hip and headed to the front door. The driver brought my things up to the porch and set them down next to a row of shrubbery.

Before I could tip him, my mother had flung the door open and was yelling, "My babies!" She snatched Dameron up and flooded his face with kisses. Embraced me with her one free hand and then pulled back to give me the once-over.

"You don't look well, Theresa. Come on in here and put your bags in your room so you can go with me."

She closed the door, set Dameron down on her gold-colored antique-style sofa and patted her hair. She was wearing it in a natural and had colored it red. A tasteful red that came closer to a deep copper. It accented her soft butter-toned complexion. She had put on a few pounds but hey, she looked happy and that was better than where I was.

"Where are you going, Mama, to one of those meetings?"

"Yeah, and I think you need to be there. These are nice young ladies who are going through hard times as well."

"What kind of hard times?" I asked, flopping down next to Dameron and fanning the bottom of my pink summer dress.

"They've been lied to and cheated on. Find it hard to trust people nowadays. Just come and listen. That's all you have to do. I think you may learn something."

"How? Have any of them been widowed?"

She turned her mouth up like she was listening to every one of their stories in her head.

"Death is a big part of their testimony. Much bigger than you know."

Mama, two young girls who appeared to be in their early twenties and I stood outside of a community center out in Stone

126

Mountain and pressed a buzzer. Mama announced herself and gained entry for us all. The two girls behind us had been quiet during most of the ride. After the introduction, unless they were doing sign language, there wasn't a word coming from the backseat.

We all took off down a long hall, with Mama directing the way as if she were leading her flock to salvation. She'd glance back at us periodically and give us all a smile of reassurance, her neatly cropped natural glistening from the bright lights above, her pink and black size-eighteen skirt swaying from side to side. When she finally reached the door at the end of the hall, she opened it and walked in. There were about fourteen black women there, ranging in age from about nineteen to forty-five. They were sitting in metal folding chairs around a long table with a sheet of paper and a pen in front of each of them. A smile crossed their faces when Mama walked in. She started with her round of hugs and then stepped back to introduce me and the other two girls.

"Ladies, this is my daughter Theresa."

"Hi, Theresa," they all said in unison.

"She's here with my grandson Dameron. They're visiting me from St. Louis."

"Oh, how nice," one woman replied.

Mama placed her hand on one of the girls' shoulders and ushered her up front.

"And these two beautiful girls are Toni and Lisa. They just realized their HIV status last week and would like to share their stories."

The two girls gave one another that look that children do on the first day of school. The lighter one with long braids stood there, head hung low, cupping each elbow with the opposite hand while the other, who wore her hair faded, cleared her throat and interlocked her fingers in front of her. She was the first to speak.

"Well, I'm about to graduate—"

Mama cut her off with, "Tell 'em what grade you finished, baby."

"I'm about to graduate from high school. And uh, well, I wanted to go into the military so I got tested and that's how I found out."

A woman with her hair wrapped up in Kente cloth asked, "Do you know how this happened, sweetie?"

The young girl dropped her head, her shoulders slumped and she slowly nodded. Mama placed her hand on her back and pulled her in for a hug. Her wailing was muffled by Mama's plentiful bosom. She was crying so hard that Mama had to take her out of the room to counsel her.

"Theresa, Lisa, have a seat. Let me tell you a little bit about what we do here," one of the women said.

I pulled up a chair and took a seat next to a woman who looked like she was the oldest in the room, which was only forty-something. Most of the ladies were quiet. Guess they figured it was enough that they were able to show up, reveal the fact that they knew their death by name. I couldn't help but wonder if they'd ever been bitter enough to wish their situation on someone else. If they ever considered doing to someone else what had been done to them. Some of these women said their lovers knew they were passing the virus on, while others had danced with demons who didn't know whether they were born to give or receive, if you know what I mean.

I felt so sorry for them all. They were so young, so beautiful. Every shade of brown one could imagine. Some were career women, others self-proclaimed homemakers. None claimed to be a victim; instead they considered themselves chosen. Told us of their desire to let God's light shine through them, to be an example of his mercy. How that blind faith and perseverance may be the very motivation that saves somebody's life. They talked about going shopping for bedroom furniture and making other plans that illustrated a determination to live the life they had left to its fullest. Made me wonder why people had to be in fear of losing life in order to exercise that philosophy. Why human beings responded so well to pain as a wake-up call. And why even then, some of us still didn't get it.

When Mama and Toni came back in the room they started a discussion about the church. How so many of them weren't informing our people of the epidemic because to promote safe sex was like giving the green light to fornicate. They were standing in a tough position. It was going against everything that they were teaching, like giving a person bail money before you suggest they *not* commit the crime.

Lisa tapped me on the arm and pointed to a message she had written on her paper. She wanted to know how long I planned to be in Atlanta. I told her about two weeks. She asked if I liked to go out to clubs. I told her no but that I couldn't wait to get to a mall. She volunteered to take me to Greenbriar later that evening.

The conversation had gone from the church to insurance and back to bisexual black men. Quite a few of the ladies had a story to tell in reference to that. I'd say maybe nine out of the fourteen insisted that was the way they were infected. They were all in monogamous relationships that they thought would take them on to marital bliss until the undercover brotha started tippin' out and doing his thing. I found myself wondering how they didn't pick up on it, how these well-educated career women couldn't figure out who they were sleeping with. What is the foolproof way of knowing when you're dealing with a bisexual black man? What signs have my sistas of every shade of brown been missing all this time? When the meeting ended we all prayed together. There was something about holding hands with a group of women who didn't expect to dance in their front yard with grandchildren forty-five or fifty years from now that brought about thoughts of my own mortality. None of us really knew when our number was up but the common thread was that we knew, HIV or not, we'd all get a turn to say goodbye.

"I really like Ms. Minerva, Theresa. She act like she been knowing me and Toni for years."

Lisa laughed, took a sip of her fruit punch and set her Styrofoam cup down on the small square table. We were sitting in the food court at the mall talking about her boyfriend, her family and Mama. As people walked by us, her attention drifted. But when the crowd thinned out, she ran off on tangents. Guess she had a lot to get off her chest, and not just with me. She still hadn't told her boyfriend Lionel yet. Her family turned their backs on her. So Mama and the support group sorta came along in the nick of time.

"You know yo' momma let me stay with her the night my momma kicked me out?"

I shook my head. "No, I didn't know that."

"Yep, that's why I'll kick somebody's ass if they mess with Ms. Minerva."

She surveyed her surroundings. Her eyes told me that she still felt like a victim. She watched everyone as though they were on to her, knew her secret.

I asked, "So when are you gonna tell Lionel?"

She peered up at me and wrapped her lips around that straw for an extended amount of time. Set the cup down and twirled the straw like she was deciding whether or not to take another sip.

"I think it's too soon to say something. I mean, he's gone already."

Zenobia

"Fine! You can have company, but not those two knock-kneed wenches that came around here looking for you the other night. And only—I do repeat, *only*—after Zaire is in bed. Got that, Maurice? And another thing before that little pea brain of yours starts ticking, Self is *not* allowed in my house tonight."

"Yeah, Z. I got it. Now be out. I gotta take a shower and get dressed."

"All right, boy. But don't make me bust a tae bo move on you."

Maurice was practically pushing me out of my own front door and into the driveway. I had to draw back on him a couple of times when he started wrinkling my outfit. I was wearing my size-eight turquoise just-below-the-knee skirt that had specks of fuchsia and gold with a fuschia V-neck sleeveless shirt. Coupled with my sexy upsweep, I looked like a goddess from the Middle East.

Truth be told, it took everything in me to even leave the house. I'd sat for over an hour and watched Zaire sleeping. Waiting to here her moan, whine or whimper, but there was nothing. I didn't observe one indication that she'd witnessed anything violent. She was as peaceful as an angel, my little brown-skinned angel.

I pulled up in front of Lainey's apartment building in the Central West End at eight on the nose. Cedric pulled up behind me, got out in his blue and white uniform, grabbed a briefcase out of the backseat and started walking me to the door.

"Hey, hey, stranger."

"'Stranger' yourself. Where've you been? You used to come over all the time. Now you just sweep through and snatch my wife away."

"Well, you know we're twenty-first-century women. Always on the move."

"Yeah, I'm learning. How's everything coming with the club? Lainey was tellin' me about you not getting what you deserve."

"Yeah, well you know how ugly things can get when you're compromising with someone you once dealt with on an intimate basis."

"Well, hang in there. You're a good woman, Zenobia. I've got a feeling things will turn around for you sooner or later."

"Thanks, Cedric. How's the real estate business treating you?"

"Things have been kind of slow. But I've got some stuff lined up. Feels like I'm working twenty-four hours a day."

"Tell me about it."

"So, where are you two headed tonight?"

"We're gonna go listen to a little jazz and have a couple of drinks."

"And I wasn't invited?"

Lainey stepped outside and leaned over the railing with a dry "Didn't know whether or not you'd be too *tired*."

She placed so much emphasis on "tired" that even I cringed from embarrassment. But apparently he'd learned to cope, because he simply looked up at his wife and blew her a kiss.

"Yeah, screw you too," Lainey said, turning to walk back into the apartment.

"Okay, did I miss something here?" I asked.

"There's never much to miss. C'mon up, I'm sure she'll be ready in a sec."

Lainey was stomping around in a cute little ivory wrap skirt and an oversized tunic shirt that hung off her right shoulder. She'd let her wavy hair hang, which was unusual. She never did this unless she was pissed and about to start cussin'. I took a seat in one of her wicker chairs and waited patiently, because if I know Lainey the curtain was about to rise.

"Zenobia, I'm a little low on cash. Would you mind loaning me a little change until next week?" she asked.

"Yeah, we can just—"

"You don't have to use Zenobia's money. Elaine, you know I'll give you my ATM card."

"No, thank you. I might notice your checking balance and that would put me in your business again!"

Cedric rubbed the top of his baldhead, shook it and then looked at me like he wanted to ask if I believed what I was seeing.

"Woman, you *are* my business. Now will you just take the card and forget about the e-mails?"

"I can't forget about the e-mails, Cedric! I want to know what they're about. Who is MrVLRuns?"

"I'm gonna tell you this one more time—it's business."

"Well, what kind of business keeps you from making love to your wife?!"

It got so quiet in that apartment you could've heard a rat pissin' on cotton. Everybody's mouth was hanging open except for Lainey's. She was standing there crying like somebody died. Mascara running down her face like it had somewhere to be.

I stood up and said, "Maybe tonight isn't a good night for you to go out, Lainey."

Their eyes were deadlocked. I waited for *somebody* to say *something.*

"No, I'm goin'. And I'll be goin' out tomorrow night and the night after that too."

Cedric said, "Elaine, calm down."

I started for the door. "I'm gonna wait for you in the car."

Lainey snatched her purse off of the counter and continued, "No need to wait. Here I come, Zenobia. It ain't a damn thing goin' on in here."

"Elaine, don't do this," he pleaded. "I love you."

"Think about what you're doing," I leaned over and whispered.

She cut her eyes at me and mumbled something in French that I was sure translated to "Shut the hell up" so I took two steps in the other direction.

"If you love me then show me. Walk over here and touch me."

"What?"

"Walk over here and touch me like I'm your wife."

Cedric chuckled in amusement, but his failure to move from his spot spoke volumes.

"That's crazy. Everybody in this room knows you're my wife."

I could almost hear Lainey's heart breaking as she ushered me out the door, then stopped on the threshold. "And unfortunately for you, one of us doesn't care anymore."

"What are you-all having?" Sheila asked, standing over our candlelit table.

She and Byron had transformed the bookstore into a serious vibe spot. The lights were out and large round tables were brought down from the deli side, covered with Kente cloth and stationed around the stage Byron usually performed on for the kids. There was a guy up front who sorta resembled Tavis Smiley, without hair, providing a soft melodic tune.

Lainey said, "I'll take the saxophone player."

"She's kidding."

"No I'm not."

"Two Chablis, Sheila."

When she walked away I bumped Lainey's knee under the table.

"What?"

"You know what. You'll only make matters worse by doing that."

"Doing what?"

"I know you, Lainey."

She pursed her lips and rolled her eyes the other way.

"Cedric is a good man."

"And what, I'm not a good woman?"

"Are you trying to become a *divorced* one?"

She rolled her neck from side to side. "And I would be losing what? Attention? The best sex of my life? I think not."

"So what's the deal with the mystery man, *Lexi?*"

She ran her hand over her wavy hair and said, "I couldn't go through with it. When I spotted him at Discretion the other night, I walked the other way. But after tonight, I wish I hadn't. At least I wouldn't be feelin' like an old maid."

I gave her an affectionate look. Didn't know what to say.

Then suddenly she asked, "You haven't forgotten about my little favor have you?"

"Have I forgotten? No. Have I decided to do it? No."

"Look Zenobia, I could be . . ."

Lainey was still fussing when I spotted David walking through the door. He was headed straight for me, so I leaned over and asked her, "Can we discuss this later?"

She followed my gaze over to David, who was in a pair of

navy-blue slacks and a tan short-sleeved button-down shirt. His rhythmic stride was consistent with the music. Strong. Confident. His friend Cliff whom we'd met yesterday was with him. Looked like he was tryin' to get with one of the women who were coming through the door at the same time. She wore reddish brown locks and looked like she'd stepped right out of the seventies in a dashiki, a denim skirt with ripped edges and brown wedge-heel sandals. She made a beeline to our table and asked, "Are these seats taken?"

As soon as I said no, Sheila reappeared behind me with our drinks.

"Well, well, the gang's all here!"

We all turned around and looked at her as she began with the introductions. Broke down how she knew everybody, whatever hobbies we had and what our momma's second cousin did for a living.

That's when Cliff exclaimed, "I thought a football player owned that club!"

I took a sip of the Chablis and had begun to share my wishful thinking with him when David turned around in his seat to face me and placed his hand on the back of my chair.

"Zenobia's doin' it all, huh? That's sweet. I like that."

Sheila interjected with, "This is one of my two girlfriends whom I plan to bring with me when I stop by your club, Zenobia."

"Oh, well you'll love it!"

I glanced over at Elaine on the other side of me. She and another woman who hadn't come in with us looked like twins. Attitudes written all over their faces, arms folded except to pick up their glasses and knock off the remainder of their drinks. It didn't help that Cliff was trying to make small talk with the bitter sista. Draped his arm across the back of her chair and leaned over in her direction every time he laughed or the sax player held a note longer than a millisecond.

"Is that invitation extended to the fellas too?" David asked.

"I was hoping you'd come. You know what, why don't we all swing by there tonight."

"Sounds good to me. Byron said we should be closing around eleven."

Elaine informed us, "I'm not in much of a mood for Discretion."

She ordered another drink. Gave the musicians her undivided attention. Sat like that for at least the next hour. By then, David and I had walked up near the stage and danced through a couple of numbers. Held on to one another like we had a history.

He whispered, "You're a beautiful dancer."

"I know when to let a good man lead."

"Are we still talking about dancing or does that go for life in general?"

"Both."

"You don't find many women who will eagerly say that."

"There aren't too many women like me, either."

David laughed. Sexy. Deep. Tossed his head back and then dropped it right against my cheek. Pecked it with his full lips and pulled me just a little bit closer.

"That's sweet. You always been this confident?"

"Is anybody ever confident their entire lives? I've moved through pain just like everybody else."

"Well, you came out smellin' like roses."

"Didn't I?" I laughed. "Just kidding, David. I don't want you thinking I'm arrogant or anything."

"I've already formed an opinion, Zenobia."

"And what's that?"

"I'm not about to let the cat out of the bag completely."

"I guess I can deal with that. So how did you get started writing?"

"I was always a quiet and shy kid, so writing was my way of voicing my opinion. I would sit in the yard back home and just listen to life. You ever hear life, Zenobia?"

I shook my head. "Can't say that I have."

"That's okay. I'll show you what I mean someday. But yeah, a friend of mine stumbled across a poem I'd written and suggested I publish my work. So I went to a printer and got about forty books of poetry printed and took them around to bookstores like this one. Thanks to Sheila and Byron I met a couple of authors and networked my way into gaining representation."

"So you have an actual agent?"

"Yeah, if that's what you wanna call him. These days he isn't doing much of anything. We've been fishing the same book to publishers for two years and nobody's interested."

"You say that like you're ready to quit working at Chrysler."

"No. I like to keep busy. I'd probably go crazy if I didn't have anything to do."

I ran my hand along his massive shoulders. "So I'm assuming you spend a lot of time working out."

"Every day. I'm not getting any younger."

"I know what you mean. I think about that from time to time."

"You mind me asking how old you are? I know that's taboo with a lot of women."

"I'm twenty-eight and holding."

"'And holding'?"

"And holding," I said in a matter-of-fact fashion.

"You know, when I was about seventeen back home, my brothers and I warned these young guys about taking their boat out before the storms. They laughed and called us punks for being afraid. Well to make a long story short, when they were about two miles out the engine just quit on them. The wind began to change directions and their tiny ship was tossed. Few of them made it back and the ones who did sulked into a state of depression and guilt over the deaths. Then an elder sat them down one day and told them to celebrate. They should certainly mourn the deaths of their friends, but they should also celebrate their own lives. They had done something exceptional. Something many others were incapable of. They'd survived. And if that isn't a reason for you to celebrate becoming twenty-nine, I don't know what is."

"That's so sad. How did their families handle it?"

"I don't know. I made that part up. The point is you need to start celebrating yourself."

I smiled at David and said, "I should've known. I thought I recognized that part about a tiny ship being tossed from *Gilligan's Island*."

He laughed.

"You have a vivid imagination," I told him.

"Thank you. You have beautiful skin."

David ran his hand down my arm, took my hand and interlocked our fingers.

"You have hands like my mother. I loved her hands."

He gently placed my slender mahogany fingers on his cheek. I looked him in the eyes a moment before he closed them and felt his definitive features—his high cheekbones, broad nose and full lips. Reached up, wrapped a couple of his baby dreadlocks around my finger and admired the soft, fuzzy texture. Wondered if he resembled his mother. Wondered if she'd had the same hairstyle. Wondered if she knew how handsome and intriguing her son turned out to be.

That's when he took me by total surprise and asked, "So what's the deal with Zaire's father?"

141

"There is no deal. We run Discretion and we take care of our daughter."

"You mind me asking how long you-all have been apart?"

"Not at all. It's been about three years and seven women."

"Oh, it ended like that?"

"Like that and then some. Payce is an okay guy. He just likes to test the waters."

"By that do you also mean *your* waters?"

"If he could, but that's not a problem. We have an understanding. I try to keep the relationship positive for the sake of our daughter."

"How old is Zaire?"

"She'll be five in early September."

"Virgo, huh? You know, Nikai is big on the whole astrology thing."

"No, I didn't know that. Actually I know little about Sheila either."

"Sheila's good people. A kind, protective sista. I met her about three years ago when she moved home with Byron."

"To the Virgin Islands?"

"Yeah. You ever been?"

"No."

"What have you been waiting for?"

"I have a child, remember? Can't just jump up and break camp like some folk."

"You ever wanna have any more children?" he asked.

"Maybe someday when I'm married. What about you?"

"I want pretty much the same but I'd like to have about four or five. I grew up in a big family. There were nine of us."

"Sounds like your parents loved one another."

"That rare kinda love, Zenobia. That's the kinda love I'm hoping for. You know, where it just flows like water and rests easy."

"You *sound* like a poet. Mind letting me hear something you've written?"

"Not at all. Let's see."

> *I was told to take my time and choose*
> *Like a nomad I was expected to roam*
> *It was they who had bachelorhood confused*
> *Yet now envy my life, our union and our home.*

I stepped a little closer, blushed and said, "I like that. You seem to be big on family and home."

"I'm big on love."

Having said that, he placed his chin on my head and hummed along with the music. David's deep voice sent vibrations down my neck and into my shoulders, but was interrupted by Lainey's finger tapping me from behind. David held my hand and trailed me as I walked back toward the table with Lainey.

"I'm about to get outta here. You think you can get David to give you a ride so I can take your car?"

"You all right?"

"My husband won't touch me below the waist. Why would I be all right, Zenobia?"

I pulled my keys from my purse and handed them to her.

"Okay, okay. I'll be by in the morning. Sure you haven't had too much to drink?"

"Is that actually possible?"

"Good night, Lainey. And be careful."

She walked away, arms folded like her time had been wasted, her space invaded. Lainey thanked Sheila as she walked her out, Nikai excused herself to the rest room and Cliff scooted over into the next empty chair while I squeezed David's hand and recited my chant to myself: *Protect your heart, Zenobia . . . live and learn.*

143

* * *

"Heeeeeyyyyyyy! We're gonna chase those crazy bald-heads . . ."

Nikai was on that dance floor doin' a reggae grind to Bob Marley like she hadn't been out since Johnny Gill had last had a hit. Sheila, Byron, David, Cliff and I watched from a table a few feet away as a couple of guys danced up to her.

Sheila yelled across the table to me, "Now watch her!"

Men had actually formed a line to wait in for a dance with Ms. Thang. Tonight was Caribbean night again and apparently Nikai was just what the guys had come looking for. She'd just grabbed the next hopeful for a thirty-second session, rocked her fit, sweaty frame to the mellow tune, then switched partners before the song ended.

Sheila informed me, "Nik is a tease."

Lonely Cliff shook his head and said, "See the games women play. Why won't she just say she doesn't want to dance any-more?"

Byron answered, "Apparently because she does want to, just not with him."

"But that's just unnecessary the way—"

I cut him off. "Drinks are on me. What's everybody having?"

Sheila said, "Byron and I will have a cranberry juice. Bring 'Angry Black Man' something with alcohol in it."

Nikai sashayed back over to her seat as the order was being given. The DJ switched the vibe to Buju Banton's "African Pride" as she grabbed a white napkin off of the table to pat her forehead dry. "I'll have a white zinfandel."

I walked over to the bar. Observed Beacon doin' a hell of a job. Had everybody at the bar laughing, smiling and, more im-portant, ordering drinks. When I stepped up, he beamed and ex-cused himself from a conversation he was having with some guy who reminded me of Maxwell, the R&B singer.

"Hey! What's up, Zenobia?"

"Looks like you've gotten the hang of things."

Just as he was about to comment, Melinda, another one of the bartenders, asked him how to make a Numbing Nobia. Beacon looked at me and grinned.

"You know, that's my contribution to Discretion."

I yelled over the music. "And we appreciate it. You're doing a great job here."

"Thanks," he said, mixing up the drink.

"Hey Beacon, I'm here with some friends. Would you have one of the girls bring this order over? Two cranberry juices, a white zinfandel, a Numbing Nobia and uh . . ."

I looked back at Cliff, who was still talking and moving his hands like he was looking for somebody to debate with.

". . . and a Hennessey and Coke."

"I thought you were strictly a wine woman."

I glanced over the other shoulder and laid eyes on Jeff. Black slacks, gray V-neck cotton shirt, beer in his hand and malice intent in his eyes. He didn't look any more interested in seeing me than I was in seeing him. I assumed his comment was supposed to be a form of greeting, easier than saying hello.

"And I thought I'd be lucky enough not to have to see you again."

"Guess that's what we get for thinking, huh?"

"No Pampers to change tonight?"

He shifted a bit and looked behind him. "I'm out celebrating a friend's birthday—otherwise I probably wouldn't be here."

"Can I get that in writing?"

"Look, Zenobia, I'm not interested in arguing with you. I don't see any reason why we can't be friends. You're single, I'm single—"

"You're engaged!"

"Not anymore. You took care of that."

He licked those Denzel lips and continued, "And I want to thank you."

I snatched the first Numbing Nobia from Beacon's hands and took a couple of sips. It hit me like lightning and warmed my insides all the way down to that last nerve Jeff was doin' the cha-cha slide across.

"Don't credit me for what your infidelity caused. *You* did that. *You* wanted to leave Leslie."

"But you helped me. You didn't have to do that. And I just want you to know how much I appreciate it."

I got it. He was setting this up so that the next time I heard it I wouldn't be totally surprised. This was supposed to be my fault and from the evil sadistic grin he was giving me, something told me my name was dragged through the mud before he walked away from Leslie.

Jeff looked around the club quickly and asked, "You entertaining guests tonight?"

"Don't ask questions you already know the answer to."

"Then maybe I should ask what I really want to know. When are you ditchin' them?"

"I'm not like you. I don't treat people like used Kleenex."

He glanced at his watch. "So let's say about a quarter 'til two?"

"Hell no! You don't get it, do you?"

He smiled, grabbed a bottle of beer off of the bar, tipped Beacon and said, "You're the one who doesn't get it. See you in about an hour."

Jeff turned and walked away like the Grim Reaper after retrieving a soul. That was what scared me the most. I'd never seen this side of him. The guy I knew brought roses to my door and took me on long walks. Listened to Stevie Wonder by candlelight and talked about his childhood. He was nothing like the ornery bastard who'd just tried to bully me.

Jeff took a seat at a table with about three or four other men in ties and slacks. He'd cleverly stationed his chair facing me, roughly thirty feet across the room. When I got back to the table, David asked me to dance. I took his hand and shook my hips to Shaggy's "It Wasn't Me" as we eased our way out onto the floor. Kept my eyes on *Leslie's baby's daddy* just in case he decided to put on a performance and made me embarrass us all. I was singin' along when I turned around and backed it up for David. Saw flames in Jeff's eyes as he took another swig of his beer and nodded his head to the beat.

"She caught me red-handed . . ."

Nikai danced through the crowd with some guy in tow and stopped next to us.

"Heeeeyyyyyyy!"

She was kickin' it. Spankin' her own butt as she danced in a circle and then stepped around us while rhymin' in her best Jamaican accent. Started a little one-leg-up move that we all caught on to. Switched partners and then broke it down like we were auditioning for *Soul Train*. We were on our way back to the table when Melinda brought the drinks. Sheila, Byron and Cliff were holding a discussion about the group of kids who were on the news for breaking into one of the middle schools on the South Side.

"They said they were students from the school where Theresa teaches!"

Nikai was yelling over the music and across me. Spraying me upside my head with chilled wine.

Sheila said, "I"m gonna ask her about talking to her class one day. Seems the age for troubled youth is getting younger and younger, doesn't it?"

Byron and David looked at one another and responded at the same time. "It's that crack generation" . . . "The families are torn apart." . . . "Momma and Daddy hovering over a bong or hypodermic needle."

I nodded my head in agreement and glanced at my watch. It was twenty minutes after one. Jeff hadn't taken his eyes off of me. Studied me like he knew me well. David placed his arm around the back of my chair while he continued. Even began to hold me tighter and massage my shoulder whenever I had something to say, which was only an *mmhmm* every seven or eight comments. The club was getting more crowded, Shaggy was switched to Beenie Man's "Girls Dem Sugar" and my martini glass was now empty. The draft from the doors opening and closing brought the perspiration ring under the arm of my fuchsia shirt to my attention. I shifted in my seat long enough to notice that every time I moved, so did Jeff.

"Hey everybody, I'm gonna run up to my office to check on something. I'll be right back."

David asked, "Can I see where you work?"

I patted his hand as I removed it from behind me. "Don't you move a muscle. I wouldn't want to lose you in the crowd."

That's when Nikai asked, "Is there a rest room up there that I can use?"

Jeff set his beer bottle down on the table. Stood up from the chair he was sitting on and adjusted his black leather belt. Rubbed the front of his shirt so that the definition in his chest could be seen and then licked those lips of his.

I told Nikai, "Yeah, come on."

We got up, and had managed to maneuver only about ten feet through the sea of people when Jeff made his move. Weaved his way in and out of the crowd until he was close enough to grab my wrist.

He asked, "You ready?"

"Ready for what?"

His shoulders dropped as he tilted his head. "Don't tell me I went through all of that for nothing."

I pulled my wrist free and asked, "Went through all of what?"

"Coming clean about us."

When Nikai overheard that, she craned her neck and stopped singing along with the music. Stepped back so she could get in on the rest of this conversation.

"I don't know what you're talking about. You had a child on the way and didn't tell me."

"What difference did that make if you were willing to be with me when you knew I had a *woman*?"

Nikai gave an empathetic grunt like she was watchin' Roy Jones beat the crap out of somebody. Those words felt like a blow. So quick, painful and unwarranted.

I shook my head and grabbed the next Cosmopolitan that passed on a tray. Nikai began with her slow rock from side to side. Her back was to me so she was bumping against my shoulder, brushing me up against Jeff. He wrapped an arm around me and smiled. I pulled out of his grasp.

"Is that your man over there?"

"Why?"

"I'm not tryin' to disrespect anybody."

"Look. I had to talk to the mother of your child while you ran home from my place after using my damn phone to call her! Let's not get on the subject of disrespect!"

Nikai backed it up again.

I continued, "And what makes you think we have anything to discuss?"

"You have something that belongs to me."

I folded my arms, pursed my lips and asked, "And what's that?"

"My heart. I just wanted to come by tonight and maybe talk to you for a few minutes since I haven't seen you in a while."

"'A while'? It's only been two weeks. Your baby isn't even smiling yet!"

"What, is that supposed to make me feel guilty?"

"I was going for humane but if all I can get is guilt, I'll understand."

"I'll take that. Now, are you gonna ditch them or should I meet you at your place?"

"You should take no for an answer."

"Not an option."

"So what do you want from me?"

"A chance."

"And if there is none?"

He stepped a little closer and whispered, "Then I wanna finish what we started."

I pictured my skirt over his head, with my leg tossed across the back of the sofa, moaning my way into ecstasy. Then I pictured the look on my face when I heard the front door slam behind him while he burned rubber on my driveway while probably trying to remember Lamaze breathing techniques. The tears that rolled down my cheeks, the mantra I stared into the mirror and chanted: *You are obligated to live and learn.*

I rebounded with a flat "No, thank you."

"Fine. Have it your way."

Nikai nudged me with her elbow, leaned back and whispered, "I gotta go before I *let* it go."

"All right."

I turned back to Jeff, who was watching some woman poppin' and lockin' her torso down to the floor. He was in a trance when I yelled, "I'm through dealing!"

He frowned and bobbed his head to the beat before silently walking back to his table.

I told Nikai, "Sorry about that. C'mon."

When we made it to the top of the stairs I started flipping the lights all of the way down the hall.

"This is nice," she said, admiring the burgundy carpet and its black and white trim. The vinelike print matched the edges of the wallpaper.

She continued, "This would be perfect for a hall of fame."

"Payce is too anal. He's not interested in seeing anybody's picture hanging in here that he can't call up personally."

"Didn't Sheila say he plays professional football?"

"Yeah. You know 'im?"

"My uh, friend, Robert . . . ahem, used to talk about him constantly. 'Payce Whittington is the best linebacker in the whole league' is all I would hear. You'd swear they grew up together."

I used the key to unlock the door to my office and said, "Well, rest assured he's not missing anything."

I hit the light and pointed her toward the bathroom in the far corner.

"Well, from the looks of the brotha you were talking to downstairs I wouldn't say you're missing anything either."

"Who, Jeff? He's an even bigger waste of time."

After Nikai closed the door, I sat down at my desk and noticed the light on the phone blinking. I picked it up and retrieved the messages. One was somebody calling about the bartending position that Beacon had already filled. Another was from the woman who wanted to throw her cousin a birthday party at Discretion. I erased it and played the last one. It was Cammie. She said she was calling to see how we were. She'd made it to California and wanted to know why Payce had gotten his number changed. I didn't even know he'd done that, but more important, for somebody who had been beaten so badly she sounded pretty disappointed about not being able to find him. When her message ended, I could just make out her saying to someone in the room with her, "She'll get in contact with me once she finds out what's going on." Then she hung up.

Nikai walked out of the bathroom rubbing lotion on her hands and adjusting her skirt. "I just love your décor, Zenobia."

"Thanks. You ready?"

"Wait a second," she said, standing in front of the two-way mirror. "You can see everything from here."

I stepped from behind the desk and stood next to her. The lighting on the dance floor had been changed from gold to a romantic red. We observed Sheila and Byron slow-dancing so closely they looked like they'd become one person. Her head lay heavily on his shoulder. Made him look even more dependable, supportive. The sight of it made my heart sink with envy. Reminded me of how I'd wasted over a month with Jeff.

I was scanning the room when Nikai pointed to David and Cliff still sitting at the table. Then I realized that *we* were being stared at—by Beacon. He was standing behind the bar with his hands in his pockets, looking up at the mirror.

That's when Nikai asked, "He's been up here, hasn't he?"

"Who?"

"The guy behind the bar staring at us."

"You noticed that too, huh?"

"Yeah. He looks sorta strange. Maybe it's the empty glare he gives people."

Hearing her say that made me think about how he'd stood in my office, perched in front of this window like he was in deep thought. Not to mention the way he took it upon himself to bring his bold butt up here without an invitation to begin with.

"I just hired him. He's kinda quiet sometimes but he knows his job. He even came up with a new drink. Guess what he calls it?"

"What?"

"Numbing Nobia."

Nikai turned to me with a suspicious grin on her face.

"Nope. It's nothing like that. As a matter of fact he hasn't tried to hit on any of the women that work here. Brothaman says he's got a job to do."

She shrugged her shoulders and went back to looking out of the window. "I don't know. I could be wrong, but I'd keep my eye on him if I were you. At least tell 'im to stop staring up here making people think you're watching them."

"You've got a point."

"What time is it?"

I checked my watch. "Two thirty-four."

"Girl, let me get outta here."

"So you-all still comin' next Saturday night?"

"Yeah, let me get a number to call you."

I grabbed one of my cards off of the desk and wrote my home and cell number down on the backside.

"Call me. You, me, Sheila, Theresa and Elaine should get together sometime. You know, have a girls night out."

"Yeah, we should."

I hit the lights and closed the door behind us. When we descended the stairs, I saw Jeff waiting at the bottom. I sashayed past him and inhaled the scent of his cologne. Shuddered at how good he smelled, and how long it lingered. But that was only because he was right behind me, following us back to the table.

I put a little distance between Nikai and me, backed up and asked, "What do you want?!"

He looked at me with heavy, intoxicated eyes and then ran his hand across my braids. "I like it when you wear them down."

"Are you *drunk*, Jeff?"

He let his head fall to one side and asked, "Do I have to be drunk to find you attractive?"

153

"Just leave me alone, okay? If I can respect yours please respect mine."

I stood there long enough to watch him rejoin his friends and then made my way back to my guests, who were standing up like they were ready to form a line to the front door.

"Leaving so soon?" I asked.

Sheila said, "Gotta get up early and open the store tomorrow."

"Won't you-all stay for one more drink? It's on me."

They all looked at one another in contemplation and agreed that it was past their bedtime.

David grabbed my hand and asked, "You about ready to go?"

"Yeah, just let me walk them out and lock the door upstairs."

I made my rounds hugging and thanking everyone for coming. Made them promise they'd be back. Then I grabbed a couple of passes for Saturday night and gave them each one. On the way out, Sheila, Nikai, and I lagged behind for a little girl talk while the guys convened in the parking lot.

"So, Ms. Lady, it looks like you two are gettin' along well," Sheila said as she opened the glass door.

"I like what I see so far."

Nikai yawned, stretched and said, "Well, I know one thing."

We both asked, "What's that?"

"I'm tired."

Sheila fanned her hand. "Girl, I thought you really had something to say. So Zenobia, you have my number. Give me a call. Nikai and I *believe* in doin' lunch. If you're not too busy, maybe you can get away with us."

Byron yelled across the lot, "All right, sistas, let's wrap it up."

"Here we come," Sheila shot back.

Nikai asked, "Cliff, you still ridin' with me?"

He nodded and matched her sleepy stretch.

Byron walked over with David, gave me a hug and kissed me

on the cheek. "Thanks again. And I hope to see Zaire next Wednesday."

"She'll be there."

I stepped back up on the curb and felt David slip his arm around my waist. I leaned in and let my head fall on his shoulder. We both waved as our friends pulled away. It seemed as though we'd done this a thousand times.

"You want me to come inside with you while you lock up or will you be okay?"

"I should be fine. I'll be right back."

I hurried up to my office, dialed Payce's number and realized that Cammie was right: The number had been changed. I pushed the flash button and called home. Nobody answered. I hung up and called back. Still no answer. I was almost out the door when the phone rang.

"Hello?"

Maurice responded, "Yeah."

"What are you doing?"

"Nothin'. Watchin' TV."

"With who?"

"Nobody."

"Where's Zaire?"

"Upstairs in the bed waitin' on her momma to come back to relieve her uncle."

"Boy, don't get smart with me. And there better not be anybody in my house when I get there either."

"Okay, okay. Trish came by but she's by herself."

"Is that one of those girls I told you couldn't come in my house?"

"Z, we decided to be together."

"Ain't that child pregnant?!"

"Yeah."

"So don't you think you need to be tryin' to put a roof—and

not mine!—over her head? And what are you gonna do about the other one? Aren't they friends?"

"Slow down. That's too many questions at once. What I look like, a rocket scientist or somethin'?"

I took my earring off and switched the phone to the other ear. "Maurice, have you been smokin' weed in my house again?"

"Why I still gotta be smokin' weed just 'cause of the past? You just harp on . . ."

That meant yes. When it came to Maurice anything but "no" usually meant yes. I hung up before he began to really get on my nerves. I had enough to concern myself with. I grabbed my purse off of the chair and hit the light. Opened the door and realized that the blinds were still up. I was turning them down when I caught a glimpse of David parked just below the window in his navy-blue Volvo. He was tapping the steering wheel and singing. I wondered what his favorite tune was, and what he did for fun besides writing poetry.

As the room darkened, I turned to rush downstairs and found Beacon standing just outside my door. I froze. Every muscle in my body clinched. I felt like I was about to lose my bowels where I stood.

"Dammit! Don't *do* that!"

"I'm sorry. I saw you come up here and I wanted to give you these."

He handed me a sheet of paper with three references on it. I put it on my desk under the glass paperweight.

"Please don't make me have to tell you this again, Beacon: You *cannot* come up here unless you've been invited."

"Listen!" he yelled as he opened and closed his hand like he had hoped to wrap it around something. Then he fell into an odd, subtle laughter and shook his head. "I understand. It's just that I knew you were . . . well never mind. Good night, Zenobia."

I kept an eye on him as I locked the door to my office and descended the stairs behind him. When I finally sat down in the car, David could see that I'd been perspiring again.

He asked, "You all right?"

"Yeah, I'm fine. Long night."

"You tired?"

"Depends on what you have in mind."

"I'm kinda hungry myself."

"Now that I'm too tired for. We can get together later this week if you like."

"That's cool. When?"

"I may be doing lunch with Nikai and Sheila so let's make it a breakfast date."

"So you're asking me out?"

I laughed. "I'm a confident, strong, independent black woman who has it goin' on, so yeah: I'm asking you out."

"Go 'head, sista!"

The ride home was filled with humor. We laughed about *Kingdom Come,* a comedy starring Cedric the Entertainer that we'd both caught at the movies last year, the goofy things he, Cliff and Byron did to get girls when they were growing up and the most outrageous hairdos either of us had ever had. But when David turned onto Tenner's Way, my mood shifted completely. Leslie's baby's daddy was parked outside my house like a bounty hunter with nothing but time to lose.

"Could you do me a favor, David, and pull around back?"

"Sure."

He drove up on the back carport, got out, ran around to my door and opened it. Walked me to the back porch and gently took my hands in his.

"I know you're tired but I wanna thank you for tonight. I haven't gone out with a woman and enjoyed myself like this since I've been in the States."

"Well, I'm happy to have been of service. We still on for breakfast this week?"

"You just call me and I'll be right here," he said, pointing down at the ground.

I had a feeling that David meant for more than just a morning meal. I pulled him in by the arms and held him in an embrace. Rocked from side to side and took in the moment. A breeze blew by us. I closed my eyes. David rubbed my back and then kissed me on the cheek.

"You should get some rest," he told me, opening the storm door.

"You're right. Call me so I'll know you made it in."

"I'll be all right. You just get some sleep."

I unlocked the door, watched David pull off and then darted around to the front. Jeff was knocked out behind the wheel. Reclined with his mouth hangin' open and a Dave Hollister CD playing. I tapped on his window. He jumped and then smiled like the annoyed look on my face was somehow soothing.

"Go home," I told him.

I walked up the front steps and put my key in the door. Turned the locks over and could hear the distinct and sickening sound of gum being popped. It echoed throughout my house like a church bell on Easter morning, slow and constant. I took a deep breath, closed the door and called out to Maurice. Trisha came around the corner from *my* living room, stood in *my* foyer and put her index finger up to her mouth signaling that *I* should be quiet.

"Zaire is asleep," she said, smiling like she was hosting a party and I was the first guest to arrive.

I stared at her blankly and asked, "Where is my little brother?"

"He's in the shower. He should be done in a minute."

"Good. He can walk you out after he dries off."

She popped that gum and folded her arms, while tapping her foot. "Can't go nowhere 'til Self gets back."

"'Back'?"

"Back."

She rolled her neck hard enough for her ponytail to sway, walked into the living room and began picking up empty cups and plates.

"I appreciate that."

"Mmhmm."

I heard the water stop as I reached the top of the stairs. After I looked in on Zaire, I stood in front of the bathroom door. Almost gave Maurice a heart attack when he opened the door and stopped wiping his face long enough to notice me. Looked like a dark-skinned Allen Iverson with his decorative cornrows, minimal facial hair and small but muscular build.

"Damn, Z! You tryin' to kill me?"

"Not yet. What was Self doin' in my house?"

"He gave Trish a ride over here, that's all."

"And how is she gettin' home?"

"That's what I wanted to ask you about."

"The answer is no," I said, walking into my bedroom.

"So what is she gonna do, Z, walk?"

"Not my problem."

"She's pregnant," he pleaded.

"Congratulations."

"And she thinks her mother might put her out."

I didn't even entertain that comment. Walked over to the window and peeped out of the blinds to see if Jeff was gone. He wasn't.

I asked, "Has Payce called here today?"

He shrugged his shoulders. "I don't know."

"What *do* you know?"

Maurice continued, "I know Trish might need a place to stay."

"Birds of a feather flock together."

Maurice draped the towel across his neck, blocked the doorway and asked, "What's that supposed to mean?"

"You *both* need a place to stay. Now move outta my way."

"That's cold. You act like we didn't even come from the same two people."

"Boy, move. You can't even honor my request for you to keep certain people out of my house."

He stepped to the side and pulled at the ends of the towel. "Don't you mean *Payce's* house?"

I had one foot hangin' off the top of the stairs when I backed up and looked at him. "*I* keep the lights on in here! *I'm* the one who buys the food, pays the water bill, provides yo' black ass with cable! Now you sit down and see how long it takes Payce to keep this place runnin'! Speaking of which, the utilities are due in five days. No more chances, Maurice! Have your share. And another thing, if I catch Self in my house again I'll have you *both* arrested for trespassing, Smart-ass! Now get that tramp outta *my* house!"

Tap, tap, tap.

Jeff was the picture of irony. He had dozed off again to Dave Hollister's "One Woman Man." I assumed that whatever he drank was ushering him into his fourth stage of sleep, because my knocks on the window were going unanswered. I walked around to the passenger's side, climbed in and startled him. He ran his hand over the top of his head and down across his face. Tried to shake the haze from his eyes.

"How long I been out here?"

"About seven minutes. You can thank me later for waking you up. Have a good life."

I reached for the door handle. He reached for my arm.

"Chocolate."

"What?" I asked.

"That should be your name. Dark, smooth and sweet to the taste."

I retrieved my limb.

"Zenobia, just listen to me for a second, please."

I sighed, folded my arms across my chest, looked at my watch and said, "You've got five minutes."

"Okay, okay. I sat in your club tonight and wondered how we could go from having so much fun to this. You said yourself that we had a lot of common interests. Now it seems all you wanna talk about is Leslie, when you knew about her from day one. I don't get it."

"It's different when you introduce children to the equation."

"And how is that?"

"It just is, okay? Now, you've been drinking. You need to go home."

"I don't want to. I want to sleep with you."

"What?!"

I opened the door.

"Wait! I didn't mean it like that. Forget what I said at Discretion tonight. It's not about sex. I wanna *be* with you tonight."

"Well, that's not possible."

"But Zenobia, I don't understand. I'm *free*. I thought this is what we wanted."

He said "free" like he'd had to smelt an iron ball and chain off of his ankle.

"You're also a day late and a dollar short. I'm seeing somebody now."

"Already?"

"What do you mean 'already'? You talk like we were in a committed relationship!"

"Do you think it's been easy tellin' this woman that I don't want her? She has been goin' on and on about how God told her differently. How I was put on earth for her and how I'm allowing the devil to interfere with divine order! *I know who I want!* And even if you don't give me a chance, I'm not going back to her."

I rested my elbow on the windowsill. Pulled the hairpins out of my braids and let them fall.

"You look so good like that."

"Jeff, please don't start with that, okay? Now I've talked to Leslie . . ."

He sat forward. "Don't remind me."

"Well, it's the truth. And from what I've heard she sounds like a good person. If not for her, go back for that baby. *He* deserves a chance."

"I don't know, Zenobia. I wasn't ready for any children. Leslie knew that."

I didn't know what to say. It seemed that Jeff was at a loss for words also because it took about a minute and a half for him to continue. Then he looked at me with what appeared to be genuine sorrow in his eyes.

"I never apologized, did I?"

I shook my head. "No, you didn't."

"I'm sorry for running out on you like that and for deceiving you. Guess I was sorta desperate to secure something with you first."

"I can't say that I understand but I will accept your apology. But there's one thing that I must warn you about, Jeff. Don't ever come to my house without my permission. I believe in callin' the police on a brotha if I'm feelin' violated. Now go home. Be a father and at least *try* to practice being a husband."

Jeff rubbed his eyes, reached down and started the engine. "Is it Payce Whittington?"

"No. Jesse Jackson will be president first."

"So it's the guy you were with at the club tonight?"

"Now you're in my business."

"All right, all right. Can we still get together from time to time?"

"I don't know if that'll be a good idea. I'm tryin' to see what becomes of something else right now."

"I got it."

Jeff opened his arms for a hug but I cut him off by holding out my hand. Didn't want to give him anything to work with.

When I went back in the house Maurice and Trisha were standing in the foyer mumbling their way through what appeared to be an argument. But when they saw me, the room got quiet.

I asked, "What's up?"

Trisha pulled at her pink and blue Mickey Mouse T-shirt, which made her look even younger, especially since her cornrows had been taken down and replaced with a lengthy ponytail. I turned to Maurice, who looked like he thought that if he kept quiet enough there was a chance we wouldn't notice he was still standing there.

Again, I asked, "What's up?!"

"Tell her, Lethal!"

I glared at Trisha. "Don't call him that in my house."

"Sorry."

"Now, tell me what?"

Maurice began to shift from the pressure in the room. Knew he had one time to say something that I didn't wanna hear and he'd be makin' small talk with a transient under the Martin Luther King Bridge.

Trish yelled, "Tell—"

"I'm about to! Me and Trisha are gettin' married."

I asked Maurice, "Are you sure that's what you *both* want?"

163

Trisha belted out, "Yes! He asked me when you walked outside."

I responded with a simple "You-all are grown."

As I approached the bottom of the steps, I called Maurice. He shuffled over as I ushered him upstairs with my index finger. We walked into my bedroom. He leaned with his back against the wall and sighed like an old man with a lifetime of regret.

I said, "Close the door."

He kicked it shut and went back to his stance while I sat on the edge of the bed, facing the dresser, and removed my jewelry. Opened the drawer to my nightstand and pulled out David's manuscript to read myself to sleep.

"You know you don't have to marry that girl if you don't want to. Nobody's gonna think you're a dog or anything like that. And even if they do, so what."

"Man, Z, this is happenin' sorta fast. That's why I was smokin' the trees earlier, 'cause she been on my head about this."

"Okay, save the excuses 'cause I wouldn't care if you had her and *her momma* pregnant—I told you to leave those drugs alone."

He lowered his head. "You're right."

"Well, what do you wanna do?"

"What you mean?"

"Boy, what you think I mean? Do you want to get married or not?!"

"I can't believe how this is all happening. Me and Self were tryin' to see what's up with this spot down in Houston."

"*What* spot, Maurice?"

"An apartment his cousin is about to move out of."

"You *do* know that in order to pay rent you have to have a job, don't you?"

"No kidding."

"Hey, you act like you didn't know. And what's the deal with the other little girl?"

"Who, Baby?"

I shook my head and rolled my eyes to the ceiling.

"Why does everybody born in the eighties have to have a nickname?"

"Don't know. But I'm sure I don't have Baby pregnant. She's just playin' games. I never touched that girl."

"So who did?"

"Don't wanna talk about that."

"I'm sorry. Did I mention that you aren't in a position to bargain?"

"Damn, Z. Self, ah'ight!"

"So you and Self are sharing women now?"

"No. I told you I never touched that girl."

"Well, you better get your business straight. So let's talk employment."

"I think I've got a job lined up already."

"What kind of job?"

"Construction."

"And you're planning on doing labor work for the rest of your life?"

"I'm only twenty, Z. I think I've got some time."

"C'mere," I told him.

My little brother sat down next to me and cupped the top of his head in his hands.

"I remember being twenty, Maurice. I was in college living the life. Me and Lainey kicked it like we'd *never* grow old. And when Zaire came along a few years later, I felt the same way Trisha is feeling."

"And how is that?"

"Desperate. That girl is concerned with everything *but* that child. Because let me tell you something, if she wasn't, she

165

wouldn't want to *force* his or her father into a union. That's not what that baby needs. That baby is gonna need *love*. I'm so glad Momma was in my ear telling me not to marry Payce that I don't know what to do. At one time we were friends, even lovers. But we *weren't* meant to be husband and wife. And it took me waiting until I was old enough to make a lifetime decision like that to realize it. Don't get me wrong now, I wanted to have the family and all of that but it didn't feel right. And from the look and vibe you were giving downstairs, this doesn't feel right to you either."

"You know me, huh?"

"The way you were sweatin', *anybody* could've met you for the first time and figured it out," I joked.

"I don't know what I wanna do."

"What did her parents say?"

"She hasn't told them yet. She wanted to be able to say that we were getting married so they won't be as disappointed."

"Have you met her parents?"

"Yeah, a couple of times."

"And gauging from that, how do you think they'll react?"

"She might just get put out."

"How old is she, Maurice?"

"Eighteen."

I sighed. "Oh Lord. Are you sure the baby is yours?"

"I'm positive. I know I was there and in full effect. Plus she and the doctor came up with the actual day of conception and well, I was there."

"And what are you planning to do about the apartment in Texas? Don't you think you need to be here for your child?"

"Yeah, I was giving that some thought too. I was gonna take my money that I saved to move, get maybe two jobs and put what I can down on an apartment."

"Well, I'm happy to see you're being a man and are willing to take care of your responsibilities. Momma and Daddy would be proud."

I wrapped my arm around Maurice and pulled him close.

"You think so?"

"I know so. There's only one thing that would make them happier."

"What's that?"

"If you got that child to stop poppin' that gum like she needs any more attention drawn to her."

He laughed. "Yeah, that shit kinda gets on my nerves too."

I sighed heavily, let my shoulders fall and said, "Well, if push comes to shove and she can't live at home, I *guess* she can stay here until you find a place. I wouldn't want Zaire on the street so I can't have my niece or nephew out there either. Momma would roll over in her grave."

Maurice looked up at me and smiled.

"But! There's a big 'but.' You have to pay one hundred dollars a month for her to stay, she can't chew gum under my roof and if she fixes her lips to say the word 'Lethal' and she ain't watchin' *Court TV,* that'll be *it* for the both of y'all."

Theresa

I was sitting in a white floral wing-backed chair at my engagement party three years ago and Don was standing behind me. Our living room was filled with his family, as well as Robert, Nikai and Kalif, as awkward as it was. Don lifted his champagne glass and made a toast. Announced that we were getting married. The crowd gasped with joy and instinctively looked down at my left ring finger. I held it up and wiggled it so that my marquise diamond could catch the light. An elderly woman who'd sat next to Nikai before she ended up causing a scene walked over and hugged me. When she let go, I felt pressure on my shoulder. I looked up and Don was gripping it tightly. Blood covered his face. Reminded me that he'd died painfully, violently. I screamed and yanked away but he wouldn't let go. I screamed again, literally stumbled to my feet and found myself breathing heavily in the middle of my old bedroom in Smyrna, Georgia. My mother's silhouette filled the doorway as the breeze danced across the room and took hold of my sweat-drenched nightgown.

"Are you okay?" she asked.

I stood there shaking, crying and wringing my hands. Shook my head.

Mama opened her arms to me. "Oh, Theresa baby, come here."

She walked me over to the bed and sat down next to me. Wiped the tears from my eyes. And tucked my auburn hair behind my right ear. She was silent, held my hand and breathed with me. I was hurting for more than one reason and she knew this. Don's death was a big part of it but there were other things involved, other unresolved issues.

I didn't bother to look up at her when I asked, "Why didn't you come?"

She sighed, gripped my hand a little tighter.

This time I tried to look her in her eyes but she wouldn't give me the privilege. "Why didn't you come and be by my side when Don died, Mama?"

"Richard and I . . . it was just that I knew that . . . I don't have an excuse, Theresa."

My tears began to flow as I unleashed something that I'd held in for so long. "You know, people tell me that Don won't die because I won't let him. But it's like I can't let him go. If I don't hold on to his memory, who will? Nobody cared that he was no longer living *but* me. His family wanted his possessions, Robert moved away, Nikai fell in love and you . . . you didn't even show up to help me. I was burying a man I loved at twenty-five years old *alone*. Do you know how that feels, Mama?"

She shook her head.

"I almost lost my mind and you let Richard, a man who *doesn't even like your only daughter,* convince you that I didn't need you?"

I squeezed her hand as she began to cry. "I hold on to Don because I don't know how not to. I did what I could. I told myself what I needed to hear in order to make it because of Dameron. And now it seems that everywhere I turn there's somebody with a remedy for mourning. And maybe I am doing myself more harm than good by clinging this way but it's the clinging that's kept me alive."

"Theresa, I prayed for you every night."

"But your prayers weren't answered, Mama, because I kept trying to kill myself, only slower. I drank because I hated my life, I drank because my mother loved a man more than her own daughter and I drank because the only person who ever made me feel unconditionally loved was taken away from me. You do more for the Women of Triumph group than you would for me . . ."

She shook her head swiftly. "No, no I don't! That's not true!"

"Yes it is. We both know that . . ."

"I was alone, Theresa! I spent so many years *alone*. I needed somebody to hold me too."

"Get in line, Mama. It ends in China."

I wiped my face and pulled her in for a hug. "I don't want to spend the rest of my life crying in my sleep but I'm doing the best that I can because while I'm getting over Don, I'm getting over what happened to you and me as well."

"I promise that I'll—"

"Don't make promises, Mama. Just do what you can."

Vince

"Ms. Irene has done it again."

I leaned back on Ray's bronze-colored sofa in his circular co-cooning combination dining room/den and rubbed my pro-truding stomach. We'd eaten like stray dogs in an alley about an hour earlier. Ray's mom came by with a carful of cooked food like pound cake, Ms. Penny's famous cheesecake, fried chicken, mashed potatoes with onion and mushroom gravy, string beans, a pan of corn bread and some homemade vanilla ice cream. I know I personally ate 'til I couldn't see straight.

She asked about Pop and I told her that he was still alive. She maintained her poker face and looked away. I could sense a ma-turity in her eyes, as though she'd outgrown him and she knew it. She asked if he'd ever gotten remarried. I told her that no one deserved to suffer like that. She laughed. Nervously. Her own past made her uncomfortable. So she finished up the dishes and left as one of Ray's friends came by. He introduced himself as Marcel. He was the same cat who directed me to the back patio the first time I came over here. He stood at about five feet eleven with a faded cut, and was a few shades lighter than me. Marcel walked back to the kitchen where Ray was going for seconds on the pound cake and ice cream. He sat on a stool in front of the breakfast bar and greeted us both with a nod of his head.

I waved from the sofa. "I'm Vince."

"Whassup fellas?"

"Shit. Chillin'," Ray told him as he opened the fridge.

"Toss me a brew while you're in there."

Ray handed Marcel a Bud Light, grabbed his bowl of cake and the remote off the island. Strolled back into the dining area wearing scrubs and a white A-line T-shirt. He took a seat across the table from me and began channel-surfing the set, which sat atop a custom stereo unit.

"So what's goin' on, Marcel? You get that gig or what?"

"Yeah, I got it. But I doubt it will last."

"Why is that?"

Marcel took a swig of his beer and furrowed his brow. "Because I'm not tryin' to be a *bartender* for the rest of my life, that's why!"

Ray laughed and looked at me. "Vince, you feel a little tension comin' from that side of the room?"

"Just a little. You ah'ight, bruh?"

"Man, fuck y'all. Ray, I need to holla at you for a second."

Without turning away from the TV, Ray put up his middle finger and said, "Just one moment." He finished off the last of his food and then watched the end of a Mike Tyson/Lennox Lewis segment on ESPN. Got up and followed Marcel down to the basement, where I figured they were discussing something that they didn't want me to hear.

I sat there with one knee on the couch, thinking about Theresa. Wondering why she hadn't called to let me know that she and Dameron had landed safely. Wondering why she hadn't called to tell me that she didn't hate me for real. Sometimes I felt like a man divided. Wanted so much on both ends. I love Theresa and I want to be with her yet I needed to push her away and give her breathing room. But only enough to keep her within my reach. Maybe it was a situation of convenience.

Maybe I was selfishly insisting that she grow, just not up and away from me. I wanted her back but only when she was truly single. Only when she was able to truly love one man.

"Ay, Babyboy," Ray called over the intercom.

"Whassup?"

"Let me get some ice down here. And let Marcel out, would you?"

By that time, Marcel had hit the top of the stairs.

"I know my way out," he told me as he headed toward the foyer.

"You sure you're all right?"

He turned around to face me and extended his hand. I noticed a tattoo in Japanese writing on the web between his thumb and index finger. He dapped me up and disappeared. I glanced out of the small window next to the front door and caught him circling my car, staring at it. More like my plates.

I hit the lights, grabbed some ice and went to the lower level of the house.

"Whassup with ya' boy Marcel?"

Ray was plugging up another controller for his XBOX when I set the bowl down on the coffee table.

"Trippin'. That's just him. I don't even hear him anymore when he starts that."

He took a seat on the sofa and took a few deep breaths. "Marcel's not an angel but then who is? I called myself helpin' him out by puttin' him on my payroll, so to speak. He was locked up, couldn't get work and I didn't want him tied up with Whose Is It 'cause that's in Mom's name. So I sent him on a little mission. Nothing illegal, but the cat's gettin' paid well. And then he brings his ass over here talking about what he don't wanna do. Had to let that cat know, you stay on 'til the mission is over. Bottom line. I don't know what he thinks this is."

I had considered mentioning Marcel's fascination with cars,

mine in particular, but by that time Ray had gotten pissed just thinking about him. So I grabbed a controller and told him to put "Madden 2002" into the system. Wasn't interested in hearing any more about another man's problems. I had enough of my own.

By eleven o'clock, I was out of it and had become bored with my effortless victories, as I assumed Ray had too. I called it quits and went upstairs to make myself another plate before heading home. Ray followed me up the stairs and into the kitchen. I stumbled and leaned against the counter as I rounded the corner.

"You okay? I noticed you weren't shy with the drink."

I jokingly waved my hand in front of my face but to tell you the truth, it was bordering on a blur to me. I had had too much, but it was getting late and unless I was gonna stop in St. Charles and crash at Rayna's, I had one hell of a drive ahead of me.

"A black woman's cooking can be addictive," Ray said, stretching out on the couch in the dining room/den.

I scooped up enough mashed potatoes to choke a water buffalo and dumped it on my plate next to three fried chicken legs. "Yeah, but it's got to be the right one. It's got to be Ms. Irene's cooking."

"I hear ya'. That's why I always say, she'll be the only special woman in my life. Takes good care of a man."

"You mind if I take a few slices of this cheesecake?"

"Go right ahead."

I opened a cabinet over the stove, looked at Ray and asked, "Got anything you don't mind me taking it home in?"

"Yeah, hang on a minute."

Silence filled the kitchen as I turned back around. Then he asked, "You got a lady friend these days, Vince?"

"Yeah, but I told you how twisted things can get when you're dealing with women. They're so emotional and unpredictable."

Ray added, "You don't have to tell me."

By now his voice was lower, much lower. He was on the floor digging through a mountain of Tupperware in the bottom of the island. I stepped to the side to give him room. He placed his hand on my leg. Ran it up the inside of my black and silver reversible mesh basketball shorts. My quads turned to stone before I could stop him from putting his lips on my piece through my clothes. I cringed with confusion as he pulled it out and placed it inside his warm, wet mouth. I'd wanted this feeling for two years from Theresa and now these moist lips on my piece and the vodka in my system didn't make me give a fuck who I was getting it from. All I knew is that it felt good. All I knew was that I was coming. I fought the desire to grab him by the back of his head as he deep-throated me like he wanted to keep my shaft with him at all times. I stood in his kitchen, gripping the edge of the island, and exploded. Ray must've known that the best head was received while standing because he began to laugh as my legs weakened. Stood to his feet and wiped around his mouth.

He smiled and asked, "You remember the locker room yet?"

I put my piece back inside my shorts and fell against the counter. Ran my hands over the top of my head. My mood had jumped from confusion to anger. Not because I felt violated but because deep inside, buried beneath what I truly thought validated manhood, I believed that if the opportunity presented itself, I'd probably let him do it again.

Ray walked back down to the other end of the room, grabbed his half-empty beer bottle and sat on the sofa. "Whassup Babyboy? You standing there looking like you just saw a ghost."

He laughed, shook his head and went back to channel-surfing. "You know your way out."

I left everything and locked his door behind me. Walked down to my car, thought about Marcel's odd ass and got in. I took a thirty-minute ride up 70 east back to St. Louis. Stopped at a gas station just inside of St. Charles County to fill up. When I got out, I could feel that my underwear was soiled with semen and another man's saliva. Could hear my father callin' me a *sissy* in my head. Could hear him insisting that I wasn't a man because I couldn't let go of the past. As I headed toward the coolers in back, I finally remembered that day in the locker room that Ray spoke of. We were showering after running through the field across the street from the school for gym class. Ray and I had to do extra laps because our teacher, Mr. Sullivan, didn't believe that we were running up to our potential. By the time we'd gotten to the locker room shower, everyone else was gone. Ray was playing around, tossing soap back and forth from one hand to another. He dropped it, slipped and fell against me. I felt his bare skin brush against mine. It was only one of a number of our awkward childhood moments—one of many that I'd failed to stop. Probably because there was a part of me that liked it, enjoyed the experimentation of it, the way I had that moment I found myself gripping that island and moaning uncontrollably.

I punched the newspaper stand next to the ATM and was cursing at no one in particular when I felt a hand on my shoulder.

Joshua asked, "Hey, what's goin' on, Vince?"

I hadn't realized until then that I was sweating. I wiped my forehead and opened the door to the freezer.

"I'm all right. What's been up with you? Finish moving all of your stuff yet?"

"Nah, not yet. I've been taking things kinda slow. I'll go back for the rest later. Did Ced ever get in touch with you?"

"Not unless he e-mailed me. I've been caught up lately."

"I hear ya'. Hey, I was wondering if you knew of a gym that I could go to. Ced stopped going and I don't wanna go too far out of the way."

I ran my hand over the top of my head. Could feel my brain aching. I could hear Josh but my mind was somewhere else. Still at Ray's place. Thinking about what he'd done, what we'd done.

"I go to the Y. I've got some literature out in the car if you wanna step outside with me."

"All right. Let me get a few things and I'll meet you out there."

I paid for my gas and took off toward the parking lot while Joshua waited in front of the microwave for what I assumed was a frozen dinner to cook. I was putting the pump back into its holder and replacing the gas cap when he came walking out of the door. I reached in the backseat and grabbed my duffel bag. A balled-up piece of paper fell as I brought it up front. When I opened it I saw that it was the note Bridget had left on my windshield that last time I was down at the Y. I put it in my pocket and retrieved a flyer from the bag. Handed it to Joshua and dapped him up. He cut his conversation about hangin' out at the drag races short. Guess he got the vibe that I was in no mood to talk. To him or any other man, for that matter.

When I got home, I dropped my stuff by the door and flopped down on the couch in the darkness. Lay my head back and closed my eyes. *He's a sissy* was all I could hear in my head. *Always thinking about the past.* Music thumped against my feet from the condo below me. The guy who had bought it two months ago was young, living a fast life. He'd have a party just because it was Wednesday, or a full moon, or his allergies weren't acting up. No legitimate reason necessary. I stomped on the floor. The bass went down a few notches. I reached in my pocket and pulled out some loose change . . . and that balled-up piece of paper. Placed it on the coffee table and stared at it. Bridget was no Theresa. But my piece was throbbing and I needed to feel a woman. I needed that softness to remove that memory, to bring me back from the immediate past I'd created.

I walked into the kitchen and dialed her number. She picked up on the third ring.

"Who is this?" she asked.

"Bridget?"

"Who did you call?"

"This is Vince. Whassup?"

"Oh, well to what do I owe this surprise? Professor Lowery is compromising his integrity and calling me? What, you trying to get directions to the Caman Cultural Center for you and your little girlfriend?"

"No, I'm calling to see if you felt like coming out."

"And where's the lucky lady?"

"I told you she was going out of town. She won't be back for another week."

"And now you want to duck behind a bush with me on the down low?"

I sat forward and moved a *Black Man* and a *Black Enterprise* magazine to the side of the coffee table. Picked up one of the white votive candles from a bowl and tossed it into the air a couple of times.

"I'm just tryin' to get to know my friends a little better. No big deal. No strings attached."

It sounded as though she'd gotten closer to the phone when she said, "What should I wear, *buddy*?"

I whispered, "Less is more."

I gave her the address and jumped in the shower almost instantaneously. Lathered up with a body gel and began to stroke myself. The moment I closed my eyes, I saw Ray's lips and my movements quickened. But before my legs became weak again, I got out, wrapped a grape bath towel around my waist and wiped the steam from the medicine cabinet. The phone rang. I looked toward my bedroom and decided not to answer it. Now was not the time.

*   *   *

"She's pretty," Bridget said, staring at a picture of Theresa on my entertainment center.

She stepped back, admiring my place. Slipped out of her black sandals and gripped the blue carpet with her toes. She was wearing a long-sleeve, white linen dress with flowers around the neckline and her hair was no longer straight but full, coiled and textured. She reminded me of a chameleon. Never knew what to expect when she came through the door.

She sashayed over to the window overlooking downtown and glanced back at me.

"C'mere, let me show you something."

She pointed across the city and said, "I used to live right over there when I moved to St. Louis. Those projects is where I grew up."

Bridget blew her warm breath on the window and caused it to fog up. Then she turned around and continued, "I hate seeing that place. Hoped I'd never have to again. Mind if I close these curtains?"

When she reached up to pull them together, I placed my hands on top of hers and let them travel along her frame. Stopped long enough to clutch her breasts and felt her pressing her butt against me. I moved her thick sandy-brown hair to the side and kissed her neck. She spun around and gave me tongue. Bridget was no longer Bridget to me. She simply represented a woman. And a woman is what I needed more than anything at that moment. I dropped to my knees, raised her dress and tongue-kissed her lower lips. Thoughts of Theresa reeled in my head but quickly vanished as Bridget began to rip at my clothes and dress me in a ribbed condom. As she knocked me over onto the dusky-brown sofa, I got the impression that we were both running from something. Trying to screw our pain away. Taking our issues out on one another. Fuckin' our sorrows goodbye.

*   *   *

Bridget lay across my bed on her back with my arm around her, toying with my fingers.

"So what are you like some kinda twenty-first-century black power advocate or something?"

I glanced at her and asked, "Why do you say that?"

She pointed toward the bookshelf across the room. "I mean, look at all of those titles. Marcus Garvey this and black civilization that. You read them all?"

"Every one of them."

Don't ask me what I was doing making small talk with a woman I'd labeled a simpleminded freak just weeks ago. And don't ask me what I was thinking when the phone rang for a second time and after realizing that it was Theresa's cell, I didn't answer. I just didn't. I was going with the flow, in every sense. Bridget had begun to ask me about myself, had asked what mattered most to me right now. I didn't quite know how to answer that. My house? My job? My relationship with Theresa? Or the fucked-up feeling I got in the pit of my stomach when I thought about how much I'd enjoyed what I'd done less than twelve hours earlier? When I asked her the same question she ran off on a tangent about dancing and making some real money someday and then switched to her childhood. Told me that she had always wanted to find her father and ask him some very vital questions. When I asked what they were, she refused to tell me. Only told me that she had not grown up with him, that she had a twin somewhere in this world and her mother had been killed early on. That all made her appear more troubled than I first imagined. But it also made her appear more human.

"You thirsty, Vince?"

"Not really. You want something to drink?" I asked, sitting up.

"I'll get it. I mean, if you don't mind."

"I mind."

I got up and walked into the kitchen with a naked, sand-colored Bridget on my heels. She made a detour into the living room and sat down on the carpet with her legs crossed. The clock on the microwave read 2:37 A.M. and she was as bright-eyed as ever.

"I think I'm gonna quit the dance troupe after this weekend's performance."

"Why is that?" I asked, handing her a glass of orange juice and taking a seat in a navy-blue chair across the room.

"I won't have time for it when I start this new job at the Nissan dealership out in Clayton. Plus, I guess I'm just tired of it. It's not going anywhere."

"And where did you expect it to go?"

"I don't know. I guess what I'm really trying to say is that I need change in my life."

She sipped her orange juice, looked at me with innocence in her eyes and continued, "So I hope you'll be there for my grand finale."

"Can't make any promises."

"I'm not asking you to make any promises. I'm asking you to be there."

I rested my chin in my hand and stared at her. Wondered what she thought this was, a relationship? Bridget turned sideways, brushed her ruffled hair out of her face and lay her head down on the sofa.

"What's wrong, Vince?"

"Why would you think something's wrong?"

"I could tell the way you held on to me earlier. It was different."

I became defensive. "Different from what? You don't even know me."

"But you know what I'm talking about. You weren't taking. You were giving, giving a part of yourself. And you don't even *know* me, which is why I'm asking. What's wrong in your life right now? What are you keeping inside?"

I shook my head. "Don't know what you're talking about."

"Okay. So why are you cheating on a beautiful woman like Theresa?" she asked, pointing to the picture on my entertainment center.

"What is this, a joke? You steal my ID, follow me through the club the other night, fuck my brains out after you compliment me on my woman and then ask me what *my* problem is!"

She remained calm. Looked at me as though she'd heard worse, had had harsher words directed at her in her lifetime. "Okay, first of all I told you I had every intention of giving that ID back. Second, I wasn't that far from you when you walked in the door that night so keeping an eye on you wasn't that hard. Third, I get the feeling that you don't truly have a woman."

"And why is that?"

"Because you move solo too much. No man in such a joyous and wonderful relationship would be out at a club on a Saturday night nor would he be as receptive as you were to me when we first met. And if that isn't enough proof, you sexed me like you hadn't had a good piece in six months."

I grimaced as this woman whom I'd initially perceived to be shallow read me like a book. She tilted her head as though she was trying to understand me further. The look on her face told me that she didn't expect anything. That maybe all she truly wanted was to be friends.

"My father raped me when I was five," she said out of nowhere.

"What?"

She nodded her head, brought her knees up to her naked chest and wrapped her arms around her legs. "My mother sent my twin away. I guess to save her."

"I'm sorry, Bridget."

"No need. I've gotten enough of that from foster parents and so on."

"So what happened to your mother?"

"You want my version or the version that was drilled in my head?"

"Either."

"I only vaguely remember it, but I believe my father killed her. My mother caught him in my room one night and just snapped. I guess it was too much to try and keep an eye on me all the time so she packed our things so we could catch a bus to St. Louis, where she'd sent my sister. I remember going next door but I don't know where my father had gone off to. Anyway, it seemed like my momma beat on that woman's door for a century. What I do remember is the look of panic on the lady's face as she stared at my father, who was running up behind us. He dragged my momma by her hair as the lady opened her door and pulled me in. I must've kicked her with everything I had in me 'cause after a few minutes, she finally let me go. When I went back home, the door was locked. My father was gone. And the house was slowly going up in flames."

"So where was your mom?"

"Locked in the basement."

She told her story with little emotion, almost as though she felt no connection to the people she spoke about.

"And there was nothing the police could do?"

"Not when you've been on the force for ten years. They believe you made a mistake, help you cover it up and allow you to move away with the promise of never coming back."

"So what are the vital questions that you want to ask your father?"

She yawned. "Why? Did killing my momma make his life any better? Why me and not my sister?"

"Don't you mean, why either of you?"

"Vince, everyone on this earth has a pivotal point in their life. Something that has happened that won't enable them to be who they were before. Something that makes people hateful, something that makes people hopeful. I guess what bothers me is that I truly believe that hers had always been hopeful."

I thought about the locker room, Ray's kitchen, my nephew's death and my pops's refusal to raise his children.

"And which are you?"

She stretched her limbs and yawned again. "I guess you can say I'm stuck in the middle."

"So where do you think your sister is? And why hadn't her caregiver sent for you?"

"Your guess is as good as mine. Nobody answers a five-year-old's questions, Vince. They give them toys or sit them in front of a cartoon to distract them. They fill the child's life with activities and dance classes and—"

"I get the point."

When she yawned a third time I offered her my bed. She crawled under my navy-blue topsheet, and I got down on the floor and did my three hundred push-ups. Thought about all she'd said to me, and about me. And I asked, "Bridget, what were *you* doing? Giving or taking?"

She looked up and pushed her bushy hairdo to the back. "At first I was giving, but then I felt your pain. So I began to receive you. I know how it feels when all you want is to be received."

She smiled. "Get some sleep, Vince. It's late."

Theresa

"I don't know if I wanna do this, Theresa."

Lisa's knee was bouncing with nervousness so quickly that the woman sitting next to her got up and moved across the waiting room. We were in the pediatric wing of Caslin Hospital waiting for her two-year-old son, Terrence, to get tested for HIV.

"Do you see that paper in your hand, Lisa?" I pointed to a line in the third paragraph. "Read that out loud!"

She whispered, "One in three new pediatric cases of AIDS are African-American."

I folded my arms across my chest and said, "Now mull over that for a minute."

I have to admit that I was cranky. I had stayed up the night before calling Vince and didn't get an answer. Wondered what he could have been doing, where he could have been sleeping, since he didn't have my place to crash at. He never slept over to Leland's unless he'd been out drinking. But this wasn't the weekend and he had to get up early for work. Wondered if he was somewhere "acting like a single person."

Lisa stared at Terrence, who was across the room putting the large pieces of a puzzle together at a colorful little desk like the one Vince bought Dameron before we left. It was the little things he did that made it so difficult to say goodbye, so difficult to make a decision and stick to it.

Lisa asked, "So let's just say the news is bad. Where do I go from there?"

I turned to her and said, "First let me ask you something, Lisa. Are you sexually active?"

"No."

"Are you sure?"

"Are you sure you're black?!"

I suddenly realized how out of place I was to insinuate that she could not be trusted, and that those were Mr. Missing in Action's shoes I was trying to stuff her into.

"I'm sorry. What I meant to say is that at some point you're gonna have to tell your boyfriend and anyone else you've slept with."

"Girl, please. Who told me? *Nobody*. It's not like I'm trying to share myself with anybody right now."

"You have to."

She shook her head. "Why? Will it change Lionel's prognosis?"

"No, but it can change the life of the next woman he sleeps with."

Lisa shrugged her shoulders. "That's what she gets for being with a dog. She's no better than me and *I* have to suffer."

She called out to Terrence in what I imagined was an attempt to shut me up. I just sat and stared at her. So young and fearful. Again, I found myself wondering what the future held for today's unprepared youth. Young people with little appreciation for life. I don't know what the hell I expected from Lisa. She was crippled with fear over the idea of learning the fate of her own child. Helping to safeguard a stranger's fate was like going to the trouble to find out who would be the next man to walk on the moon. Completely irrelevant in her eyes. After all, like she said, the only thing she could focus on was her own suffering.

We had to wait a full week. And it was the longest I'd endured since Don had died. Surprisingly, he hadn't appeared in my dreams since the night I got some things off my chest with Mama. This was probably because Vince had occupied my every waking thought. I'd only spoken to him twice and both times he was short with me. During the first conversation he asked the general questions that I'd expected but I felt that he was dancing around some things. The second was only because I needed a ride from the airport and Nikai hadn't been answering her phone. I imagined she was somewhere sliding down the firefighter's pole. So Vince was my only other option, and I didn't like it. I mean, damn, I came down here to get away from my habits, and not once did he ask how things were going. So I chose not to inform him that I hadn't had one drink. Nor did I have a desire for one. I think part of it had to do with the fact that I was pouring myself into the support group and helping others. That turned out to be the best way to forget my own troubles. And hanging out with this promising bunch, it wasn't hard.

I told Lisa that I wanted to take her out for pizza after the meeting to discuss whatever the results were. I figured even if they were good, her perspective on this situation was still skewed. She needed to talk before she ended up hurting someone, or worse: causing someone to hurt her for passing along her misfortune.

When Mama and I walked into the community center the ladies greeted us with the usual lighthearted smiles. I instantly began to search for Lisa's face in order to read her expression, but she wasn't there.

I asked, "Where's Lisa, ladies?"

They all looked around at one another. Then one of the older women said, "I called and asked if she needed a ride and she said that she was coming with you two."

Mama had no clue why I was looking for her so intently. I had kept our little visit to the hospital between Lisa and me. I wanted to show her that she could trust me, trust anyone. But it appears that *she* was the one who couldn't be trusted.

Vince

Guilt will wear you down. And shame will make you hate other people who have nothing to hide. Theresa walked toward me in the east terminal of St. Louis's Lambert Airport carrying a small bag on her shoulder and a pink paperback book in her hand. The look on her face told me that she wasn't excited about being home, wasn't eager to keep company with me either. She needed a ride and that was all.

Dameron wasn't with her on the return flight. She had mentioned during one of our very brief phone conversations that her mother begged to let him stay in Atlanta for the summer. Now that her load had been lightened, her pace was a little faster than usual. She swept past me, heading toward baggage claim. Slightly brushed my shoulder with the gray hooded jacket hanging over her arm that matched the cotton sweat suit she wore. No eye contact, no greeting. I followed a few feet behind as if admitting to some kind of wrongdoing. She folded her arms and pursed her lips when I finally stood next to her.

"How was your trip?"

No response. I put my hands in my pockets and glanced at my watch.

"Was the flight long?"

She turned and glared at me. I tried to keep my composure. But I knew I looked suspect.

"I only called you because Nikai wasn't available. You don't have to talk to me, Vince. Especially since you were at a loss for words when I wasn't in your face."

"What are you talking about?"

"I realized that I've got to stop looking at you as anything more than a friend because that's all you intend to be. It was my fault for expecting you to miss me."

"I did miss you."

She tucked her hair behind her diamond-studded right ear and rubbed her temples like I was annoying her.

"Look, we don't owe one another anything. There is no more us, remember?"

I shut up and waited for her luggage to spin around. Grabbed it and followed her out to my car. When I opened the passenger side door, I heard a car horn blow. We both stopped and looked to our left. But I was the only one who began to sweat. Ms. Irene was waving and checking for traffic, then opening her car door. When she got out, wearing tan capri pants and a white button-down shirt, I tried to hurry Theresa on into my car, but I'd left a folder from work in the front seat. She bent over to pick it up but didn't sit down.

"Hey, Vincent, how you doin' baby?" Ms. Irene said, wrapping her arms around my neck.

Then she turned to Theresa, while patting me on the stomach. "Don't be jealous, Babygirl. I been knowin' this boy here since he was a baby. Use to look after him like he was my own son."

Ms. Irene's demeanor shifted a bit as she put her hand above her eyes to block the sun.

"You heard about my baby, didn't you, Vince?"

My insides felt like I'd been hit with a stun gun. I didn't ever wanna hear his name again if I didn't have to.

"No ma'am."

"Ray's in the hospital. Got pneumonia. I took him 'cause he was having more frequent dizzy spells. That's why I'm here to pick up my sister. She's flying in from Tennessee."

A flushed look came over her face as she grabbed the gold cross she wore around her neck and began to rub it.

"It's hard on me, staying out there at Missouri Medical all night."

Then Theresa placed her hand on Ms. Irene's shoulder and asked, "Is he gonna be all right?"

"Babygirl, doctors can only do so much. God is the only one who can heal my baby."

Theresa looked at me. "And this is a childhood friend? Vince, you should go and see him."

I gritted my teeth for a moment and got a sick feeling in the pit of my stomach. The same one I'd gotten every time I thought about what my actions would mean to the world, to Theresa, to my father. *He's a sissy . . . won't let go of the past.* In that short amount of time, Ms. Irene had begun to cry. And before I could console her, Theresa had wrapped her up in her arms. I took a step back as the sun beat on my back. Wiped the sweat from my brow and ran it across my denim shorts.

"Say a prayer for him, would you Babygirl? I'm having my cousin come out so Ray can give his life over to Christ as soon as possible."

She wiped a tear. "I . . . I don't know if he's gonna make it."

"Oh, Ms. Irene."

This was Theresa. I cringed and felt a sickness come over me. My saliva glands went into overdrive. My stomach rumbled one good time. My lunch flipped and earned ten points for the dismount onto the curb. They stopped having a sentimental moment over an asshole long enough to notice me.

"Vince!"

I closed my eyes and pictured myself inside that kitchen, gripping that island, when the floodgates burst again. I fell against the car, taking deep breaths, as Theresa ran to my side and fanned me with my work folder.

"Sit down, Vince. I'll drive."

Ms. Irene shut my door and asked, "Are you gonna be okay, suga'?"

I nodded my head and held up my hand.

"All right. If you're able to make it out to the hospital, Ray is on the fourth floor. I hope you'll get a chance to see him."

Theresa leaned across my lap and promised, "Vince will be there, Ms. Irene. Just tell 'im to hold on—his friend Vince is coming."

Theresa

I drove Vince back to his place and helped him up the stairs. I was still pissed about him not calling me in Atlanta as frequently as I'd hoped but I had to be honest with myself. I still had issues with Don's death and instead of working through them, I was seeking to replace him with someone else. It was as though I was walking around with a dresser and a mattress tied to my back and instead of lightening my load, I was changing my shoes. Coming up with an easier way to cope but never getting to the root of the problem. And besides, if I had agreed to simply be Vince's friend, helping him clean up vomit and visiting a dying childhood buddy definitely fell under that criterion.

I unlocked the door and helped him over to the sofa.

He told me, "I'm all right."

"You sure?"

"Yeah. I just need to take a shower and brush my teeth."

He'd started toward the bathroom when I asked, "So who is your friend?"

Vince spun around and asked, "What friend?"

"The one who's in the hospital. What did Ms. Irene say his name was?"

"Ray, and he's not really a friend."

"Then why did she say that you were like a son and you two grew up together?"

He gave me a curt "She didn't say we grew up together. I hadn't seen Ray since we were twelve or something like that."

I asked, "You haven't or you hadn't?"

He dropped his shorts around his ankles and braced himself in the threshold.

"What's with all of the questions? What's the big deal?"

"The big deal is that he's dying! Don't you want to say goodbye?"

"Theresa, not now, okay? Let me take a shower."

Having said that, he shut the door and started the water. I walked into his bedroom, picked up the phone and dialed my mother's house, but she and Dameron weren't there. I left a message. Asked if she'd heard anything from Lisa and let her know that it was okay to give her my phone number in St. Louis if she ever did call. Sitting there on Vince's bed made my mind race with possibilities of us being more than friends so I got up and went into the living room. Opened the curtains and got a glimpse of downtown. St. Louis was a place for families. The Midwest. Where adults worked hard and the teenyboppers prayed a hip-hop show rolled through piggybacking on a release party in Chicago or Kansas City. People like Cedric the Entertainer, Joe Torrey, C'Babi and Nelly and the St. Lunatics put our hometown on the map so quickly that the East and West Coasts were forced to take notice. But still there was an undeniable Southern-like tension. Being ranked number four on the list of most segregated cities in the U.S. made you feel as though time had not brought about change. Depending on what side you rested on, you either pretended you didn't notice it or pretended you didn't feel it. But ironically, I was happy to be back home in this place where miraculously everyone sorta knew everyone or had at least gone to high school with their second cousin's in-laws. In that respect, there was an unspoken unity. Black-owned businesses were popping up all over the place. In the Delmar Loop you could find natural hair care salons and bookstores that greeted you with the sweet smell of incense as you strolled along sidewalks lined with everything from vintage clothing shops and print galleries to top-of-the-line shoe stores and jewelry spots. Living here was all about knowing where to go.

I turned around and took a seat in one of the blue chairs that faced away from the window. Put my feet up on the coffee table and noticed an envelope sitting next to a bowl with white votive candles in it. It was addressed to a "Professor Lowery." It was also open. And I know I was out of order but I was also still into this man. When I picked it up, I found two tickets to a "New Era Dance Troupe" performance.

Vince opened the bathroom door and yelled, "Theresa, would you bring me a towel out of the closet?"

"Yeah! Hey, what's up with these tickets on your coffee table?"

"Oh, that's some dance thing. They were giving the tickets away."

"To who?"

"To whomever wanted them."

I handed him a black bath towel and asked, "Well, who is Professor Lowery?"

Vince sighed. "Wait a minute. I'll be out in a sec."

He shut the door as my cell phone rang from the living room.

I grabbed it and answered, "Hello."

Nikai asked, "So how was the trip?"

"It was okay. I left my baby down there so you know I'm feeling strange."

"I guess so. Hey, what are you doing tonight?"

"I don't know. Why?"

"Gotta talk to you."

"About what? Wanna give me the lowdown on your little dinner?"

At that moment Vince came out of the bathroom, wiping the excess water from his head. He glanced at me and then started toward the bedroom.

I told Nikai, "Hold on."

"Hey, Vince, are you going to this performance tonight?"

"No, I'm going to bed."

"Do you mind if I use these tickets?"

"Go right . . . Wait a minute."

Sounded as though he was doing some serious thinking. Like maybe he had promised them to someone else.

Then he told me, "Sure. Take 'em."

"You sure?"

"Positive."

"Hello, Nikai. Meet me at the Caman Cultural Center at eight."

"For what?"

"To catch a show. I'm bored. Need to get out. If I go home I'll just think about the fact that my baby is gone."

"I understand. I'll be out front at a quarter 'til."

"See you then."

I walked back into the bedroom and leaned inside the threshold. Watched his oiled muscular body as he bent over and grabbed a pair of black boxer briefs out of a dresser drawer.

"Hey, Professor Lowery."

Vince didn't turn around when he answered, "What's up?"

"You need me to spend the night tonight and nurse you back to health?"

"Nah, I've got some editorial letters that I'm trying to get done. I just wanna be alone."

* * *

Nikai was standing outside on North Grand near the Fox Theatre waiting for me in a colorful little two-piece outfit that looked like she'd snatched it right off of India Arie. I waved as I entered the crosswalk but she didn't wave back. She was wearing her locks wrapped up in some orange material, but her usual smile was absent. When I hopped the curb, she put her arm through mine and led us toward the Cultural Center.

I asked, "Are you okay?"

She shook her head.

We took our seats in a room that wasn't much bigger than a movie theater. Observed our surroundings. The crowd was mixed with white and black, young and old. I crossed my legs and straightened the tail of my red, white and gray diagonally striped skirt. Then checked to make sure I didn't have too much cleavage coming out of my white top. A lady walked up to us and asked if the seat next to Nikai was taken. I told her no. Looked at Nikai. She was staring at the back of the chair in front of her. I grabbed her hand. She squeezed mine. Felt a sadness and a sense of struggle oozing from her palm.

I said, "Well, until you decide to talk about whatever's on your mind, why don't you tell me about your dinner with Robert."

She didn't bother to look at me when she closed her eyes and shook her head. Squeezed my hand a little harder. I put my other hand on top of hers and said, "Okay."

The lights went out. In the darkness, I felt some of her tension escape. Seemed as though she wanted to hide. Maybe even from herself.

Nikai stared at the stage and asked, "How is your mom?"

"She's good. Got more energy than me and you put together."

"So you and Vince are still hangin', huh?"

"We're friends. I've got to get used to us not acting outside of those roles. Sometimes, I want my friend to be my man, you know?"

She gave a laugh that sounded as though she was making an observation in retrospect.

"Sometimes, you can have both."

I didn't comment. About nine or ten women dressed in pastel leotards and flowing skirts with tattered edges danced under bright lights with pure enthusiasm. Each taking their turn stepping forward and showcasing their obvious talents and ability to wow a crowd.

I leaned over and whispered, "They're good."

She leaned over and whispered, "I'm pregnant."

"What?!"

Shhhhhhhh! A large black woman holding a flashlight stood in the aisle next to me and put her hand on my shoulder.

I said, "I'm sorry. Won't happen again."

Then I grabbed Nikai's hand and did a little dance in my seat. She wasn't moving.

"What's wrong? You've waited on this for forever."

A single tear rolled down her cheek. I stopped smiling and wrapped my arm around her.

"Do you wanna leave?"

She nodded her head, followed me out into the hall and over to the ladies' room. Leaned against the counter, rested her face in one hand and snatched the material from her locks with the other.

"Okay. No more silent time. What's the deal, Nikai? This is what you wanted, right? You cared about having a baby more than you did music. Am I correct?"

"Yeah."

"So, Kalif will be happy, won't he?"

She looked up at me with a face full of self-deprecation.

"Yeah, if it's his."

I felt the air escape my lungs, and a face flashed in my mind. I winced and closed my eyes. This couldn't be happening. She couldn't have been so careless. She parted her lips to say something and I held up my hand. I couldn't stand to hear the words that I felt in my heart were coming.

"Theresa, what am I gonna do?"

I walked over to one of the chairs in the lounge area and flopped down. I wanted to cry for her. I wanted to petition Father Time to move the clock back in order to help my sistafriend out. But more so, I wanted to kick Robert's ass myself.

I pounded my fist on the arm of the chair and asked, "Where is he?"

"What difference does that make?"

I leaned forward on my elbows, scooted to the edge of the seat and asked, "Why, Nikai? Why?! Honey, I don't understand."

I was sitting in the bathroom begging her to tell me this wasn't so. She turned her back to me and couldn't stand to see her own reflection in the mirror. Snatched a paper towel from the dispenser and saturated it with water from the faucet.

"Sheila's gonna eat my ass alive," she said, placing the towel on her forehead.

I jumped up instantly. "*Sheila's* your biggest concern?! What, are you kidding me? You're pregnant . . . Wait, let me back this up. You've been waiting for years to get pregnant by a man who worships the ground you walk on and now that you aren't sure if it's his or the asshole's who paid off family members to fool your ass into believing he truly loved you, all you can think about is what *Sheila* will say?! Girl, have you lost your *damn* mind? Lord, this beats all."

She turned to me. "No it doesn't. 'Cause I'm thinking about having another abortion."

That was it. I turned, slammed my hand against the door and

walked out on her. Accidentally bumped into a woman who looked like she was arguing with the group's choreographer, who had introduced the troupe at the beginning of the performance. She placed her hand on my back and said, "Oh, excuse me."

When I turned around, she studied my face, and the apologetic smile she wore faded.

Then she continued, "I'm just finished with dancing, okay? I don't wanna do this anymore."

"Bridget, the least you could have done was given some sort of notice."

"You mean you didn't 'notice' that I wasn't showin' up to rehearsal?"

The choreographer looked at me and told the woman, "We'll discuss this later."

"Fine, but I need my refund now."

"Don't have it."

Their voices trailed off as I spotted Nikai walking out of the rest room. She glanced in my direction, and yelled, "He says he's gonna call you."

"Dameron is out of town. I have nothing to say to Robert."

She lowered her head in shame and exited stage left out onto North Grand.

Zenobia

Sheila and I spent that entire morning on the phone discussing volunteer work. She wanted me to come into the bookstore once a week to teach a class on sewing to some thirteen- and fourteen-year-olds. I had shown her the quilt that I was working on one day when she came by to drop off some books I'd ordered for Zaire. I had to give it to Sheila, she was putting more back into the community than I had seen one person do in a while. Sewing, cooking, hair braiding, African dance and computer skills classes were going on around the clock. Byron was also putting in time, with the young men. Showing them how to rebuild fans and engines and, more important, how to express an appreciation for the black female. They were even generous enough to donate a certain amount of books a month to black men who were incarcerated. Sheila's current project was an AIDS seminar, and her next mission was to find people who were willing to talk about how their lives have been affected by it. She said she didn't care if she had to go to the hospital and hang out in waiting rooms to talk to the families. I found that to be a bit much, but she had a determination that was unmatched.

My other line rang as she was running through her plans for the Juneteenth celebration.

"Hold on a second, Sheila. Hello."

"Hi, may I speak with a Zenobia Hall?"

"This is she."

"I'm Elizabeth Burke, Jim Shoner's secretary, and I'm calling about your inquiry for the human resources management position. I'd like to apologize on behalf of Mr. Shoner for taking so long to get back with you but he wants to know if you would be willing to fax your resume over this week."

"This week? Yes, I could do that."

"Great. Here's the fax number: 555-0991. Mr. Shone would like to have all of the applicants' resumes by no later than five o'clock on Friday. He's got a family emergency so I'll be reviewing them and interviewing. Do you have any questions?"

"Yes, Elizabeth, I noticed that the ad mentioned that a bachelor's degree was required. How lenient are you-all with this policy?"

"Well, do you have any human resources experience?"

"Yes, I do."

"Well, Ms. Hall, just fax your resume over and I'll take a look at it. There are always exceptions to be made. However, it would behoove you to at least pursue a bachelor's degree. We have other openings and it is more often than not preferred. I should also inform you that in the event that you are hired for the position, there's a great possibility that Shoner Industries will offer tuition reimbursement. May I ask the highest level you've completed?"

"I have three years of college."

"Oh, Ms. Hall! You are so close. Would that be a human resources degree?"

"Business management."

"Well, fax your resume over and I'll look at it immediately and get back with you. Any other questions?"

"No, not as of right now. Thank you, Elizabeth."

"Call me Liz."

"Thanks, Liz. I look forward to your response. Bye."

I pressed the flash button and heard silence.

"Hello."

Sheila said, "Yeah, I'm back. That was Nikai on my other line. She wants to get together tomorrow but that's my day for research. I told her we could do something this Thursday. How's Elaine?"

"Still tryin' to get laid."

"What do you think it is?"

"Time to give up."

Sheila chuckled and sighed slowly.

"Well, let me go. I've got some folks to interview, errands to run and souls to pray for. You take care, Zenobia, and call me if you need anything."

"Sure thing."

I hung up, sat back in one of the wicker chairs and heard someone knock on my bedroom door. "Come in," I called.

Trisha cracked the door wide enough for a malnourished squirrel to squeeze through and peeped her head in.

I laughed a bit and said, "I don't bite."

"You busy?"

"No. You can come in and have a seat."

She walked over to the chair on the opposite side of the small table I had put my feet up on. She wore a pair of white pajamas with little cartoon characters and large furry zebra-printed slippers. Her hair was curled on top and stood out horizontally in back.

I asked, "How are you?"

"I'm fine. Maurice told me that it was okay to make breakfast this morning. I didn't know if you wanted some or not but there's some bacon and eggs left."

"No thanks. I'm all right."

She asked, "Would you help me pin my hair up, Zenobia?"

"Yeah, c'mere."

She sat on the floor between my legs, extended hers and handed me some bobby pins.

"Zenobia, can I ask you a question?"

I took a pin out of the corner of my mouth and said, "Yeah."

"I know you don't really like me and everything. What made you decide to let me live with you and Maurice?"

"To be honest, Trisha, I don't know you well enough to not like you. And I let you stay because I felt that this would help my brother accept responsibility for his actions. It had little to do with you."

"So if I wasn't pregnant, you wouldn't let me stay?"

"Probably not."

"That's what I told Maurice. He always makin' it seem like he got some pull."

"Well, I told you that from day one. Maurice ain't runnin' nothin' in here but his mouth."

She laughed. "You know what? If I wasn't pregnant a whole lot of things would be different. Like for one, I'd probably graduate with my class next year."

That yanked me back to a time when Zaire had put a halt to my life plans. Part of me felt sorry for Trisha. I had gotten a lot further with my education but I still wasn't where I wanted to be. Felt the pinch of time wasted on a daily basis. I was twenty-eight and hadn't ever worked a job that couldn't be technically labeled as a favor. Payce knew like I did that the door swung both ways. He was pimping me for my skills and calling it a family business when I didn't own a fucking glass in the place. I had put my faith in a man just like Trisha appeared to be doing with Maurice. The only difference was she had something I didn't see anymore when I looked into my own eyes: the desire to believe that something real and attainable was on its way. And I wasn't about to let that wither up inside of her and die.

"Who says you can't graduate with your class, Trisha?"

"My counselor. He told me that I should just start thinking about getting a GED."

"Well, you know what I think? I think you can walk across the stage with your class, *and* start college with them too. You don't have to go away, you know? There's UMSL, SIUE, Webster University, Washington U, St. Louis University . . . or you could go to one of the three junior colleges here in St. Louis. You know what you want to major in?"

"I like numbers. I used to talk to Mr. Gilmore, the counselor, about majoring in finance but he always had something negative to say so I stopped bringing it up."

I put the final pin into her hair, held her by the shoulders and turned her around so that she could look into my eyes.

"Listen, Trisha, anytime you need someone to talk to about furthering your education, come and see me."

She smiled and stood to her feet. "I talked to my momma last night. She wants me to come home but I told her that Maurice wanted me to stay here with him."

"And what did you finally decide upon?"

"I told her that I wanted to be with my future husband."

I saw myself standing there in her shoes almost ten years ago, full of optimism and belief in a man who didn't know where he was going or what he would be doing the following year, let alone how he would manage to fit me into the framework of his life. Thought about how many years I wished I would have come back to be with my mother instead of chasing a promise. Because the one thing I've learned if nothing else is that while we wait on others, the world keeps on spinning.

"Trisha, go home to your mother. You need her more now than you ever will. And you just never know—she may really need you too."

Vince

I'd say it was about two days before I could eat anything. In the meantime, I tackled those manuscripts that I'd been foot-dragging on. Actually got two of 'em out of the way. Theresa called and checked up on me periodically. Asked if I needed my car anytime soon. She said she'd have someone follow her over so that she could drop it off. But I didn't particularly feel like company. And if I weren't a man of my word, I probably wouldn't be bothered with Joshua either. He'd invited me to join him over in Madison, Illinois, for the Gateway International Raceway, a drag racing series, since Luke didn't have much time between his deer hunting trips to Fulton, Missouri. We'd shared a laugh over how different they were. Joshua had traveled the world in the military, played basketball in college for a couple of years and lived in cities like Seattle, Miami and Chicago. He told me Luke was lucky if he made it any farther west than Kansas for a horseshoe tossing convention, and to him that was note-worthy. Confided that he thought Luke and Rayna's relationship was odd, damn near resembled an experiment. Two people with absolutely nothing in common, including race, upbringing and social perspective, claiming to love one another. Just didn't make sense to either of us.

I sat up in bed to call and ask Leland to give me a ride to the grocery store to pick up a few items before the races. I also wanted to see what was up with him. He'd been out of sight for almost three weeks. He didn't answer, and I was leaving him a message to get back at me when someone rang my doorbell.

I got up and asked, "Who is it?"

"Bridget."

I opened the door to find her in a red cotton dress that stopped at her knees and a pair of sneakers with the backs out. Her sandy-brown Afro was pushed back and secured with a red headband. A sweet scent drifted inside my apartment when she entered without permission and dropped her purse on the couch like I'd been anticipating her arrival.

"I finally quit the troupe."

"Really? Good for you."

"And I found my daddy too."

"How was that?"

She pulled a sheet of paper from the inside of her purse and handed it to me.

"Looked him up at work. Wasn't hard."

I pretended to look at the paper and then handed it back.

"You don't look like you feel any better about it."

"That's 'cause I don't. I've wanted to see him for so long, probably because I felt that I couldn't. But now that I can, I feel like what's the use. My life is my life, right?"

"I guess."

"You gave the tickets away, didn't you?"

"Yeah, how do you know?"

"I don't forget a face. She bumped into me and I recognized her immediately. Everything okay with you two? She looked upset."

"We're not exactly a couple right now. We're just doing the friend thing."

"Like us?"

"I'd say it's a bit different. You want something to drink, Bridget?"

"Yeah, let me get some water."

I walked into the kitchen and turned the light on. "So how's the dealership gig?"

"I feel like a preacher sometimes, like I'm just performing. Saying all of the right things at the right time to get the right reaction out of people. It's a job."

"Seems like you're having regrets."

I handed her the glass of water and walked back toward the bedroom.

"Am I interrupting something, Vince?"

"I was about to get dressed to leave in a little while but you're okay."

When I sat down at the foot of my bed to get a T-shirt out of the dresser I found her standing on the threshold. Wearing her hair natural made her facial features more prominent, gave me an opportunity to appreciate her beauty. Her face clouded with uneasiness, she cleared her throat. When she tried to speak, her voice wavered.

"I've got a ticket to Miami and friends fly free. You interested?"

"Nah, I'm cool. Got too much to do here. What about your new job?"

"What about it?"

"You trying to lose it?"

"Honestly, I'm trying to lose myself. I'm still broke and I want a new start. Thought it would be nice to have a little company while I do it."

"Well, I'm not the type to run away."

Bridget sat down on the bed next to me. "And that's what you think I'm asking you to do?"

"That's what it sounds like."

She held my hand. "Vince, the only difference between me and you is that you're treading water. Celebratin' the fact that you ain't drowned yet. I don't see happiness on your face either."

"Well, you damn sure don't see a ticket in my hand. Listen, Bridget, you're the one with the missing twin, neglectful father and jacked-up past. That has nothing to do with me. You wanna get away? Great! You don't owe me or anybody else an explanation. But to tell me what I need to do is overstepping boundaries."

She shrugged her shoulders. "Whatever's clever. I don't leave until next month. If you decide you want to go, the ticket is yours. If not, good luck on locating a buoy."

"I told Cedric this morning that we're still on for Saturday's meeting. He says he's got five pieces of property picked out already."

Joshua yelled over the revving engine in a red racing car covered in Budweiser decals and being driven by a show-off. Tires were spinning, smoke billowing into the air. The animated, half-drunk crowd cheered as I sipped on my bottled water.

"What areas has he lined up?"

"Don't know yet. I'm still not that familiar with St. Louis. I can get from here to there with directions but that dip-shit Luke hasn't been helpful at all."

Joshua raked the top of his brown hair like he wanted it to appear wild and uncombed. Leaned back on his elbows and sipped the beer in his plastic cup.

I asked, "So what's the deal with him? Between me and you."

He didn't look at me when he replied, "What do you mean?"

"I'm sayin' he's an asshole."

"No need to celebrate the obvious."

"Have you ever noticed the way that he looks at me? Not to

mention what he tried to do when my nephew Percy died. He didn't even want to give him a respectable burial."

"Vince, stop beating around the bush. What are you gettin' at?"

"I'm sayin' Luke is a racist."

"And why is that?"

"Because of the way that he degrades Rayna and despises me."

"And you-all are the only two black people in the world?"

This time he glanced over in my direction. More so at a blonde who was walking up the metal bleachers in a canary-yellow midriff shirt and a short white skirt.

"Back when he came into our lives I was making that transition from being a boy to wanting to be a man. Like any brother, felt the need to protect my sister, which I still do."

"Understandable."

"My pops was drinking, and staying out at night with women. Completely ignoring the fact that we were practically raising ourselves. Rayna worked after school, splurged on Percy when she could while dropping me a few dollars whenever it was feasible. But she had to save for her college tuition and she knew it. She was going to Xavier University in New Orleans. She wanted to be a doctor, a pediatrician. Kept her mind on the books, hardly ever dated. Said guys would get her off track. And then that day came, when Luke started coming around. Buying her flowers and taking her out. I can remember lying in bed wondering where they'd gone off to and sometimes I dared to think that maybe he wouldn't bring her back. I didn't understand her interest in him. He was seven years older than she was, he was suspicious—"

"He was white?"

I nodded my head. "And he was white. I didn't believe he loved her. You couldn't even convince me that he liked her because after a month or so I'd catch him yelling at her. She was changing right before my eyes, cowering, and insisting that her child do the same."

"So maybe you don't really have a problem with Luke. Maybe your real issue is with your father for not being there. Sounds like Rayna wanted a father figure and the first one that came along would do. It just happened to be Luke. Listen, he's an asshole. The jury's no longer out on that one. But to call Luke a racist is a bit of a stretch. He is what he is. No one has made him that way and no woman can change it, whether she's white or black. The only thing she can do is decide whether or not it works for her."

"I see where you're coming from. You're one of those white boys who will acknowledge racism but won't do anything to change it because the cards always fall in your favor."

"No. I'm one of those white boys who understand that sometimes white people do what they do because that's the way that they're cut. It has nothing to do with the color of their skin. That would be as stupid and closed-minded as saying that all black people who live in low-income housing steal cars, or sell drugs. If you're cut like that, you'll do it whether you're white, black, crippled, cockeyed, retarded . . ."

"I get your point."

Cars sped by on the track like the thoughts in my mind. Maybe my beef really was with my father. But to blame him would mean that I would have to acknowledge him—something that I wasn't quite ready to do. In order to admit that he'd let me down, I'd have to submit to the truth. That I had in all of my anger still expected something of him. That somehow, even after all of my attempts to ignore him and push him out of my life, my father was still able to affect me. His words, as negative and counterproductive as they were, had stuck with me. Infiltrated my thoughts and actions. Sent me running with no direction. I just wanted to get away from everything he approved of, everything he touched. Not realizing that by running I was doing the very thing that he wanted me to. I was being that *sissy*, the weakling who was afraid to let shit go. Even my desire to have his love.

Joshua's cell phone rang as the race started. He held one ear closed and answered it. When he hung up, he turned to me with a troubled look and declared, "C'mon, Rayna says we need to get back to the house, quickly."

PART THREE

"... Remnants of Joy and Disaster"
—SADE

Theresa

The lunch hour couldn't have arrived soon enough.

I was sitting at my desk grading some papers thinking about Lisa. What plans she had for her future. What her son's HIV status was. Whether or not she'd be willing to seek counsel with the Women of Triumph support group. They were a blessing but her young eyes had been closed for so long that she probably couldn't see that.

I had made a mental note to call Mama to see if she'd heard anything when I saw a small figure dash down the hall past my door. I stood up from my desk and spotted Tiwana running like she had lost her mind.

I yelled, "Young lady!"

She stopped, turned to me so quickly that she almost lost her footing on the polished floors.

"Ms. Downing, Ms. Downing! Please, you gotta help Deon. The boys said there's something wrong with him!"

"Where is he, Tiwana?"

"In the bathroom! Follow me."

We took off down the hall and she stopped right outside of the bathroom door. When I stepped inside, Deon was lying on the floor near a row of urinals, convulsing violently. What was even more disturbing was that he had been left alone. I ran over, sat on the floor behind him, grabbed his head, placed it in my lap and yelled for Tiwana.

She peeped around the corner and answered, "Yes, ma'am."

"Run to the office and tell them to call 911. Then go to the cafeteria and get me a spoon and tell anybody in the hall to come here! Hurry!"

I'd just stuck my finger in his mouth to keep him from swallowing his tongue when a little boy from a fifth-grade class walked in slowly and stopped next to a stall.

"Baby, there's no reason to be scared. Could you please get me some cold water?"

He stood there clutching the wall like he thought it would fall if he moved. That's when Deon bit down on my finger hard enough to bring tears to my eyes. He moaned loudly. His outcry rattled my soul and unleashed something in me. The understanding that there are some things in life that people should not have to experience alone. I wanted to cry out as well because I *was* Deon. Neither of us were given what we needed at very vital times by those we relied on for unconditional love and we both longed for something more. The only difference was the way we chose to act out our frustration. I sat back on my legs and cradled him like he was my own child. Rocked him the way that I needed somebody to do me on the night that changed my life three years ago. His eyes opened and closed with the rapidness of a butterfly flapping its wings, as I began praying.

"Save him, God. Please, spare him, Give this baby another chance."

He clenched his fists, spastically fighting for his life. With muscles tensed, he let out hollow moans that quickly died down into a whine. Suddenly, Deon stopped moving and slowly began to open his eyes. The school nurse; Deon's new teacher, Ms. Strong; and the principal, Mr. Edwards, ran inside the bathroom, and all imparted the same look of relief.

I asked him, "Where are you, Deon? Do you know where you are?"

He shook his head.

"An EMS unit is on its way," Ms. Strong informed me as she stooped down at Deon's feet.

When he struggled to sit up, it took Mr. Edwards to help us make Deon lie back down. Mr. Edwards stood, pulled a hand-kerchief from his pocket and handed it to me. I hadn't realized how profusely I was sweating until then. He looked at me and said, "I guess I owe you an apology for not backing you when you were only looking out for the children. If he had been in your class, you might have seen this coming. The other kids say that he had taken some ecstasy an hour before this started."

"You can only hope, Mr. Edwards. I can only be his teacher. Like I told you before, the children come here to learn academics. I'm not responsible for drug intervention, anger manage-ment, social development, abstinence encouragement and other moral issues. What people tend to forget is that these children have parents who are dropping the ball at home. They are prac-tically bearing no responsibility, have no shame. And I can't be that teacher who makes life easier for them."

"I understand."

The paramedics walked in and took Deon from my lap and placed him on a stretcher. He attempted to curl up like the vul-nerable and scared child that he really was. Began to cry as he reached out for me.

"Wait a minute!" I yelled. "What hospital is he going to?"

"Missouri Medical."

I grabbed Deon's hand and asked him, "Would you like for me to go with you?"

He nodded and secured his grip on my hand, secured a place in my heart.

* * *

I was getting a cranberry juice from the vending machine in the hospital waiting room when I heard someone behind me apologize. I turned around and Deon's father was standing there giving me a remorseful stare.

"I thought you were like a lot of other teachers who take their frustration out on kids. I mean you hear about it all the time. Half of them aren't interested in children or even qualified, just there to do head counts."

I didn't know if this was making him feel better about what he wasn't doing for his son or if he was just building a case against the school system. But I listened. Because when he was done, when he sat alone with his own thoughts, his conscience would eat him up alive.

Mr. Coleman continued, "But I want you to know that I'm sorry and that I can see that you really were concerned about my son."

I reached out to hug his pudgy frame and he broke down in my arms.

"Deon could've died. And after the way I yelled at you, you could've let him."

"No, I wouldn't have, Mr. Coleman. The reason I was so frustrated with Deon is because I knew he possessed the potential to be a great young man, but it takes work. I wanted you to match the work I put in and when you didn't, I became angry. I shouldn't have lost my temper. But now we see where we are and how far we have to go. He was using a drug. Did anyone tell you that?"

"Mr. Edwards called and informed me. That boy has shamed his whole family."

"If you had to be informed then you obviously didn't know. Had you known I'm certain you would've intervened."

"Yeah, I would have."

He took a seat next to an end table filled with magazines and rested his hands on his large stomach.

"The doctor said that he would be okay," he said, pulling a painful smile across his face.

"He sure will. But, Mr. Coleman, *you* have to raise him to be the man that you want him to be. I'm only here to reinforce it. I can't be his parent. We've all got a job to perform and that's yours."

"I guess now you have the right to say that I've been doing it poorly."

"I'll just say that now you know that what you were doing wasn't working. It's time for a new approach. It's time to let *him* be the child. He doesn't need any more friends—he needs a father. Believe me, I know from experience."

As I was talking to him, I spotted Sheila getting off of the elevator and walking down the west corridor wearing a dark brown dress with a mudcloth bag over her shoulder. I excused myself and ran over to her.

"Hey, sis, what are you doing here?" she asked, hugging me.

"One of my students had a seizure and I'm here to make sure he's all right."

She tapped me on the shoulder and smiled. "Oh, now see, that's what I'm talking about. Looking out for the youth. I'm here trying to do some research. I met this guy up on the fourth floor who has a friend dying of AIDS and he agreed to talk to me. I left my tape recorder in the car so I'm going back to get it. You wanna walk with me?"

"No, I think I"m gonna wrap up here and go on home. You talk to Nikai yet?"

"She called me but I haven't been able to get back with her. Why? What's up?"

I sighed. "Nothing. If you talk to her, tell her to call me."

"Okay. You've been all right though?"

"Yeah. I'm good."

"All right. Well, we may even stop by later on. Nikai made this Cajun fifteen-bean soup that she's been trying to share with everybody. But if not, we'll shoot by tomorrow so you can tell us about your trip in Atlanta."

I let her go and watched her walk away. Wondered if Nikai had any intentions of mentioning what was going on. Wondered if Robert was even man enough to call me.

Vince

"He had a stroke?!"

"Yes, and I think right now is a good time to bury the hatchet."

"So you trick me into believing there was an emergency—"

"This *is* an emergency, Vince! Dammit, can you just get over yourself for one minute?! Jesus, he's your father!"

We'd left Josh at the house and sped down I-40 east in Rayna's white Acura Legend like the world was coming to an end. I got off on Ballas Road, turned into the parking lot and let Rayna out at the door. Told her I'd be up in a minute. That I needed some time.

She bent down and replied, "Time waits for no man, Vince." And then slammed the car door. My momma once told me that there will come a time when everything a person fears will be placed before them with an opportunity to show themselves just who they are and what they're made of. My biggest fear? The lack of my father's respect.

He always told me that it didn't make a difference if people liked you. If they respected you, they wouldn't *disrespect* you, which meant the rest could be worked on.

I wondered as my sweaty palms gripped the steering wheel in the parking lot of Missouri Medical Hospital if we'd ever get a chance to work on the rest, if he'd ever get a chance to respect me. I mean, I had gone down this road before. I'd made countless attempts to visit him two years ago which only resulted in heated arguments and me being called out of my name. Loving my father was like running into a brick wall and hoping the next go at it would bring it down.

I just wanted to sit in there in his hospital room, breathe the same air he breathed. Watch him lie on his side facing the window, facing the world but not being able to face me. I wanted to give him a chance to rethink his rejection. I wanted him to know how his inability to even imply that I meant something to him was killing me deep down. But Vincent Ramone Lowery Sr. was stubborn and he only loved when a person appeared to be lovable. Anything that was inconsistent with the norm was not lovable, not tolerable, and definitely would not occupy his world.

And so now that I was faced with invading his world against my own will, it felt like hell. I took a few moments to gather myself, got out of the car and walked through the large glass sliding doors. Approached the front desk and asked the lively young Asian woman who was pointing visitors in the right direction for my father's room number.

She observed my demeanor and smiled. "It takes more muscles in your face to frown," she said without a hint of an accent.

I nodded and gave her what she wanted. After all, that was about the only thing that I felt was negotiable at that point. I took the piece of paper she wrote his room number down on, hopped on the elevator at the end of the hall and rode up to the sixth floor. When I stepped out, the distinct smell of illness and recovery was in the air. I've always hated the atmosphere of hospitals. And balloons and flowers only relay one of two messages: Either you'll be here for a while or shit is looking real bleak.

As I walked down the long hall toward room 604, I observed the elderly and the youthful alike. Wondered what their stories were, how they'd ended up stuck in limbo. Caught between fate and their normal lives. Thanked God that it wasn't me checking in for an overnight stay.

The sixth door I came to on my left had my father's name listed outside. I could hear the soothing tone of a woman's voice as I entered the room. She was a sista. Dark-skinned with a braided coif and shapely legs. I got a chance to notice them as she closed the curtains for Pops while maintaining a one-way conversation.

When she turned around and spotted me standing there she jumped and covered her mouth as though she hadn't expected anyone, not even Pops, to be listening.

"Hello," she chirped. "You *must* be related to Mr. Lowery."

I smiled. "I'm his son."

I heard a moan from the figure that lay on the bed facing the nurse. A shift under the white blanket let me know that he was still alive. The sigh that followed let me know that he hadn't forgotten why I'd kept my distance in the last year.

"You are the spitting image of him. Well, he's doing a lot better than he was this morning. He's more settled."

"Has my sister made it up here yet?" I asked, sticking my hands into the pockets of my dark blue denim shorts.

"Yeah, she went around the corner to talk to the doctor. Someone else called a little while ago. A man. He only gave his first name. Lou or Luke I think it was. Mr. Lowery asked me to take a message. Hasn't been in a talkative mood. And that may have something to do with his left side."

She stepped closer and quietly mouthed that he was unable to move anything aside from his right arm and hand. I glanced at him. She touched my shoulder, lowered her head and left the room. When the nurse's footsteps had blended in with an uptight conversation in the hall, I stood at the foot of his bed and watched his chest rise and fall. Watched his pupils dart from one side to the other under strained eyelids, playing a futile game of possum.

Pops was a six-foot-three, broad-shouldered, salt-and-pepper-haired ex-marine who had constantly reminded me throughout my life that the road to hell was paved with people who had failed to plan ahead. And the moment I laid eyes on him every word I thought would be appropriate escaped me. All of the things that I had *planned* to say somehow didn't make any sense.

I asked, "How you feelin'?"

He opened his eyes. The left side of his face sagged a bit while the other let me know that he wished I hadn't come. His look reminded me of me. Torn between desire and need. He was a man divided. A force stronger than him had taken over.

He let out a perturbed grunt. I figured I'd better say something that he was interested in hearing before he called the nurse back in with a request that I leave.

"You know Rayna came too. She'll be in here in a minute."

No response.

"She tell you I'm about to look into buying a house?"

Another annoyed grunt. He gripped the blanket with his right hand and repeatedly clinched his fist. I felt like I was on *The Gong Show* and the little buzzer above his head was all the commotion he needed to make in order to get me quickly dismissed.

"Sometimes, I sit and think about just where things went wrong with us, Pops. Back when I was thirteen."

I glanced over and noticed a yellow notepad and pen on his night table. Someone had scribbled a few words down. I wondered if it had been Pops. But when I moved towards the pad, I heard another grunt. This time it was in unison with my cell phone ringing. Pops closed his eyes and rested his right arm on his abdomen. I grabbed the pad and pen and handed it to him—no, more like poked him with them until he finally opened his fist.

I answered the phone. "Yeah?"

"Hey, what's goin' on? This is Cedric from Arch Line Realty. Just calling to confirm our four o'clock appointment for Saturday."

"Yeah, we're still on. I'll be there."

"I spoke with Josh a little while ago and he says he'll shoot through with me. That all right?"

"No problem."

I hung up and sat in the wooden chair with the burnt-orange cushion by the door. Our silence gave way to conversation that existed all around us. I folded my hands in front of me, determined to wait Pops out. I had given in enough just by showing up.

Another half hour dragged by and we were no closer to reconciliation than Mama was to coming back from the dead. By then I had turned the television on while Rayna cuddled up next to him in the hospital bed as if to remind him that no matter how old she got, how many nights he left us alone in that house, she was still his little girl. He and I ignored one another.

When Rayna had finally pulled away long enough to go to the bathroom, I glanced over at Pops and observed him writing something. I hopped up and held the pad in place so that it wouldn't be as difficult. It was as though we had reversed our roles. I was able to show him the simple things in life that I wanted from him, like concern. As he struggled, I stepped closer. But when my hand touched his, he dropped the pen with a contorted face and a heavy, sickened sigh. I looked into his eyes and grabbed his hand, almost as if to lay claim on him as my blood. He pulled away but I held on, forcing Pops to see me, touch me, because *this* I could control. Him loving me was something that still hung in the balance.

"I love you," I told him.

I felt him flinch like my words were a blow to his manhood.

He closed his eyes, went back to his game of *If I can't see you maybe you aren't really here.*

"Pops, I'm your son. You don't have to hate me to prove that you don't agree with me. I'm not here to make you feel bad. I'm here because I care."

He picked up the pen and scribbled the words *No regrets* on the pad.

"I'm not asking you to regret anything. I'm asking you to put your pride aside now."

He wrote *kds?*

I sat back down in the chair and said, "No kids yet."

He wrote: *Kids tke car of u.*

"Was that your reason for having us?"

He flung the pad on the floor and closed his eyes. He was still the selfish man he'd always been. So busy receiving that he had no time to give of himself. And now that he was older, he clung to Rayna because she represented another woman he could use, and she was too blind to see that. When I bent over to pick the pad up, my cell phone rang again.

I answered, "Yeah?"

"What are you doing?" Theresa asked, sounding dispirited.

"I'm at Missouri Medical with my pops."

"Really? I'm on the highway. Just left there. How's your stomach?"

"I'm all right."

The thoughts of Ray that I'd hoped I could run from were front and center again. Made me realize that Pops could never take anything from me that I didn't let him. I didn't feel like a man because of *my* issues, because of what *I* believed my action represented. Pops only reinforced what I was already thinking.

Theresa exhaled and asked, "You wanna come over and spend the night? I could really use some company right now."

I bent over, rubbed my forehead and asked, "Why do we keep trying this, Theresa? We already know what we're good at."

"And what's that?"

"Being friends. Taking the sting off of loneliness. I don't want to keep regretting my actions. You aren't ready for a relationship and neither am I. I'm just sick and tired of regrets."

Silence.

"Just be honest with yourself, Theresa. We've known each other—"

"That's the point, Vince! I *don't* regret any part of our relationship, and I don't know what that means. You treated me like shit when I was in Atlanta!"

Guilt and confusion straddled my back and weighed me down.

"Listen, I'll be leaving here in a little while. I've got a few things to take care of today but I'll be over to your place tomorrow so we can talk face-to-face."

"No sex, Vince, just talking."

"None of that, Theresa. I'll see you later."

I turned the power off on my cell and checked the time. It was a quarter after three and I was out west when I needed to be heading south. Rayna exited the bathroom and caught me looking at my watch.

"What do you have to do?"

"I've got some stuff to get squared away."

When I stood up, Pops handed me the pad. He had written: *Do u luv her?*

"I love the way that she used to make me feel."

He pointed toward the pad as though he wanted to remind me that he still knew a bullshit line when he heard one.

"I can't say whether or not I love her. I've learned that life isn't as simple as loving or not loving a person. I've loved you all

227

of these years and you still don't really know me, Pops. Still haven't taken the time to work through the past."

Rayna yelled, "Vince, dammit, *I'm tellin' you* to get over it! You can't move forward looking at the past."

"But forgetting the past is how history repeats itself, Rayna."

She pointed at Pops. "Look at your father! He can't move one side of his body and you're still trippin' 'cause he didn't tuck you in at night?!"

And that's when I realized that Rayna really didn't get it.

"I'm trippin' because nobody showed up to watch me play basketball all of those years! I'm trippin' 'cause I couldn't put a face on the man I bragged about when everyone else ate lunch with their fathers on the one day out of the year I needed him to come to my school! I taught myself to drive! Mr. Jenkins up the street showed me how to knot a tie. The fuckin' janitor at school helped me build my go-cart for Boy Scouts, not Pop! But I was there to mow the lawn and take out the trash. He never taught me how to be a man, and he never taught me how to protect you from—"

"From what, Vince? Or should I say who?"

"He never taught me to protect you from *Luke*! Maybe if he had been a man himself, Luke couldn't have snatched you up so easily."

Rayna stepped closer and looked me in my eyes. "Vince, I wasn't snatched up. I went willingly."

"But only because you hungered for the same thing from him that I did. You wanted a father."

"I *have* a father."

"What you have is someone to call Daddy. And unfortunately, I've always needed more." I looked over at Pops, and he had scribbled, *luv u both, sorry*. He even had the nerve to cry.

"Not being accepted by your family is a hurtful thing," I told her. "I've hurt all of my life and now, *now, Rayna,* I'm ready to let it go."

Pops gave me a repentant stare and then underlined the word *sorry* on his pad. And all I could think to say was "I believe you."

The nurse who'd been with Pops when I first arrived returned.

She asked, "Is everything all right?"

"Yeah, I was just about to leave anyway."

Rayna clutched my arm and stopped me as I walked into the hallway. Placed her hands on her hips and stared at the floor for a minute. Then she sighed, tucked her lips and looked up into my eyes. "I never knew you felt this way, Vince. Hell, I never even knew that all of that was happening. I was so busy trying to raise Percy and—"

"Don't worry about it, Rayna. I'll be fine. I've gotten it off of my chest now."

"Where are you going?"

"I'm gonna go call a ride home."

She pulled her car keys out of her pocket. "Here, take my car. Someone will be out to get me."

"I know Luke is coming, Rayna. And that is the very reason why it's so hard for me to believe that you're happy. You're so reluctant to be open and honest with me. You chose that man over me and practically put me out of your house. But that's your husband and your choice. I just want you to know that you're about as far away from me as Pops is right now."

"Can you understand that the same things won't constitute happiness for two different people? We grew up together but we didn't suffer the same way, Vince. You chose to let Daddy's actions hinder you and keep you from growing. My memories are a lot happier. So naturally, our views on a lot of things will be different. And I'm okay with that because you're still my brother and I still love you. Believe it or not, love has a lot to do with relationships. It's what we allow to cloud our vision and what we harbor in our hearts that will make all of the difference in the world. It's what helps me to love that man in there no matter what."

I watched from the hall as the nurse pushed a food tray aside and proceeded to check Pops's blood pressure. Found the strength and forgiveness in my heart to walk back in there, took the pad and tore off the page that we had used to communicate. Folded it and put it in my pocket. Then I told Pops that I would be back the following day to see him. Surprisingly, he nodded in acceptance of that idea.

I wanted badly to hug him but thought that this relationship had to be rebuilt one brick at a time, so I left with my heart intact and my father's wisdom in my pocket. As I rounded the corner I could hear the nurse asking if I was his only son. Pops must've said yes. But when she asked whether he was proud of me I quickened my steps. Ran from his response. I guess Rayna was right: You have to hold on through the rough times because a little love going one way will always outweigh none at all.

I walked down to the elevator and cringed when the doors opened.

Ms. Irene yelled, "Vince! You made it. I knew you would. I told my sister that you and Ray were like brothers and if nobody else came to see him you would. C'mon baby, hop on here with me."

She grasped my hand the moment I stepped on the elevator. As we descended two floors I felt as though the breath was escaping my body. I inhaled and stared at the light jumping from one number to another.

"You all right? He doesn't really look that bad. Just lost a little weight."

When the doors opened, we exited and took off down the hall. Passed a sitting room where Ray's homey Marcel was talk-

230

ing to a tall brown-skinned woman who looked like she was into the black movement. He cut his eyes at me when I waved and began pointing as though he was disclosing information about where he knew me from.

"You must've gotten lost, huh? Were all the way up on the sixth floor."

"No, actually my pop is up there. He had a stroke."

"Oh my goodness. What room is he in? Unless you think it'll be a problem. I'm just an old friend."

"Nobody's up there but Rayna, Ms. Irene."

"Well, do you think he'll mind me seeing him? You know how men can be. Especially your daddy. He was always so strong and independent."

"Yeah, a little too independent."

"Well, that was always his way. I always told Ray that the only thing you can ask from a person is that they remain consistent."

"Is that truly all that you can ask, Ms. Irene?"

She tilted her head and gave me a look that let me know she'd probably always view him through the same eyes that Rayna did.

I told her, "Seems that if you truly love a person you always want more for them, you want them to grow. It's easy to be stagnant. Anybody can do that."

"Yeah, but everybody has got their own cross to bear, Vince. Your father loves you."

"I don't dispute that. He just never *expressed* this love everybody keeps speaking about. What good is it if I don't feel it?"

She reached out to hug me to and whispered, "Show him, Vince. Teach him how to love you. I never could."

And then she walked away. I watched her pass back by the sitting room, smile and wave at Marcel. He appeared in the doorway and started toward Ray's room, where I stood. I turned and greeted an older woman in a pair of black slacks and an orange blouse who I assumed was Ms. Irene's sister. Her eyes widened as a smile grew on her peach-toned face.

"You *do* look just like him."

"Who?"

"Ray. Irene told me that there was a resemblance but my God. I never knew that it was this strong."

I looked down at the man who had managed to unlock a forgotten chamber in my mind just three weeks ago. He'd dropped a considerable amount of weight and there were dark circles around his eyes. He was asleep, with his hands at his side and the white sheet pulled up to his waist. Part of me was wishing that it was over his entire body when a woman called my name from behind. It was the same sista that Marcel was talking to in the sitting room.

She smiled. "How are you? My name is Sheila Francis, and I'm sorry about Ray. This is truly unfortunate. Would you mind speaking with me about his life? I'm trying to gather information in order to benefit the youth at an AIDS seminar that my husband and I are holding at our bookstore, African Impressions."

"I don't know much about his life."

"Well, would you be willing to discuss the little that you do know? Possibly something about yourself? How this is affecting you?"

Ms. Irene's sister suggested, "Go on, baby. You could change somebody's life."

So I followed this woman down to a small pond outside of the hospital and wondered where Marcel had gone off to. He had a chip on his shoulder and by the look he was giving me, his anger was directed my way. We walked less than half a mile and managed to find a quiet spot where people weren't consoling one another. It wasn't long after we'd sat down on an iron bench that Sheila pulled a sandwich bag filled with bread from her purse, walked a few feet away and began to feed the ducks. She talked as she tossed crumbs at them.

"So what's your story, Vince?"

"'My story'?"

"Everybody has a story. What's yours?"

I shrugged my shoulders and rested my arm on the back of the bench. "Give me an example. What's yours?"

"Well, I'm a wife, a teacher, a mother, an entrepreneur, a friend and a goddess."

I gave a fake Jamaican accent, "You work many job, mon."

Sheila looked back at me and smiled. "I'm an only child. My parents died when I was twenty-seven. I graduated with a bachelor's degree from Spelman in Atlanta. For a long time I didn't love myself the way God intended for me to. Had sex with men because I felt I had little else to offer. I didn't feel beautiful because my nose is so broad and my lips are so full. Feeling ugly led me into isolation, where I sat with myself, heard the God in myself. I learned to pray, to love God back, to love myself. I met my husband one night at a club and married him so quickly my friends thought I was crazy. They thought I was even crazier when I left the country with him. We moved back to the States three years ago, after his mother passed. I opened a bookstore in order to create an inviting environment for my people. I'm not rich, at least not in finances. But in spirit, I'm loaded. I haven't given birth to a child but I nurture the children who are already here on earth for me to teach how to love their self. Now again, I ask you, what's your story?"

"Damn, I don't know if I'll be able to top that."

"I'm not asking you to. I want to know about *you*. What makes you you?"

"I thought we were here to talk about Ray."

"We will. In due time."

"Well, I grew up in what could be considered an imperfect

family. My sister Rayna and I both spent a lot of time missing my mother when she passed. My father is another story. I was a Boy Scout, ran track throughout high school and went to college on a basketball scholarship. I was one of the best on my team. I got hurt in my junior year, graduated and decided that I would make St. Louis my permanent home. While I was recuperating, I fell in love."

"With a man?"

She caught me off guard with that. Reminded me of why we were out here in the first place.

"Why would you ask me something like that?"

"Well, it's my understanding that you and Ray were intimate, right?"

"Where would you get some *shit* like that?"

"Marcel told me about your relationship when you came in. Is this not true?"

"Of course not! Like I told you, I don't know much about Ray's life."

"Okay, okay, well let's get back to you. You fell in love with a woman, graduated from college and moved back to St. Louis."

I gave a curt *"And the rest is history."*

"So how long have you been friends with Ray?"

I looked at Sheila, tossed my other arm across the back of the bench and breathed deeply. She smiled, nodded her head and went back to feeding the ducks.

"Take your time. Think about your answer."

"I don't need to think about my answer, and I don't need you to be condescending either. I ran into Ray about a month ago. We hooked up . . ."

She raised her brow as if I was accidentally telling on myself.

"We watched the basketball game, had a few drinks, played video games for a while. I know his mother well."

"Is that all that happened when you went by his house in Lake St. Louis?"

"Look, Sheila or Mrs. Francis or whatever the fuck you go by, don't play games with me, ah'ight?"

She backed down a bit.

"Is there anything else you want to tell me about your relationship with Ray Lippons?"

"My *friendship* with Ray Lippons."

She shrugged her shoulders. "Okay."

"The Ray I know is selfish. No pretending. He gives it to you straight. No pun intended. He never dresses up anything he has to say. That's what some people loved about him, but it was the very thing that others hated. He never judged. Took people as they were, as flawed as that may have been. Did that *ex-convict* Marcel tell you he helped him out with a job? Well, he was that kinda guy. Looked out for you, treated you like family."

"You ever feel you've been judged by people?"

"Well, that's inevitable. In this world, if you do anything that isn't consistent with the masses you'll be judged. Even if what the masses are doing is backward as hell."

"So what do you go for?"

"What do you mean?"

"I mean as far as dating."

"I never said that I'm dating anyone right now."

"Okay, if you were to date, what type of women would you go for?"

"Beautiful, smart women. I love a thinker. I usually prefer ones with a little bit of college under their belt. Someone at least as beautiful as my sister."

"Where is your sister?" Sheila asked, finally taking a seat next to me on the bench.

"She's upstairs visiting our father."

"Any other relatives?"

I thought about Percy, Mama and their untimely deaths.

"Nope, it's just the three of us."

"So what would you say to young African-American people in reference to the AIDS epidemic and the way that it's affecting the community?"

I looked out across the park and pondered that question for a minute. Saw myself holding Theresa from behind and watching the sun set on her beautiful face. Then I pictured Ray lying up there in that hospital bed, unable to fast-talk and manipulate his way out of this one.

"I'd have to say, give yourself a chance to live because tomorrow is not promised. Not much is in this world. But we should make the most of our lives. Few of us are foolish enough to play a true game of Russian roulette so why participate in a modified one? Live your life as though it'll be an open book someday and know that it's usually the stuff you'd rather not talk about that'll be referenced over and over again."

"Is that it?"

I caught a glimpse of the sun glistening on the water as I closed my eyes and took Sheila's advice on thinking carefully about my answer. Saw the last thirty years of my life, the people I've known who were no longer there to share it with me and, lastly, Ray.

"AIDS is real."

Theresa

Nikai and I were sitting at a table outside a trendy restaurant in the Central West End waiting for Sheila. I hadn't seen or heard from her since the performance at the Caman Center and my instincts told me that she was ducking and dodging me.

I asked, "So what's new?"

She sipped on a clear soda and sighed. "Nothing's changed."

"Sorry to hear that."

She looked across the street at a couple walking hand in hand and tapped the edge of the table with a silver ring on her thumb. She was embarrassed, and she had every reason to be.

I leaned forward on the table and asked, "So what happened, Nikai?"

She looked over at me and stopped the tapping. "I guess I wanted to prove myself. Wanted him to know that I was doing good, looking good, felt good."

I scoffed. "I'm sure he got the message."

"Theresa, please don't do that."

I apologized. She continued, "I guess deep down even though I had moved on, I was still hurting. I never had any intentions of being with Rob again. My meeting him was to show him what he'd lost out on, what he'd never get a chance to enjoy."

I gave a sarcastic, "Oh really?"

"*You know what I mean.* And I guess I wanted to know that I had that sort of power over him as well. The power to make him turn his back on the woman he's seeing now. I needed to feel like our three years meant so much to him that maybe he was still struggling to get over me too. To tell you the truth, he had really torn me down, and every time I stood before him knowing how long I'd played the fool, I felt just as small. That is, until I saw that he was ready to risk what he had for just one night with me."

"Well, guess what? You did the same, and chances are that woman he's seeing now will never know about that night. Especially considering what you have planned."

"I haven't made up my mind completely. I may still have the baby and deal with the consequences. So what's with you? You still dreaming?"

"Not as often but when I do, it's horrible."

"Listen, I think it's time you talk to somebody about not being able to get over Don. Death is serious."

I leaned back in the green plastic chair.

"It's not as simple as a lot of people think," I told her.

"So if we're all thinking the wrong thing, give us the right perspective."

I sat forward and cupped my forehead with my hands.

"What, Theresa? What is it?"

Nik was rubbing my arm.

"Greetings, sisters."

Sheila appeared out of nowhere—cowrie shells, Kente cloth handbag and all. Sheila had a regal look about her. The type of sista thugs humbled themselves to. She always walked with her head of decorative braids held high and had a way of making mature men cease conversations just to watch her maneuver her way across the room.

I looked up, pulled a smile across my face and responded, "Greetings."

"Girl, you put the C in CP time," Nikai said.

Sheila looked at me. "Will you tell Nikai there's a thing called being fashionably late?"

"So that still doesn't explain your tardiness," Nik joked.

We all laughed as Sheila gathered the bottom of a long tan rayon skirt that seemed to go on forever and took a seat next to me.

"Did you-all order yet?" she asked.

"Yeah, I got your favorite, the Portobella mushroom thing."

"Great. So what's new?"

Nikai looked over at me as if to say this was an opportunity to cleanse my soul. I stared back, undaunted. She had a lot of freakin' nerve.

Sheila repeated, "So what's new, ladies?"

Nik wouldn't take her eyes off of me. "Sheila, you remember when my ex, Robert, thought he had another woman pregnant and kept it from me for almost the entire pregnancy?"

"Uh-huh."

By now Sheila had rested her elbows on the table and leaned in like she was determined not to miss a single vowel of this conversation.

"It was Theresa here who convinced him to admit it to me so that I would have an option to either live my life or die of heartache in that relationship. One might've thought that her loyalty would lie with Robert because he was her fiancé's best friend but even then, she was on my team. Living in truth was important to her."

I interrupted, "And it still is."

"She understood that a lot of our problems could be solved if we just remove fear from the equation."

"And I still do."

Sheila's head was ping-ponging back and forth as she did her best to keep up.

Nik's eyes were still locked on me when she said, "Sheila, Theresa is in pain."

Sheila lightly placed her hand on my arm. "You ready to talk?"

My first instinct was to get upset.

I looked at both of them, and decided to lay my burden down, but only part of it.

"I'm having these dreams about Don. He wants me to be with him. I don't know if that means his spirit is preparing me for my end in the near future of if I just miss him. He shows up almost every night. Always smiling, never asking about Dameron. Just wants me to come and be with him."

Sheila finally leaned back in her chair and sighed loudly enough to let me know that this was going to be a challenge. The waiter brought our food out. Gave Sheila a couple more seconds to think. Gave us all a couple more seconds to think. Nikai thanked him in a tone that said: Get away from our table. We're really here to talk, not eat.

Then Sheila started with, "The mind is powerful. Few truly understand it completely. I'm not amongst those few. But what I do know is that dreams are stemmed from thoughts that are in our minds, even if you aren't aware that they're there. Let me give you an example. You can fall asleep with the television on, mentally absorb certain events and take them into your dreams."

I was hoping for clarity. My sixth-grade class could've come up with a more interesting explanation. She hadn't told me anything I didn't already know.

"My point is whatever the reason you are having dreams about joining a dead person it's stemmed from your conscious belief or fear that you will die, soon."

"Why the emphasis on 'soon'?" Nikai asked.

"Because if it were just about dying period, she wouldn't be as worried, the dreams wouldn't be as frequent and she wouldn't need the familiar face of a loved one to cushion her transition. These dreams are taking over you, Theresa. That's the one thing about the mind. It'll shift according to each individual's strength. That's why some people pass out in tragic situations. Others may only remember certain incidents. In your case, by feeling that Don is waiting for you, you seem to be coming to grips with death because your mind knows that if you move any further in fear, you'll lose it."

"I don't know."

"I could be wrong, sweetie. But if you aren't moving in fear, why hasn't he asked about his son in your dreams? Why do you think your mind is telling you that he only wants to see *you*? It sounds like you feel your life is in danger, but only yours, not your son's. That's no coincidence."

Sheila grabbed both of our hands and began to bless the food. "Amen" was heard from all around the table. Then, while slicing into her huge mushroom and the fresh vegetables inside it, Sheila asked, "So, what have we given of ourselves?"

I took a sip of my bottled water and asked, "Excuse me?"

Nikai laughed and tried to catch a piece of green pepper before it could bounce off of her chin and hit the table. "Every week that Sheila and I get together we ask that question. In order to tell whether or not we're honoring ourselves, we ask what we've given of ourselves to other people."

Sheila added, "For example, I've given patience to one of the distributors for the store. He's a week late getting back with me about some figurines."

"Well, on a sadder note I gave away my peace when my mother and I began arguing about her putting Uncle Lucky in a home. He's aware that she's tired of the responsibility 'cause you know she don't believe in holdin' her tongue. But he was doing so good. Now it seems he just wants to sit back down in that old musty recliner he's got and stare at the wall. And my mother just acts like he's got one foot in the grave and the other on a banana peel."

Sheila turned to me and asked, "Well, what have you given, Theresa?"

I sighed and crossed my legs. "Hell, I don't know. I'm sure I've given up something or another. I'm gonna have to think about that one."

Then she asked, "Theresa, are you still teaching?"

"Yes, that and trying to influence these little grown people at Collins School of International Studies to slow down."

"I know what you mean. I started doing volunteer work when I'm not at the bookstore. Going around to high schools, sitting in on leadership classes and talking to teenagers about self-worth. You know, some of these kids have never even heard of the seven principles of Kwanzaa?"

Nik chimed in with, "They probably asked what Kwanzaa's last name was. Which video she danced backup in."

We all laughed to lighten the mood, but we knew that there was nothing funny about it. Sheila pulled a newspaper from her handbag and placed it on the edge of the table. It had been folded in half and was bent around the edges, indicating that it definitely wasn't the latest edition. She took her index finger, pointed to some names that she had scribbled above a picture of the owner of Whose Is It and damn near made me fall out of that cheap plastic chair.

"This is why these kids need to slow down. This brother, Ray Lippons, is only thirty-two years old. His mother shouldn't have to bury him. *He* should be carrying on after *she's* gone. I don't question his lifestyle, because that plays such a minor part in his death. His irresponsibility is what is shortening his days. These kids aren't taking this stuff seriously. A future isn't an option with them. For example, the other day I spoke with a young girl who is supposed to graduate from Woodson High. She's pregnant and wants to go to college. She wants the father to join her so that they can raise the child together but he won't go."

Nikai asked, "So what did you tell her?"

"I told her to bring his butt up to the bookstore and let Byron have a few hours with him. Make that brotha think some things over."

Nikai added, "That's the only way, get all up in their mix. Show them that you're watching."

"No, what we want to do is show 'em that we *care*. So I worked some of my connections and found these brothas right here who knew this guy Ray. One of them admits to being his lover for some time. The other doesn't, but I've got my suspicions. His name is Vincent Lowery. He says—"

And right then, I lost it.

Realized *exactly* what category *I* fell into when it came to personal psychological strength and passed out in my plate of fettuccine at the mere mentioning of Vince's name.

"Why haven't we heard from you?!"

I wasn't even fully awake. My head was throbbing to the beat of Nelly's video on the television. He was moving across the screen wearing a cowboy hat and picking up women along a country road. Flashing his platinum medallion and representing his hometown like it was nobody's business. I realized I must've left the set on while waiting for Vince. I had a serious bone to pick with him and what I wanted to know couldn't wait.

"Theresa, you hear us talking to you!" my mother and stepfather yelled into the receiver.

Richard had picked up the other line, I'm assuming to make the situation appear as severe as possible. I was used to it by now.

From the time I was sixteen he's always pitted my mother and me against one another. I ignored him and answered, "I'm here, Mama."

"So what have you been doing that's keeping you so busy? You don't return my phone calls. I don't know what's goin' on with you. Dameron has been begging to speak to you for two days. I'm assuming you haven't stopped drinking yet! Have you?"

Richard yelled, "Probably not!"

"Would you please hang up the phone, Rich? I'm talking to my mother."

"Yeah but on my dime!"

"Then send me the bill! Now *please* hang up."

He slammed the receiver down so hard that it rattled my eardrum.

"Do I have to come up there to St. Louis and rescue my only child?"

Yeah right! When I needed that you were nowhere around. Don't try to sell me cheap now!

"Mama, I've been working and meeting with parents in the evenings. One of my kids at school—"

"And what about *your* parents and *your* kid?"

I rubbed my forehead and answered, "I know, I know. I was gonna call you this weekend. Is Dameron awake?"

I looked up at the large round chestnut Eddie Bauer clock above the bed. It was about eight-thirty in the P.M.

"He's asleep right now but the moment he gets up, he's gonna be whining. Don't you have to go to work in the morning?"

"Yes, Mama," I said, running my fingers through my tangled hair.

"So what's keeping you in bed all day? You'll never get to sleep tonight."

Vince knocked on the back door in the kitchen. I walked

through the apartment and unlocked it for him. Turned and
walked back into the bedroom.

"Theresa?"

"I'm here."

"It was nice having you home. I wish you would come back
for my birthday."

I hated it when she referred to Georgia as my home. It almost
sounded like she was waiting for me to come to my senses and
move back to Smyrna so that the four of us—she, Richard,
Dameron and myself—could all live happily ever after.

"I *am* home, Mama."

"Well, you know what I mean. Your cousins will all be here
from Chicago. You know your aunt Regina thinks she's something special 'cause Laura and Landers are bringing their kids
down for the weekend. She says they're gonna fly in that Thursday so they can get a full tour of Atlanta. You know, their kids
ain't been down here since they were babies, probably about
Dameron's age."

"Mama!"

"What?!"

"I'm gonna have to call you back, okay?"

"So are you coming home, baby?"

"I don't know. Can't make any promises right now."

"Well, I wanted to let you know that Lisa finally made it
around to the Women of Triumph meeting. And Terrence is
fine. She said his status came back negative, thank God. She
wants to talk to you, too. I gave her your number."

"That's fine."

"I know you. You must have company."

Vince removed his shirt and shorts. Lay down across my bed
on his back and stretched like he'd had a trying day. Made a
slightly irritating clucking noise, which I'd forgotten about, to

scratch the back of his throat and then tried to massage my shoulders from behind.

"Tell Vince I said hi."

"I will."

"Tell him now!"

I moved the receiver away from my mouth and said, "My mother says hello."

Vince lifted his hand and waved.

"He said hello."

"That's a good man you have there, Theresa—about as close as you'll ever get to Don. You better hold on to him because a lot of women would be willing to snatch him up."

"Yeah, he's a special kinda guy."

"All right, Theresa, I expect to hear from you."

"Talk to you later, Mama."

I hung up and sat down next to him as reality set in. I didn't know who the hell I was dealing with. We sighed at the same time and then looked in opposite directions. I doubt either of us knew what to say. Felt like we'd walked into a dead end. Our options were limited.

"So what happens now?" he asked.

"What do you mean?"

"I mean what do we do about us?"

I braced myself against the headboard to put a little space between us. He was giving off a negative vibe and I didn't exactly know how to come out and ask this.

"First things first. I need to talk to you about something else. Since we're friends first, I can trust that you won't lie to me."

"About what?"

"Did you meet with a woman by the name of Sheila?"

He held a poker face. "Yeah. She wanted to know about my boy Ray who grew up next door to me. His moms, Ms. Irene, dated my pops for years and when I went to see Pop at the hospital, I ran into her. You remember when she asked me to come and see Ray so I did. That's when that Sheila chick started asking me all of these questions like I'm fuckin' the cat or something. I didn't even know he was gay until she started insinuating that maybe *I* was."

I stared at him for a minute and prayed that he was telling the truth. I didn't want to have to second-guess my friend, didn't want to imagine him being a blatant liar.

He turned to me and quizzed, "So what happens now?"

Before I knew it the words had fallen off of my lips. "Are you HIV-positive, Vince?"

He gave a simple "No. Is that what Sheila told you?"

"No, I'm just asking."

I'd stood there staring at him, searching his face, for what felt like an hour when someone pressed the buzzer downstairs. Vince and I looked at one another.

"Who could that be?"

I shrugged my shoulders. "I don't know."

I got up and walked over to the apartment phone.

"Who is it?"

"Me and Sheila. We got a small package for you. I made some soup."

"Hold on a second."

I jogged back to the bedroom. "Get up!"

"Who is it?"

"Remember the woman you met with about Ray?"

"Yeah," he said, catching his airborne shorts as I tossed them across the bed.

"Well, she's right downstairs and waiting to come up."

"So?"

"So, she doesn't know that we know one another. Especially like this!"

"So what, you don't believe me?"

I threw on a pair of shorts and assured him, "Look, my back is against the wall right now. Just stay in here until they leave."

"So you *don't* believe me."

"I want to."

"But you don't."

Vince's shoulders slumped. The way he furrowed his brow reminded me of a neglected orphan. Then Nikai impatiently pressed the buzzer again.

"Let me put it like this: I'll always be your friend."

"Don't worry about it. Let me know when they're gone and I'll leave out the back door."

"Vince, you don't have to—"

Buzz, buzz, buzz.

"Sheila's waiting, Theresa."

I walked back toward the kitchen and pressed the button to release the door downstairs. Turned the television on in the living room, unlocked the door.

Nikai walked in behind Sheila carrying a large plastic bowl.

"Well, I"m glad the boogeyman wasn't on my heels."

"Be quiet, Nikai."

"Hey sis," Sheila greeted me.

She was wearing a long denim skirt and a red shirt with chiffon sleeves that flared out at the wrists. Nikai was in a simple black V-neck T-shirt dress that I remembered from back in the days when we first met. Sheila took a seat as Nikai seemed to head toward the bedroom.

"Where are you goin'?" I asked.

"To the bathroom. What, I didn't raise my hand and ask first, Ms. Downing?"

"I think the toilet is broken," I lied.

"You're kiddin'?"

I shook my head and began sniffing at the bowl of soup.

"Well, I'll just have to reach down into the back of it 'cause I've been holdin' this. Got a little nervous energy."

When she danced toward the back, Sheila scooted to the edge of the couch.

"You missed a good time last month when you went to Atlanta. Zenobia's club is really nice."

"I've heard a lot of good things about it. We still goin' this weekend?"

"It's up to you-all."

"Maybe that's just what I need, a night out."

"So what's the deal on the dreams?" she asked.

"I haven't had any more but right now, Sheila, real life is frightening enough."

"What do you mean?"

"You ever feel the need to second-guess everything you thought you knew?"

"Depends on what it is. First I had to learn to trust myself, trust my instincts. Otherwise, I'd probably be off point every time."

We could hear Nikai dropping something in the bathroom.

I asked, "What is she doing?"

"Nervous energy. She's been waiting to get over here and open a letter she got yesterday. Wanted us to be around in case she'd gotten rejected again. Kalif told me that this was the last one she'd try for."

"What is it?"

"She's trying to get an agent so she can get on with the next step in her singing career. At least land a few backup gigs."

Vince must've gotten up and moved around because Sheila darted her eyes at me when the hardwood floors in my bedroom creaked.

She asked, "Were we interrupting something?"

"Nope. The building is just old."

She looked up at the ceiling and then down at my Paul Good-night print called *Listen to the Hipbones*. It was a mint-green, brown and orange-reddish picture of three black women with their backs turned and their hands on their plentiful hips. I'd had it matted and framed at Lithos down on Delmar three months ago.

"I like that, Theresa."

"Thanks. I want to collect as many of his pieces as—"

"NOOOOOO! God, NOOO!!!"

There was a crash in the bathroom that was all too familiar. Wisdom or sincerity had hit the floor. I could hear that the glass candle holder had broken. My heart skipped a beat. Sheila jumped up. And to my dismay, Vince bolted from the bedroom wearing boxers and a T-shirt.

"You all right?!" he asked.

Sheila yelled, "Vince? Vince Lowery?!"

Nikai screamed again—but not as loudly as I was screaming on the inside. I pursed my lips at Vince and rolled my eyes. He looked at Sheila, then at me. Pivoted and scurried back into the bedroom like she was speaking German to a retarded child.

She asked me, "Wasn't that—"

Then came another piercing scream.

"Wait a minute, Theresa. We need to *talk*."

Sheila made a beeline to the bathroom, which gave me a chance to check on the retard.

I opened the door and he started with, "I didn't know what was happening. I thought you were hurt. Who was that yelling?"

"You don't know her."

"Sorry about that, Theresa."

"Not as sorry as I'm about to be. Please, just get dressed."

I could hear Nikai crying all the way in the bedroom. I stepped out and closed the door behind me, and walked down the hall. Sheila was holding Nikai by her head with one hand

and rubbing her back with the other. They were surrounded by shreds of paper, a small puddle of glass at their feet, and a dented candle.

I told them, "Don't worry about that stuff."

Sheila nodded and closed her eyes while she rocked.

"God will give you just what you need when you need it. Trust him, Nikai, trust him."

They stood in the bathroom rocking, crying and praying. Then Vince exited my bedroom, fully clothed.

He asked, "Everybody okay?"

"She should be fine," I said, walking him toward the front door.

I felt Sheila's eyes burning a hole in the back of my head as Vince hesitantly reached out to hug me but couldn't manage to dodge her judgmental stare. He finally settled for a one-arm embrace and started down the steps. I closed the door and went back to the bathroom.

Sheila squinted her eyes and looked at me like a displeased mother.

"You know all about him, don't you?" she asked.

"He's part of my past."

"But if you heard anything I said earlier, why are you making him a part of your present?"

"He says it's not true. It's a long story."

"Is that what you want your *tombstone* to read?! '*It's a long story.*' That brotha could be dangerous!"

"Sheila, that 'brotha' is my friend."

"Get in line, Theresa. He's also befriended a *dead man* in the same fashion."

"I know him! He's not HIV-positive."

Nikai looked up and wiped her eyes like she'd been in a three-year coma.

"What are y'all talkin' about?"

251

Sheila asked me, "And how do you know this?"

"He told me."

"And you honestly believe that he would tell you otherwise?"

"What are you basing this on, the fact that you *think* he's bisexual? For all Zenobia knows, David is HIV-positive. Do you think he's told her his status? Hell, we could all be lying!"

I was becoming louder and angry. I don't know, maybe it was because I didn't have any test results to support my defense. All I had was Vince's word, which to Sheila didn't amount to shit.

Nikai asked, "Who are we talking about?"

"The guy I interviewed about Ray Lippons, the club owner who's dying of AIDS."

Nikai looked at me. "Theresa, is that true?"

"Is *what* true?"

She tilted her head like she didn't want to have to repeat the accusation.

"Yes, I've slept with him. We had protected sex but no, I don't know for certain if he's negative or positive."

"And he knew Ray Lippons?"

Sheila interjected with, "Knew him *well.*"

"They grew up together!"

They went on scolding and badgering me like a Jerry Springer audience does trailer trash. I had to stand there and defend not only my honor, but Vince's as well. An honor that I wasn't even certain he was worthy of. He had hurt me. But he'd also been more than a lover at one time. And he'd damn sure been more of a friend than these two were looking like at the moment.

Nikai asked, "What were you thinking?"

"She couldn't have been."

"You wanna know what I was thinking? I was thinking about the fact that neither of you understand me or what I'm going through. When I'm sittin' here sifting through boxes of Don's things, nobody comes along and wipes my tears. Nobody is re-assuring me that I'll ever find real love again. But of course you-all wouldn't. You have it already. So if I have to take the word of someone who is considerate enough to be there for me even if it's only from time to time, then protected, emotionally safe sex will just have to suffice."

Sheila folded her arms and leaned heavily on one leg.

"Are you through?"

I didn't respond. Rolled my eyes and threw my hands on my hips.

"Did you ever consider the idea that just maybe Don's death was intended for you to grow? You spend so much time coming up with reasons why you can't move past this and it's killing you to move past that. Nikai has told me all about how you lock the door, turn off the light, grab a bottle of whatever and feel sorry for yourself. Now tell me, has it helped? Has putting your life on the line with careless sex made you feel any better? Has it changed the fact that you're single? Because not once have you mentioned that your homey-lover-friend has denounced his bi-sexuality for a monogamous relationship with you."

"He's not bisexual!"

"*Whatever!* You better think, girl! I spent thirty-four years of my life waiting for my husband to find me. You've only been at this for twenty-nine. So you cry? You're not the only one who feels pain. But the same sun will shine upon a new day for you just like it did for us. Nikai went through pure *hell!* You saw it. You were there. So no, I don't want an invitation to your pity party! When you decide to start celebrating your life and the life of your child, call me. I'll be the first guest present."

Sheila brushed past Nikai, walked into the living room, grabbed her purse from the couch and stormed out of the door.

"I don't even know why you brought her over here," I told Nikai.

She stooped down and began picking pieces of glass off the floor. "Maybe it was meant for her to see Vince."

"But you do see where I'm coming from, don't you? I should be able to have anyone I want as a friend."

"But I thought you said he cheated on you, Theresa. The most I would think you would want to do is be cordial. Speaking on the street is one thing but this is just a recipe for trouble."

"So you're agreeing with Sheila?"

"Let me put it to you like this: When you stumble around in the dark, you never find what you're looking for. You only get bumps and bruises, which you usually end up having to explain when you finally step into the light."

The nerve of her!

Zenobia

"Z! Yo, Z! Wake up!"

"What, boy? Quit callin' me like that!"

Maurice had cracked my bedroom door and was yellin' like the house was on fire. Caused me to knock David's manuscript, which I'd fallen asleep reading, onto the floor.

"Payce is downstairs."

I rubbed the sleep from my eyes and pulled my panties out of my butt. Ironically, I was wearing one of Payce's triple-XL gray T-shirts from '96. It was about the only thing other than Zaire that I'd hung on to of his. I lay back down, tossed my braids over onto the other pillow and pulled the blue and green plaid sheet up to my chin.

"What time is it?"

"Seven-thirty."

"Send 'im up here."

"Ah'ight. I'm about to be out too."

"Where you goin'?" I asked from under the covers.

"I'm goin' to check on some summer classes at the community college."

I looked up and asked, "For real?"

"Yeah. Me and Trisha started talking about what we're gonna do with a baby and can't get a decent job. So I decided that I'd take a step in that direction so she can finish up high school next year."

"She tell her parents yet?"

"Nope. Oh yeah, some dude named David called this morning too. I told him to call you back in about an hour. That was almost forty-five minutes ago. And Trisha just took a message for you from an Elizabeth. She wanted to know if you could come in for an interview this morning."

"All right. Well, you be careful."

"Always," he assured me, pulling the door open.

"Hey, Maurice!"

"What's up?"

"I'm proud of you."

He grinned and then rubbed the corners of his thin mustache. "You be careful too, Z. You the only sister I got. Oh, and by the way, I gave Zaire some cereal. She's downstairs playin' with Payce. And it looks like he signed another contract."

"Why do you say that?"

"You'll see. You still want him to come up?"

"Nah, I'm awake now. Tell him I'll be down in a minute."

When Maurice closed the door, I grabbed the remote to the stereo and pressed play. Track number eight on my *Who Is Jill Scott?* CD permeated the air in my bedroom. Put David on my mind—his sense of humor and rhythmic stride *made* a woman wanna sing. Not to mention the fact that it was looking like I'd finally get a chance to tell Payce to kiss my ass.

I did a little two-step while I drew the curtains back so some sunlight could shine in, then made my bed. As I was bending over to tuck the ends of the sheet, I heard a knock at the door.

"Who—"

Payce walked in, with Zaire straddling his neck. She ducked as he cleared the threshold and sat in one of the two wicker chairs Lainey and I bought at Pier 1 last summer. He placed

Zaire on his lap, stretched his arms and yawned like I was making a bed we *shared*.

A gold Ecko shirt fit his linebacker build with precision. Anyone could see how cut up his form was, even through the baggy denim shorts. Payce had gotten bigger over the years—hell, it appeared over the last week. His thick and massive neck housed a platinum chain that offset the one-carat-diamond stud in his ear. I could tell it was new by the way he fondled it when he pulled Zaire over his head and set her down. He was about as used to it as I was to him lounging in my sleeping quarters.

Payce asked, "What's up?"

"Nothin' you couldn't wait downstairs to hear about."

"Looks like you're missin' me," he said, pointing to the T-shirt of his I was wearing.

"You wish. Did you bring her new clothes?"

"No, I'm gonna bring 'em when I drop her off on Sunday. Looks like Maurice has been liftin'."

"He works out a lot."

I pulled a pair of shorts from the dresser drawer and put them on. Felt his eyes moving up my thighs along with the material. His voyeur's grin made the act seem dirty.

"What's up with you gettin' your number changed? Runnin' from somebody's brother again?"

"Cute. Real cute, Zenobia. Too many people had it."

I sat down in a matching wicker chair across the room next to the window. That's when I noticed a big-ass black Hummer truck parked in my driveway. I leaned back and asked, "Is that you down there?"

"Got it yesterday," he said like he'd pulled up in a pea-green '87 Nova instead.

"You're doin' it like that but can't hire somebody to help me in the office?"

"The money I make in the league is separate from the money

257

I make at the club. I don't even count that when I'm goin' over losses and earnings."

"What, it spends differently? It's all green if you ask me."

"Looks like *you* are too."

I flipped him the bird and asked Zaire to go in her room until I could finish talking to her daddy. When I heard her skip down the stairs, I looked at Payce and asked, "So who is she?"

"Who is who?"

"The woman you had to get your number changed for. I know you. There's a story behind everything you do."

"You got the wrong man."

"So you goin' to another team? I know something has happened. You're walkin' around here lookin' like you just won the Best Rap Album of the Year Award."

"Why, you tryin' to hop around butt naked in my video?"

"Only if I'm dancin' in the spot right next to yo' momma."

That shut him up. Payce gave me a twisted look. Then asked, "You sure you and Cammie aren't workin' together?"

"Cammie's too slow to work with me. Plus she don't know you like I do. And come to think of it, I think she is a habitual liar 'cause I've been watching Zaire and she's not cried in her sleep once."

Payce gave me a look as if to say I should have believed him in the first place.

"What did I tell you? She's a drama queen and she probably just wanted to turn you against me. She knows I love Zookie and she knew you keeping her from me would hurt. That's her whole objective. Plus I think she figured as long as you hated me you wouldn't want to be with me, you know?"

"Well, I guess that says something about you. Have to ask yourself what it is about you that attracts drama queens."

"All right now, Zenobia. How is that new cat doin'?"

"What 'new cat'?"

"Beacon or whatever you said his name was. The bartender."

I crossed my legs. "He's all right, I guess. A little strange."

"What do you mean by that?"

"I don't know. I may be overreacting but he always seems like he's trying to get close."

"To who, you?"

"Yeah."

Payce sat forward and began to rub his fist with his other hand. "How long has he been pushin' up on you?"

"Nothing like that!"

I shrugged my shoulders and then fanned my hand in dismissal of the subject.

"I don't know. It's probably nothing."

"Are you sure? Because—"

The phone rang and cut him off. I jumped up and answered it.

"Hello?"

"It feels so good to hear your voice," David said.

He had more of an accent in the morning. His voice was even deeper, more intriguing. I looked back at Payce and turned around to face the wall and the large oil painting of my mother that hung over my bed. "It feels good to hear yours too. How are you?"

"Everything is cool. I was just about to get in the shower and I wanted to make sure we're still on for today."

"Still stands. I've got to make a run but I'll be available this evening."

"So I'll see you later."

"See you then. Be careful."

As soon as I put the receiver down, I could hear Payce sighing. When I turned around he was standing closer to the door.

"You could've asked me to wait downstairs."

"And you could've asked before you brought your ass up here."

Payce pointed at the phone. "He new?"

"*He's my business.* You don't ask me about mine and I don't ask you about yours, remember?"

"That's tacky, Zenobia. Real tacky. You know, you're a mother now."

"And I'm also a woman!"

"But you're a mother first. You have a responsibility to my child that far outweighs some chump tryin' to get in your bed!"

"What?!"

"You heard me."

"You don't even know David!"

"Yeah, I never know any of them. Coincidence?"

"Well, it's better than the tired-ass sista-girl relationships you expect me to form with every amateur crackhead, beauty pageant reject you decide to drag home from the security gate at the dome!"

"They're fans!"

"They're *groupies!*"

"If you have a problem with me, you keep this between me and you. Nobody else!"

"My point exactly! You don't know David from Beacon so leave his name out of your mouth."

He turned his lips up, squinted his eyes with fury and shook his head. "You think this is gonna get you married? Nobody is gonna marry you, Zenobia. You got that black woman attitude problem, no education and you're too fuckin' hard to get along with. You did good gettin' this house and that change I kicked you down."

"Go to hell, Payce!"

"No, *you* go to hell. You don't know the first thing about what a man wants—how are you gonna make somebody happy?

You'll get screwed until he's sick of your mouth and needy ways. Just like I did."

"Get out!"

He walked down the hall and scooped Zaire up in his arms. Descended the steps and then turned around just inside the foyer. "Tell me it didn't happen that way. Show me a man who didn't take advantage of you and I'll show you a fool."

As I listened to the front door close, I ran back into my bedroom and flopped down on the side of the bed. Glanced over at David's manuscript on the nightstand as tears slowly blurred my vision. I hated Payce with every fiber of my being. But what I hated more was that he'd come frighteningly close to the truth. I had allowed myself to be used by men, had been called needy by more members of the male species than just him, and sometimes I wondered if maybe it was all my fault. I knew in that moment that I needed to regain control of my situation. I grabbed the phone from its cradle and dialed Elizabeth back and told her that she could expect me at eleven. Then I left David a message to let him know that he shouldn't be expecting me at all.

It felt strange to be on the other side of the desk shaking hands.

I tossed my braids over my shoulder, straightened the back of my simple black business dress and took a seat in one of the chairs across from Elizabeth. She had thick, curly, dark brown hair and an oval face. Bright eyes and a pleasant smile. Made me feel as though she really wanted me to have this position.

She toyed with the tip of a pen and perused my resume again. Placed it down on the desk and folded her hands in front of her. "So we finally meet. I was very impressed with your resume, Ms. Hall."

"Call me Zenobia."

"Okay, Zenobia. And although we prefer a bachelor's degree, I get the feeling that you would be an asset here. Would you tell me a little bit about yourself?"

"Well, I attended the University of Missouri for three years and majored in business."

"Specialization?"

"Management. And then my beautiful daughter came into my life. Let's see, I'm goal-oriented, I learn quickly and I'm a self-starter."

She smiled. "When I had my son I took some time off, but the thing is that you have to get back into the saddle."

"I agree."

"So tell me what attracted you to the position."

"Well, I'm looking for a company with opportunities for growth and creativity. I'm interested in expanding my knowledge from a business aspect."

"Well, I like what I see but I can't make any promises today because there are other applicants applying for this position. But you should be hearing from me very soon. I'd also like to remind you that Shoner Industries offers one hundred percent tuition reimbursement after the first year of employment with the promise that you'll remain with us for three years. I want to thank you for coming in on such short notice. As I've mentioned, Mr. Shoner dropped this in my lap pretty much in the same manner."

She stood and extended her hand. "Again, it's nice meeting you and I hope that you have a good day, Ms. Hall."

I ran the brief interview through my mind during the drive home. It was sorta hard to read what the outcome would be. At times she gave me promising looks and then at others she made it seem like it was all a toss-up. I pulled up on Tenner's Way and put the gearshift into park. Closed my eyes and lay back against the headrest. This job would make a big difference in my life. I looked over at my large beautiful home and suddenly it didn't look like shit to me. It was a shell, a toy that Payce hung over my head to keep me in check. Maurice was right—it *was* Payce's house. And I wanted something of my own.

In the rearview mirror, I caught sight of a car pulling up behind me. When I focused, I recognized David's face. He got out in a pair of khaki pants, a tan ethnic short-sleeved shirt and brown sandals. Walked up to my driver's side window and tucked his hands into his pockets. I rolled the window down and leaned against the door.

"Hi. I guess you got my message."

"Yeah, I did. What's going on?"

"Life is going on, David."

"You mind if I get in and sit with you for a while?"

"Go right ahead."

He stared at me as he walked around the front of the car and got in. We sat and didn't talk until he broke the silence.

"I went and saw a movie this morning."

"Really? Was it good?" I asked.

"I don't know. I saw it but didn't hear much. I was thinking about you. Wondering where things went wrong, what changed in the matter of minutes between the time that I'd last talked to you and when you left that message."

I turned to him and said, "You want to move full speed ahead and you don't even know me."

"I know enough."

I shook my head. "No you don't! You don't know if I'm needy or . . ."

"Are you?"

"Yes! Very!"

He shrugged his broad shoulders. "Okay, who isn't to a certain degree?"

"I'm just saying that you don't know me."

"Okay, Zenobia, tell me who you are. Where are your parents?"

I scoffed and shook my head again. "Are you serious?"

"Yes. Tell me about your parents."

"They died about six months apart. My father had a heart attack, my mother died in her sleep."

"Any siblings?"

"I have a little brother who lives with me."

"You-all taking care of one another?"

"More like me taking care of him. But Maurice is a good kid, just a little misguided."

"I'd like to meet him sometime."

I smiled. "Well, we'll have to arrange something then, won't we?"

"So did you get a chance to read the excerpt?"

"I sure did, and it was truly moving. The way the guy was torn between all of the women in his life was so unfair. You can be loyal to someone and not let them control you, but his family couldn't see that. What happens in the end?"

"Well, his family raises so much hell that his wife takes his daughter and leaves. At some point she is obligated to take her happiness into her own hands. Especially considering the way that her husband turned a deaf ear to the way his family made her feel. That's not love. That's what you call being desperate to pull things together even at the risk of sacrificing someone who has done nothing to cause you any pain."

"Is that your story?"

"No, but a lot of mama's boys who haven't gained respect as adults are living this story."

"So have you decided on a title?"

"Nope. Have you thought of one for me?"

"No, but I can. I mean if that's what you want."

"I would be flattered."

"Then flatter you is what I'll do. But you can't laugh if it sounds corny. I'm no writer."

"I promise."

I blushed. Then David took my hand in his and asked, "So tell me, Zenobia, are you a hot or a cold person?"

"By that you mean, what?"

"Well, I'd say a hot person is full of energy, looking for a good time around each and every corner. A cold person would be someone who's content and is able to alter their surroundings according to their needs without searching for a good time else-where."

I said, "I guess that would make me warm."

David laughed. "And why do you say that?"

"I'm never one way or the other. I'm usually in between hot and cold."

"Safe answer."

"And what about you?" I asked.

"I'm a cool brotha. I'm leaning more toward cold. My focus is home. I want a wife and kids so maybe after a few years we can move back to the islands, buy some property."

He had me until that part about moving to an island. That was nowhere in my plans. Plus, there would be no family here for Maurice. All we have is one another, and no man or love affair is strong enough to break that bond.

David asked, "Why so quiet on me all of a sudden?"

"No reason."

"A penny for your thoughts."

I smiled. "Lainey says be careful what you wish for."

"Well, I wish you would consider taking this relationship one day at a time and not duck out before even trying."

I laughed. "You put more pressure on a sista than a bill collector."

265

"Figure if I throw enough mud against the wall something ought to stick."

"Or fall and leave a mess for you to clean up."

"Some things are worth the effort."

"For instance?"

Before he could answer, my cell phone rang. I held up my index finger and answered on the second ring.

"Good afternoon, black woman. What's goin' on?"

I smiled, looked at David and told Sheila, "I'm sitting here talking with our friend."

"And who might that be? David? Tell him I said hello."

I moved the receiver from my mouth. "Sheila says hi."

He waved his hand. "Greetings and salutations."

"So what's goin' on with you and Nikai?"

"She's upstairs talking on the phone with Theresa. I had to get off of the line with that girl before I exploded. She's making mistakes, life-threatening mistakes."

"What kind, Sheila?"

"Wait a second. Hol' on."

I could hear her yelling over a long distance to someone—annoyance lacing her every word.

"Yeah, Nikai says Theresa's gonna go with us. We're gonna do a little shopping and then get together later. You still hanging out with us?"

"What time are we talking?"

"We'll be ready at about two."

"Can you meet me at my house?" I asked.

"Yeah, give me the address."

"4219 Tenner's Way."

"That's out by Hazelwood East High School?"

"Two miles south of it. But David and I have a date later so I can't hang out for long."

"All right, sweetie."

When I hung up and placed the phone back in my handbag, I could tell that something had changed. Then David said, "I've been known to voice my desires too quickly. I hope I haven't scared you?"

"No, I've got some fears to move through but I don't scare *that* easily."

"Well, I'm gonna try and make sure that you're never afraid again."

"That's a big job, David."

"Like I said, some things are worth the effort."

I pushed my braids over my shoulder and fell into his arms. Relaxed as I sank into his massive embrace. Felt that maybe he was the one man that I could trust and there was no longer a need to protect my heart. So I gave myself freely to the passion of his kiss.

I opened my eyes and said, "You've just got all *kinds* of plans for me, huh?"

He nodded. "Now if I can just get you to relax and stop fighting."

David leaned back and rested one arm on the windowsill.

"I'm not fighting you, David."

"I'm just kidding with—"

"It's just that I'm bracing myself for a struggle."

He sat forward and gave me an inquisitive stare. "And why is that?"

I sighed and continued, "You sort of get used to certain things after so long. I've struggled with Payce, I've struggled with my parents, struggled with work, struggled with my little brother. Sometimes it seems that struggle is all I know."

"You ever stop to think that maybe nobody else really wants to fight and are maybe just acting in self-defense?"

"What do you mean? Like I'm the one who initiates confrontation?"

He shrugged his shoulders. "Okay, we can entertain that thought. Seems as though you feel like you're gonna lose something."

"Something like that?"

"What don't you want to lose the most?"

"My child."

"Next to that."

I laughed. "My mind."

"Okay, next to that."

The car became quiet as I remembered the battle with my parents. How they wanted me to move back to St. Louis and how I really had no reason not to other than the fact that it wasn't initially my idea. Then I thought about how crippled I felt when Payce toyed with me about Zaire. Thought of how I beat myself up with disappointment over wasted years. Years that could have been spent getting my degree so that I could work the type of job that I chose. Lastly Maurice flashed through my mind and how I'd been checking on him four or five times a day for the last six years. How maybe it was my fault that he'd been so irresponsible, since I had never truly made him responsible for anything. I was a puppeteer promising freedom to someone who knew from experience that nothing would go down without me approving of it first. And that's when it became clear to me what I feared most, what sent me barreling into a frenzy.

"Control."

David asked, "Excuse me."

"Control. I don't want to lose control of my life and the situations that occur in it. I guess I feel like if I have my hands in everything, or shall I say *on* everything, nothing can go wrong."

"Do you believe in a higher being?"

"Of course."

"Do you believe in fate or would you say that a lot of events that take place are random?"

"It depends. Where is this going?"

"I'm just wondering if you really believe that you *have* been in control this far. I mean, the way I see it is you can want something for your entire life but if it is not yours, if it is not what the Creator desires for you, you won't receive it. No fight, no struggle and no level of control is more powerful than divine order."

"So what are you saying?"

"That everything is being controlled by the Creator—everything, Zenobia. Even this relationship between me and you."

"Hell, she might as well have crawled in the bed with the both of 'em!"

I said, "Be quiet, Sheila! These walls are paper-thin."

That was the second time I'd had to warn her. We were hanging out at my house after Nikai and Sheila picked Theresa up for an afternoon of shopping and lunch. And as soon as Theresa had asked to use my bathroom, Sheila started in. She had rolled the red chiffon sleeves up on her shirt, taken a seat on the sofa in my living room and proceeded to give me the lowdown on Theresa's apparent death wish.

"I'm tellin' you I thought I would fall out on the floor when I saw him come runnin' out of her bedroom. It was almost like it happened in slow motion."

"Sheila, please," Nikai begged.

Sheila looked at me. "Nobody thinks this is a big deal but me."

Nikai retorted, "I think it's a big deal but repeating it a thousand times won't change the scenario. You know something has truly got to be wrong with that girl if she's making sense of sleeping with a—"

Nikai stopped there, looked up at Theresa, who was now

standing on the threshold, and then shook her head at Sheila as if to say that it was her fault for even bringing it up again.

"What am I sleeping with?"

Nobody said a word. We sat still, like insects trying to blend in with our surrounding.

"Sheila?" Theresa asked.

Sheila looked up, undaunted. *"What?"*

Theresa walked down the two steps into the living room and sat in my cream leather chair against the wall.

"Tell me what I'm sleeping with. You should know. You just talked to him the other day, got all up in his business like you were in the least bit concerned about him as a *brotha*. That *is* what you refer to all black men as, right? Unless of course they're a . . . Now that's the part I didn't get. So tell me, *what* is Vince? What am I sleeping with, dammit?!"

"Theresa."

I stood up and reached out for her but she moved her leg, and on any other day I would've sworn she tried to kick me.

"Stay out of this, Zenobia. You don't know Vince like Sheila does. Apparently *nobody* does, so give her a chance to fill us the fuck in!"

Sheila rose to her feet. Theresa followed.

Then Nikai reasoned, "Come on, y'all. It's not that serious."

I chimed in with, "Will somebody *please* change the subject?"

"I swear. I thought this was *my* pity party. I'm the one who keeps getting rejected by record companies."

It was as though Nikai and I hadn't uttered a word. Theresa and Sheila stood there, hands planted firmly on their hips, scowls across their faces with pride dangling from a thin thread.

Then Sheila broke the silence with, "Theresa, I'm only trying to help."

"Okay, well how about this? Keep your fuckin' opinions to yourself when it's concerning me."

"You didn't seem to think my opinions were so useless when you couldn't get a decent night's sleep, or did that have something to do with the fact that you knew your little escapades with your homey-lover-friend would eventually prove to be fatal?"

"All right, Sheila, you're out of order," I warned.

"She's always trying to help somebody but can't see the shit that's goin' on right underneath her nose," Theresa said.

I asked, "What are you talking about?"

"Tell her, Nikai!"

Nikai sank farther into the sofa and covered her eyes with her hand.

"Tell me what?" Sheila asked. She looked over at Nikai and then back to Theresa, who finally said, "You wanna help somebody? Help Nikai figure out who the father of her baby is!"

"*What!?*" rang throughout the first floor of my house.

"I'm tired of y'all looking at me like I'm the only one in the room with issues. Age ain't got a damn thing to do with wisdom! You're dealing with shit like the rest of us. The only difference is that the older you get, *the less you tell* 'cause you feel that we think you should know better. But you're no better than me! *Anyone who has a heart* will have problems, can be fooled and can fall in love for all of the wrong reasons! So all of y'all, just leave me the hell alone!"

Theresa's flawless vanilla complexion turned to a beet-red shade of hurt as the tears welled up in her eyes and spilled forth like a dam of denial had burst inside of her. Her pride, still dangling from that thread, wouldn't allow her to move, to break that statuesque form of strength, even after it had become clear that it was no longer part of her being. Her body began to shake and as if on cue Nikai and I both jumped up to hold her. We could barely hear Sheila's frustrated sigh over the painful moaning that rose from the pit of Theresa's stomach.

She cried, "Don't *do* this to me, Sheila. *Please,* don't *do* this to me."

Her words of weakness and vulnerability touched a corner of my soul and brought forth tears from both me and Nikai.

"I don't deserve this, y'all. I haven't done anything to anybody. I've *never* hurt anybody."

We had formed a circle around her. One that wasn't complete because Sheila was still standing across the room like a mother refusing to admit a wrongdoing to her children.

Nikai comforted her with, "We know, honey. You were only doing what you felt in your heart, and you are not wrong for that. Nobody can say you're wrong for that."

Sheila slowly lifted one foot at a time and started toward us, the heavy denim of her lengthy skirt grunting reluctantly as it rubbed against the carpet. Nikai and I opened up the circle for her to complete, offered a shoulder for her tears, which she now found hard to control.

"We are all flowers, delicate flowers, each with our own set of issues," Sheila preached. "Though Nikai has proven to be the most hardheaded of us all."

We nodded in agreement.

"And I don't want to see any of you-all hurt."

She looked me in the eyes. "*Any* of you."

"Sistas have been sacrificing one another since the beginning of time. We do it by not warning one another about foreseen heartache, and I can't be that kind of friend. In fact that's not a friend *at all.* The relationships that I've formed since Nikai and I met are important to me. I'm the oldest here by about six years and sometimes I want to help you-all so badly that I end up doing more harm than good. I'm sorry, Theresa, but it's my desire to nurture and protect you as my sister that makes me so angry, that makes me careless with your feelings. And for that, *I* am wrong. Please, please, forgive me."

"I forgive you," Theresa said.

Then Nikai yelled. "Well, I don't. I don't believe you, Theresa!"

"Shut up! You've been sittin' back like the Virgin Mary while I get *bashed* over the head, and your news is worse than any I've heard in a long time."

Sheila said, "Just don't tell me the brotha puts out fires for a living. Anybody but him. Tell me you think it may be Bob Barker's baby, Enrique Iglesias'. Anybody but Robert Hayes."

Nikai mumbled, "Then I won't tell you anything."

The sudden ringing of the phone interrupted our moment. When I walked up into the kitchen and answered it, Lainey was on the line yellin' like a wild banshee.

"Where have you been?!"

"I had an interview and then I was with David. Why?"

"There's been a change of plans. MrVLRuns sent an e-mail this morning. They're gonna meet at his apartment at four o'clock."

"Okay."

"'Okay'?! So we need to be there!"

I sighed and leaned against the island in the kitchen.

"All right, Lainey, but I've got a date tonight."

"What time?"

"Probably about seven-thirty."

"With who?"

"David."

"So you like him, huh?"

"He's nice."

"I remember you said the same thing when you met Payce in Chicago."

"Well, believe me there's a big difference between Payce and David."

"Oh yeah? And what's that?"

273

"I wouldn't hit David with a moving vehicle."

We both laughed. Hers dwindled into a dim exhale.

Then Lainey asked, "You think I'm stupid, don't you?"

I glanced down into the living room, where the imbalanced female energy had caused tempers to flare, and observed how everything seemed to have calmed down once love, comfort and the Creator had been placed back into the equation.

Then I told Lainey, "You know what? You're just struggling."

"'Struggling'?"

"Yeah, you're fighting a losing battle against yourself. Nobody else has a strategy but you. Cedric is not sitting somewhere devising a plan the way that you are."

Silence stretched across the line, and I imagined that some of David's gems of knowledge were seeping in. Then Lainey broke the silence with a brusque "Shut up, Zenobia, and have your ass ready at three-thirty. I'll blow."

As she let me go, I realized that our circle still wasn't complete because Lainey was part of our floral arrangement too, whether she knew it or not.

Zenobia

"Okay, the address is 2043 West Keller Place."

I closed the door on the driver's side and looked over at Lainey. She acted as though she was giving me directions to Six Flags Over Mid-America instead of some unknown man's home who she suspected was sleeping with her husband.

"I don't believe we're doing this," I said.

That was intended to make her rethink the whole idea. It went in one ear and out the other. She brushed the lint off of her black cargo capri pants and buckled up like I hadn't opened my mouth.

Lainey asked, "You hungry? I got some coupons for a two-piece and fries with a biscuit."

"I don't believe you."

"What?"

"You're sittin' there like this is no big deal."

"What would you like me to do, pull matchin' skullcaps out of the glove compartment? We're just gonna park up the street and see what goes on there."

"Which is none of our business," I countered, pulling off.

"Speak for yourself. So what's been happening?"

"Well, I told you that David and I are having a good time, and that I interviewed for that human resources position I was telling you about and I think I may get it. I should be hearing soon. I'm thinking about moving out of Payce's house. I had to send Jeff back home to his baby's momma and Maurice decided to get married."

"What?!"

"Yeah, married. He's got a baby on the way. My little brother is growing up. He's not a little knothead kid anymore. He's making his own kids."

"What about making his own living?"

"Oh, yeah! He's going to school and he's gonna get another job so he can save some money. But they're gonna stay with me until he gets on his feet."

"All right now. Don't become a crutch. I've seen situations where people say they're gonna eventually move out and the next thing you'll know Maurice's kids will be registered for school under your address."

"Well, trust me, that's not gonna happen."

I took I-170 south to I-70 East. Rode through what some consider the hood, and past the Bissell Mansion where dinner-theater shows reminded me of the game Clue. Lainey pressed the play button so that Amel Larieux's "Infinite Possibilities" would pour from my back speakers and then reclined her seat. We rode in the quiet of our own thoughts. My mind had wandered back to the way that I felt in David's arms, then on to him sharing his desire to eventually leave the United States to go back home. That was the only thing that made me fearful of getting close to him—I couldn't leave my family. All I had was Maurice, and I couldn't imagine being without him. I glanced over at Lainey and thought about what little she had as well. Cedric had become her life. Her parents were dead, she was an only child and she had lost contact with the few family members she had back in the town of Lafayette, Louisiana. If she found what she was afraid she might today, I couldn't imagine what kind of condition it would leave her in.

I pressed the pause button on the CD player and asked, "So what exactly are you looking for, Lainey?"

She didn't bother to open her eyes when she responded.

"The truth."

"Okay. Could you be a little more specific?"

She lifted the back of the seat and said, "I need to know whether or not I should be packing up and going back home."

"What?"

"You heard me, Zenobia. If Cedric is gay, I'm going back down South. I don't need this shit. I'm only thirty, in good shape, making decent money and I don't have any kids yet. I'm ripe for pickin'."

"Sounds like you're getting ready with your southern clichés," I said laughing.

"Call it what you want but today determines my tomorrow. I don't have anything here. You've got your child, a house, your brother and you're about to fall in love with a big-dick Virgin Island native. I've got to start layin' some foundations too."

I wanted to say that going back down South didn't guarantee that, but with the way she'd just sized my life up as opposed to hers, I thought it would sound selfish.

"And if he's not gay, Lainey, then what?"

"Then I need to know why he's not in love with me."

We rode another two miles and then I asked, "Are you in love with him?"

"Jesus loved Judas, too," she said.

"Lainey, why did you marry Cedric? And tell me the truth."

She ran her hands down her legs like she was attempting to wipe sweat from her palms and then propped her elbow up against the window. Rested her forehead on the tips of her fingers and then sighed.

"Because I knew he wouldn't do what my grandfather did to my grandmother and what my father did to my mother. I married him, Zenobia, because I knew that he wouldn't ever leave me. Love had nothing to do with it."

As she spoke, tears formed in her eyes. Couldn't tell if they were from guilt or from fear that maybe what she thought she'd prevent was happening anyway.

I held her hand and whispered, "You know that's not fair, don't you?"

She nodded and then shamefully stared down into her lap.

"I did it because it was a sure thing, not to hurt anybody. I knew that I would never leave him."

"But you're prepared to."

"But only because I will have been wronged."

"And Cedric hasn't been?"

I could tell by her refusal to respond that she had answered the question. Lainey had been moving in fear, hurting her husband whether he knew it or not, yet trying her best not to get hurt. And all this meant was that regardless of the outcome, the only victim here would be Cedric.

When I-70 turned into I-55, I took it around to I-44 and hopped off on the Grand/Louisiana exit. Made a left and passed Tower Grove Park. Crossed over Shenandoah and Magnolia. I had ridden less than two miles when rainbow flags that lined storefronts and quaint retro and vintage spots began to pop up all over the place. Lainey looked over at me as she continued wiping her palms on her pants.

I asked her, "What's the address again?"

She repeated it through a shaky voice, not one which someone bold enough to be watching a stranger's house should possess. We killed the air conditioning, rolled the windows down and observed blocks of restaurants and barbershops. There were restaurants to visit for everything from Indian to Vietnamese to Mexican cuisine. Spots where one could buy erotic material of all sorts were sandwiched between pet shops and coffee houses. Men strolling with the sashay of Diana Ross back in the day when the Supremes ruled the world maneuvered their way through huddled masses of women with the nonverbal intimidation method of the NFL's Warren Sapp on a bad day. It was a world neither Lainey nor I had ever known about. As I reached inside my handbag and pulled out a piece of the quilt and began to rub it, Lainey said, "This is it right here, West Keller Place. Turn right at this corner and see if it's down here."

I followed her instructions and found myself on a street of large two-story brick houses. Another two blocks down and we ran into a group of condominiums with the same address as the one that was sent to Cedric.

I said, "Okay, Lainey, the entire building is 2043. There's got to be at least thirty condos up there."

I was trying to get her to change her mind so we could get the hell away from there. This was a *man's* home we were spying on, not that of some catty woman who maybe at least *one* of us could take down just in case some shit jumped off.

"All right, shut the engine off."

"What?"

"Shut the engine off. We're already lookin' suspect. Let's just try to blend in."

"And just how in the hell are we supposed to do that without me leaning over and kissing you in the damn mouth?"

"Don't play," she joked. "I keeps a shank in my purse."

I cut the engine and pressed the pause button on the CD player so that I could at least mentally escape. More cars began to pull up behind us as Amel sang of sweet misery and Lainey continued to stare out of the window at smoke billowing in the air.

"Smells like bar-be-cue," she said.

I glanced in my rearview. "Looks like we just pulled up into the middle of a party, and you know what that makes us."

"What?"

"Uninvited guests."

Vince

The only bad thing about living in my neighborhood was the parking. When I got back to my place from dropping some manuscripts off at the office, the guy downstairs who was always blasting music had allowed what looked like ten or twelve cars to park in spaces that are usually occupied by tenants.

I ended up parking about a block away. Started up the sidewalk and had only gotten halfway when a light-skinned woman sitting on the passenger side of a car near the steps smiled and beckoned me with her index finger.

I nodded my head as I approached the car and said, "Ladies?"

"How are you doing? I was wondering if you liked"—

Then the brown-skinned driver wearing braids cut the passenger off with, "Wondering if you liked living over here. It seems a bit noisy."

I looked back down the sidewalk and noticed two guys walking toward the condo under mine, where there was apparently a party being thrown.

"We've got a few new people but it's usually quiet. You-all thinking about moving in?"

"We're just observing. Seems like a mixed crowd."

"Yeah, we've got the elderly and a lot of middle-aged people with families in the area. You're welcome to come up and see my place. I'm not the best interior decorator but you can get the general idea."

"Sure, we—"

That was the passenger.

"We'll have to think about it. Let us sit here a little while longer so we can decide if the noise would become an issue. Thanks." That was the driver.

"All right, I'm on the fourth floor, unit G. You ladies take care."

I tapped the inside of the passenger door twice and continued on my way. When I made it upstairs to my condo there was an envelope at the bottom of the door. My initial thought was that Theresa had some things to get off of her chest again but when I recognized the tiny writing I knew exactly who had darkened my doorstep. I unlocked the door, walked in and dropped my keys on the coffee table. Looked at the envelope and decided that I stood nothing to lose.

I found that Bridget had sent a copy of her one way E-ticket to Miami and had written the message:

I'm serious, Vince. I've got nothing here and I stand nothing to lose. Come with me. Start anew.

Bridget

She had placed one of her dealership-issued business cards with her home phone written on it in the envelope as well. I opened the door to the balcony and grabbed the phone off of the coffee table. Knocked a *BM* magazine onto the floor as it rang.

Rayna asked, "Hey Vince, you busy?"

"No, just getting in. What's up?"

"I was calling about Daddy. We're gonna have to put him in

a nursing home or something because I can't take care of him and I'm sure you don't have the time."

I drew the curtains and sat down on the sofa.

"Who's got money for that? You? 'Cause I don't. You know all of mine is tied up."

She sighed. "I don't know. But we've gotta do something."

"What did Pop say?"

"Well, what sixty-year-old man doesn't want to be in his own house? But that's impossible. He's gonna need help and he says he doesn't want some stranger hanging around making him feel like a child."

"Well, if you ask me, he's not really in a position to talk about what he doesn't want. If he can't do it himself, he'll have to have a nurse. Bottom line."

"But I was thinking that if he moved into a facility, he'd have people to socialize with. I don't want my father to be alone, Vince. Ms. Irene came by and talked to him for a little while today. He was fussy when she left. I guess he didn't want her to see him like that. Unable to do much except ask for help."

With all of the bridges he'd burned, he was lucky he had someone who was *willing* to help him, I thought.

"And Ms. Irene looks good, doesn't she? She wanted me to tell you that the funeral arrangements are still pending but she needs to talk to you."

"About what?"

"I don't know, but I told her I'd be there for the funeral. I was just happy to see her after all of these years. She says she's gonna give me her recipe for sweet potato pie."

"Good, I'll expect to be your guinea pig until you get it right."

She laughed, and we let a quiet moment between us begin to bridge the gap.

"Vince, I'm sorry."

"For what?"

"For you having to hurt all of these years, for me thinking that your gripes were unwarranted. I thought you hated Luke because he wasn't black, when your biggest issue was that you wanted to protect me."

"You don't have to apologize, Rayna. You were the only one besides Mama who was there for me. In a way, when she passed, you became her. I couldn't stop her from dying, felt so helpless. But I'd sworn to protect you even though I didn't know how. And when Luke took you away from me, that was a blow to my manhood. I'd lost the two women who meant the world to me and there was nothing I could do except hate someone, anyone. Inside, I was blaming him for what Pop didn't do."

"Well, let me go. Josh said he was coming that way. When he gets there would you ask him to pick me up some lightbulbs? And don't forget to call Ms. Irene. At least offer your condolences."

"Yes, Mama," I joked.

"Go 'head, Vince. I love you, baby brother."

"I love you too, big sis."

I placed the phone in its cradle and stared up at a framed 8x10 photo of Theresa that sat atop my entertainment center. It was the picture of her sitting in the park under a tree of changing leaves. I took it the summer we met, before Percy died, before everything was what it is now. I'd shaken the memories loose, gotten up and started toward my bedroom when I heard a knock at the front door. I walked back through the living room and looked through the peephole. The tall, thin, dark-skinned Maxwell look-alike from downstairs was standing there dancing to the sounds of Craig David that were drifting up the steps and invading my mental space, derailing my train of thought.

I opened the door and asked, "What's up, man? You tryin' to wake the dead or what?"

"Don't tell me you're gonna be the fourth person to complain about the music."

I held on to the corner of the door and warned, "This is a quiet neighborhood and they're not afraid to call about a peace disturbance."

"Already have. I explained that we would keep it down."

He doubled over with laughter and began slapping his hand against the wall outside my door.

I asked, "Let me guess, they bought that."

"Yep."

"I hope so, for your sake."

"So you comin' down? We've got ribs, hot dogs, veggie burgers and all. Whatever you like, it's down there."

"Nah, I'm cool," I said, shaking my head. "I've got some business to take care of."

"You sure?"

"Sure."

"Well the door is open. Just come on in if you change your mind."

"Thanks."

I shut the door and glanced at the clock. It was five 'til four. Cedric and Joshua would be here any moment. I walked back over to the sofa and sat down. Grabbed Bridget's business card and dialed her up. She answered on the third ring.

"Well, isn't this a pleasant surprise. Change your mind?"

"No. What's up, Bridget?"

"Well, my note should speak for itself. Where've you been?"

"The hospital. My father had a stroke."

"Oh, Vince, I'm sorry to hear that."

I scratched at the top of my head and flipped the business card over.

"But he's gonna be okay, Bridget."

"I've given my two weeks' notice already so I'm gonna be

leaving soon. I hate that you won't be joining me. We could have really had some fun together."

I didn't respond, didn't really know what to say.

"So listen, I'm in the neighborhood. You mind if I come by and see you?"

"I'm about to have a meeting in about thirty seconds."

"Oh, okay. Well, you know how to reach me. Take care, Vince."

Zenobia

Lainey asked, "Okay, so what was I supposed to say?"

"I don't even know why you called that guy over here in the first place."

"He was *cute*."

"Look around, Little Stevie Wonder—there are a lot of cute guys around here. That doesn't necessarily mean that they think *you're* cute."

"I know gay when I see it."

"Yeah, that's right. So tell me again why we're parked on the far end of town hoping to spot *your husband* walking into a condominium?"

"That's different, Z. That guy I just talked to was *not* gay. I could see it in his eyes. He's all man, and fine too. Truth be told, I caught him looking down at my thighs."

I fanned my hand. "If that's what helps you sleep at night."

"You don't wanna hear about what will help me sleep at night."

"Keep ya comments to ya'self."

I turned around, looked out of the window and was just about to slide a Billie Holiday CD in when I spotted Beacon getting out of a white Blazer across the street. Since Inspector Gadget was next to me so intently watching to see if her life would change drastically, I decided to sit quietly and observe where he went without letting her in on it.

Beacon crossed the street, hopped the curb in a pair of lengthy black shorts, a black and white Fubu T-shirt and what looked like a new pair of white tennis shoes. He dodged a pile of mud and almost lost his balance. When he leaned against a large tree at the foot of the long ascension of steps that curved around to the condos, his eyes shifted in my direction. He did a double take and then started toward me.

Lainey asked, "Who is this coming over here?"

"He works at the club. He's the new bartender I hired, Beacon."

"He's cute too. Gay or not gay?"

"Who cares?"

"Just answer whether or not you think he may be gay."

"I'm gonna have to say no."

Lainey squinted her eyes and brushed her hair back with her palm.

"I'll put my money on him being gay."

"Thank God you didn't maneuver your way into the judicial system. We'd all be in trouble based on appearance."

"You didn't know? We already are."

"Chill out. Here he comes."

Beacon leaned in my window, folded his hands and smiled at both of us.

"Hey, what's goin' on? I didn't know you hung out on this side of town."

I looked over at Lainey, who had gone back to watching the building.

"Yeah, we were supposed to meet one of our girlfriends over here but can't figure out which one of these condos she lives in. What are you doing over here?"

"A friend of mine is throwing a bar-be-cue and he invited me so I decided to stop through for a minute."

"Oh, I'm sorry, Beacon. This is my girlfriend Elaine. Elaine, this is the bartender with the grand ideas that I was telling you about."

Lainey extended her left hand to shake his but Beacon hesitated for a moment before giving in.

"Nice to meet you, Beacon. What's up with this tattoo?"

Lainey turned his palm down so that the web between his thumb and index finger could be viewed. He flinched and gritted his teeth. Got the same disturbed look in his eye that he'd had when he was in my office staring through the window.

"It's a symbol," he told her.

"A symbol of what?"

"My love for someone."

Beacon glanced at me, no longer smiling. Made me want to look at his hand again, pay attention to what concerns were churning inside of him. The tattoo was some kind of Asian writing, in black ink. I don't know what it is about Asian writing that implies depth. Maybe it's the fact that it's simply not understood. It's the mystery behind the writing that draws you in. And some people, particularly people like Beacon, possess the same ability. Leave you convinced that there's something more than what catches the eye.

As he retrieved his limb my cell phone rang. Beacon stood up and took the opportunity to make a clean getaway.

"Okay, Zenobia, I guess I'll see you at work. And it was nice meeting you, Elaine."

"Same here."

I waved to Beacon and answered my phone with an unenthusiastic "What, Payce?"

His words were stiff and calculated. "Zenobia, just tell me you have Zookie."

"What are you talking about?"

"Tell me you have her!"

"But I don't! Where is she? I gave her to you!"

"Shit, shit, shit!"

"Shit my ass, Payce! Where is my baby?"

"Hang on a second. I think I know where she is."

"Where?"

"With Cammie."

"Cammie?! I thought she was in California!"

"She was. She's back now."

"For what, Payce? Y'all can't continue to go for twelve rounds in front of Zaire."

"I told you before, Zenobia, Zookie wasn't even here. Cammie's a habitual liar and a—"

"Then don't you think you need to have your ass out there tryin' to find my child?!"

"*Your* child?"

"Payce, now is not the time, okay?"

"Just stay where you are and I'll hit you back in a minute."

"You've got four minutes, Payce, and then I'm coming to your house."

"No! Don't do that!"

"Why not?"

"Because . . . because I asked you not to. Respect mine. Isn't that what you've always told me?"

I sighed. "Four minutes, Payce, four minutes."

As soon as I hung up Elaine asked, "What's going on with Zaire?"

"I don't know," I answered, starting the engine, "but we've got to cut this party short."

Lainey grabbed my hand, still resting on the keys in the ignition, and wouldn't let go.

"Wait. There he is."

"*Where*, Lainey?"

She pointed at a briefcase-carrying Cedric as he and a tall muscular white guy with an obvious sex appeal stepped out of a dark blue Mazda Protégé.

"Right there," she said, scooting down in the seat.

Lainey was moving with such swiftness that her bun of hair flipped on the headrest, came undone and gave her one more good reason to curse.

"Goddammit! What is he doing?"

I scooted down in my seat and leaned to the right a bit.

"They look like they're going to that bar-be-cue. He's speaking to a couple of the guys outside. Wait, now they're opening the door and going inside. My bad, he's not going to the bar-be-cue."

Lainey sat up and took her hair down. "Well that's a relief."

"Look, I know this is eating away at you but my child is missing. I *have* to go."

"Well, let me drop you off and then I'll meet you back at Payce's place in an hour."

"And just what do you plan to do in the meantime?"

"I'm gonna come back over here and see what I can see."

"All right, Lainey, but don't do anything stupid."

She combed through her wavy dark hair with her fingers, a definite sign that she was about to get loose.

"You know me, Z."

"Don't remind me, please don't remind me."

I was beatin' on Payce's front door like a Jehovah's Witness with a quota to fill. And I know he heard me. Actually, whosever drop-top BMW was parked outside next to his brand-new Hummer truck had to have heard me too.

I stepped back off of the porch of his six-bedroom home on two acres of land in Ladue and looked up toward his master bedroom. When I saw a sheer curtain fall closed, I raced back up the steps and lay on the doorbell with the determination of one of those reality show participants who thrust themselves into death-defying situations that they know damn well may not fall in their favor. I didn't know who was in this house but Zaire *wasn't* so I was prepared to show Payce that Cammie would be the least of his concerns if I didn't get some answers soon.

Finally a stick figure with a bad weave opened the front door and peeped outside.

"Is Payce here?" I asked.

She shook her head and wrapped her arms around herself long enough for me to realize that she was shaking. I used a bit of deductive reasoning and asked, "Do you know Cammie?"

She slowly nodded.

"Has she been here?"

Another nod followed.

"Is my daughter Zaire with her?"

When she shrugged her shoulders I felt like giving her a badge for Mute of the Year, but instead I threw my hands weightlessly in the air and sat down on the top step. Girlfriend was still casting a shadow over my shoulder as I cupped my face in my hands and calmed myself with the piece of quilt. I didn't know what to do, where to turn or who to ask for advice, so I opted to be still.

"She knows you too," the mute behind me said in a barely audible tone.

I quickly turned around and wiped the tears that were forming in my eyes.

"Yes yes!"

I was now nodding my head like I was on foreign land and the translation book wasn't doing either of us any good.

I stood from the steps and asked, "Did she mention me? What did she say?"

"She said that you were the only person in St. Louis that she could trust. She and Payce were arguing and he went out to the garage to get the rest of her things. That's when she took Zookie and left."

"Did she say where she was going?"

Girlfriend went back to nonverbal responses.

"Do you mind if I come in and use the phone?"

She stepped out of my way and held her arm out for me to enter Payce's domain. The first thing I laid eyes on as I walked through his foyer was a shadow box on the wall with a jersey hanging in it—a different jersey. It was a jersey that would cause my child to fly to another time zone in order for Payce to spend any time with her.

I asked Girlfriend, "What's up with this?"

She smiled like she'd been there from the very start, back when Payce's broke ass didn't have eye water to cry with.

"He got traded. We're moving to the East Coast in a month and a half."

"What?! When was he going to tell me?"

She took two steps back and began hugging herself again. Buried her head in her chest like if she had the opportunity to disappear she would have.

"Where's the phone?"

She pointed toward the kitchen. I walked through his high-ceilinged home, grabbed the cordless off the wall and paged Lainey so she could bring me back my car. After I hung up, the mute and I both sat there in the kitchen. Silent. Distant. And maybe even wondering who the other really was.

I glanced up at the round chrome-rimmed clock above the stainless steel counter. Five minutes had passed. I tapped my nails on my thigh and hummed aloud, hoping she would leave, disappear into another room. But she was anchoring that bar stool like an anvil was tied to her ankle.

I placed the phone on the green marble-top island, leaned over on my elbows and asked, "So how long you been doin' Payce?"

Vince

"Care for anything to drink?"

"No, I'm all right," Cedric and Josh answered in unison.

I closed the refrigerator door, walked back into the living room and took a seat in one of the navy-blue chairs across the coffee table from them. Cedric scooted to the edge of the cushion on the sofa and folded his mocha-brown hands in front of him. The black slacks and blue tie he wore contradicted his posture. He was dressed for business but his mood was more relaxed. Joshua had shown up in jeans, a white T-shirt and sneakers.

"Looks like there's a party goin' on downstairs."

"New neighbors. I think a few of 'em are college students."

"That explains it," Cedric said, placing his black briefcase on the sofa in between the two of them.

When he popped the locks we both heard a pager going off. I looked at him. He looked at Joshua.

Then Cedric asked, "That you?"

"Nope."

"Probably someone partying in the hall."

I asked, "So, Cedric, how long have you been a real estate agent?"

"Not long. I'm just getting started but hey, I figure if I play my cards right I'll be in the big leagues soon. Gotta strike while the iron is hot. A buddy of mine sold that club Whose Is It downtown just yesterday. A guy named Ray Lippons owned it, and he just passed away. Apparently his mother wanted nothing to do with it so as you can imagine my partner will get a nice little commission off of that."

He pulled out a stack of papers and stared at them for a minute.

"Okay, what we've found so far is four homes in Ballwin Hills, Chesterfield and Wildwood."

Cedric scooted to the edge of the sofa and placed the listing on the coffee table to show me. "This one is a vaulted great-room ranch in the Parkway South school district—"

"No kids."

"No problem. We've also got a two-thousand-forty-square-foot three-bedroom two-bath in Chesterfield with blond parquet flooring that flows from the entry through the kitchen area. It has a finished lower level with a built-in office. If that's not enticing enough, I've also got a three-bedroom two-bath with a hearth room and fully furnished lower level. The master suite is vaulted, with a luxurious Jacuzzi. Covered porch . . ."

As he talked, the thumping bass below us and the constant beeping of a pager from partying guests in the hall caused my attention to drift. I was thinking about how lonely I'd become in these wonderful houses he was describing. I'd never imagined actually living in one without Theresa by my side. I guess deep down I'd hoped that she would shake Don's memory and realize what she had in me, but I didn't even know what was in me anymore. I knew I'd let go of part of my hate for Luke, had healed a corner of my soul that had been aching since I was thirteen when I poured my heart out to Rayna and Pop, but still, I wasn't complete. The fear that maybe I had contracted something from Ray was wrapping around my throat and choking the life out of me every night. And I knew running off with Bridget to another time zone would make me feel no better. What I needed was Theresa to say that she believed me, and to break down and fill my mind with a memory of her.

Ced asked, "So what do you think?"

"I like the sound of the first two. When can we go and see them?"

"You name the time," he answered.

"Monday afternoon. I've got someone else that I want to view them with me. And I'll let her decide which one she wants."

Cedric asked, "You about to get married?"

I sat back on the sofa and rubbed at my goatee. "I hope so."

"Well congratulations. There's no better feelin' than sitting a black woman down in a nice house so she doesn't have to work if she doesn't want to. I've got a beautiful wife who hates her job, and the fact that I've been keeping this whole thing a secret is killing her. I'm ready to make some things happen. I've taken on real estate to help her pay off her credit card debt and things like that. After that's out of the way, I can surprise her with the news that Cedric Cummings's wife doesn't have to punch anybody's clock!"

"I hope she sees what she's got in you," Josh said.

"Sometimes, fellas, I don't believe she does."

Theresa

I lay on my back across the bed after talking to Lisa. She said that she needed time away, which was something that I could relate to. She also asked when I was coming back to Atlanta. She decided that she would tell her boyfriend about her status but she wanted me to be there. Told me that I reminded her of Mama and she didn't think she could do it without me.

When I finally reached a comfortable position, a million and one thoughts flew through my mind. Did I really want to teach anymore or could I be more of a help to the Women of Triumph? What in my frustrated state did I have to offer to anyone? Could I stand a move back down South? Did I want to say goodbye to Vince? And what reason would Sheila have to lie on him?

I closed my eyes, allowed the soft humming of my mother's relaxation tape to sooth me into a light sleep. And then there I was standing outside of Don's engine house over on the south side of St. Louis. He walked from behind the shadows of a pumper in his blue uniform. His broad robust shoulders, coffee-brown skin and bushy eyebrows were just as I remembered them. When I looked down at myself, I realized that I looked different. I was pregnant. Don started toward me with his arms extended, and that's when I began to cry. He stopped walking, smiled and told me that he loved me. I couldn't speak but I shook my head when he asked me to come and be with him. I felt the baby kick inside of me and held my stomach. I was having contractions but Don was still smiling. I felt a scream build from the pit of my stomach and interlock itself with pleas of helplessness.

"Stop it, Don! I can't do this! Please leave me alone!"

"Live then, Theresa," he whispered as the smile disappeared from his face.

I told him, "I love you and so does Dameron."

"I know. I've watched you-all for years."

I desperately wiped the tears from my flushed face and said, "I know, but we don't need you to look over us anymore. You're scaring us."

"I'm only scaring you, Theresa. Dameron is not afraid."

"Then watch over *him*, Don, please. You are killing me inside."

"I still love you," he uttered as he backed away into the darkness of the engine house. "And I'll go when you no longer need me."

I stood there crying until the phone's ringing pulled me back to consciousness. I snatched up the receiver before checking to see who it was.

"Hello!"

Robert asked, "Were you sleeping?"

I wiped my eyes with the back of my hand and pulled the floral sheet over my feet.

"You'll never guess who I was just dreaming about."

"Don?"

"Yeah. I can't take this anymore. Every time I close my eyes, I see him."

"That's called true love."

By then, I'd gathered myself and remembered the bone I had to pick with him.

"Robert, what do you know about true love? You bring your butt back in town like you're some kinda Egyptian king and screw that girl's life up like that!"

"Hol' on now. Nikai is grown. I can't make her do anything she doesn't want to do. Now, I'll tell you just like I told her. Yeah, we went through some things and I'll admit that I fucked up but if you're asking me to stop loving that woman, then you're wasting your time. I didn't go off having kids by another woman and I still haven't gotten married."

"Well, I hope you don't intend to ask her."

"And why would that be so bad?"

"Because if you had any intentions on getting married, you would've done it by now! Don't play with me. Now the first time we had this discussion about you doin' your thing three years ago, I had a different take, a peaceful take. But now, I'll stay in her ear all the way down the aisle reminding her of just who she'd be dealing with."

"You *wouldn't*."

"You don't know me very well, Rob."

"Nah, Theresa, *you* don't know *me*."

Zenobia

"Ray Lippons."

"Wait a minute. I know that name from somewhere."

Lainey and I were pulling out of Payce's driveway when she brought this guy up. I was still experiencing mixed emotions. I was nervous about Zaire, pissed at Payce and held a certain level of guilt in my heart for interrogating Girlfriend, whose name turned out to be Amira. Once I'd talked to her, I found her to be a really nice person. She let me know about the house that Payce had already bought out in Philly, that he emphasized how important it was to him that she develop a healthy relationship with his daughter and then he threw in a bit about me being crazy. I cleared the last part up and we exchanged numbers. Nobody had seen "crazy" yet. I was still waiting to check out how the day ended.

"Think long and hard, Zenobia."

I was trying to but I kept drawing a blank.

"Well what else did they say?"

"I don't know. I couldn't hear very well and then you started blowin' my pager up. *Then* this elderly woman across the hall opened her door, caught me on my knees trying to listen through the crack at the bottom of that guy's door."

I laughed.

"What did she say?"

"Something about 9-1-1. You know I didn't stick around to find out. But get this—they were in unit G."

"You mean the cute guy that we stopped on his way in?"

"Yes!"

"NO!"

"Yes!"

"He's not . . ."

"Yes!"

"Oh my God."

"Yes!"

We both found the energy to laugh our way back to my house. And when Lainey pulled up to the curb, my heart leaped with relief: Zaire and Trisha were on the porch blowing bubbles. I jumped out of the car and rushed over to hug Zaire, but she held up her index finger for me to wait a minute. She blew a bubble large enough to cover her entire head and then let it explode on her face. I couldn't help but laugh.

Trisha proudly exclaimed, "I taught her that trick!"

Zaire began to use the very same gum to remove the sticky mess from her cheeks, nose and chin. "All right! Cut that out. Where is your father?"

Trisha said, "Him and that Mexican girl said they was going to his club to talk about getting back together."

"He *told* you that?!" I asked.

"Well, no, but I heard them when they were making up. Oh and a man named David called you too. He wanted to know if you liked fresh flowers. I went ahead and told him yeah. I think all pretty women do."

I reached down to hug Zaire and grabbed Trisha with the other arm.

"C'mere girl. You tryin' to get your ghetto pass revoked or something?"

"Yep. Mine *and* Lethal's . . . I mean Maurice's."

"Thanks for being here to take care of my baby at a time like this."

"No problem. She's my niece too."

I stood up and asked, "And how is *my* little niece or nephew doing?"

"Pretty good."

"Where's Maurice?"

"Him and Self were looking for you. Self wanted to talk to you about gettin' on the microphone tomorrow night for the party. They said that they would stop by the club to see if they could catch you."

"He any good?"

"He's no Tupac but he'll do."

"Well, we'll see. Do you mind watching Zaire just a little while longer while I get some things squared away?"

Trisha shrugged her shoulders. "Where am I gonna go?"

"Thanks."

As Lainey and I walked into the house her pager went off, and we ended up grabbing the phone at the same time. She was in the living room and I was in the kitchen.

"Hang up, Lainey."

"*You* hang up. This is Cedric paging me."

"And David is expecting me to be ready for dinner in less than two hours. I'd like to touch base with him."

"I promise I'll make it quick."

I let her win that one and hopped in the shower. The more I lathered up, the more tired I became. And that's when I realized that I was in no mood to go out. I still had to get to the bottom of this Cammie and Payce issue. Someone would need to let me know who would be over my child and in what state they would reside.

I stepped out of the warm water, grabbed a burgundy bath

towel off of the rack, wrapped myself up and went into my bedroom. Sat down on the side of my bed, took a moment to breathe and called David.

"Hello?"

"Hi there."

"Zenobia! How are you?"

"A little tired. Well actually, I'm beat. That's the reason I'm calling you."

"You're not going to cancel on me, are you?"

"I'm afraid I'm going to have to, David."

"Okay, well how about you come over and I'll cook for you?"

"I have a child, remember?"

"What are you saying, you don't think I can make fries too? Bring Zaire with you. It'll be fun. I'll rent some movies and we can all sit around and guess how they end."

"She likes cartoons, David."

"Good, I won't be the only one. So can I pick you two beautiful ladies up at eight?"

I shook my head at his persistence and switched the phone over to the other ear.

"I guess so. Sheila, Nikai and I were talking about doing a little something special for Theresa at Discretion tomorrow night. You think you and Byron would be willing to come through?"

"If you're there, I'm there."

"All right, baby, see you at eight."

By the time I finally found the energy to pull myself up from the mattress and get dressed in some gray sweats, Cedric had arrived to pick up Lainey. They were sitting in the living room. Well, it was more like Cedric was sitting and Lainey was standing by the fireplace crying.

When I got to the bottom of the stairs I asked, "Is everything okay in here?"

"We're fine. I'm just letting my wife know that I love her and that she doesn't have to follow me. I'm reminding her that I know everything about her . . . the wave of her hair, the ring of her pager, every inch of her body—*even if* I'm unable to make love to her."

I was completely floored. Lainey leaned against the mantel right in front of their wedding photograph and began to cry harder. Her whimpering rose louder and louder as she repeatedly made futile attempts to form words.

"Elaine, I'll tell the world. I have erectile dysfunction, which makes it difficult to get an erection, but I *love . . . my . . . wife,* Zenobia. I was ashamed, but I'm not willing to lose her to *anything.* I want her to be happy and to enjoy her life. I don't want her to have to work if she doesn't want to. She is too intelligent and beautiful not to be given a choice. I know what I have in her but I also know what I'm temporarily incapable of giving. But I promise to *God* that I will do everything I can to make you happy, Elaine. My right hand to *God!*"

I wanted to yell that I believed him even if Lainey didn't. Cedric stood from my eggshell-colored sofa, walked over to Lainey, kneeled down and humbly hung his head, waiting for acceptance. And it took a second, maybe even two, but she grabbed and hugged that man in the spirit of reception until he too cried. I knew from that moment that she *had* grown to love Cedric over the years. And sometimes the best kind of love is the one that overwhelms you and takes you by surprise.

I parked in between Cammie's Sebring and a brand-new white Corvette, which I assumed was Payce's. Got out, walked across the parking lot and up to the side door of Discretion. It was ajar but when I went inside there was no one around. I flipped a couple of light switches and checked the bar. Signs of Payce's presence became very apparent then. There was an empty shot glass with only a few drops of dark liquor left. Next to it was a half-full wineglass. I turned on my heels and headed for the VIP section in the back, where Payce had been known to drag a hoochie or two. I descended the four steps that led to a room of sofas and another bar, only to find them in the middle of the floor half-naked and clawing at one another fervently.

I leaned inside the threshold, folded my arms and cleared my throat.

"Oh shit! Damn, Zenobia!" Payce yelled, reaching for his pants.

Cammie simply looked away in shame. I thought of giving her a sermon on how she brought about her own problems, how she would never get away from Payce if she didn't stop worshiping him on the physical level, but like I said, she was half-naked and fully shamefaced.

"Would you mind doing this elsewhere? People have to walk on these floors."

"If you knocked before you entered—"

"What? You would've had time to move up to a couch?! You disgust me, Payce!"

"Look!"

"No, *you* look! I'm sick of watchin' you mistreat women! Do you want some man *fuckin'* Zaire on the floor in a vacant building?! And then you have the nerve to say that women cause their own problems. You're the dumb-ass, Payce. Your daughter has met more promiscuous unemployed women than a goddamn gynecologist at a free clinic! And now you've got Amira over there packing her stuff and dancing to the tune of another one of your lies."

I looked at Cammie and asked, "Did you know that he and Amira have plans to move to Philadelphia in less than two months?"

She snapped her neck in Payce's direction and then pulled her naked thighs closed.

As he stood up and began to get dressed I continued, "You might also wanna ask him how long it took to replace you. Girl-friend is over there answering phones and the whole nine."

"She's answering our phone, Payce?"

Cammie looked about as pitiful as she did the last time I'd seen her. Her beautiful face wasn't battered and bruised but her integrity and pride were down for the count. She stood up and put her clothes on as her man-of-the-moment nonchalantly ex-ited the room—make that the building—and left her standing there to fall victim to my I-told-you-so's.

"Let me ask you something. What made you think you were so special that you could get him to straighten up and fly right?"

"I just thought—"

"What did you think that you could try that I didn't? You were lucky enough to have the signs laid right out there for you. Some people don't get that chance. You wrote me that dramatic letter about how he mistreated you, but you mistreated your damn self! Back then I didn't know what I was dealing with and by the time I did, I had a child on the way. Your story is totally different. And now look at you. You're serving yo' coochie up on the floor to Payce just like the woman you caught him with. Cammie, leave my establishment. And if you ever think about touching my child again, Payce will be the least of your con-cerns."

And having said that, I let her have some time to herself. I walked back across the dance floor as someone knocked on the side door. I walked over and opened it. A tall muscular guy with skin the color of a paper sack was standing there with a bouquet of red roses eyeing me like I was a piece of meat.

"Who are you?" I asked.

He extended the flowers. "I'm Leland. You busy?"

"Yeah, very. What can I do for you?"

"Let me come in and talk to you for a minute."

I looked at him like his head was on fire. "Uh excuse me, but I told you I'm busy. I appreciate the gesture with the flowers and all, but I don't take gifts from strangers."

I pulled the door and he jammed it with his foot. Extended the flowers again like maybe I hadn't heard him the first time.

"I came all the way down here just to meet you. The least you could do is take these damn flowers that I spent all of my money on!"

"Fine!"

I snatched them, quickly shut the door before he had a chance to get another word in and walked upstairs to my office. As soon as I unlocked the door and turned on the lights, my cell phone rang. When I answered, Lainey was on the other end whispering.

"Zenobia, what are you doing?"

"I'm walking in my office. What are you doing?"

"I'm at home. Can you believe what Cedric said?"

"Actually, yes," I told her, cracking a window and sitting down at my desk.

"I feel so bad."

"And so you should."

A breeze blew in and sent some paperwork dancing under the glass paperweight on my desk.

"So what now?"

"What am I, a doctor?"

"No, but you're my friend and I need you."

"Oh, speaking of friends, I think the two of you should come out tomorrow night. We're celebrating Theresa's birthday here."

"What time?"

"The usual. Come through about nine."

"Okay, but back to my husband's issue."

"What about it, Lainey?" I asked, reaching across the desk to move the annoying paper.

"Have you ever heard of it before?"

I glanced over the references that Beacon had given me and experienced a huge epiphany.

"I've got it!"

"Okay! What should we do?"

"No, Lainey. Now I remember where I heard the name Ray Lippons before. That's the guy who died not too long ago and Sheila said that Theresa was seeing one of his lovers."

"What?!"

"Yeah. We all had a big talk about it. Sheila says she's sleeping with the guy. I think his name was Victor or Vince or something like that."

"Vince what?"

"I don't know but Ray Lippons's name is on this sheet of personal references that I got from Beacon. It says here that he worked for Ray Lippons from January 2000 until indefinitely."

"Well how can he still be working for him if he's dead?" Lainey asked.

I heard a noise coming from downstairs. Sounded like someone was scooting the stools across the floor.

"Lainey, let me call you back."

"Why? What are you doing?"

"About to go downstairs and tell Cammie that I'm serious about her leaving me and my child alone."

"I thought she swore she would move out of town for good."

"She did. She's back."

"Okay, well call me, and keep me in mind."

"I will."

I hung up the phone and walked over to shut the window. When I peeped through the blinds, I could see that Cammie's car was gone. I grabbed the glass paperweight off the corner of my desk and stood alongside the two-way mirror. I took a quick glance but didn't see anybody. I pressed my back against the wall and tried to slow my breathing. My heart was pumping to the beat of go-go music on D.C. nights. I took a deep breath and another quick glance, and this time spotted a shadow starting up the steps. I fought back the desire to cry as I wrapped my braids up into a bun on the top of my head and gripped the paperweight.

"God, if I have to beat somebody to death today please let my cell mate be friendly." I could hear footsteps coming down the hall, heavy masculine footsteps. Once they stopped, I watched my doorknob turn counterclockwise. I hit the light switch and ducked behind the file cabinet.

"Stop playing with me, Nobia. I know you're the only one left here."

I didn't move a muscle. Sweat trickled down my forehead like a midsummer rain.

"You pissed Payce off so he's not coming back. I think Cammie hates you too. But who could blame them? I mean, I wasn't even good enough to come and sit with you in your office without having a justifiable reason. I just wanted to hang out with you!"

I tried to slow my trembling but it seemed impossible. My nose was running and when I sniffled it rang out in surround sound.

Then suddenly, my cell phone rang. The nutcase began to laugh again. Leaned against the file cabinet and started humming the theme song to *Cheers*.

"Wouldn't you like to get away?" he sang.

I had a choice. I could either listen to Li'l Crazy go on for I didn't know how long or I could press the talk button, which would inevitably encourage him to pin me and my cell phone between the file cabinet and the wall. I opted for the latter, and that's when the chaos began.

"Hello! Hello!" I yelled into the receiver.

I could hear Sheila yelling back, but only for the second it took for Beacon to grab me by the top of my braids and drag me around the cabinet and to the floor.

"Don't interrupt me, Nobia!"

His eyes were red, his light blue jeans were filthy and he wasn't wearing a shirt. It was then that I realized how cut up he was. He was built like he'd done hard time. Zero percent body fat, and if that wasn't proof enough the seven or so braids that now rested on the floor next to my foot after being yanked out of my scalp were.

"What do you want with me, Beacon?"

"I go by Marcel, okay? Kill the 'Beacon' shit. Only my momma and the police are allowed to call me that."

"Well, Beacon . . . Marcel . . . whatever the hell you go by!"

He pulled out one of my chairs, calmly sat down and rested his foot on his knee. Let it dangle like he didn't have a care in the world.

"You feelin' froggy, Nobia? Leap then."

"Hello! Zenobia!" Sheila yelled into the receiver.

Beacon stomped on my cell phone and then kicked it across the floor.

"Now, where was I? Oh yeah, I was gonna tell you about Vince. Ray started talking about givin' Vince a chance to bump me out of my position when he started hangin' out in Lake St. Louis all the damn time. I had a room there, I had a history with Ray. He made sure I had everything I needed. In fact it was his idea that I get a job here, to see just what you were doing to keep the crowds packin' this place. And before I know it, I'm being disrespected in front of people. Couldn't get respect from you, Vince or anybody else!"

In that moment, I decided that it would be in my best interest to make this Vince guy look worse than he already did. At least he had absence in his favor. Li'l Crazy was right here, *hoping* I gave him a reason to cut loose.

"Okay, I'm not doubting that Vince is a horrible person, but I have nothing to do with Vince."

"Yes you do. Don't lie to me, Zenobia."

"I'm not lying! I don't even know him."

Beacon sat forward and rested his elbows on his knees.

"I saw you talking to him before I got out of my truck earlier."

"Saw me *talking* to him?!"

"Yeah, you and redbone called him over to your car. Then you make up that bullshit story about trying to find some girlfriend's condo!"

I jogged my memory back and realized that he was talking about the cute guy who invited us up to his place, the same cute guy whose door Lainey was squatting in front of.

"But that's all right, you don't have to remember him. My problem is with you, right now."

"But I didn't do anything!"

His temperament was mellow, almost as though he was about to take a trip down memory lane. I was foolish enough to let my guard down for a second, but when he got up and started bustin' Shaolin-style kung fu moves in the air, my nerves stood at attention. It became very obvious that I'd do myself more harm than good trying some tae bo right about now.

"You ever feel used?" he asked, imitating what looked like a crane.

I scooted my butt about four inches across the floor alongside my desk.

"Yes."

"Some people will just use you for whatever they can get."

312

"Uh-huh."

"Prison changed my life, Zenobia. It was the worst six years of my life. But you would be surprised how you adapt."

He swiftly changed into a snake as he darted toward nothing in particular with precision.

"Most people think prison teaches criminals to be citizens, but it doesn't work like that all the time. Sometimes it teaches citizens to be criminals, rapists and thieves to be murderers. It can change your way of thinking completely. Leave you living two lives when you finally get out. You struggle with who you were and who you've been labeled as.

"You see this tattoo?" he asked, stopping long enough to show me.

I nodded my head as he went back to his display of agility.

"This is Ray's name. I got it put there on my hand because he meant so much to me. He was the first person to show me love when I got out. He didn't care what my record showed. He gave me a job and a place to stay. But he used me. I found myself petitioning for his attention just like I had to do with everyone else. I never raped or burglarized anybody, but over six years I was forced to adapt to the mentality of someone who had or else I would've perished. I was a citizen, but now . . . now I'm a criminal."

He did a graceful back flip and landed on his feet. I felt like I was watching Spiderman's alter ego prove to me that following whatever he decided to do to me, he could get away without a problem.

"Okay, but what did *I* do, Beacon?"

"What did you call me?"

"Marcel! What did I do, *Marcel*?"

"It's what you didn't do, Nobia. You had an opportunity to break the cycle. You could've been different. You could've given me a chance."

"But I did. I gave you a job."

"But only because you didn't know about my past."

"Okay, Bea—I mean Marcel. But what else was I supposed to go off of?"

"If you had let me talk when I came up here the first time you would've known how I felt, but I was too insignificant to—"

We both heard a noise coming from downstairs. Beacon looked toward the door and then ran to shut it.

"Who is that?" he asked.

"I don't know but they'll probably be coming up here in a minute."

He beckoned, "C'mere."

I shook my head and held on to the corner of the desk.

"C'mere!" he yelled.

I slowly stood to my feet, trying to kill time and to think of a little friendly conversation to further stall him. "I like your work here, Marcel. You're the best bartender we've ever had."

"Shut up!" he yelled, grabbing me by my collar and pulling me close.

He looked me over from the top of my aching head down to my breasts. Began breathing heavily like he was taking in my scent. Sweat rolled down my forehead, ran along my jawline and landed on his hand.

"I was married once," he whispered.

My hands dangled at my side. Unsure of what to do with them, I reached up toward Beacon. He pulled me closer and kissed me on the mouth. I pressed my closed fists against his chest and he backed off, right as my breakfast worked its way backward through my system. I caught it and took a deep swallow.

"Whoever that is downstairs will be looking for me, Marcel."

"I know. That's what I'm waiting for."

He walked us over to the two-way mirror and peeked down-stairs.

"They're on their way up here. Do you wanna see this or would you rather be knocked out?"

Instantly, I thought about Maurice and Self coming by to talk to me.

"What are you planning to do? Leave them alone!"

"Listen, the whole world is fuckin' with me! I'm broke, can't get a decent job!"

"But what do *we* have to do with that?"

"Everything!"

"Listen, Beacon, I mean Marcel! I *said* Marcel! Life is never about what other people can do for you but what you can do for yourself. Nobody is responsible for your happiness. Yes, society owes you for being a victim of circumstance, but c'mon—we'd all have reparations if that were the case. If you sit around wait-ing for somebody else to change the way they look at you before you gain some sort of happiness or personal value, you will die a miserable longing old man."

A second later I realized that I was talking to my damn self, 'cause Beacon was standing beside the door in another kung fu stance.

He looked at me as though he'd only recently noticed that I was talking and yelled, "Didn't I tell you to *shut up*?!"

"That's my brother down there!"

"Thanks for the memo."

"Why do we have to pay for what society did?!" I yelled in a fit of anger.

"Don't you see that everything you do, every thought you think shapes this society? Crime isn't the way that it is because people are bored. People don't generally rob and steal for sport. They do it because they are running a rat race. Every person plays a part. Life is like a play and nobody realizes that we determine the ending. You don't have to be stuck-up but you choose to. See, this is about choices, Nobia. We're making a choice to stifle others, ridicule one another. Things could be different and I hoped that they would, but that would make us all even. And most times the ones on top are afraid that they'll lose their position."

"So you take it upon yourself to make them suffer?"

He shrugged his shoulders as the doorknob turned counter-clockwise.

"We've all got a role to play," he told me.

"Go back downstairs, Maurice!"

Beacon pulled the door open and shoved a dark figure into a six-foot ficus tree that stood next to the window. Took him by total surprise. I know this for sure 'cause it took him longer than anybody's crippled grandmomma to get back on his feet. That was when I realized that it was the guy who had brought the flowers. Beacon hit him in the face and chest like he was the society who needed to pay. I stepped back and kicked the glass paperweight on the floor next to my braids. As soon as I bent down to grab it, Leland stood up. They were turning and moving so quickly that I couldn't get a good shot from where I was. And right before I could hurl the paperweight across the room, Maurice appeared in the doorway, then Leland picked up one of my chairs and cracked Beacon over the back. He fell over onto my desk and then down to the floor. Maurice and I stood there looking at a bloodied and bludgeoned Leland. His shirt was torn, and the right side of his forehead was bleeding. He dropped to his knees like a limp rag doll. I scurried to his side and set him down in one of the chairs.

Maurice asked, "What is this about?!"

I glanced over at Beacon, lying unconscious on the floor. He reminded me of a defiant child acting out for attention. His actions paralleled those of the self-destructive youth of today so closely that I wondered if that was how he'd begun. If society had been too preoccupied with chasing a dollar and a handful of status to notice that this was where we were headed. The only difference between Beacon and the children from Theresa's school who had been on the news was that there was still time to help them. And Beacon—he was an example of what we would have if we didn't wake up and change the ending of this play.

I ran into the bathroom to get a cup of water and a paper towel to clean Leland's wounds. Sorta expected him to snatch them away but then it occurred to me that he probably didn't have the energy right at the moment.

Leland glanced up at me with his one good eye and asked, "You okay?"

"Yes, thanks to you."

He grinned and then said, "I couldn't help but protect you with all of that booty on duty. Now what are you gonna give me?"

I playfully nudged him with my arm. "A head start if you don't quit acting up. Learn how to introduce yourself to a lady first. You'll get a lot further. Plus you would've known by now that I've already got a man."

Later that evening, after I had gone over the story about a thousand and ten times to a thousand and nine people including the three police officers who arrested Beacon, Zaire and I ended up over to David's house—a beautiful ranch-style two-bedroom home over on Bellefontaine Road.

I was in the kitchen with the remainder of my hair tied up in a red scarf, cooking my specialty vegetable lasagna while David and Zaire watched Bugs Bunny classics on his DVD player. Found myself eavesdropping on their conversation from time to time. I wanted them to get along. I wanted her to grow to trust him but even more I wanted stability for my child, which was something David and I had in common.

Once we had all eaten and Zaire fell off into a deep sleep I took her into his bedroom, which looked out onto a creek from a window seat with storage underneath. I laid her down on his blue and gray comforter. Watched her ball up into the fetal position. I wanted to hold her and keep her safe from all of the Beacons yet to come.

David walked up, held me from behind and said, "Dinner was great, Zenobia."

"Thank you."

I tucked a piece of the quilt into my pocket as David grabbed my hand.

"What's this?"

Embarrassed, I answered, "It's part of a quilt my mother was making for Zaire when she died. I keep it with me most of the time. It's comforting."

I shrugged my shoulders and continued, "And I guess it sort of makes me feel safe."

David turned me around, looked into my eyes and said, "*Use me,* Zenobia."

"What?"

"Use me. That's why I'm here. That's why we're all here on earth. Just don't *mis*use me. I want to be that quilt. I want to make you feel safe. Will you allow me to do that?"

I laughed and waited for him to join in but he didn't. David wanted me to realize just how serious he was. "I guess I owe you the opportunity to do that."

"Don't guess. Like I told you before, I don't like wasting time. If you weren't the woman for me I wouldn't have pursued you the way that I have. I don't want any restrictions when I decide to fall in love. So please be sure."

"'Fall in love'?" David, it's only been two months."

"How many hours in the day do you think it takes to recognize the sun? I have observed and recognized you, Zenobia. Women like you come along only once in a blue moon. I consider myself a wise man and this, I'm sure of. Are you?"

"I am, David. I'm sure."

As he held me, I looked up at an enlarged photo next to the bookshelf: a woman and a child standing by the ocean.

"Who is that?" I asked.

"My mother and I back home. I was seven. This picture was taken near our house."

"Your mother is beautiful, David."

"I told you you remind me of her."

"I wish I could've met her."

"Well you definitely would've had to go to VI because she didn't believe in flying."

"You say that as though you think I wouldn't want to go."

"I don't know," he said, taking me by the hand and leading me out of the bedroom. "Your mood seemed to change when I mentioned going back there to live someday."

"Well, it's just that . . . I guess it's that . . ."

I couldn't come up with anything to justify needing to stay here in St. Louis. Payce would be gone to Philadelphia, Lainey had a man who was determined to love her come hell or high water and Maurice . . . well, he had truly become a man.

"What is it, Zenobia?"

"I guess there's nothing for me to control here. At first I wanted to stay because I thought Maurice needed me, but he's starting his own family now. And Payce is leaving as well."

"So he did get traded?"

"Philadelphia. He'll be gone in less than two months."

"I don't know if it's rude to be happy about that or not."

"Well, let's both take our rude butts in here and listen to some music."

David put Musiq Soulchild's CD in and we slow-danced closely, just as we had at the bookstore. But when he held me this time, I felt something new. I felt the ability to let him lead, in more ways than one. There were no games to play and no prices to pay for his attention and loyalty. And in that moment I realized that sometimes the best things in life really *are* free, because they're too valuable to put a price on. I lay my head on his chest and listened to his heart beat.

He asked, "You hear that?"

"Yeah, so calm, so rhythmic."

"That's life, peace. Stay here with me, love. Help me make my house into a home."

I looked up at him and asked, "Are you serious, David?"

> *I was told to take my time and choose*
> *Like a nomad I was expected to roam*
> *It was they who had bachelorhood confused*
> *Yet now envy my life, our union and our home.*

"Is that serious enough for you?"

Theresa

Do you know that Nikai had the nerve to show up to my birthday gathering at Discretion the next night with that clown Robert? Sheila and I were pissed, which is why she stayed at the far end of the club for most of the night. I thought about inviting Vince but changed my mind. When he called earlier about coming over, I let the answering machine pick up. I wasn't ready to talk to him just yet, wasn't ready to make a decision. What I was really beginning to consider was moving back to Atlanta. St. Louis had drained me, and the fact that I had no family here only compounded things. I loved the girls; they were good for me. But I needed another start, not one tainted with bad memories that left a foul taste in my mouth. Didn't have any intentions of maintaining relationships on the down low. Ducking and dodging my friends because I was ashamed of Vince. And then getting mad at him twenty-four hours a day because I'd always wonder in the back of my mind if maybe he was lying and Sheila was telling the truth. The message that he left was that he wanted me to go somewhere with him on Monday. I hadn't ruled it out completely but it wasn't something he could bet his money on either.

Sheila lifted her glass of cranberry juice and proposed a toast:

"To the end of Theresa's twenties, and hopefully her nightmares as well."

I put my glass in the air. "I'll drink to that."

Sheila, Byron, Zenobia, David, Elaine, Cedric and I clinked glasses and looked around for Nikai.

I asked Sheila, "What do you think she's gonna do?"

"She'll be okay. She's only hanging out with him because Kalif is out of town and I think she's lonely."

Zenobia chimed in with, "And thickheaded."

I lifted my glass. "I'll drink to that."

Sheila lowered my hand. "No you won't. I thought about what you said last week, and you were right. Anyone who has a heart can make mistakes, and people learn at their own pace. Forcing them into doing what you want them to will only send them scurrying in another direction."

She sipped her juice and stared across the dark club at Nikai. "That's probably how she ended up where she is. But my point is that we all at some time believe in something or someone we shouldn't. Why do you think the divorce rate is at fifty percent and rising? People are having starter marriages like they used to have starter homes. Single-parent families are about as common as mailboxes. Whether we think a man will love us or that a new house and a fancy car will make our personal value go up or even if we buy into that overnight weight loss crap, we've all been made a fool of. So celebrate your wisdom but don't believe you're in a position to punish others for not using theirs where *you* see fit. You can bend down and yell at a flower for as long as you want, but it will still grow at its own speed."

Elaine yelled, "Can the church say amen?!"

"Well!"

Nikai finally made her way over to our table with a glass of juice and a frown painted on her face. "Nobody waited for me before y'all toasted."

Lainey's inappropriate butt blurted out, "We thought you were over there lettin' that firefighter put out the fire in your bosom."

"Ha ha," Nikai retorted. "We've agreed to leave one another alone. I just had to be honest with Rob. I can never trust him again. When I needed someone to catch my drift, he served his purpose. But I'm in a new place now."

Sheila smiled with approval and winked at me.

"See, I told you. My girl's got wisdom dripping from those pretty brown locks."

"Eeww, why does that not sound good?"

"Y'all know what I mean! I'm the oldest here. Don't make me get physical."

"All right, Momma Sheila. We get your point."

Once the clock struck twelve we all huddled together for a group hug. And at that brief moment, I knew there would be a lot I'd miss about St. Louis, especially this crew. I'd miss the memory of Don and our relationship, but hopefully with it would go the nightmares. Since I'd be doing things differently, in a different place, he'd know that I didn't need him to look over me anymore. That I was able to maintain without him.

"Happy birthday, Theresa! How do you feel?" Sheila asked.

"Like I'm gonna cry. I'm gonna miss you guys."

"Oh, we'll miss you too, sweetie. Now don't cry. There are too many fine men in here watching you for that."

Vince

Ms. Irene gave Ray a memorial that Monday, which Rayna and I attended together. She was my rock, even though she was unaware of the storm raging inside of me. I was still unable to get past what I'd done, what I'd allowed to surface in me. I'd rationalized that men in prison had engaged in the same behavior and weren't even inebriated, yet the act had not constituted bisexuality. I loved women. But more important, I loved Theresa. I finally got her to agree to meet with me. She didn't know that I was taking her to see the house that I planned to move her into. I was gonna ride back to Rayna's and hook up with Josh and Cedric after the memorial, after I'd said goodbye to this man and everything about him.

Rayna and I were standing on the steps outside St. Matthew's Church waiting to offer our condolences to Ms. Irene. There was a line of people. As curt and brusque as Ray was sometimes, it was clear that he was loved by many. He had obviously changed lives, more than just mine. When Ms. Irene made her way down the steps in a powder-blue dress, dabbing her puffy, swollen eyes with Kleenex, she reached out and embraced me. Cried harder. I felt so bad at that moment for despising her son, but it was a fleeting moment.

She released me, hugged Rayna and asked, "How is your father?"

"He's doing good."

A woman in a black pantsuit came by and tapped her on the shoulder. She leaned her head over and thanked the woman for coming. Then turned back to us.

"Do you think you'll be able to come back to Ray's house for the reception? I stayed up late last night and cooked a bunch of food. Got your favorites. Even whipped up some sweet potato pie."

I could tell that she was desperately trying to hold it together for the other mourners. She smiled like the woman of the hour, like maybe her healing had already begun.

"No, Ms. Irene, we won't be able to make it."

"Oh, but I really need to speak with you two. I've got something I've been needing to get off of my chest for some time. You know I'm getting old, and my soul . . . well, it's gettin' heavy with guilt."

Rayna held her by the arm. "Guilt about what, Ms. Irene?"

She began to cry, which made Rayna start with the waterworks.

"Your mother was a good woman," Ms. Irene said.

She held Rayna by the face. "You remind me of her so much, Rayna. So sweet. She was good to your father, even when he didn't deserve it. And Lord knows most of their marriage, he didn't deserve it. And it's eaten me up for years when I think about how I called on him when I should have called on the Lord. I was young. Just felt like I needed a man in my bed at night to make me feel safe. And when I got pregnant with Ray, I convinced myself that I had fallen in love with Vincent Sr. But what I was in love with was the idea of not being alone anymore. I gave Ray your daddy's middle name just to show him how much he meant to me. Even though he wasn't his child."

Ms. Irene reached down and held both my and Rayna's hand. "I let him play with you, Vince, because I wished you too were my own. When your momma died I offered to take you-all in but your daddy didn't want that. He thought I might tell you-all about all of those years that we messed around while your mother was still living. Soon after, Rayna got married and, well, I had had enough of your daddy's selfish ways. So I left. Never told a soul the truth, not even my own sister. Wanted everyone to believe that I was special to your daddy, that I had given him children. Everyone I told was so far away, I didn't worry about none of you finding out. But when Oleatha told me that she mentioned your resemblance at the hospital with her blind self, I knew that I'd carried this burden for too long. I'm sorry, babies. I'm so, so sorry. If it were up to me, he would've been your brother. I finally confessed to your daddy that the secret he was holding was a lie. I didn't want to let him go on believing something that wasn't true, even if he wasn't man enough to act on it."

Ms. Irene broke down in Rayna's arms, and a huddled mass of mourners swarmed around her. She told them that she would be fine and offered to walk us to our car. Rayna and I just stared at one another, speechless. We stood on the curb and all three of us held hands as the sun beat across my back in that black suit.

"Here," she said, reaching into her purse. "Since you-all were *like* brothers, you two get a share of his club. I sold it, and here is half of the profit."

She planted folded checks into first my palm and then Rayna's. I opened mine, and found the dollar amount was one hundred and seventy-five thousand. The smile that grew across my face was almost sinful. We grabbed her at the same time and kissed each side of her face.

Then she asked, "Now y'all are sure you don't wanna come

by and get something to eat? There's plenty. Maybe you can take your daddy a plate."

"Well, I guess *I* could, but Vince has got a prior engagement. He's buying a home."

"Oh really? Well, that's good, baby. Well, if you change your mind, you know the way. I'll see you in a minute, Rayna."

When Ms. Irene had walked back up the front steps of the church, Rayna turned to me and asked, "Well, what do you think about your father now?"

I opened the car door and told her, "The one thing you can ask of people is that they remain consistent. And I can say, he's been the way he is for years. Who am I to ask him to change?"

Joshua, Cedric, Theresa and I pulled up to a beautiful brick-front three-bedroom ranch on the 4700 block of Sparrow's Way in Chesterfield late that afternoon. It was the one with the blond parquet flooring, the vaulted master suite with the Jacuzzi and the finished lower level.

Theresa turned me and asked, "Who lives here?"

"You, if you want to."

She furrowed her brow and immediately looked in the backseat at Joshua and Cedric.

"Vince, may I speak with you in private?"

Josh said, "I know my cue."

They opened the back doors, got out and walked around to the rear of the house.

She tucked her hair behind her ear, fondled my gold ring on her thumb and asked, "What's this all about?"

"It's about me loving you as my friend and knowing that this was meant to be."

She studied me for a second. "What are you talking about? You told me that what we do together is take the sting out of loneliness. I don't want a relationship based on that for the rest of my life."

I didn't respond. She was right and I knew it, but I was afraid of losing her.

"Listen, Vince, I'm strongly considering moving down to Atlanta with Dameron and my mother. I've given it some thought and my mother agrees that maybe this would be a good move. There are a lot of women down there that need my help."

I stared out of the window at a child playing alone in the yard across the street. Tried to think of the right words to say, ones that would let her know how she was hurting me. She'd said herself that we were closer than most couples. I'd helped her get over Don's death, she'd helped me bury my nephew. I was as much a part of her son's life as any of her friends, including Sheila's intrusive ass. I didn't get it. When had history become irrelevant in a relationship?

I turned to her and asked, "Well, what about what *I* need?"

She propped her elbow on the windowsill and rested her chin in her hand. "Let me ask you something: Were you being completely honest with me at my apartment the day Sheila and Nikai came over?"

"About what?"

"Don't play on my intelligence, Vince. Were you?"

"Was I what?"

Theresa tilted her head like she didn't want to repeat herself. I had to turn away from her. Grabbed my head in frustration, rubbed it abrasively and banged the steering wheel. Scared the hell out of her. Theresa jumped and leaned away from me.

"I'm sorry," I said, and reached for her.

But she dodged my touch.

"What? What's wrong with you?" I asked.

"No, the question is what's wrong with *you*? You still haven't answered my question. Were you intimate with that man?"

"Are you asking me . . ."

"Were you, Vince! Just tell me!"

"No! I mean, yes, but I was drunk! It wasn't even what you would call—"

She put her hand up to cease conversation. "Let's just call it the end."

"What? But I stayed with you after the dreams."

"No you didn't!"

She snatched my band off of her thumb and tossed it in my lap.

"Remember? You walked out on the alcohol and the dreams, the time when I really needed you."

"You needed help!"

She lowered her chin and stared at me in a matter-of-fact fashion. "Oh and *you don't?*"

Theresa folded her arms across her chest and pursed her lips. "Tell your story walking, Vince. I'm not tryin' to become part of that circus act."

I grabbed her arm and she quickly pulled away. "Don't touch me!" she yelled as tears formed in her eyes. "I defended you! Had everybody looking at me like I was crazy and you really were—"

"Theresa, please, please hear me out."

"What are you gonna say? That you didn't enjoy it? You didn't finish? I don't even want to hear the specifics!"

"But you know me!"

She squinted her eyes with a look of hatred. "I know who you *showed* me."

"Ahhhhhh! You gotta be kiddin' me! The moment a brotha tells the truth he's persecuted?"

"You know what? You spend so much time talking about how selfish your father is and how you never want to be like him, but look in the mirror for once. All you are concerned about is yourself—what you want, how you feel, what you need. Who gives a damn! I don't anymore. It's about time you get to see what it feels like to be walked out on. Now take me home."

"This can *be* your home," I said, pointing to the house.

"This can only be my hell. Now drop me off where you picked me up!"

Zenobia

There is one thing in life that is certain, and that is change. And David has changed my belief in true love. The way he rubs my feet at night and prays over them, asking God to direct my path away from danger, has given me a renewed hope. I am no longer struggling because the real thing puts all of the distrust and reservations at ease. The real thing doesn't leave a woman looking for evidence of infidelity. Love is true and exact, honest and transparent, when there's nothing to hide.

Theresa is alone now. She threw a packing party for her move to Atlanta. We all miss her but with the way she's been rambling on about the Women of Triumph support group, I get the feeling that she will be okay. Initially she was a little heartbroken and embarrassed, but Sheila has reminded her that she can bear no responsibility for someone else's actions. Vince stopped calling her a few days before she left. And from time to time, when we're reaching out across the states, she breaks down. Not because she misses him, but because of the years she feels she's wasted. That's when I remind her that time is never wasted unless you simply aren't paying attention. Those years were her preparation for something better; the experiences she had during them helped her to realize who she really was. She hasn't dreamed about Don again either. Sometimes I think he was only there to watch over her. David says if you aren't eager to live, you're waiting to die. And maybe Don was lingering around until she'd decided which way she wanted to go.

Now, Ms. Nikai Parker is another story. I think I'm gonna call Leslie first thing in the morning and tell her to rally up her prayer group so they can all come lay hands on that child. When Kalif got back in town from one of his DJ tours, she had disappeared like a prop in a magic trick. Got us to help her move out and into her own place. Said she didn't want any stress. That this was the baby she'd been waiting on for years and she would enjoy the pregnancy, surrounded by us. So every time I go shopping for Trisha, I grab something for Nikai's little one too. After all, I've got two nieces coming in the middle of Black History Month.

Lainey and Cedric goes without saying. Those two lovebirds rekindled the flame once Cedric understood the power of honesty. And the fact that he's allowed her to stay at home and become a "domestic engineer," as she likes to be called, has only made a good thing better. They've got a trip to Cancún planned and she says she's ready to start having babies now that he's swallowed his pride and sought help.

Sheila and Byron just left for a week in New Orleans to take in the Essence Music Festival. Which has left little Miss Zaire upset that she'll miss her story time, but I'm allowing Payce to take her on a camping trip this week since he's in town and has a lot of free time. It seems he broke his leg and injured the same shoulder he'd had two previous surgeries on and, well, let's just say he's not considered the team's most valuable player. So he'd better use his "Discretion" wisely when it comes to budgeting his finances. Surprisingly, we've made peace. I had to truly be honest with myself about why I was doing what I was. I guess a part of me was bitter. It wasn't that I still loved him, but I was afraid that maybe he would love someone the way I'd always wanted him to love me. But now it doesn't matter anymore, because trips to a quaint and comfortable little home in St. Croix, Virgin Islands, have a way of clearing up a lot of bitterness and frustration.

I started my job as a human resources manager four months ago, and believe me it was a huge adjustment. But a welcomed one. This is something *I've* earned, and at the end of next year, my bachelor's degree in business management will fall into that same category. And as I sit by the window in our two-bedroom ranch, watching David type the revision of his soon-to-be-published novel and finishing the quilt of Africa, the one that my mother started, I get a sense of completion. Things truly do come full circle. And having learned just how human we all are has left me free from regret, free to love and free to tell the world: I have a heart that's been broken once or twice, but I'm nobody's fool.

Vince

Bridget resided in St. Louis a lot longer than she'd anticipated, and maybe it had something to do with me. But I wasn't enough to make her stay. She called me this morning and asked me for a ride to the airport. She wanted to say goodbye but deep down, I think she wanted to give me a chance to change my mind. Joshua and Leland agreed to ride with me because we intended to catch the drag races in Illinois again after I'd bid Bridget farewell. It was only the second time that the three of us had gotten together since Leland had fallen in love a few months ago. He is now living proof that the right woman can mold a man. He doesn't curse, club or drink anymore. It was always in him, just needed to be brought out.

We were standing in the east terminal of Lambert Airport when Bridget heard the boarding call over the intercom. She was wearing a burgundy, ankle-length sundress and had an overnight bag slung over her shoulder.

"Well, I guess this is goodbye."

She hugged me, and I felt such solace in her arms. I wanted to ask her to stay. But I knew that would only be me trying to satisfy the need to fill Theresa's space, the need to have someone there with me in the quiet of that empty home I'd bought out in Chesterfield.

"Take care of yourself, Vince. And remember that you can come see me whenever you like. I won't have much to start with but you're welcome to the little that I've got."

I held her hand and placed a folded cashier's check for seven thousand dollars in her palm and rolled it closed. Kissed her cheek and thanked her for everything. For listening to me and being the only person that I could tell about Ray and me.

She looked at the check and asked, "What did I do to deserve this?"

"You received me at a time when I needed it."

She reached in her purse, pulled out my ID and said, "Here, I was gonna keep it to remember you but take it. Don't wanna send you through any more trouble."

Then a skinny woman behind the counter yelled into the microphone, "All passengers with a boarding pass from one to sixty . . ."

"That's me." She stepped closer and caressed my face. "Don't be so hard on yourself, Vince. You're not your father. Remember who you are and you'll find everything in life you need to make you happy."

We hugged and I let her go as Josh walked over from the gift shop. He's turned out to be a more honest and loyal friend than Leland. And for that I not only learned to respect him, but came to realize that the true racist was me. Once I removed the blinders from my eyes, I found the ability to see people as who they are, not who society says they should be.

"What are you thinking about?" he asked.

"The fact that I keep coming up short in life. Guess my momma was right: A man's gotta eventually pay for his sins before he leaves this earth."

"Depends on who it is," he said, placing his hand on my shoulder. "'Cause some of us have already paid for all of our *future* sins."

And in that moment, as another woman in my life turned and said goodbye, I found it hard to believe. The count was up to four: Mama, Rayna, Theresa and now Bridget. They'd all slipped away at one point or another. I guess the real sin was my wanting them to stay, asking them to remain stagnant, asking them to love a younger version of my pop. Even as I'm struggling to embrace the original. Struggling to keep from sinning. Struggling to love myself.

I pulled the sheet of paper that I'd torn off Pops's pad in the hospital from my wallet and stared at two of the words he'd written: *No regrets*. Like Bridget had said, this truly was a pivotal point in my life. One where I could choose to be hateful or hopeful. Some decisions aren't that hard. I would never be like Pops again. And in that moment I let go of the past.

AUTHOR'S NOTE

HIV/AIDS has claimed too many lives already, so I reiterate the fact that it is paramount that safe sex is practiced. The startling rate at which this epidemic has spread is due, in part, to ignorance and denial. Become educated on the subject of HIV/AIDS so that we may share more than memories of loved ones whose lives were shortened.

HIV/AIDS among African-Americans

The 2000 rate of reported AIDS cases among African-Americans was 58.1 per 100,000 population, more than *two* times the rate for Hispanics and *eight* times the rate for whites. [*Source:* CDC (Center for Disease Control and Prevention) National Center for HIV, STD, and TB Prevention]

CDC National AIDS Hotline 1-800-342-AIDS
www.cdc.gov

DISCUSSION QUESTIONS

1. How much of a role does Vince Senior's belittling play in his son's self-contempt? Was Vince using his father and his past as a scapegoat?

2. How possible is it that a man like Jeff, who could turn his back on a newborn, would make a good husband and father?

3. Based on her actions when Vince came to visit, do you believe that Rayna was searching for a father figure when she married Luke?

4. Do you believe that Zenobia still possessed feelings for Payce? If so, was the reality that he'd never be the man she wanted him to be the cause of her bitterness?

5. In the event that Robert was the father of Nikai's baby, do you believe that there was potential for them to get along for the sake of the child, *without being intimate*?

6. Is it possible that Elaine developed a love in her heart for Cedric, or was she still operating on the basis of her own insecurities?

Discussion Questions

7. In the event that the baby was not Robert's, should Kalif have been willing to take Nikai back?

8. Do you believe that Theresa's move to Atlanta was smart, considering the strained relationships with her mother and step-father?

9. Are there truly any signs that aid in determining if a man is bisexual? And if you believe so, were there any that Theresa missed from Vince?

10. What is the most important thing you learned from reading *Anyone Who Has a Heart*?

PG